Anna Johnston is a former baby, aspiring octogenarian and emerging Australian author with a love for the heartfelt and hilarious. She grew up in country Victoria before moving to Melbourne where she lives joyously with her husband and daughters by the beach. Anna left an imminent career in medicine to follow her heart into her grandfather's nursing home where she became the social support coordinator, taking great delight in shaking up the usual program. When injury left her unable to continue working in aged care she began to write about it, channelling her love for older people onto the page. Anna has enjoyed a life-long passion for screenplay, theatre and creative ageing.

THE BORROWED LIFE OF

Frederick Fife

ANNA JOHNSTON

MICHAEL JOSEPH
an imprint of
PENGUIN BOOKS

MICHAEL JOSEPH

UK | USA | Canada| Ireland | Australia
India | New Zealand | South Africa | China

Michael Joseph is part of the Penguin Random House group of companies
whose addresses can be found at global.penguinrandomhouse.com

Penguin
Random House
Australia

First published by Michael Joseph, 2024

Cover illustration 'Elderly couple flying kite on beach' by The Laundry Room
Photograph of Anna Johnston by Angelica James
Photograph of Anna Johnston with her grandfather, Fred Parkes,
from the Rosen family collection
Cover design Debra Billson © Penguin Random House Australia Pty Ltd
Typeset in Adobe Garamond Pro by Midland Typesetters, Australia

Printed and bound in Australia by Griffin Press, an accredited
ISO AS/NZS 14001 Environmental Management Systems printer

A catalogue record for this
book is available from the
National Library of Australia

ISBN 978 1 76134 759 7

penguin.com.au

We at Penguin Random House Australia acknowledge that Aboriginal and Torres Strait Islander
peoples are the Traditional Custodians and the first storytellers of the lands on which we live
and work. We honour Aboriginal and Torres Strait Islander peoples' continuous connection
to Country, waters, skies and communities. We celebrate Aboriginal and Torres Strait Islander
stories, traditions and living cultures; and we pay our respects to Elders past and present.

For my best friend Fred,
who was also my grandfather.

Please note that the story, setting and characters portrayed within these pages are completely fictional. The love is entirely real.

There is no remedy for love but to love more.

– Henry David Thoreau

Chapter 1

The single drop of wee made a pitiful splash. Fred sighed as he stood over the cracked toilet bowl that, like him, had seen better days. The public restrooms at Wattle River Reserve weren't as dirty as he'd feared, though the walls hosted a colourful array of ageing graffiti.

Another couple of measly drips. Was there a job in the armed forces for people who could urinate in Morse code? If so, he'd be an ideal candidate, though it was unlikely they'd accept 82-year-olds.

He glanced around the cubicle for something to distract his prostate – a watched pot never boils, after all. He didn't want to 'call Caz for a good time', as some peeling purple writing on the windowsill suggested, and he was getting nowhere, so he zipped up and unlocked the stall door. The damp concrete toilet block was pretty roomy. Could he possibly sleep here tonight? Surely if he asked around, he could find somewhere a tad cosier that didn't smell like urinal cakes and lost dreams.

His knobbly fingers protested as he rinsed them under the freezing tap water. The dryer was cactus, so he made the most of his wet hands to smooth out his unruly moustache. A foggy mirror above the sink reflected blue eyes flanked by deep crow's-feet. Not a bad price to pay for eight decades of laughter – well, seven decades at least. Fred coughed. Grief's blunt force could still wind him on bad days. He shook it off and headed back outside to the river, where he'd come to clear his mind before his bladder got other ideas. The welcome scent of eucalyptus filled his nostrils from the rows of sage-green gum trees lining the bank.

It was the sound of the river that usually brought him peace: the monotonous babble could drown out whatever was rattling around the corners of his mind. But not today. Today's mental cacophony was too loud even for the river.

'I'm sorry but I gave you notice over two weeks ago, Fred. You've got to be packed and out of here by tonight, mate.'

His landlord's words from earlier this morning echoed in his ears. They hadn't been unkind (Fred hadn't been able to scrape together rent for months) but they'd meant business, and he had nowhere to go. He'd rustled up some packing cartons, but they remained empty. How could you seal precious mementos in a box, not knowing when or if they would ever be reopened? It wasn't as though he had anywhere to store them. He was terrified that the memories would suffocate in their carboard prison, and that he would forget her. It was all too much, and his procrastinating feet had led him here.

He kicked a fallen gumnut into the water, his eyes following its descent down the grassy bank. There, by the river's edge, sat a man about his own age slumped in a wheelchair, an open bag of sliced bread at his side, now the prize of fighting seagulls. Hair the colour of aluminium foil waved carelessly in the breeze, with a matching, neatly trimmed moustache sitting below a substantial nose. The man's narrow face tilted to the side, one large ear directed at the sky like a wrinkly satellite dish. His watery blue eyes, magnified behind thick round glasses, were slightly open and appeared to be squinting at something. Fred stepped closer.

'Hello? You all right there, mate?' The lack of response alongside the stare – which was as vacant as Fred's flat would be tonight – said that he wasn't.

Fred always took great joy in meeting new people, but usually they were alive.

He stooped down, craned his saggy neck forward, and peered into the man's eyes. Yep, definitely dead. His breath, or lack thereof, smelt of tuna and Vegemite. A long strand of drool from his open mouth had made a damp patch on his blue flannel shirt. Fred's pulse quickened as he stared at the torn piece of bread that sat abandoned on the bloke's lap. He swallowed hard. More troubling than the realisation that he was face-to-face with a dead body was the niggling feeling that he knew the man. He looked so very familiar.

A babble of voices sounded from further up the riverbank near the barbecues. Some old folks in knitted cardigans sat on parked walking frames, crocheted blankets over their knees. Two women in turquoise uniforms poured them tea from a thermos and handed out biscuits. Fred's tummy growled. Behind them in the distance stood a minibus with *Wattle River Nursing Home* painted in big navy-blue letters along the side. The old boy must belong to them.

Taking a deep breath, Fred grasped the handles of the wheelchair and pushed the old man towards them – they would surely know what to do.

It was an unusually warm April day and beads of sweat prickled his skin. He hadn't exerted this much force in years. Except for that time on the toilet when his back passage had been so clogged up the neighbours had called emergency services, fearing his wails were that of a woman in labour.

'Mind this for me, would you, mate?' he said as he removed his heavy jacket and laid it over the man's shoulder. He pushed on. A flash of grey and white appeared as a bold seagull made off with the bread from the man's lap. With a sudden rush of air, an entire flock descended upon them, a whip of feathers assaulting Fred's face.

'Go on, get, you mongrels!' Fred blurted, trying to dodge a second group attack. He grabbed the stale Vegemite scroll he'd been saving for lunch from his pocket and threw it at the birds in an attempt to divert them. The wheelchair gave a sudden jerk and tipped sideways, flinging its occupant out like a discarded piece of wrinkly fruit. The body tumbled down the bank, landing half submerged, his yellow-trousered bottom pointing upwards towards the sky. Bugger! Bother! Blast!

Fred ambled down the bank and with a gargantuan effort tried to haul the man out, the immense physical strain causing Fred to pass wind repeatedly, bringing to mind last night's dinner, the single remaining item in his pantry: a tin of home-brand baked beans. He apologised profusely between each emission before realising whom he was talking to.

'Lucky for you, you can't smell, old boy.' Fred could always find the silver lining in things.

With one almighty tug, he fell backwards onto the grass, pain searing through his skull as the side of his head knocked against a rock. When the body slipped from his grasp and was taken by the current, it was only Fred's eyes that screamed. His mouth, along with the rest of his body, froze as if meeting liquid nitrogen.

The blob of silver, blue and yellow became smaller and smaller as it floated down the river and out of sight. Fred flooded with a type of panic he had never experienced, except in his recurring dream where he had to fill in for Dolly Parton at one of her concerts. A dull throb pulsed through his skull as his eyes darted from side to side, up to the nursing-home crowd and back to the water.

'Oh my god! Bernard! Bernard's fallen!' The shrill nasal voice came from one of the uniformed women, whose matronly bosom would have been disproportionate if not for her mass of frizzy red hair to balance it out. 'Bernard!'

Fear rose like heartburn in Fred's throat, questions jackhammering his brain. Did she think he'd pushed the man? She couldn't have known he was already dead. Would he go to jail? On the positive side, at least he'd get food and a bed in prison . . .

'Oh dear, Bernard!'

The woman's voice, now close, snapped him back into the present.

'You've fallen out of your chair, you silly sausage! Come on, let's get you back in.'

He blinked slowly, glancing over his shoulder to see who she was talking to. Certainly not to the body; that had disappeared altogether. There was no one else there. She was staring directly at *him*, talking to *him*.

'It was an accident. I didn't mean to . . .' he trailed off.

'Yes, yes of course. That's okay. No broken bones, I hope? That'd be the last thing I need.' She patted him down, looking at him as one might a small, inconvenient child. 'Oh, and I see you've lost your specs, too! Never mind. We'll get you sorted.' She picked up the man's glasses, which had fallen near the water.

Fred winced as she spat on them and wiped them with her blouse.

'There we are!' She placed them on his nose and everything became a complete blur. He felt himself being firmly assisted into a seated position then wheeled forward, smudged flashes of colour passing in a whir.

'Excuse me . . .' he tried again, but it hurt to speak.

'Don't worry, we'll get you a nice cuppa and a bickie. Did you enjoy feeding the seagulls?'

He paused, his eyebrows furrowed in contemplation, not wanting to be impolite or untruthful.

'Well . . . if I'm completely honest, no, I did not.'

Fred exhaled as they finally came to a stop, now surrounded by the hazy figures of the other old folk he'd seen before. A thick plastic mug was thrust into his hand.

'Thank you,' he managed. Never one to refuse a cup of tea, he drank. A lukewarm fluid tasting more like dishwashing liquid filled his mouth. As he forced a swallow, something pink and red was placed on his lap on a piece of paper towel. Assuming it to be the aforementioned bickie, he tasted it. The first bite confirmed that not only was it indeed a biscuit, but it was what he considered to be the queen of all biscuits: the Iced VoVo. When had he last splurged for a packet of these? For a moment, he forgot about his predicament and felt nothing but gratitude as the glorious bursts of raspberry and coconut waltzed on his tongue. The flavours coated a delicious memory – they had been his dear Dawn's favourite. He closed his eyes to visit her in the only way he now could: in his mind. He saw his younger wrinkle-free hand in hers as they sat on their sun-dappled porch drinking coffee, two VoVos on a plate nestled side by side – just like the two of them.

'You, my darling, are the froth on my cappuccino!' he would chuckle as he spooned the chocolatey foam from his cup into his wife's mouth. The memory wrapped itself like a warm blanket around his broken heart.

Then, like clockwork, it came. The thought, so familiar it had become part of his body, spat its poison.

I should have come home sooner.

Fifty-seven years had done little to dull its jagged edge. An ache too great to bear crescendoed in his heart. He took one more longing look at Dawn's face before forcing his eyes open to what was now his reality.

The fuzzy outline of the redheaded woman came into view as she pulled the paper towel from his hand and used it to roughly wipe his mouth, making his moustache prickle.

'Bet you feel much better now, Bernard. You've certainly got a lot more colour in you than when we got here this morning – you were as pale as a corpse.'

Fred gulped. Good grief.

'But I'm not Bernard . . . I'm Fred, you see. Frederick Fife. Wait a second, I'll show you my ID.'

But she had already moved on. He reached for his wallet in his jacket pocket, only to feel his shirt. Bugger. He'd taken his jacket off. It must have washed down the river with the dead bloke!

'Time to go,' the woman bleated as she returned and grasped the handles of the wheelchair once more.

Memories of being on one of those dreadful amusement park rides rose to the surface as he bumped along the path; still unable to see anything because of the glasses. Dizzy, queasy and scared, he searched for words of protest but found none. A mechanical noise sounded as the wheelchair lift raised him into the van. Two elderly ladies whispered loudly in front of him, the scent of potpourri thick in the air.

'Did you see the trousers Denise was wearing?' said one, her voice as raspy as that unfortunate hairless chap in *The Hobbit* who was obsessed with the ring.

'Toilet-brush Denise?'

'No. Denise Denise. The carer.'

'Ahhh, redhead Denise.'

'Yes, well, her trousers were falling down, and I could see her bottom shining like the rising sun. Almost fell off my chair, I did! Absolutely disgraceful!'

Perhaps it was a good thing he had the wretched glasses on after all. As the engine of the bus sprang to life, Fred's hands tightened over the armrests.

He managed a meek 'Wait!' but it was lost in Michael Bublé's voice oozing through the speakers. His skin twitched. Did they honestly think *he* was that poor bloke? Were older people so invisible that they all looked the same? The body had probably floated to ruddy Sydney by now. Perhaps it was all a dream . . . but the pounding in his head and the coconut stuck in his teeth told him otherwise.

A wave of nausea interrupted his thoughts. Fred was prone to feeling carsick at the best of times, even when he wasn't wearing someone else's glasses and sitting at the very back of a bus. He shut his eyes and tried to keep the VoVo down.

Chapter 2

'You're it!' squealed Hannah as she tagged her sister. Sadie was three years older than her but Hannah was almost as tall, with the same short curly brown hair and green eyes. Her bare feet zipped past the garden shed, jumping over the patch of bindies just in time to avoid the dreaded sting.

'If I'm it, you're it too!' laughed Sadie, catching up to her little sister, pulling her in close for a bear hug.

Hannah proudly let out the big juicy fart she had been holding in for just this moment, a sure-fire way to escape her sister's clutches. It was so loud it gave her the giggles. Normally she was the queen of silent-but-deadly, but this one was noisy *and* deadly, a winning combo.

'Hannah! *Gross!*' Sadie scrunched her nose just like the time Hannah had dared her to put seven sour Warhead lollies in her mouth at once.

As Sadie released her, Hannah felt something dripping on her forehead. She rubbed her fingers over it. It was red. She squinted at Sadie in confusion.

'Am I bleeding, Sayd?' But as she looked at her sister for an answer, she saw it was Sadie who was bleeding. Big drops of blood fell from her nose and onto her rainbow tie-dyed T-shirt. It seriously made it look even cooler, though. It needed a splash more colour after Mum had accidentally washed it on a hot cycle.

Sadie touched her fingers to her nose. 'Argh, rats! Not another one!'

Hannah slapped her hand over her mouth. Holy cow! Her farts were even more powerful than she thought if they could make your nostrils bleed. Perhaps she should try holding them in more.

'Come on, let's go inside,' said Hannah, running past the rusted washing line towards the house. Sadie clutched her nose and followed alongside, drops of blood dripping onto the brown grass below. Hannah opened the screen door with a creak.

'Dad! Where are you?'

Mum glanced up from the kitchen bench where she was making a sandwich, her messy hair tied up in a bun.

'Mum! What are you doing back? I thought you were at work.'

'Oh hi, love, I just ducked home – forgot my lunch. Dad's out the front.'

Hannah pointed to her sister. 'Sadie needs some tissues. She's got a blood nose!'

'Oh dear, never mind. Here you go, you silly sausage,' Mum said, handing Sadie a box of Kleenex. 'Don't get blood on the carpet!'

Sadie obediently stepped off the beige shag rug and onto the white kitchen tiles.

'Careful, or your brains will bleed out, sis!' Hannah teased.

Sadie poked out her tongue and pinched her nose with the tissue. Within seconds, it was bright red just like Hannah's all-time favourite food: tomato sauce. Tomato sauce went with *everything*, despite what Sadie said. She was such a weirdo and liked vinegar on her chips! Who would prefer vinegar to TS? Her tummy rumbled. She really felt like some sauce now.

'Mum! Can we have tomato sauce on toast for lunch again, please?'

Mum didn't answer.

'Mum? Mum?'

Mum frowned as she handed Sadie her favourite purple teacup, the fancy one that Aunty Jane had given her from London. 'Try to have a sip of water, love. Gee, you're getting a few of these, aren't you? My darling girl. I think we'd better take you to see Dr Parkes.'

Hannah scrunched up her face. This meant no more tag for today. Rats. The front door swung open and Dad walked in carrying the newspaper, his brown hair flopped in his face. He *really* needed a haircut. Maybe he'd finally let her do it this time. The practice run on her Cabbage Patch doll Maggie hadn't been *too* bad, and Maggie looked better in hats anyway.

'How's my little Han?' Dad asked, tickling Hannah under the chin and sending her into fits of giggles.

'Daaad! I'm not little anymore!' She placed her hands on her hips and gave her father her most serious, grumpiest look, the one she saved for the psycho cat next door who she was pretty sure had stolen Maggie's underpants from the washing line.

'I know, I know,' said Dad wrapping his arms around his daughter.

As hard as she tried to push them down, Hannah couldn't stop the corners of her mouth from turning upwards.

'Achoo!' Dad roared, covering his nose. If there was a competition for who could sneeze the loudest, her dad would be world champ for sure. His sneezes could even set off the car alarm.

'Sorry! I couldn't resist patting the neighbour's new puppy!' He went to grab a tissue and stopped when he noticed Sadie. 'Oh dear, what's going on here? You didn't try any kung-fu moves on your sister, did you, Han?' He raised his bushy eyebrows and winked at Hannah.

She grinned, but Mum's freckled face remained very serious.

'We need to take her to the doctor,' she said, glancing back at Sadie, who now looked like she was holding some sort of bright-red flower under her nose, the scrunched ball of Kleenex soaked in blood. 'In fact, you'd better take her right away. I'm so sorry I can't come – I've gotta get back to work, they're short-staffed. Don't forget to tell him about those night sweats as well.'

Dad nodded and tossed the newspaper on the table, his face now serious, too. 'Han, can you get an old towel for Sadie, please?'

Bum. Hannah sighed, her hopes of Dad teaching her to play chess later down the dunny. She ran to the linen closet in the laundry, looking up and down at the rows of folded towels. There were so many colour options . . . Should she pick a red one to match the blood? Could someone run out of blood? She'd be happy to lend Sadie some of hers if she ran out. Better get some just in case.

She grabbed an empty glass jar and Mum's sewing kit from the cupboard then took the biggest needle she could find and pricked her finger hard, biting her tongue to distract herself from the pain.

She held it over the jar, disappointed to see that only one drop came out. Maybe she'd have to make her nose bleed, too? Her teacher always told her not to pick her nose as she'd get nosebleeds, so she stuck her finger up and gave it a good pick, but all she got was snot. She narrowed her eyes. What else had Mrs Hudson lied about?

'Hannah! What are you doing?' Dad ran in, catching her in the Great Nose Pick. Why did dads always choose the worst moment to enter the room? It was like when he'd walked in on the kissing scene when she and Sadie were watching *Charlie's Angels* that time . . .

'We need that towel now!' He pushed past her and grabbed the closest towel, even though it was white and would probably stain. Silly billy!

'Come on, Hannah, we need to get Sadie to the doctor straightaway!'

She ran after him, her heart beating fast. Dad pushed the towel under Sadie's nose; she was so pale now, like someone had coloured over the top of her face with a white crayon. Hannah glanced at the jar with the drop of blood in it. She'd better bring it, just in case.

Chapter 3

'Idiot!' hissed Denise to no one in particular, as she read over her colleague's near-incomprehensible notes in Bernard's file. *And* in the wrong section to boot. Did she have to do everything herself? If there was one thing she couldn't stand, it was proper procedure not being followed. Just put notes in the right freaking place, Sandra, it's not hard! She rolled her eyes and let out a forceful sigh; she'd have to talk to her about it tomorrow.

She closed the file and adjusted the seat of the black office chair. Her back spasmed. They didn't design these chairs for people her size. They didn't really design anything in life for someone like her, whoever *they* were. She rubbed her forehead, trying to erase a pending headache before it grabbed hold.

She didn't need this on her plate, what with Bernard's fall on her watch and the worry about her daughter. Of course she shouldn't google the symptoms yet there she was, typing away with her sabotaging fingers. The search results slammed into her chest, snatching her breath. Shit! The doctor would no doubt need to order tests and the wait of not knowing would be absolutely excruciating. On one hand, she wanted nothing to be wrong. On the other, it would be a relief to know what was causing all this, to have a reason, a name for what was happening to her darling girl . . .

Did this make her a shit mum, wanting there to be something wrong?

She glanced at her Apple watch, scowling at the indentation it made on her wrist. Should've bought a larger wristband; buying a smaller size didn't magically make you that size. *Idiot.* The new nurse would be here soon. He'd better not be an imbecile like Sandra.

She really ought to check on Bernard again now but he was asleep, and she needed a rest, too. Denise would need more than a bloody sandwich today. She grabbed a Mars Bar from the residents' lolly trolley and scarfed it down.

Bloody Bernard. Should never have left him alone to feed the seagulls, but he was so freaking annoying sometimes. Grumpy old fart. Why did this have to happen on her shift? At least Bernard had the early signs of dementia, so any other changes from a fall could surely be explained away by that.

She opened an incident report form in his file. At least she had control of what would be written down. And for once, it was going to be in her favour.

Chapter 4

It was Fred's nostrils that woke first. A disastrous combination of urine and disinfectant assaulted his airways, tumbling the contents of his stomach like socks in a dryer. Smears of fuzzy colours filled his eyes. He went to rub them, his fingers meeting something hard. Why was he wearing glasses? Removing them from his nose, a small salmon-coloured room came into focus, generic pictures of sailing boats adorning the tired walls. The TV on the sideboard was off, but the unmistakable rise and fall of David Attenborough's muffled voice drifted from the next room. A soft breeze blew in from an open door that led to a tiny courtyard lined with neglected potted pansies. Where on earth was he? And why was he in a wheelchair?

In the corner sat a hospital-like bed, the red light of a call button illuminating the beige doona. As he looked across at the bedside table, his mouth went dry.

He rubbed his eyes. It couldn't be.

There, next to a telephone, sat a gold-framed photo of *him* with a birthday cake, two red number candles making up the '83'. He was pretty sure he was still just eighty-two, though. Or *was* it eighty-three? He frowned, racking his brain for a memory of his last birthday.

There'd definitely been no cake, although he had splurged on a choccy scone from Baker's Delight. But he'd been alone, as he had for his last ten birthdays. No one would have been with him to take a photo. He rubbed the side of his head, his hand meeting a sizeable bump that left a smudge of blood on his fingers. Had he knocked his head? Was he concussed? Or was this it? Had he finally lost his marbles? And, if he had in fact lost his marbles, would he have the clarity of mind to question if he had?

Taking a deep breath, he picked up the photo for closer inspection. Stuck to the frame was a label with *BERNARD's 83rd BIRTHDAY* written in neat capital letters. Fred pinched the bridge of his nose. Surely he hadn't forgotten his own name? He studied the unsmiling face and the blank eyes. That was the first clue. He always had a smile on his birthday, even if no one else was there. Phew! It was not, in fact, him. Marbles intact. For now, at any rate. He was indeed eighty-two after all. Probably.

Then, like a fast-acting laxative, it all came flooding back. The river. The seagulls. The body. The name.

He squinted at the photo, swallowing the golf ball-sized lump that had formed in his throat. There were minor differences of course – the size of their ears, the angle of their eyebrows, the width of their eyelids – but by and large the two of them looked almost identical, especially if he put on the glasses. His lungs searched for air as a glimpse of the pale, slumped face flashed in his mind. So that was why the man – Bernard, he presumed – had looked so very familiar. It was practically the same face Fred saw in the mirror every day. He pictured the blob of colours being swept away by the current and then looked down at his own blue check shirt and mustard-coloured pants. They even dressed alike.

Crikey. No wonder they'd thought he was Bernard.

He shifted, his cotton trousers sticking to the fake leather of the wheelchair. His bottom felt wet! And what was that smell? The relief of seeing that his crotch was dry was soon overcome by the alarming realisation that Bernard's hadn't been. Argh. Must've been too disorientated to notice it earlier. He needed a shower pronto and to sort out this frightful mix-up. He stood, listening for voices outside but hearing none.

'Excuse me, please!' he called down the hall, his heart racing. Where was everyone? Drawing attention to himself was as appealing as applying haemorrhoid cream, but desperate times called for desperate measures. When no one came, he pressed the call button repeatedly like an impatient child eager for a walk signal to turn green. It made no sound. Little bugger must be broken. He waited for ten more sticky minutes before the thought of someone else's bodily fluid on him became too much to bear. The sliding door in the corner revealed a hospital-like ensuite. With some difficulty, and trying not to gag, he removed his clothes and gave himself a quick rinse with the hand-held shower.

'Bernard?'

Strewth! Fred's heartbeat quickened as the door began to open. He stumbled onto the plastic shower chair, placing a face washer over the area that was, well, *not* his face.

'Why are you in the shower?' The nasal voice of Denise was unmistakable now. 'You aren't meant to do that yourself; you goose!' she said in the same tone Fred's mother had used when she'd caught him eating a whole jar of strawberry jam. 'I've got a new nurse with me today, Bernard. He's learning the ropes and has come to check you over after your little fall at the river. This is Kevin.'

Despite his state of embarrassment, Fred, always the perfect gent, managed a weak smile. 'How do you do, Kevin?' He craned his neck to see the young man with ginger hair waving hello.

'G'day, mate. Lovely to meet you,' said Kevin, his thick Kiwi accent and freckly face brimming with a level of enthusiasm that would've been less awkward if Fred weren't starkers.

'Oh! I see you've had an accident! Oh gosh, Bernard,' Denise scolded, glancing back at the wheelchair and the wet pants on the floor.

'No, well, that's the thing I've been trying to say,' said Fred. 'You see, it wasn't me that had the accident – it was Bernard.'

A look of confusion flashed across Denise's face before she nodded, giving a knowing smile and wink to Kevin. 'Oh, yes, honey . . . It was *Bernard*,' she said, making air quotes around the name with her pale fingers.

His chest tightened. 'But . . . I'm *Fred*!' he attempted again, though neither of them were listening.

'Here, let's get you sorted.' Denise turned the water off and began patting him dry with a white towel, starting at his feet. As the towel rose higher, so did Fred's dread.

'I think I can manage this part,' he said, just in time.

'Okay, I'll clean down your chair while you do that, then we'll be back to help transfer you, all right?' Denise said, as if talking to someone whose first language wasn't English.

She closed the ensuite door, but Fred could still hear their voices clearly.

'Bernard came to us a few months ago after a fall. Doesn't have any visitors. He's divorced and his ex-wife died, so no family on the scene. Used to work in advertising or something. Heard he lost most of his money – sad story. Grumpy old bugger he is. Oh, and a bit deaf, so you need to speak up. He can walk but we always take him in a wheelchair for longer distances. He used to be quite good mentally when he first came in November but had a mild stroke on Christmas Day, of all days. Hasn't been quite the same since. It's caused some vascular dementia, so he can get confused and sometimes forgets who he is, or where he is. The fall this morning can't have done him any good, either. He needs lots of reassurance and guidance.'

Fred buried his face in his hands. Blimey. This was going to be harder than he thought. He glanced at himself in the mirror, his silver eyebrows in a furrow once more. A tiny spot of dried blood peeked from behind his right earlobe. Perhaps he could trouble them for a bandaid? Even the home-brand ones were pretty dear. He heard them spraying the chair and quickly dried his nether regions. If only he had some spare jocks on him. He'd even settle for some budgie-smugglers at this point.

The two staff members returned with a navy-blue shirt, grey tracksuit pants and a pair of light-brown underpants that Fred feared may once have been white. Helping him to his feet, Denise promptly pat-dried his bottom before he could say a word, then helped him into the fresh set of clothes. They fit perfectly.

Once dressed, he was escorted to the armchair by the window where Kevin began his examination. Fred's bicep protested as the inflating blood pressure cuff squeezed it, relinquishing its grasp seconds before he thought his arm might drop off.

'Gee, your blood pressure is better than ever, Bernard,' said Kevin, glancing at an iPod – or was it an iPad? 'Oh golly, I can see you've got a bit of a cut behind your ear, too. Let's take a look at that, shall we? Does it hurt anywhere? Any other problems at all?'

'Er, no,' Fred replied, wondering if this was a good time to mention his weak stream and the mole on his scrotum that he'd been meaning to get checked . . . Perhaps best not. Kevin shone a small torch in Fred's eyes and asked him to follow his finger.

'Looking good, no sign of a concussion, mate.' Removing a dressing kit from a trolley, he gently cleaned and dressed the wound.

'Thanks, Kevin.' Fred sighed inwardly. Thank goodness he hadn't had to ask for that bandaid. This was some first-rate service.

'Right, well, we'll leave you to it. Oh look, just in time – here's your lunch!'

Kevin stepped aside to let a petite young woman in a canary-yellow uniform pass. At the sight of her, the nurse's face reddened and he dropped his clipboard with a clatter.

'Oh, um, er, sorry about that. I'll, um, leave you to it, Bernard.' Kevin gave a strange little bow, then, as if realising the absurdity of what he had done, slapped his palm to his forehead before hurriedly exiting the room, Denise following behind.

The young woman gave a bemused smile then looked at Fred with warm, brown eyes. 'Hello, Mr Bernard!' Her chirpy voice was soft and sweet. 'It's just Linh here. I've got your lunch and the activities schedule.'

Fred paused, still coming to terms with what seemed to be his new name. Linh placed the tray on the wheelie table in front of him, brushing her thick black fringe from her face.

'Oh, lovely! Thank you ever so much.'

He took a deep breath, determined to try again. 'I'm sorry to bother you, love,' he said as she turned to leave, 'but I've been trying to tell someone that I don't belong here. I came by mistake —'

'Oh no, Mr Bernard, you haven't made a mistake,' she said, rubbing his shoulder. 'This is your room. Twenty-three, remember? We talked about that yesterday?' She pointed to the gold number on the door.

He shook his head. 'But I'm not who you think I am. I'm not *Bernard*, I'm *Fred*, you see . . . *Fred*.'

'Fred?' Linh frowned, tilting her head to the side.

'Yes, Fred!' Dare he hope someone would finally listen?

She paused before nodding enthusiastically. 'Ah, I see! Yes . . . Fred! Just wait here a moment.'

He sighed, relief washing over him. Finally. This whole debacle would be sorted out at last.

Fred rubbed the soft fabric of the navy shirt between his fingers; it was much nicer than his usual scraggly ones from the op shop. Could he keep this outfit? He certainly didn't want to put the urine trousers back on.

Linh returned, breaking his train of thought. He leaned forward in anticipation. In her hand was a DVD. A man's black-and-white face smiled at him from the cover.

The Fred Astaire Collection.

He flopped back in his chair. Bugger.

'Fred! He's a great dancer, Mr Bernard.' Linh pointed to the case as she did a little boogie.

Fred forced a smile as his mind groaned. If only he was as recognisable as the greatest dancer of all time. Fred wasn't really the greatest at anything – well, apart from eating jubes, perhaps. He was exceptionally good at that.

Linh put the DVD on to play and left doing a waltz down the hall. As the music started and his namesake and Ginger took to the floor, the smell of gravy intoxicated his nostrils. He'd totally forgotten about lunch, a very rare occurrence indeed.

The tray before him resembled those his mum had been given when she was in hospital: thick, insulated beige plastic covers on a plate, bowl and mug. He'd never forget having to feed her like a baby, that non-identifiable mushy stuff resembling brown cottage cheese. Fred sent up a silent prayer that old Bernard hadn't been on vitamised food as she'd been at the end. Still, his grumbly tum would be grateful for anything at this point.

Excitement spritzed over him as he lifted the cover to reveal slices of roast beef, spherical peas, cubes of roast pumpkin and oval roast potatoes covered in gravy. You little beauty! He clasped his hands together – must've been at least ten years since he'd had a roast. There was even jelly and custard for dessert!

Dawn had always cooked marvellous meals for the two of them. She'd taught home ec part-time at the local high school and her expertise showed in every dish she created. Since her passing a decade ago, he'd been largely surviving on toast with baked beans or tinned spaghetti. Meat was too expensive anyway, even if he'd been able to cook it. He'd tried his hand at rice a few times, but it always ended up either crunchy or gluggy. He ate it nonetheless.

'Better belly busted than good food wasted,' his dad had always said.

Fred glanced at the roast, a quiver of guilt rising in his gurgling stomach. Could he at least stay for lunch? Surely it couldn't do any harm? Poor old Bernard certainly didn't need it where he was.

Fred deferred the decision to his tummy, who made the executive decision to tuck in. The warm food and his mouth were a match made in heaven. He scraped every last bit of gravy from the plate, and even gave it a lick after checking no one was watching. Sinking deeper into the chair, he savoured the delectable yet long-forgotten sensation of being truly full. But it wasn't long before the peas began to roll around in his gut, his conscience as heavy as an udder in need of milking. He *had* to tell someone the truth – this poor blighter must be found and buried. Ignoring his aching knees, he rose out of the chair and left the room, running into Linh in the hall.

'Mr Bernard! Please don't try and walk after your fall!' She looped her tiny, tanned arm in his and escorted him to his wheelchair.

Crikey, she was strong.

'You gave me a fright, Mr Bernard!' she said, patting him on the back. 'Where do you want to go? Are you finally going to come to Bingo?'

'Oh . . . no. I'm sorry to be a pest, love, but would you mind taking me to see whoever's in charge of this joint, please?'

'DON?' she questioned.

'Er . . .' Fred shrugged. 'I'm not sure if his name is Don.'

'No, I mean the Director of Nursing – Sharon. She's new. She took over from Helen last week, remember?'

'Oh, yes. Well, I'd be awfully obliged if you could take me to her, please.'

'No worries, Mr Bernard – can do!' She grasped the handles of the chair. Not this again. At least this time he wasn't wearing those dreadful —

'Oops, better not forget your glasses!'

Bugger. He sighed as the spectacles were once again placed on his nose, rendering his vision as useless as a chocolate teapot.

She wheeled him down a long corridor, coming to a stop at a blurry green door. 'Sharon, I've got Bernard Greer here to see you. I'm not sure you've had the chance to meet him properly yet. He's the gentleman in room twenty-three.'

'Ah yes, Bernard. Hello, we only met very briefly last week. I'm Sharon Young. What can I do for you?' she said, many decibels higher than necessary.

Fred moved the glasses further down his nose so he could look over the top of them. A formal, middle-aged woman in a black pantsuit with short peroxide-blonde hair and red glasses closed her laptop.

He cleared his throat. 'How do you do, Ms Young. Well, it's just that, I'm sorry to say, there has been a bit of a misunderstanding, an accident, as it were, and I've been trying to tell someone —'

'Oh, you're a darling. Don't worry, Bernard. Denise has already told me about the fall at the river and we've filled in an incident report.' Her voice dripped with a sickening sweetness as if she were talking to a baby koala.

He shook his head. 'But I'm *not* Bernard, you see. I'm afraid there was a terrible accident and poor Bernard has gone down the river!'

Sharon glanced at Linh. 'Yes, that's right, you did go down to the river this morning. Did you have a good time?'

Fred frowned. Was he speaking a different language? 'But he fell in! He was all wet, and I tried —'

'Bernard, it's okay.' Sharon leaned forward and placed a sympathetic hand on his shoulder. 'You weren't wet from falling in. We are going to look at adjusting your medication to help with the . . . *accidents*.' The phone rang and she glanced at the number, raising a finger to Fred's face.

'I'm so sorry, Bernard, but I have to take this. You go and have a nice rest, okay?'

Tears pricked Fred's eyes while exasperation gripped his chest. 'I'm Fred,' he said to no one in particular. 'Fred, Fred, Fred . . .' But the words died in his mouth.

'Ah, yes! Good idea. Let's go back to your room and watch another Fred video! Or one of your bird documentaries? I know you love those.'

Fred felt himself nodding, too exhausted to fight anymore.

6d

After a thoroughly appreciated dinner of chicken Kiev and pavlova with a surprisingly smaller side of guilt than he'd consumed at lunch, Fred watched the daylight surrender to the dark sky. The six o'clock news on the telly told him that a late thunderstorm was forecast as Denise burst into his room.

'C'mon, into your PJs, Bernard,' she said, not making eye contact.

He glanced from her to the window where the wind was already agitating the trees. Perhaps he'd stay just one night? What harm could it do? Be much better than the public loos. He could take another crack at sorting things out tomorrow.

Denise removed a pair of red flannel pyjamas, not unlike Fred's own at home, from the chest of drawers. Perhaps this wouldn't be so bad after all? A moment later, when she pulled out what appeared to be a gigantic nappy from the bottom drawer, he changed his mind. But the thought of attempting to explain again brought a wave of crushing exhaustion. It was pitch-black outside – how would he manage to get home? Not that he could even call it home anymore. Yes, he'd get some sleep and try again tomorrow.

Denise approached with the white monstrosity.

'Um, do I have to wear that? I think I can manage without, please?'

'Yes, Bernard, you duffer. You've already had one accident today, remember?'

If only she knew the extent of Bernard's accident. Poor bugger. Fred clenched his jaw. The protest of his aching bones had whittled down any last scrap of resistance, so he simply nodded. At least the grass was greener on this side; wearing incontinence pants was definitely preferable to lying at the bottom of the river. Another nip of guilt pinched his belly. An awkward dressing ensued before

Denise led him to the bed and said an abrupt goodnight. What little dignity he had left had passed away with Bernard.

He climbed under the covers, allowing his body to sink into the squeaky plastic-covered mattress. The bed was comfy enough, yet he searched in vain for sleep. The image of Bernard floating down the river clasped his mind with an unwavering grip. What had happened to the body? Surely it would be found – and then what? Would he be implicated in Bernard's death?

He pictured his tiny flat. What would the landlord do when he found Fred gone but all his things still there? His muscles tensed. His belongings held little value, except for the contents of the left side of the wardrobe. For it was there he kept his treasure – everything he had left of his darling Dawn. Her favourite cornflower-blue dress she wore on their Friday night dates. The reindeer pyjamas that she proudly paraded in year-round. The suspiciously small cashmere jumper that she had given him for his forty-ninth birthday then promptly claimed as her own. The 'stinky jacket' she wore on their camping trips, so named after a possum had weed on it. The golden necklace he'd given her for their fiftieth, and last, wedding anniversary. She hadn't cared that it wasn't real gold.

He'd never been able to part with those things. Perhaps the act of clearing that wardrobe had been more frightening than homelessness itself, and now it would be done for him in one terrifying sweep. His breath caught in his chest. The photo albums! What would become of them? A slideshow of pictures ran through his mind, illustrations of their story. Tangible proof that such a glorious love could exist. Their 40-degree wedding day, their first dilapidated house, their handmade Donald and Daisy Duck costumes for a fancy-dress party. He closed his eyes and inhaled, trying to still his tumultuous heart. At least the image of her face could never be disposed of, for it was engraved in his mind – though he would have done anything for a physical photo, too. His thoughts turned to the small plastic container that sat alone in his freezer, housing an eleven-year-old chicken casserole. The last remaining meal that Dawn had made, one of many she'd lovingly prepared before her first round of chemo so he wouldn't have to worry about cooking. After she died, he kept putting off eating it, his tastebuds unable to handle the grief. Before he knew it almost a decade had passed and he then worried that consuming it might lead to the expulsion of more than just tears. His eyes shot open. He still had a new nine-pack of two-ply toilet paper he was saving for a special occasion . . . Hopefully *that* wouldn't be chucked out.

The rain drummed steadily on the roof as gratitude for the lovely meal and the warm bed drummed in his heart. If – that is, when – he left here tomorrow, there would be no bed. He couldn't even pay for a motel room for one night. The wind howled and he pulled up the covers to his quivering moustache. Eventually he succumbed to a fitful sleep, dotted with nightmares of being chased by seagulls while singing Dolly Parton songs and wearing nothing but a gigantic nappy.

Chapter 5

Fred woke with a start. Or possibly a fart. He groped in the dark for his bedside table lamp, which didn't seem to be there. He shifted onto a wet patch of pillow where a puddle of drool had accumulated, the size of which indicated that he must have been out for the count. Glancing around, he tried to make sense of the long shapes in the darkness as he rubbed his aching lower back. Why was his mattress so squeaky, and why did his bottom feel enormous? He reached a hesitant hand down his rear and his heart skipped a beat as it met plastic. He was in a nappy. It hadn't been a dream. The river, the body, the stolen roast dinner.

The digital clock on the nightstand told him it was 5.51 a.m. He patted behind his ear and felt the dressing. Yesterday's headache had mercifully gone, allowing a single thought to shine clearly in his mind: why didn't he simply leave? He could just walk out the door and go. Why hadn't he thought of it earlier? Better get dressed first, though; a man in pyjamas would no doubt arouse suspicion.

Removing his PJs and giant nappy (triumphantly dry), he opened Bernard's cupboard and selected underwear (the least stained pair he could find), brown corduroy pants, a khaki shirt and a green woollen jumper.

'Hope you don't mind me borrowing these, old boy,' he whispered to Bernard. Thinking it best to hide his face, he took a cap adorned with the Sydney Swans logo from a hook inside the door. He shrugged. At least it wasn't Collingwood. He dusted off a pair of sunglasses from the top shelf and put them on. Bugger, they were prescription. Having the vision of a blind bat would not aid his grand escape, so he left them, walking out of the room and down the easy-clean carpeted hall. A series of identical corridors confronted him. He said a silent prayer and chose the middle one.

Halfway down, he came face-to-face with an elderly woman in a hot-pink nightie, her raven eyes and eyebrows standing out against her long, pale hair. Her face glowed with an eerie intensity as their eyes met.

'Hello, my lover,' she crooned, reaching up to turn on her hearing aids. 'Haven't seen you in a while!'

A nervous laugh escaped Fred's mouth. 'Oh, hello . . . I'm afraid I can't stop now, sorry.'

'Ohhhhh!' Her lips and eyebrows dropped in a synchronised dramatic frown. 'Isn't Mr Chicken Twistie happy to see me?' she pouted, making a phallic gesture with her index finger.

Good Lord. Fred cringed as his face flushed with heat. He tried to walk past but she stepped closer, her long spindly fingers grabbing hold of his shirt collar. Her surprising strength caused him to stumble towards her, the scent of mothballs and Glen 20 creeping up his nostrils.

'Come on, lover-boy! Let's slip into my room right now – the nurse thinks I'm still sleeping!' She giggled with the vivacity of a schoolgirl. 'You know I don't like to sleep alone.'

He shifted uneasily, looking down the hall for an escape. 'Oh, that's a very, er, generous offer, but not today, thank you kindly.'

'You can't get away from me that easily!' she screeched, grabbing both of his bottom cheeks with such vigour that Fred almost lost his balance. She continued squeezing like she was checking for ripe avocados. As Fred hadn't done any notable exercise in the last decade, his were very, very ripe.

'Oh, dear me, no! I have to go,' he said, pulling away. This was the last thing he needed when trying to fly under the radar.

'Don't you find your Patricia-poo beautiful anymore?' she pouted.

His heart galloped. 'Oh, you are, er . . .' he stammered. Dawn had been the very definition of beautiful. Once he had seen her, every other woman fell short of the word.

'I won't go without a smoocheroo!' Patricia insisted, reapplying red lipstick from her handbag with the precision of a drunken clown.

Fred tried blowing her a kiss.

'No deal!' she cried, making a cross sign with her bony arms. She advanced, clasped his jumper and pulled him into her room.

'Oh dear! Kindly release me, madam!' His protest fell on deaf ears. Exactly how deaf, he didn't know.

In a shockingly sprightly movement that would have been impressive if not for the circumstances, Patricia pushed him onto her bed, upsetting an array of colourful fluffy cushions. Her hearing aid whistled as she pulled herself up next to him, ready to pounce. He gagged. Her breath smelt worse than Bernard's, which was rather disturbing considering she was – unfortunately for him – still alive.

As her nightie drooped, Fred gasped as he caught sight of what looked like a tattoo of a man's private parts. Why on earth was it green!? As she moved to the left to kiss his neck, the emerald phallus stretched out, like a wrinkly accordion, to reveal (to his relief) what was actually a cactus, bringing to mind the fold-in pictures in the *Mad* magazines he'd had as a young man.

His heart convulsed, his mind searching for an escape route. The red emergency button on the wall next to the bed gave him his answer. He'd never liked to bother people and had even felt guilty for summoning the flight attendant on the plane to Queensland when she'd given him a packet of peanuts despite his mild peanut allergy. As Fred's own 'peanuts' (this time minus the 't') came alarmingly close to being grabbed, he felt assistance was indeed warranted and slammed the button, praying that help would arrive swiftly.

A loud alarm immediately sounded: *'CODE BLUE, ROOM THIRTY-EIGHT! CODE BLUE, ROOM THIRTY-EIGHT!'*

In the confusion, Fred scrambled away down the hallway, leaving a disorientated Patricia on her bed.

Chapter 6

After several more dead ends, an aching hip and many expletives, Fred finally arrived at the automatic glass doors at the front of the nursing home, which looked out onto a manicured garden and the street beyond. It was still early, so the reception desk was unmanned – all the more reason to leave now. He walked right up to the doors, his nose bumping against the cold glass as they failed to open.

Bugger.

He walked backwards and then forwards again, waving his hands, trying to provoke the sensor in a series of dodgy steps resembling the cha-cha that would've made Astaire turn in his grave. Nothing. His eyes rested on a keypad next to the door and his heart sank. A code was required to get out.

Blast.

He pressed the numbers 1-2-3-4, just in case. No. He mashed the keypad like an impatient toddler. Nothing. Exhaling defeat, he sank into one of the nearby lounge chairs, pondering his next move. Moments later, a teary middle-aged couple entered holding some rosary beads.

Seeing his opportunity, Fred made a beeline for the open door. The man looked him up and down.

'Are you a visitor?' he asked.

'Er, yes, I suppose I am,' Fred replied, quite truthfully, as he strode out, not waiting for a response.

The brisk autumn air nipped at his fingers, and he tucked his hands into his pockets. He would head straight to his flat, even though by his estimation it would be an hour's walk at octogenarian speed. On the bright side, that may help to firm up his avocados. He clenched each buttock sequentially.

The sign of the McDonald's on Gould Street, where he'd occasionally splurged on a soft-serve cone, was visible above the rooftops, giving him an orientation. Wattle River was a sizeable town, though much easier to navigate than sprawling Sydney two hours south. He and Dawn had moved here in search of a quieter, greener place to raise a family – a dream that never eventuated.

I should have come home sooner.

A lump formed in his throat. He swallowed it and tried to distract himself, picturing his little flat, with its soft green armchair and friendly yellow walls. How he hoped his things would still be there.

His wallet had ended up in the ruddy river, but his birth certificate was somewhere. With ID, he'd be able to prove he was *not* Bernard and set the record straight. Even if what Denise had said was true and Bernard didn't have any relatives on the scene, the bloke deserved a better resting place than the bottom of a river.

What he'd do after sorting out the mix-up was another question. Where could he sleep tonight? Perhaps his landlord would give him a freebie, or the local church had a shelter in the area? He shivered as the distressing thoughts and crisp air burned his ears.

Light rain began tapping the ground like fingers on a typewriter. He rubbed his hands together, wishing he'd borrowed Bernard's coat, too. What would Dawn think if she saw him now? Dressed in another man's clothes trying to escape a nursing home and the clutches of a nonagenarian nymphomaniac? She'd be laughing, for sure. Her beautiful laugh, more contagious than chickenpox. What he wouldn't do to hear it now.

He breathed in deeply. Somehow, everything would be okay.

The wind slapped his face, the cold air exacerbating his arthritic joints. He wrapped his arms around himself, wishing they were Dawn's. These were the only kind of hugs he got these days.

After what could have been no more than half an hour, the wet road reflected red and blue lights as the intermittent burst of a siren filled the quiet street.

The police!

They were slowing down. Fear seared his stomach – could they be after *him*? The body must have been found and he was about to be convicted of murder. Well, maybe not murder, but at least manslaughter, or impersonation charges. Or grand-theft roast dinner.

His breathing shallowed. Fred had always prided himself on being a calm and grounded man, but at this moment an illogical childlike panic took hold of him. His already-racing heart began to sprint.

'Sir?' A young, tanned police officer stuck her head out of the window, halting his barrage of thoughts.

Fred pretended not to hear and quickened his pace. Though he recognised the absurdity of an octogenarian outrunning a police car, it didn't stop him from trying.

'Sir! Please stop . . . Sir!'

He made a sharp right into a lane between two houses, too narrow for a car to follow. The engine of the vehicle clicked off, the ensuing sound of the closing doors bringing a fresh wave of panic.

Any minute now . . .

He surveyed his surroundings and quickly stepped behind a gum tree, picking up a fallen branch to hold in front of his face for extra camouflage. It was rather fortuitous that he'd chosen brown pants and a green jumper. A memory of playing 'Tree number 3' in his primary school production popped into his mind. Ironically, acting had never been his forte, yet he apparently played a very convincing Bernard. Footsteps approached, and Fred suppressed the urge to vomit.

'Sir? Sir, we can, um . . . see you.' The tanned officer was accompanied by a lanky male colleague holding an umbrella.

Fred poked his head around the trunk and offered a cheesy smile, placing the branch down. Beads of sweat formed on his forehead despite the cold. At least the embarrassment was warming his face.

His mouth went dry. Here it came. He was going to die a criminal.

'I didn't mean for any of this to happen!' he blurted. 'Bernard was already gone when I found him!'

'They said he might be confused,' the tanned officer whispered loudly to her colleague. 'It's okay, we've found you now,' she said, slower than necessary.

Fred glanced from one to the other. 'What's going to happen to me?'

The male officer smiled, revealing the perfect teeth that Fred could have had if not for his life-long soft spot for jubes. 'We're taking you back to the nursing home. They were very worried when you disappeared this morning and asked us to keep an eye out for you, Bernard.'

And there it was: *Bernard*. The name hit him like a punch in the guts. Not them, too . . . Weariness drizzled through him, washing away his last traces of energy. Yet somewhere, deep down, he was greeted with an unexpected wave of relief. He was freezing, wet and hungry, and his flat (which in reality didn't promise anything) was still a good half-hour's walk away. His eyes began to water as a feeling long forgotten stirred within: someone actually cared about him. He had been missed. After Dawn died, no one had cared, let alone known where he was.

'Let's get you dry.' The tanned officer brimmed with kindness as she produced a blanket, and wrapped it around his shoulders. 'There's a cafe just down there,' she said, motioning to the street beyond. 'We were about to get a coffee. Would you like one?'

Fred rubbed his eyebrow and looked down at his soggy brown loafers. 'Thanks ever so much, but I'm afraid I don't have my wallet on me.'

'Nah, this is on us, mate.' The lanky cop placed a large reassuring hand on Fred's shoulder.

Minutes later, he sat cocooned in the blanket in the back of the police car, a takeaway cup in his hands.

'Yes, we've found him and are bringing him back now,' the male officer said into a fancy mobile phone.

A strange sense of relief again calmed Fred's body, followed by a wisp of guilt, but not as big a wisp as he expected. The warmth of the cappuccino felt marvellous against his cold fingers. He only wished Dawn was there so he could share with her the chocolatey froth she so adored.

They soon pulled up to the entrance of Wattle River Nursing Home, where the officers helped him out of the car. Uniformed staff stood at the door, wheelchair at the ready.

'Bernard! What did you do? We were so worried about you! I can't *believe* you made it that far!' A frazzled-looking Denise ushered him into the chair.

He smiled sheepishly, unsure of what to say.

'Let's get you into some dry clothes.' She took him to his room and helped him change into another of Bernard's outfits. 'You've missed your brekkie, but there's some sandwiches on the tray. And you're late taking your morning meds.' Denise rolled her eyes and thrust a small plastic cup containing two pink tablets into his hand.

Fred glared from the cup to Denise. 'But I don't take any medication,' he said, his heart picking up pace.

'Now, Bernard, don't give me that nonsense again!' She raised a hand to stop his words. 'You've given me enough grief for one day. You know you need to take these for your heart.'

Fred's body turned to jelly. How bad could it be to take someone else's medicine? Would it kill him or just make him sick? Was he about to join Bernard in the afterlife?

The phone clipped to Denise's belt rang and she stepped out of the room to answer. Fred didn't waste his chance. He opened the courtyard door and flung the pills outside, making it back to his chair just in time.

As Denise re-entered the room, he tipped the non-existent contents of the plastic cup into his mouth, took a sip of water and made an exaggerated gulping sound.

'Open your mouth so I know they've gone down.'

Fred's jaw dropped as he stared out the window behind Denise where a mangy seagull was making off with the pink pills in its beak. Denise, who must have assumed he was obeying her command, took a quick look in his mouth and left. He breathed a sigh of relief. Disaster averted; although he was frightfully worried that he had now in fact murdered someone, even if it was a bird. Poor little brute.

Fred turned his attention to the small triangular sandwiches, which he gobbled down like a famished teenage boy after a sporting match. The empty pantry cupboards at home loomed large in his mind. Bernard's bed beckoned loudly, and his aching feet and weary eyes gave in to its call, sinking into the mattress and then into sleep.

Denise threw Bernard's wet clothes in the laundry trolley. The cops had told her that they'd picked him up in the neighbouring suburb, over two kilometres away. How the hell had the old bugger made it that far? Something was definitely up. She rubbed her chin. Or chins, more like. At least he hadn't escaped on her watch; he was already gone when she clocked on. As if she needed another thing to worry about. She was already in borderline deep shit over yesterday's debacle at the river; she hadn't even noticed Bernard's bump on the head until Kevin pointed it out. That old man would be the death of her.

Her mobile rang and she silenced it quickly. She couldn't risk being caught with it again during work hours. 'Hello?' she whispered, ducking around the corner to answer the call.

It was the doctor. The results were in.

Chapter 7

'Hello, Mr Bernard!'

Fred looked up from the telly to see Linh's jovial face as the soft aroma of strawberry tickled his nostrils. He was feeling slightly more human after a nap, a cup of tea, and four Teddy Bear biscuits.

'Happy Hour is starting soon!'

The words took a minute to place. They couldn't possibly be going to a pub, could they? Did Happy Hour here mean the same thing as at his local? He tried to erase a terrifying vision of a group of over-medicated old farts in a circle clapping along to 'If You're Happy and You Know It'. Surely not. He would be happy *and* know it if he could have a shandy, all right.

Before he could speak, Linh had helped him to his feet and transferred him to the wheelchair, placing Bernard's wretched glasses on his nose. He surrendered like a giant doll being played with by a child.

'Maybe you don't need this chair anymore, Mr Bernard? We all heard about your little adventure this morning!' Linh giggled.

Fred smiled, shifting the specs down his nose again. The stinging blisters on his feet were very grateful for the wheelchair at this present moment, and he made no protest. Linh wheeled him down the corridor into a large room with maroon carpet and high ceilings, the words *Wentworth Room* painted in gold cursive letters on a wooden sign above the entranceway. Several round tables were placed throughout, the elegance of their white linen tablecloths somewhat diminished by the thick, clear plastic covers that protected them. A few padded wooden dining chairs sat interspersed with spaces in between, while some wall-mounted speakers pulsed softly with the Beatles singing 'Penny Lane'.

'Where do you want to sit, Mr Bernard?' asked Linh, bending down to his seated position to make eye contact.

Fred scratched his moustache as he surveyed his choices. The table to his left hosted a sea of pale-blue-haired ladies, laughing loudly and chattering nonstop like a warble of magpies. Pass. At the far table sat a group of residents in what appeared to be La-Z-Boy armchairs on wheels. They all stared vacantly ahead, an expression that Fred could recognise anywhere: advanced dementia. He sighed. Then, shouted above the music, came a single clear word that made his stomach flip.

'Fred!'

Had he imagined it? Where had it come from?

'Fred!'

There it was again – unmistakable. Fred stood and turned to see a gangly man in a tweed flat cap and glasses, waving enthusiastically and gesturing to the empty seat next to him. At almost six feet Fred was not a short man, but he had to look up to meet the fellow's gaze.

'Fred! Freddy boy! I didn't expect to see *you* here! Come sit with me!' The man beamed delightedly, removing his cap to reveal what remained of his white hair.

Fred studied the man's face, searching the weathered contours for a trace of anything that might jog his memory. An oval-shaped head framed a wide crooked grin that, with the balding scalp, gave the impression of a cracked watermelon. This bloke obviously knew him, but from where? He didn't have the foggiest.

As Fred stepped closer the man enveloped him in a long, tight bear hug of musk and mouthwash. When finally released, Fred's lungs reinflated as he smiled through gritted teeth. 'Oh hello . . . um —'

'You remember Mr Albert?' Linh interjected, just in time, as she pulled out the neighbouring chair for Fred to sit.

'Oh . . . yes, of course. Albert,' he lied, his voice higher than usual. Thank goodness she'd divulged the man's name, but it still did nothing to aid recognition. 'So how have you been . . . Albert?'

Albert's beam grew, burying his eyes under a sea of wrinkles. 'Marvellous. I'm simply marvellous. Can't wait for the wedding!' he said, replacing his cap and doing an enthusiastic little hip wiggle. His voice was warm and creaky, but it rang no bells.

Fred squinted, flipping through the diminishing mental Teledex of people he knew who were still alive. Could he be the husband of one of Dawn's many cousins from Newcastle? He'd only met them a couple of times. Perhaps one of their grandchildren was getting married?

'I'm so very glad you said yes when I asked, Fred. I wouldn't want anyone else there, you know, by my side at the altar,' gabbled Albert as he took his seat, polishing his large, gold-rimmed glasses. 'We're going to look so handsome!'

Fred let out a nervous laugh. Surely he didn't think the two of *them* were getting married?

'You've got your speech ready, haven't you, Freddy?'

Fred's stomach lurched. Speech? Public speaking terrified him even more than heights, which was saying something given he couldn't even brave the Ferris wheel at the Sydney show with Dawn. Perhaps his fall at the river had been harder than he thought after all, and had knocked any memory of this man out of his brain. Fred looked back at Albert, who was now staring at him as though he were Santa Claus.

'Ahhh . . . I . . . um,' he began, searching for answers that weren't there. He was saved by a tiny, frail woman in a cream cardigan who hobbled over to the table, slowly lowering herself into the adjacent chair.

Albert turned to her, his grin on full display once more. 'Hello, I'm Albert, and this is my big brother Fred.' Fred glanced from Albert to the woman and back again.

'How do you do, Fred?' She offered a sparrowlike hand, smiling through tortoiseshell glasses that magnified her grey eyes.

'I, er . . . um . . .' He frowned, fidgeting with a button on his shirt, which was now damp with sweat. Brother? Had Bernard been Albert's brother? But if so, why was he calling him Fred? He sank his teeth into his bottom lip, but the pain didn't match that of his aching brain.

Linh placed her hand on Fred's shoulder, her small face appearing between the two men. 'Don't worry, Mr Bernard. Remember Mr Albert has dementia? He thinks you're his brother, Freddy!'

'Ohhhh.' Fred exhaled the confusion. So Albert didn't know his true identity after all. Was he relieved or disappointed? He didn't have a moment to consider before the woman spoke again.

'I'm Ruby. But I could have sworn your name was Bernard?' she said in a loud whisper, scrunching up her mouse-like nose.

Fred leaned in. 'Yes, well, that's what people usually call me around here. I gather poor Albert there isn't in his right mind.' Fred tapped the side of his head.

Albert turned to him again, his blue eyes now looking somehow out of focus, like they were staring beyond him into something Fred couldn't see.

'Hello, I'm Albert,' he said, offering his hand to Fred.

Fred hesitated for a moment before shaking it. 'Hello, how are you?'

'Very well, thank you,' said Albert, tipping his cap again to reveal some moles that probably needed to be checked by a doctor. 'Actually, I'll be much better when I can remember where I parked the car. I have a wedding I need to get to.' Albert glanced at his watch with its hands stuck at nine o'clock.

Fred moved his chair closer. 'Ah, I see. So, tell me, Albert, where are you from?'

'Well, I'm from Tassie, but I'm moving to Sydney next week because I'm getting married. But I must find my brother first. He's my best man and I need to check if he's written his speech – he's terrible at these kinds of things, and I'm worried he's forgotten.' Albert rubbed his wrinkly hands together as the words tumbled out.

Fred nodded, the pieces now slowly falling into place. 'I always wanted a brother, you know.'

'Ha! They can be a pain, brothers can,' Albert retorted, sticking his tongue out and going cross-eyed.

Fred laughed. Albert was his cup of tea.

'What can I bring you gentlemen?' Linh reappeared with a big smile and small notepad.

'Shandy for me, thanks, love,' said Albert, not missing a beat.

'A man after my own heart. I'll have the same, thanks.' Fred smiled. Thank goodness Happy Hour meant what he'd hoped it would. No clapping old farts in sight.

Linh returned shortly with the drinks and a platter piled with sausage rolls and party pies. Fred's eyes widened as his stomach let out an excited growl. Many goals were being kicked tonight!

'Cheers, mate!' He raised his drink to Albert. The clink of their glasses brought a wave of déjà vu, yet Fred couldn't quite recall the last time he'd had someone to toast with.

The shandy wasn't very cold, but Fred thoroughly enjoyed the bubbly beverage nonetheless. He surveyed the other tables in the room. Some residents hadn't been so lucky. Those in the padded chairs on wheels clasped thick plastic mugs, like the one he'd had tea in earlier. A young male staff member sat next to a large woman with thinning white hair who was cradling a baby doll. The man spooned a thick yellow liquid into her mouth from the mug, stopping now and again to dab her mouth with the giant bib around her neck.

Fred's tummy tensed as he caught sight of Patricia sitting at the table beyond, sipping champagne from a curly straw, her eye contact with him unwavering. Fred crossed his legs tightly and turned back to Albert, whose unsteady gaze now searched the room.

'You all right there, mate?' Fred asked.

'He's not here. He's still not here! Where's my brother? He's going to miss his speech,' said Albert, wringing his hands more frantically now.

'He's always looking for his brother,' Linh said, handing out some paper serviettes. 'But his brother is dead. It's the dementia, poor Mr Albert.'

She turned to Albert and before Fred could stop her, she said, 'Your brother is gone. He died, Mr Albert.'

Fred cringed, wishing he could take back her words. The expression on her face said that she did, too.

Albert stared at her in disbelief, his head shaking. Tears slipped down his face as he rocked his body back and forth. 'No, no, that's not right. Where is he? Help me find him! Please, please, it's almost time for his speech.'

Fred's insides jumbled.

Linh shook her head. 'I really shouldn't have said that. His wife always comes to Happy Hour, but she's sick today, Mr Bernard.'

Fred's already-soft heart liquefied. 'It's okay, my friend,' he said, taking Albert's bony hand and looking directly into the poor man's eyes. 'I'm here and I'll make sure everything is all right. I'm not going anywhere, okay?' He placed his arm around Albert and felt the tension release from his new friend's body. 'Now then, why don't you tell me about living in Tasmania? I've never been there, would you believe? Whereabouts did you live?'

Albert stopped rocking. His breathing slowed and his darting eyes came to rest on Fred. 'Launceston. It's a beaut place. Would you like to come and visit?'

'I'd love to! Let's have another shandy, shall we? Do you think they'll let us?' He winked at Albert, and Albert winked back, tapping his nose with his index finger.

'I've been waiting for you. I'm so glad you're here, Fred,' Albert said, squeezing his hand.

A smile crept across Fred's face. 'You know what? I think I'm glad I'm here, too.'

Chapter 8

Flashes of coloured light from the television caught Fred's eye. He'd just been wheeled into another lounge with some fellow wheelchairees. He removed his glasses so he could focus on the words appearing on the screen: *In the Night Garden*. A gardening show – that'd be all right. Fred didn't mind the odd potter, though his flat only had room for a few pot plants on the tiny balcony. As the title disappeared, a strange-looking train and alienlike creatures ran around speaking gibberish. Jeepers. No Don Burke in sight. He promptly put the glasses back on.

The morning light snuck through a small rip in the curtains that were disappointingly still closed. Thanks to the shandies, he'd fallen asleep quickly last night but had frequently woken beaded with sweat and panic. A bit of sunshine on his face right now would be just the ticket to revitalise his sluggish body. He peered over the top of his specs, his gaze resting upon the woman opposite him, the one from last night with the doll. She sat in the same recliner, which he had just heard referred to as a 'princess chair'. Funny what constituted royalty around here. It did look like it would be much softer on the old caboose than his wheelchair, though. He needed to get out of this thing. Why was he so hesitant?

The woman let out an indecipherable word. Her sparse grey hair framed vacant eyes that looked like Bernard's had when Fred had found him: staring but not focusing. Yet the rise and fall of the crocheted blanket over the woman let him know she was not in quite the same predicament. Late-stage dementia was like an empty house that the tenant had checked out of. It was the same distant stare his mother had had in the years before she passed away from complications related to early-onset dementia, the very cruellest of diseases that stole the mind and soul without mercifully taking the body as well.

Fred had loved his mum Penny with his whole heart. Wasn't hard to. Things weren't always great growing up, yet she found the positive in everything. She had a knack for making people feel shiny and good about themselves and their achievements, however small. Mum had never bought any framed artwork; instead, the lounge-room walls boasted every drawing and painting Fred had done as a child. The woman could find the bright side of a burnt piece of toast.

He sighed. That's what made losing her extra cruel. It was small changes at the start. Her gung-ho optimism became less sparkly. Snide little remarks began sneaking into their conversations like pinpricks, adding sharpness to what was once smooth. At first, Fred wondered what he'd done to upset her. It was when other changes came – forgetting where she'd put her purse, or not finding the word for flour – that they'd all realised something else was going on.

'Hi, Kathleen.'

Fred glanced up to see Kevin approaching the woman. He bent down to her level, made eye contact and gently placed his hand on her shoulder, complimenting her baby doll and explaining what he was doing before taking her blood pressure. Fred smiled. It said a lot about a person, the way they treated someone with dementia.

A little bit of kindness and patience spread further than butter on a hot crumpet.

A faint rattling sound made Fred turn. Linh entered pushing a cart stacked with board games. Her face brightened when she spotted him. He wasn't the only one who had noticed Linh's entrance – Kevin was staring at her like a child who's just seen a Christmas tree for the first time. Linh gave the boy a shy wave. The action broke Kevin's trance, his face flooding to match his ginger hair. Fred caught Linh's eye and raised his eyebrows up and down.

She giggled. 'Mr Bernard, you're so funny! See you at Bingo this afternoon!' She exited, shaking her head.

Fred saluted and turned back to Kevin, who was now staring at the blood pressure cuff like it was a bomb he had to dismantle. After Linh was well out of sight, Kevin, still the colour of tomato soup, walked over to Fred.

'Hi, Bernard, it's Kevin here. We met yesterday?'

'G'day, mate.'

'Now, let's take a look at that dressing.' Kevin pointed to Fred's head.

Fred touched his hand to it. He'd forgotten all about it.

'So how are you feeling, Bernard?'

'Not too shabby, thanks.' The words came without thought, but if he was honest, his arthritis was particularly bad that morning. He'd been diagnosed with it last year and prescribed some great meds but had to stop taking them after the first box. It was just too expensive to keep up. Fred studied his hands, scrunching his knobbly fingers in and out.

Kevin frowned, leaning closer. 'Are your hands bothering you, mate?'

'Oh, it's nothing really, just part of being old.'

The young nurse took Fred's hands gently in his and turned them over, examining the misshapen carrots that were his fingers.

'Seems to me like you have a bit of arthritis, mate,' he said, whipping out the iPad and tapping the screen.

'Hmm, it doesn't seem to say anything about it in your file. Has Dr Rosen mentioned it?'

'No,' said Fred slowly. 'Dr Rosen hasn't.' It had been some other random doc he couldn't remember the name of, at the bulk-billing clinic.

'Hmm, well, he's on long service leave at the moment but we'll get the locum to check you out. In the meantime, I'll give you some Nurofen.'

'Oh, well, if it's not too much trouble, that would be super. Thanks, mate.' Golly. What a treat it would be to be pain-free! Even if it was only for today. 'So, how's the new job treating you, Kev?'

'Oh, it's awesome,' he said, gently removing the dressing. 'It's actually my first job – well, first proper job. I just finished uni last year.'

'That's great. There's nothing like earning your own way in the world, is there?'

A chuffed grin spread across Kevin's face as he dabbed the wound with antiseptic. 'Yeah, it's pretty cool. I'm saving for a new car.'

'Nice one! Any ideas what you'll get?'

'It'll be a matter of what I can afford, sadly. Would love one of those new Jeeps if I had my pick, but a second-hand Corolla is probably more within the budget, I reckon.'

'Nothing wrong with a Corolla, mate. My wife, my late wife, had one back in the day.'

And for a second he could see Dawn, singing along to the radio at the top of her voice behind the wheel of her little white car.

He tried to grasp her – the memory of her – but it slipped away. He exhaled.

'Speaking of great women, that Linh seems like a nice girl.'

Kevin gulped, his colour rising again. 'Oh, um . . . I don't, um, really know her,' he said, dropping a gauze wrapper on the ground.

Fred grinned. He recognised the gleam in Kevin's eyes. 'I felt the same way when I first saw my wife. The "falling for" often comes before the "knowing", I've found.'

'Ha! Is that so? Tell me about your wife.'

Fred closed his eyes. Dawn's amber irises with the gold rim came instantly into view. Eyes that had battled age and won, never losing their spark, even at the end when her body had conceded defeat.

'She was pretty special my Daw— my wife,' he said, catching himself, although it was unlikely that Kevin would know the names of spouses, especially exes or deceased ones. Bernard was divorced, wasn't he? Or was it widowed? He frowned, rubbing the back of his neck. Who was he trying to be? Why did he care if Kevin found out? Wasn't that what he wanted? To fix up this mess?

He wasn't so sure anymore. Guilt prodded at his ribs.

'How did the two of you meet?' Kevin's voice broke through his thoughts.

A guttural chortle escaped Fred's chest as the memory sprang out like a jack-in-the-box. 'I broke her arm! I accidentally ran over her with my bike.'

'Oh, gosh!' Kevin tossed back his head and laughed. It was a proper laugh. Loud and generous, not holding anything back.

'Yes . . . probably not the best way to attract a girl,' Fred chuckled, glancing in the direction Linh had gone. Kevin suddenly developed a great interest in his Reeboks before hastily resuming his duty. 'Yes, well, I won't go trying that one.' He smiled, applying a new dressing to Fred's head.

Fred inhaled, breathing in the memory of seeing Dawn for the first time.

'I was riding my bike to the milk bar and there she was, in a blue polka-dot dress. A 24-carat beauty, so dazzling that I lost my footing, knocked her over and rode over her arm! She had to go to the hospital to have a cast put on. I felt absolutely dreadful about it, but I visited her the day after and took her a bunch of gardenias, and the day after that, chocolates. That was the true way to her heart, the chocolates.'

Kevin grinned.

'And, well, you get the idea. We were practically inseparable after that.'

'How long were you married for?'

Fred rubbed his ring finger once hugged by a golden band that had only been removed when his arthritis had demanded it. He hadn't had the money to resize it, but his devotion to her was engraved onto his very being.

'Fifty years before I lost her ten years ago.'

I should have come home sooner.

He swatted the unwelcome memory away.

Kevin's eyes filled with sympathy. 'How did you keep the love alive for all that time?'

'Well, I guess you can't always rely on feeling in love. That comes and goes. It's a decision, too, you know. You have to look after it. The more you can make the other person feel loved, fill their tank as it were, the more they have in their reserve to make you feel loved. It's a cycle. I used to try and plan little surprises when I could if ever things were getting stale.'

Fred stifled a laugh as a memory of answering the front door naked to surprise Dawn appeared. Unfortunately, she'd been running late from work – but at least no more Jehovah's Witnesses had visited them again after that.

Kevin popped the blood pressure cuff around Fred's arm. 'That's quite the story. Very inspiring stuff, mate! My folks got divorced when I was three. I've never been great with the ladies. Never quite know what to do or say. Everything is online now, swiping right and swiping left.'

Fred nodded politely, without the faintest idea of what Kevin was talking about. It must have something to do with a credit card. Surely you didn't have to buy dates these days?

Kevin noted the blood pressure and removed the cuff. 'Anyway, I'm a bit old-fashioned, I guess. I was kind of hoping to just meet someone naturally, you know? I wish —' The phone clipped to Kevin's belt rang, cutting him off.

'Sorry, Bernard, gotta go. It was really nice talking to you, mate.'

'You, too. Cheerio!' called Fred as the nurse walked away, chatting animatedly on the phone.

Ah, young love. There was nothing better. Except, perhaps, for old love – love of fifty years. But you had to start somewhere. He scratched his chin, glancing in the direction Linh had gone, then back to Kevin.

Some people just needed a bit of encouragement.

Chapter 9

Hannah lay on her unmade bed, studying the *Human Body* sticker book her parents had bought her yesterday. She whispered the heading aloud, not wanting to wake Sadie, who was taking a nap in her room next door.

'Blood cells,' she muttered, slowly pointing to each word as she said it. There were different coloured cells in blood, and each had a different job.

'Sadie has cancer that affects her white blood cells,' the doctor with the big nose had explained to her.

That was weird. The white cells in her book had boxing gloves. Weren't the white ones meant to *fight* the infection, not *be* the infection? Which cells were going to fight it if the white cells were sick? Maybe they had understudies like in the school play? Usually, understudies weren't as good, though. Margot Jenkins had done a terrible job of filling in for Sadie when she'd had to pull out of her role as Tinker Bell in *Peter Pan*. Margot was allergic to the pixie dust and sneezed for most of the play, while poor, un-sneezing Sadie was home in bed, too tired to move – let alone fly. Hannah wrapped herself in her rabbit doona.

Dr Big-nose's voice replayed in her head. 'Sadie's going to

have a type of medicine called chemotherapy that will make her very sick.'

That sounded silly. Why make a medicine that would make you sick? The medicine that Mum gave her when she had a cold always made her feel better, even though it tasted like a five-cent coin. And she knew that from experience, as Sadie had once offered her two bucks to suck on one for five minutes. She'd accidentally swallowed it after three, but Sadie had still come good with the money – and she'd eventually got her five cents back the next day, too.

She looked at the picture of white blood cells in her book. Did they really have smiley faces? Probably Sadie's would have sad faces if they weren't feeling well.

'She will lose all her hair,' the doctor had added, 'but that's normal.'

Hannah put the book down next to her piggy bank and stood up to look at herself in the oval dresser mirror. She ran her hands through her brown curly locks. Her hair was too short to be any good for sharing, but she knew whose wasn't.

Bounding down to the kitchen, she removed the big scissors from the drawer. She was meant to ask to use the big ones, but Mum had a shift today and Dad was nowhere to be seen. She'd been allowed to use them for her Antarctica diorama project last week, so assumed she could use them for this 'project', too. This was far more important than penguins, after all.

Half an hour later, her dad appeared in the doorway, his eyebrows so far down he reminded her of Sam the Eagle from *The Muppet Show*.

'Hannah! What on earth are you doing?'

Hannah looked from his reddening face to her bedroom carpet. She'd cut the hair off every one of her Barbies and superglued it into one big rectangle, like a patchwork quilt. It was mostly varying shades of blonde with some red thrown in for good measure. She glanced up at her dad, who stood frozen like a raspberry Zooper Dooper.

'Sadie always said she wanted to be blonde. Now's her chance. I'm making her a wig for when she loses her hair. The Barbies don't mind, Dad, they really don't. You needn't worry, I explained everything to them.'

'Argh,' he snarled, making Hannah flinch. 'You've got superglue in the carpet, Hannah! How are we going to get that out? This is the last thing we need right now!' His face was scrunched up in a way she'd never seen before, except possibly that time when he slipped on his bum playing tag and broke his coccyx. He began grabbing at the pile of hair.

'No, Dad! It's still wet!' Hannah cried, jumping to her feet to stop him. His fingers were covered in the sticky glue and the more hair he tried to pick up, the more it stuck. It was a mess. Hannah covered her mouth to hide a smile – his hands looked like Bigfoot's! She searched his eyes for that familiar giggle, waiting for his worry to turn into laughter as it often did, but it never came. His body shook as he frantically tried to pull the blonde strands off.

'I just can't . . . I can't . . . I . . .'

His voice sounded scratchy like an old record she'd heard at her grandma's house.

Hannah's tummy tightened.

He took a deep breath and collapsed on the floor, sobbing. 'I can't do this. I c-can't d-do it, Hannah.'

'Don't worry, Daddy.' She put her arm around his big shoulders, trying to ignore the banging in her chest. 'I'll do it. I'll clean it up. I'm sorry I made a mess.'

Hannah's lower lip trembled. His crying scared her more than his yelling had. She'd never once seen Dad cry, not even at Aunty Jane's funeral or when she'd accidentally flushed his new car keys down the dunny.

He stood up, still shaking, his face the colour of tinned beetroot. 'I'm going to wash this off. Don't you dare make any more mess!' He stormed out, slamming the door behind him.

Tears filled Hannah's eyes as she finished picking up the hair, which left her hands very hairy too. Would she have to start shaving? Probably best not to borrow Dad's razor today, though. She stared at the clumps of hair and glue in the bin and her rows of semi-bald Barbies.

'Sorry, girls. We tried,' she whispered.

Sadie would just have to wear a beanie. Lucky Mum had taught Hannah to knit last summer. Well, tried to, at least, but practice makes perfect. She ran to her chest of drawers and pulled out some leftover green wool, images of her dad's face flashing in her mind. New thoughts whispered in her ear.

Maybe she couldn't fix things after all.

Maybe it wasn't going to be okay.

Chapter 10

Denise picked at the loose bit of wool in her scraggly scarf. It was bloody freezing outside, but she'd needed some fresh air after a rotten toilet incident with Kathleen. She shuddered; she'd never quite got used to the smell of faeces despite her decades of work in care. Her feet and head throbbed in unison. Shouldn't have had that fourth glass of chardy last night. The mum guilt was through the roof today. Working when the girls had a curriculum day was the pits. Bingeing *Bluey* with them on the couch would've been a million times better than cleaning up shit, but they were so short-staffed.

It was a miracle that their dad had been able to take the day off work to look after them.

Denise pictured Greg's deep eyes and clenched jaw. His smile was rapidly becoming a fuzzy memory; she couldn't quite see the outline of it anymore. A shot of fear pulsed through her veins.

Please don't let him lose his temper today. Not with the girls.

Greg was losing it more than ever these days, along with any desire for her. They were *all* more stressed since they'd found out, but she was determined to trust the experts. Things had to get better soon. She buried her face in her hands. Greg seemed to think that everything was her fault, even their darling girl's diagnosis. She told herself it wasn't logical, but a small part of her had begun to believe him. She'd had half a mind to bring the girls into work today instead of leaving them with him, but how could she explain that to the DON? It wasn't like she could ask one of the residents to mind them, though half of them – especially those with no grandchildren – would probably love a visit from kids.

Denise sighed and went back inside. The elastic of her enormous Bridget Jones-style undies, the ones that were supposed to provide the support of a steel beam, were digging into her in bad places. She glanced down the corridor and seeing the coast was clear, bent over and plucked out a giant wedgie. She straightened, flinching as she spotted Bernard outside his room. Heat flushed her cheeks. How long had he been bloody standing there? His expression was neutral and pleasant. If he'd witnessed anything, he didn't let on.

'Hi, Denise! How are you?'

She narrowed her eyes. Bernard *never* asked her how she was. In fact, he never remembered her name. And just where did he think he was going with his glasses on his head? They only work if you wear them, you galah. She frowned at the newspaper and crossword book under his arm. The old man could barely read anymore, let alone do a puzzle. Was it possible that Bernard's knock to the head had somehow improved his vascular dementia? Her uncle had once told her that his bad back had miraculously improved after a car accident . . .

She shot Bernard a gruff nod as he walked – not hobbled – down the hall. Denise pursed her lips and made a mental note to look up his condition.

Chapter 11

The large maroon armchair in the lounge was supportive in all the right places, though Fred couldn't be one hundred per cent sure it wasn't also the slightest bit damp. He pushed the thought aside as he dabbed a lingering skerrick of breakfast from his moustache. This morning's offering had been porridge with brown sugar, followed by toast with lashings of butter and marmalade. Gosh, the porridge here was so delightfully creamy! Must've been made with milk, unlike his poor man's water and oats at home. His tummy let out a contented purr as he closed the newspaper, having read it from top to bottom. Still nothing about the dead body. He placed his hand on his sternum to still his beating heart, which seemed in a constant state of overdrive.

'Enjoy every moment – life is not a dress rehearsal.' Dawn's sage advice echoed in his memory. She always knew just what to say, even now.

He relaxed deeper into the chair, allowing himself to forget his predicament and marinate in the moment. A delicious sense of calm washed over him, reminiscent of a feeling he'd had as a child, waking up on a Saturday morning and realising he didn't have to go to school. The sun streamed in and Fred shut his eyes, allowing its gentle heat to seep into his wrinkled face. The beauty of being this old was that you didn't have to worry too much about sunscreen anymore. Something was sure to take you before a melanoma would.

The sound of a creaky wheel echoed down the hall, and Fred opened his eyes to see Albert being led in by a young female carer. He hobbled uncertainly on his walking frame, his watery eyes blinking rapidly, his movement jerky. The poor bloke was frightened. Fred motioned to the chair next to him and the carer sat the old man down.

'Hello? Hello? Please, please help me,' Albert pleaded, but the carer had already walked away.

'Hi, Albert. I'm here – it's okay, mate.' Fred reached out to hold Albert's trembling hand.

'No, no, it's not okay, something's not right. It's not right at all.' Albert's lips quivered, tears sprouting in his eyes.

Fred looked him up and down. The carer had brought Albert out without his glasses on. He sighed, touching the thick frames on top of his own head. Why couldn't they have forgotten Bernard's specs instead? If he wore them much longer, he was going to need them for real.

'Oh dear, you haven't got your glasses, cobber. No wonder you don't feel right. Let me get you sorted.'

Albert hadn't seemed to register his presence, but Fred didn't let go of his hand. He motioned to a blonde nurse coming down the hall. 'Hello there! My friend doesn't seem to have his —' But the nurse just rushed by.

'Oh, dear. What will it take for two old codgers like us to get a look-in, hey? Seems like we don't turn heads anymore. Don't suppose you know what room you're in, mate?'

'I live at 4 Banksia Street, Launceston,' Albert said clearly, springing to life. 'I just want to go home, please.' He closed his eyes, causing a solitary tear to break free and travel down one of the many ravines in his cheek.

Fred scratched his moustache. He needed to find his friend's room, but how? The answer glared up at him from a faded sticker on Albert's walker: *Albert Higgins, Room 43*. Bingo (for the second time that week).

'I'll be back in a jiffy, mate.'

Fred left Albert and made his way down the green-carpeted corridor. Hopefully he wouldn't run into Patricia again. He didn't think his avocados or Chicken Twistie could withstand the force.

This place was like a ruddy labyrinth, worse than that dreadful Swedish furniture store where he'd once lost forty-five minutes of his life and a perfectly good pair of jocks just finding the loo after one, or more accurately fifteen, too many meatballs. He checked the room numbers as he went. Were they repeating themselves or was he just going in circles like a lab rat?

He backtracked and, turning yet another blasted corner, finally spied room forty-three. It was a pleasant room, brighter than his, with light-blue walls. An emerald wing-backed armchair and matching ottoman sat in the corner next to a potted peace lily. A wall of faces greeted him, smiling from the many framed pictures that hung opposite the bed. He stepped closer, studying them with interest. Each had been carefully labelled with a sticker. There were old photographs and some more recent ones with Albert and his daughter Sarah, daughter-in-law Cassie and exceptionally cute grandchildren Eve and Norah. He smiled at the girls' cheeky little faces. How Fred would love to have been a grandfather. He'd have been good at that. Perhaps Eve and Norah would come to visit Albert, and Fred could say hello? It would be the closest he'd get.

His smile vanished, plucked away by the familiar, never-ending pang of longing for offspring of his own.

I should have come home sooner.

He closed his eyes and tried to squash the thought, to catapult it out of his mind, but it took hold, dragging him into the dark, haunting memory. The bloodstained sheet and his young wife's dark hair came into view.

It had been a silly argument, so silly he would have forgotten it if it weren't for the events that'd followed.

They were renovating their first home. He had wanted to do everything himself to save money, but she kept insisting they get some help. After more than three years of trying, the miracle they had thought might never eventuate had finally happened and, even though they'd had over six months to go before the birth, Dawn had wanted everything to be ready as soon as possible.

For the first time in his twenty-five years, he'd ignored his mother's advice to never leave the house in anger. He'd stormed out and gone to the pub, intending to cool off. When he came home tipsy at midnight, the first thing he'd seen was the splash of red on the bed. Initially, he wondered why Dawn had her Christmas scarf out, but then he heard the crying and the words, paralysing and incomprehensible.

'I've lost it, Fred. I've lost the baby.'

She'd mentioned feeling a bit funny earlier that day, but he'd reassured her it was probably just indigestion after they had decided to eat all of the leftover Easter chocolate in one hit. Later, the doctors told them again and again that it almost certainly wouldn't have made a difference. That it probably would have happened regardless, whether Fred had been there to rush her to the hospital hours earlier or not. But for Fred, the words sat like air outside an airtight container, unable to penetrate, heal or be believed.

Fred stared at the picture of Albert and his daughter, sadness filling up every cranny. If his own child had lived, would he still be suffering this dreadful loneliness?

A faded sepia shot in the left-hand corner caught his attention. Two similar-looking boys grinned at the camera, flexing their biceps. He traced his finger over their faces. The label underneath confirmed his suspicions: *Albert and Freddy, Port Arthur, 1946.* So, this was Albert's brother. Surrounding the print were more photos of the two as teenagers and young men, the affection between them radiating from the images.

No wonder Albert missed him. How old had Freddy been when he died?

Fred was an only child. He'd been conceived before his dad, a naval officer, went to war. Having sustained severe injuries, his father wasn't able to have any more kids when he returned. Fred's parents had loved him fiercely, pouring everything into their son – but he would have done anything to have had a brother or sister to play with or even fight with. Once, around his eighth birthday, he'd thought his mum was up the duff, but it turned out she'd just overindulged over the festive season. It was with great disappointment that he'd realised he couldn't be a brother to mince pies and plum pud.

The closest thing he'd had to a sibling growing up was his neighbour and best friend Bruno Gallo. Bruno's family had emigrated from Sicily, and although he spoke little English when they first met, they united over their love of food.

The boys attended the local primary and secondary schools together. Neither one was much of an academic, but they worked hard – and played even harder. Bruno, the extrovert of the two, loved practical jokes, and Fred more than willingly obliged.

While Bruno had gone straight to work in his father's house-painting business after finishing school, Fred, who loved his tools, had earned his crust as a handyman, becoming affectionately known as 'Fix-it Fred' by the local community.

Bruno married Roberta, a first-generation Italian immigrant, and they had four beautiful, dark-haired children. 'I wish we could give you one of ours, Freddy, but the wife might realise they're missing,' Bruno had once said, with a sad smile, his brown eyes full of compassion.

Bruno and Fred had remained friends their whole life. Or for Bruno's whole life, at least. He had died two years before Dawn – yet another wonderful soul lost to the dreaded C. Roberta moved back to Italy to be with her sister shortly after, and the kids dispersed interstate.

Fred turned his attention back to the pictures of Albert. Which was worse, the dreaded C or the dreaded D? He leaned closer, taking in the wall of memories that were no longer remembered. Dementia may well be the cruellest. Above all the other photos hung a gold-framed black-and-white wedding photo showing a young, dapper Albert dressed in tails and a top hat, a beautiful fair-haired bride by his side adorned in a long lace gown and veil. At first glance they appeared stunning and happy, but something about the photo seemed off. Fred studied their faces. They were smiling, but only with their mouths. Their eyes were eerily vacant and pained.

A small cuckoo clock chirped behind him, making Fred jump and pass wind simultaneously, a feat he hadn't thought possible. Thankfully, no one was in earshot. Or nose-shot, for that matter. Fred smirked. Bruno would surely have applauded if he'd been there.

Why had he come in here again? Glasses! He searched around and soon saw them on the bedside table. Their obvious location would have angered a different man. Albert deserved better care, but Fred always gave people the benefit of the doubt; he knew how busy the carers were.

He navigated his way back to the lounge where Albert was still sitting, and gently placed the glasses on the bridge of his friend's nose. Albert blinked as a smile spread slowly from his magnified eyes to his mouth. He placed his icy hands on Fred's and squeezed them tight.

'You're just wonderful. Simply marvellous, you know that? Thank you, Fred.'

Fred didn't think twice about hearing his own name now.

'You're the best brother I could have asked for,' Albert grinned.

'You aren't too shabby yourself, old boy,' replied Fred.

Evidently, brothers didn't always come when you expected them.

Chapter 12

Back in his room later that day, Fred watched Fred Astaire twirl Ginger Rogers effortlessly around the dance floor. He had surprised himself and was actually enjoying these videos. How he'd loved to dance with his Dawn – at parties, social events or even just in their lounge room. Fred could almost smell her if he tried hard enough. An intoxicating blend of orange flower and bergamot, an aroma that brought comfort, desire, love and joy all at once. He had kept her perfume, Fleur de Lys, on his bedside table. On the nights when the loneliness grew extra heavy, he'd spray it on the pillow next to him. Occasionally, if he could trick his brain into thinking she was there, it helped him fall asleep. More often it brought on streams of tears so great that he had to change the pillowcase.

'I wish men still danced like this!' Linh entered the room with the weekly activities schedule and a smile that would have gladdened even Eeyore's day. 'It's so romantic. There's no more real men out there, Mr Bernard, not like you.'

Fred blushed. 'Do you like dancing, Linh?'

'I *love* it, Mr Bernard! Back in Hanoi, where I'm from, I used to take classes.' Her eyes waltzed in the wistful memory.

'How wonderful. Vietnam is a beautiful place. I think of it often.'
A flash of jungle and sticky legs marched through his mind.

'Oh, you've been to Vietnam?' She cocked her head to one side.

'Yes,' said Fred softly, his eyes meeting hers. 'During the war.'

Linh's usually upbeat demeanour dropped away. 'My grandfather died then.'

'I'm so sorry,' Fred replied. 'I lost some mates, too.' He could
still see their eager young faces. Must have been about the same age
as Linh, come to think of it. Hard to even imagine now.

She placed a hand on his shoulder. 'Do you like Vietnamese
food, Mr Bernard?'

'Oh, yes, I love it!' Fred's tastebuds tingled at the memory of
fragrant stir-fries and hot spicy noodle soup laden with chilli and
handfuls of fresh aromatic herbs. 'Though if I'm honest, I haven't
had it in yonks.'

He pictured the little Vietnamese restaurant in Manly he'd taken
Dawn to for their anniversary. They had laughed until they cried
over their less than professional chopstick skills that resulted in
noodles all down Fred's shirt.

Linh clapped her hands, her eyes filling with delight. 'Oh, I'll
make you some, Mr Bernard! I love cooking. Do you like it spicy?'

Fred nodded eagerly, his tummy rumbling in anticipation.
'That's very kind of you.'

She leaned in and whispered in his ear, 'I'll bring it tomorrow.
Not really supposed to, you know, but for you, Mr Bernard, I will.'
She took a few steps and paused. 'You know, there is something
different about you . . .'

Fred's heart skipped a beat. 'Is there?'

'Yes. You seem happier lately, Mr Bernard, and more talkative.
I see it a lot. It's a big change moving into a nursing home – sometimes

it takes a few months to settle in. You're doing really well. What do you think the secret is?'

'The secret?'

'To happiness, I mean? You seem to have found it.'

Fred leaned back. 'No one's ever asked me that before. I don't have all the answers, but it's definitely not money, that's for sure. That comes and goes – as does youth.'

And a strong stream, he thought. 'I reckon being grateful helps. Grateful for whatever you have, whether it's a new car or a new packet of chips.'

Astaire took Rogers in his arms and whirled her around the dance floor, catching the attention of both.

'And having someone to share it all with, of course – someone to love, and be loved by. You'll be richer than a millionaire if you can find that.'

Linh's eyes sparkled. 'You're very wise, Mr Bernard. I'm so glad to see you coming out of your shell.' She moved her white sneakers to the beat then danced out of the room. 'See you later at Music!'

'Wouldn't miss it for the world!' he sang, waving his arms like a conductor. His eyes returned to the screen. There was a knock at the door and Fred turned to see Kevin. He'd had more visitors this morning than he'd had all year.

'Hiya, Bernard. Just come to check you over, mate.'

'You know, Linh was in here just now,' said Fred, raising his eyebrows.

Kevin dropped his stethoscope and gave a strange little cough.

'She was? That's, er, nice.'

'Have you had a chance to speak to her yet?'

'Speak to her?' Kevin said the words like Fred had suggested the lad get an early prostate exam.

'Well, you know, mate – ask her out?'

'Oh, I, um . . . well, I would like to but I just wouldn't know what to say.' He took Fred's pulse, which was likely lower than Kevin's own.

'Maybe talk about something she's interested in. She likes cooking, oh and dancing, you know.'

'Dancing?' His ginger eyebrows shot up, wrinkling his freckled forehead.

'Yes, ballroom dancing – like that.' Fred motioned to the telly where Astaire and Rogers were still spinning around the floor.

Kevin gave an audible gulp. 'I don't know the first thing about dancing.'

A carer burst in and whispered something into Kevin's ear. He gave Fred an apologetic look as he made for the door. 'A resident's got hold of some meds again. Gotta run – sorry, mate.'

Fred waved and glanced back at the TV, tapping his fingers on the arm of his chair. Maybe Cupid needed a little help.

👓

The next morning Linh entered the room carrying something wrapped in a white towel.

'Quick, Mr Bernard, I've got your pho. I heated it in the staff microwave. It's our little secret, okay? Shhh!' She touched her index finger to her lips.

Fred nodded like a cheeky schoolboy. She removed the towel to reveal a glass container of soup, and placed it on the table. He clapped his hands together as the hypnotic smell of lemongrass, ginger and coriander wafted through the room.

'Ooooh, whacko! Thanks so much, Linh.'

He took a spoon and was about to dig in when he paused, an idea taking hold.

'Oh, gosh, Linh, I'm actually not feeling too well all of a sudden,' he said, placing his hand on his forehead and emitting a dramatic groan. 'I think I'm going to need the nurse.'

Linh squatted next to him and looked on in alarm as he pressed the call button (now thankfully fixed).

He knew who was rostered on today. Sure enough, Kevin popped his head in a minute later. Fred gave his bottom a victorious wiggle.

Linh's presence caused the young man to blush, but he focused on the task at hand. 'What's up, Bernard? Are you okay?'

'Oh, well, I'm just, um, feeling a bit dizzy, you know? I think you might need to check my blood pressure?'

'Okay . . .' said Kevin slowly, 'I did just check it twenty minutes ago . . .'

As Kevin placed the cuff on his arm, Fred caught his eye and gave him a big wink before letting out another loud groan.

'You absolute bugger,' Kevin whispered, though there was no trace of anger in his voice.

Fred glanced at Linh, who was looking on, concerned.

'So,' said Fred, a little too loudly, 'Linh here has just made me some amazing Vietnamese soup. Do you like Vietnamese food, Kevin?'

'Oh, I, um, I haven't ever tried it, actually, I'm ashamed to say. My mum's cooking repertoire is meat and three veg, I'm afraid, and I don't eat out much.'

'Well then, you must taste this! I haven't touched it yet.'

'Oh, um, I don't want to take it away from you . . .'

'I insist, why don't you put some in a cup?' Fred glared at Kevin imploringly, giving a not-so-subtle cough.

'Is Mr Bernard okay?' Linh's dark eyes were full of worry.

Kevin glanced at the monitor. 'Yes, his blood pressure is surprisingly as right as rain. Fancy that! Though I suspect his *head* may need examining.' He shot Fred a knowing glance.

'Oh, yes, I'm feeling better already. How fortuitous!' Fred smoothed his moustache.

'That's good,' said Linh. 'I'll get a mug for you to try the soup, Kevin. Back in a sec.'

'Bernard!' Kevin said, as soon as she'd left. 'What am I meant to do?'

'Compliment her on her cooking? Ask for the recipe? I'm sure you'll figure it out! Quick, here she comes.'

Linh returned and carefully poured some of the pho into a white paper cup, handing it to Kevin with a spoon and a smile.

His lanky hands trembled as he took it. 'Ooh, thank you so much – smells amazing,' he said, bringing the cup up to his nose before popping a generous spoonful in his mouth. 'Oh, wow, that's super delicious, Linh, I-I . . .' Beads of sweat began to outnumber the freckles on his forehead. He tried not to cough, which made him cough all the more, causing some of the hot soup to spill onto his trousers. His attempt at stifling the resulting yelp was grossly unsuccessful. Placing the soup on the wheelie table, he stared in horror at his wet groin, his eyes now watering profusely. 'It's, um, very, er, spicy, isn't it?'

Linh and Fred couldn't help but giggle.

'I'm sorry, maybe you don't like spicy?' Linh covered her mouth with her hand.

'No, no,' said Kevin, rasping like a chihuahua with emphysema. 'I like it – it's just, I might, um, need some water.' Another coughing fit ensued as Linh dashed to the ensuite to get him a glass.

'Bernard!' Kevin, half angry, half laughing, croaked, giving

Fred's shoulder a playful push. 'She'll *never* want to go out with me now!'

Linh placed her arm gently on Kevin's back as she gave him water. Her touch had an even greater effect than the chilli, causing the youth to turn a deeper shade of red, the kind that belonged in a medical magazine.

'Next time I'll make it less spicy for you, Kevin, okay? You enjoy yours, Mr Bernard. I'm glad you're okay. I must go now – it's almost time for Knitting Club.'

As she left, Fred and Kevin met each other's gaze. A glint of hope spread from the younger man's eyes to his lips, which broke into a broad smile.

'Did she just say "next time"?'

'She certainly did,' said Fred, grinning from ear to ear.

'Hopefully next time I won't look like I've wet my pants!' He grimaced at his soup-stained crotch.

'Ah, that's good practice for when you are my age, my boy!' Fred chuckled, motioning to the packet of incontinence pants in the open closet.

Kevin laughed. 'Bernard, I was wondering,' he said, shuffling his feet. 'I finish work early on Tuesdays. Do you reckon I could possibly come for a chat and maybe watch some of those dance videos with you? You're so easy to talk to and, like, my old man isn't around. Absolutely no stress if you don't want to though . . . or if you're busy '

Busy? Fred wouldn't know busy if it bit him on the bum. He gazed out the window at the smudged clouds. The body could be found any day now, so he probably shouldn't be making any commitments here. He'd soon have to face the music and work out where he was going to live. A shelter? A housing commission? He turned back to Kevin, whose brown eyes held a fragile hope that Fred couldn't bear to break. Bugger it.

'Yes. In fact, I'd like that,' he said, shooing the impending exit date out of his mind like a stray cat.

Chapter 13

Hannah scrunched up her nose at the terrible, awful sight. She sat up, rubbing the sleep out of her eyes. Why did her doona have Super Mario Brothers on it? Video games sucked! A grunt came from the corner as their friend Liam opened his eyes, stretched and waved good morning before picking up his Nintendo comic. She rolled her eyes. That's right. They'd slept over here last night as Mum was on night shift and Dad was busy – again. She gave Luigi a greasy stare. It was bad enough that she'd had to sit through the movie last night, which was even worse than the game. Especially when they could have watched *The Little Mermaid*, but she and Sadie had been outvoted. She looked around the room, the sound of snoring tickling her ear. Her sister lay sound asleep on the lilo next to her, her pale face peaceful as she dozed.

Hannah's tummy rumbled as voices came from the kitchen. It was Liam's little twin brothers, arguing about who could burp the loudest. She giggled. It was always noisy here, and she liked it. Things were quiet at home. Too quiet, and she had begun to fear the silence. Dad hadn't been around as much recently, and he was always cross, like he'd forgotten how to be happy. Perhaps Mum had forgotten too. She was always sad, a permanent crease between her eyebrows like a missed crinkle on an ironed shirt. They hadn't been holding hands recently. Why didn't they hold hands anymore? Dad didn't even give Mum a kiss on the cheek before work like he used to. Mum was always criticising herself, saying how awful her hair was or how saggy her bum had become. But Hannah thought she was the most beautiful woman in the world.

She'd tried to cheer Mum and Dad up by making them a nice brekkie on the weekend. How was she to know that if you put butter and Vegemite on bread before putting it in a toaster that it would catch fire? They say it's the thought that counts, but she didn't feel like the thought, or the scorched bread, had counted. It hadn't cheered them up at all. Dad had even got angry at Mum for not teaching Hannah better. It wasn't Mum's fault.

Tyres crunched on the gravel driveway. Hannah checked the time on Liam's silly dinosaur clock. Rats! They must've slept in.

Gently, she shook her sister awake. 'Mum's here, Sayd – wake up.' Sadie groaned and sat up. A clump of brown hair remained on the pillow. Hannah gasped and quickly scooped it up, putting it in her pyjama pocket before Sadie could see. So it was starting. The nasty chemo medicine was stealing her sister's hair.

The girls collected their things, thanked Liam's parents, and hopped into their mum's blue Mazda. Mum looked particularly bad today; her bloodshot eyes matched her splotchy red skin.

'Hi, girls,' she said with a smile.

But the smile looked fake, like the kind Hannah gave when she went to the dentist. Hannah studied her mother's crinkled uniform, smudged make-up and extra boofy hair. It would've been a big effort for her to collect them straight after a shift. When they got home she'd return to bed. Work and bed were the only two places Mum seemed to manage at the moment.

Hannah hugged her close, wishing she could take on her pain for her.

'Is he home?' Hannah asked, her heart beating fast. Dad just wasn't the same person anymore, and she was beginning to believe that no amount of Vegemite on toast could change that.

'No, love, he's at . . .' Her eyes dropped. 'He's at work.' Her lips pulled into a skinny line.

Again? On a Saturday? Hannah frowned.

Dad seemed to be at work a lot lately. Hannah didn't know exactly what he did, but he always came back in a very bad mood. Mum was quiet on the drive home, but Hannah reckoned her thoughts must have been loud – she had her thinking face on, the one she used during Trivial Pursuit. They pulled up to the house and Mum unlocked the door. The pile of bills on the hall table with the red writing on them looked even bigger than it had yesterday.

Sadie went straight up to her bedroom, no doubt to get stuck into the new Marvel comic she'd been itching to read, another thing Hannah had no interest in. As Sadie climbed the stairs, Hannah spied a bald patch at the back of her head. Her tummy felt off. Probably the five packets of Nerds lollies she and Liam had eaten as a midnight feast. She put her hand in her pocket and felt the soft clump of her sister's hair. Could you stick hair back onto the scalp? She'd used up all the superglue but had plenty of clag, though that may not be sticky enough. The phone rang, making her jump. Mum answered, turning her back to Hannah.

'Yeah, I know it's overdue. I'm sorry. I'm taking on extra shifts and I'll pay it next week. Yep. Thanks. Bye.' Her mother placed the receiver back and closed her eyes for a long time. 'I've got a shocking headache. I'm just going to lie down for a bit, love,' she said finally, her fingers rubbing her temples as if she were trying to erase a mistake, like Hannah did in her maths book. 'Sadie's got her appointment this afternoon – I'll be up by then. You can watch some telly if you like.' Mum walked slowly to her bedroom and shut the door, leaving Hannah all alone.

And there it was again: the silence.

Chapter 14

Two small beads of sweat slid down Fred's forehead and made a tiny wet patch on Bernard's blue shirt. The Move-it Monday exercise class Linh had convinced him to try had pushed him hard, though he still couldn't quite figure out how one became exerted from balloon tennis. He pinched the crinkly skin under his arm as a giggly memory escaped from deep within. Dawn sat next to him on their faded yellow couch, seeing who could stretch their wrinkly tricep skin out the furthest. It was serious business involving a measuring tape, and the winner had to do the dishes for the week. Dawn had beaten him by two centimetres, but he'd insisted on doing the washing-up anyway, maintaining that glorious soft, stretchy skin like hers should be celebrated, not punished.

Albert, not quite as sweaty, tapped Fred on the shoulder and gave him a wink, flexing his arms in a strongman's pose. Fred laughed as a well-dressed elderly woman with a smart grey bob walked up behind Albert and placed her hands on his shoulders.

'Hello, my darling Albie – it's me, your adoring, wonderful wife.'

A huge grin spread across Albert's face, his eyes vanishing within the folds of his crinkled skin. 'Ohhh, hello, Vally darling!'

He grasped her hand, kissing it repeatedly like it was the most fabulous thing on earth.

'Hello, I'm Valerie – Albert's wife,' she said, extending a manicured hand to Fred.

'A pleasure to meet you. People call me Bernard,' he replied, getting a small kick out of his accurate choice of words.

'I haven't seen you at exercise before. I come here every Monday after class.' Valerie picked some lint off Albert's shirt.

'Well, it's never too late to get fit, they say,' Fred said with a wink.

'Touché!' Val beamed.

Albert pointed to Fred. 'I found Freddy, Val! I knew he'd come. Isn't he just marvellous?'

Val cocked her head to the side, her shaped eyebrows furrowing as she looked from Albert to Fred. Fred shrugged his shoulders.

'I see,' she said slowly. 'Well, would your marvellous "Freddy" like to get a coffee with us at the cafe? My treat.'

Albert's eye's widened and he nodded vigorously at Fred, silently urging him to take up the offer.

Fred didn't need to be asked twice. 'I'd love to, thanks.'

The cafe near the entrance of the nursing home was designed specifically for visitors and residents. Someone had obviously tried to make it look inviting with jars of gaudy fake tulips and battery-operated tea-light candles. You could almost forget you were in a nursing home but for the faint smell of urine and the thick plastic tablecloths.

Val ordered a Devonshire tea for her and Albert to share, and Albert quickly busied himself by licking the cream off a scone. Fred chose a blueberry muffin and a cappuccino, which he inhaled as soon as they were placed in front of him.

'So, what are you in for, Bernard?' Valerie asked, confirming Fred's impression that, like her husband, her sense of humour was on point.

He shrugged. 'Old age, I guess, like the rest of them.'

'I'm so glad Albert has made a friend,' she said, spooning some more cream onto Albert's now-bare scone. 'It's not easy, you know, with the dementia. He has his good times and bad. We get through them one day at a time.' She placed her hand on Albert's cheek. He beamed at her like a lost child who's been reunited with his mother.

'I'm just so grateful that he still knows me, although he often thinks we aren't married yet.' She shot Albert a coy smile, causing his eyebrows to dance up and down. 'So, I take it he has mentioned his brother Fred to you?' Val lowered her voice, emptying a sachet of Splenda into her tea.

'He has a bit. Does he often mistake other people for him?' Fred scraped the last bit of delicious froth from his cup.

'No. Funny, that. I think you might actually be the first. I can't say you look alike, but there is something about you that reminds me of Freddy, too. He was a lovely man, like my darling Albert.' She squeezed her husband's hand.

'I was told by the staff that Fred passed away. I'm so sorry.'

Val took a slow sip of tea, staring into the steaming amber liquid. 'Yes, he did. On the way to our wedding, in fact.' She paused, the words causing visible pain. 'In a horrible car crash. He was the best man.'

A chill came over the room. It made sense now, the wedding photo with the unsmiling eyes. What a brute life could be. Fred reached out and patted the couple's intertwined fingers, searching for words.

'I'm sorry, love, I'm so very sorry.'

Valerie gave a slight nod of her head as he saw decades of grief pool in her eyes.

'It was too late to cancel. Albie was already standing at the altar. It wasn't until after the actual ceremony that we got the news. No mobile phones back then, of course. We just thought Fred was very, very late, as he often was, the larrikin. We didn't even want photos but the photographer insisted on one, said we'd regret it forever if we didn't. I'm just so glad Albie doesn't remember it. That's the only bright side of all of this. But he looks for him, for his Freddy.'

'Freddy!' sang Albert, grinning at Fred. 'It's just so great he's here, isn't it, Val?'

'Yes. Yes, it is.' Her words seemed genuine.

As they finished their morning tea, Val gushed as she told Fred about the people he'd seen in the photos; their daughter Sarah, her wife Cassie, and their beautiful granddaughters Eve and Norah.

Albert's mouth stretched into a giant yawn.

'I'm going to take him back to his room now for a rest,' Val said, wiping away Albert's cream moustache with a Kleenex. 'So lovely to meet you, Bernard. I'm sure I'll see you again soon. I'm so happy he has someone to talk to.' She shook his hand warmly.

'Don't you worry, love. I'll keep an eye out for him.' While I'm here, that is.

'Marvellous, you are!' Albert pointed at Fred with both his index fingers. 'Simply marvellous!'

Fred saluted him and hoped for the first time that 'here' would be a long, long time.

He wandered slowly back to his room, thoughts of his own wedding day keeping him company. Bruno had made a wonderful best man. Fred had always wanted to return the favour but, as much as Bruno loved Fred, he had four six-foot-three Sicilian brothers to not offend, so he hadn't quite made the cut.

Fred reached his room, and no sooner had he sat down than Linh entered with a tray. Surely it couldn't be lunchtime yet? The clock showed 11.38 a.m. He shrugged. Close enough.

'Hello again, Mr Bernard! Here's your lunch, and the newspaper!' She placed the tray on his table. It smelt of bacon and optimism.

'Thanks, love, that's fabulous.' He removed the plastic lid from the mug of tea and took a sip, immediately spitting it out again. Not because of the terrible taste but from the newspaper headline that caught his eye and froze his blood.

The body had been found.

Chapter 15

BODY OF LOCAL MAN FOUND IN RIVER

At 4.30 p.m. yesterday, the body of an elderly man was found on the bank of Wattle River by a passing jogger. The man has been identified as Frederick Fife, 82, a local to Wattle River, who was last seen by his landlord leaving his apartment for a walk in April. Mr Fife, a quiet widower with no known relatives, is said to have been facing financial problems. However, police are not treating the death as suspicious. He is believed to have suffered a heart attack before falling into the river. Photo ID found on his person, along with a positive ID from the landlord, Martin Belford, confirmed the body's identity.

'You okay there, Mr Bernard? You look like you've seen a ghost!' Linh dabbed at the spilt tea on Fred's shirt. If only she knew the half of it! A coldness pervaded his core. The masking tape that had been holding his mind together was quickly becoming unstuck. *Had* he in fact died, and was now in some strange kind of afterlife? Surely the tea wouldn't be this bad in heaven?

'Er, fine, thank you,' he managed, lowering the newspaper to finally answer Linh.

'Okay, then, if you're sure. I'll see you later.'

He nodded, taking another sip of the ghastly tea, regretting it wasn't something a little stronger. He stared at the article again to check it was real.

They think the dead body is me! I'm not going to be implicated in anything. No one knows that Bernard is dead!

The case was closed, the body accounted for, no loose strings to tie up. He exhaled slowly, a mixture of guilt and relief in equal measure, as four words illuminated his mind.

I can stay here.

He gazed out to the potted pansies in the courtyard, now watered and thriving much like he was, then back to the bed, desk and telly. His little flat would no doubt be vacant now – not that it could be called his anymore. The left side of the wardrobe would be emptied and bare – the impossible task of letting go had been done for him. He was a skydiver pushed from a plane. Terrified. Airborne. Light. Free?

A seed of possibility sprouted in his mind. Could it be that he was being offered a very rare and unusual gift? A gift from his Dawn, even? He tapped his fingers on his cheek. Staying on here meant he would be looked after for the rest of his life. He'd have a home – no more rationing food or worrying about the electricity being turned off. The thought of spending someone else's money sat in his belly like a week-old ham sandwich, yet from the sound of it, Bernard didn't have any family to share it with. He didn't know Bernard's monetary situation, but it had to be better than his own if he was able to pay the fees here.

Though Fred's financial decline had taken place gradually, it had all seemed to creep up suddenly. He'd never forget handing over the keys to the beloved Californian bungalow he and Dawn had shared. After Dawn died he'd had to sell it to pay her medical bills, including the costly experimental treatments they'd tried, none of which were covered by Medicare. Their meagre super had evaporated. He was grateful for the pension, but it was a drop in the ocean. The in-home nurse and medical equipment alone had cost an arm and a leg, though it had meant Dawn could be at home with him. He'd have given his whole body if it would have saved her. None of it had worked in the end. They say that time heals, yet the ache still caught his breath. Grief is often invisible to the outside world – Fred was like still water whose reflection mirrored the sun but concealed dark and murky depths underneath. He often wondered how his body still held together when his soul had broken into a million pieces.

The loneliness grew bigger at night. Darling Dawn had always felt the cold, so every evening throughout their marriage he would hop into bed ten minutes before her to warm up her side of the bed, moving over when she got in. The night she had passed, he'd instinctively climbed in on her side. Then, like death itself was upon him, he'd been winded with lament. There was no longer anyone to move over for.

A warmth spread across his face as tears fell with abandon. What he'd struggled with the most since Dawn died hadn't been the times of wanting a bit more to eat or the uncertainty of how he would manage, but the loneliness. The ache-in-your-bones kind of loneliness. The loneliness of all the shared memories with loved ones now being yours alone. The feeling of being left behind by everyone he held dear – his wife, his handful of friends, Bruno, their lost baby. All those he cherished stood in his past now, and he had no one to look forward to loving. The ever-constant sting and guilt of never having children grew even greater. Dawn, like her name, had made all his days begin. She'd been his only light.

He plucked a Kleenex from the box and began dabbing his eyes, but it did little to stop the great plopping tears. His mother had always said that Fred had been born with an extra helping of love in his heart, and he thrived on sharing that love with those around him. The problem was now he didn't have anywhere to put it. Grief was love with nowhere to go. He often went to the supermarket twice in one day just to talk to people, even when he didn't have enough money to buy anything. His dear old cocker spaniel Lulu, with her comforting chestnut fur, had passed shortly after his beloved wife. He hadn't had the heart to get another dog, who would undoubtedly outlive him.

But here at the home, he had Albert and Linh and Kevin. Even Patricia's company was almost better than none. Almost. Here he was *known* – even if it was by another name. For so many years he'd taken for granted the significance of being known by another person, until it was all snatched away and he was suddenly a stranger to everyone he met.

Now, for the first time in a very long time, he felt useful, wanted, as if his presence made a difference to someone in a small way. He could keep an eye out for Albert and maybe, just maybe, he could help Kevin win over the lovely Linh. Here he felt the physical touch of other human beings, even if it was just a brief handshake or a pat on the shoulder. Besides, if he wanted to confess the truth now, he doubted anyone would believe him after so many failed attempts. He'd been swimming upstream for too long and wanted to let go. Bernard had been swept away by the current life had dealt him, and maybe he could be, too.

Fred closed his eyes. His thoughts drifted to poor old Bernard slumped in that wheelchair. A timid breeze made its entrance through the open window, caressing his eyelids. He opened them and spoke softly.

'Would you mind terribly, old boy, if I borrowed the rest of your life? I mean, I know you're not using it, you see, and it seems a shame for it to go to waste. I promise I'll take excellent care of it. I wouldn't normally ask – it's just that I'm a bit down on my luck and really have nowhere else to go. I did try to set them straight but they just won't listen – and now, well, I could do with a friend or two.'

A lone seagull landed on a pot of pansies, looked directly at him, and squawked. Fred's body flushed with peace. He had the old boy's blessing: he could let go. So he tucked the lie away into a little box deep inside himself and shut the lid.

It was at that moment that Fred decided to be Bernard.

Chapter 16

At 7.30 a.m. Denise stepped into the linen supply closet, slamming the door behind her. She rubbed her lower back. The ibuprofen had not targeted the pain like the ad said it would. She looked into the garbage bag containing Bernard's incontinence pants. She'd thought it felt light – they were even drier than the wine she'd drunk last night. They were *always* wet. Was something up with his kidneys? Had there been a change in his medication? She'd have to ask the doctor when he came.

Tossing the bag into a bin, she rubbed her eyes. She was too tired to worry about things like this with all she had going on. She sucked in the thickened air, trying to still the throb in her chest. The overwhelming smell of bleach didn't help. Grabbing a pile of folded white sheets from the steel shelving unit, she screamed into them. Why hadn't she called in sick today? But she had needed the distraction – things were so fraught at home. She was grateful to her friend for taking the girls for the second time that week. They'd be safe and happy with Kristy's young boys for company.

Memories of last night played in her mind in slow motion. The panic-stricken expression on Greg's face as he lurched naked from the shower, drops of water spitting off him like a sprinkler.

Him grabbing for his phone, which lay next to her on the bed, dinging with text messages.

He was definitely hiding something. Or someone.

A wave of nausea spread through Denise's gut. How she hoped it wasn't someone. When she asked him about it he screamed at her, accusing her of keeping too tight a leash on him; then he'd been crabby with the girls.

Her chest tightened and she screamed into the sheets again, willing her desperation to transfer to them. She pulled away, leaving behind a smear of cakey beige foundation on the linen. Her flesh crawled with disgust. Why did she even bother anymore, with the make-up, with any of it? If he was seeing someone, she would probably be a lot better-looking than Denise. Wasn't hard to be. Skinny, blonde, big boobs, no doubt.

Denise looked down at her own chest. *She* had big boobs. Huge boobs. But not the good kind. At least she had finally found a decent bra at Target on the weekend. If only her bloody husband gave her the same level of support.

She caught a glimpse of herself in the glass cabinet on the wall. A clown on steroids looked back, her frizzy red mop resembling Ronald McDonald having a bad-hair day. A sour taste rose into her mouth. She hated her hair. Hated her body. Hated herself. Stupid, fat, ugly, useless – just like Greg said. The soundtrack of her life on loop.

Her watch beeped twice. Time to shower Ruby.

Denise took a long, deep breath. No way was she putting up with any nonsense today. Unlike everything going on at home, at least her job was predictable. Well, except for Bernard. She couldn't quite put her finger on it. She'd googled his condition more than once, but it seemed that nothing could reverse vascular dementia. He appeared to have had a personality transplant, and now the change in continence.

She couldn't afford to be pulled up for any more mistakes. Denise needed this job, needed the money. God knows the bills were piling up.

Tossing the foundation-smeared sheet into the dirty-laundry basket, she gave her face a sharp slap, put her shoulders back and exited.

She knocked abruptly on Ruby's door, not bothering to wait for an answer before barging in.

'Ruby! Wake up! Time for your shower!'

The old woman lay bunched up in the bed, eyes shut tight, a pale-pink doona forming a cocoon around her fluffy hair and see-through skin, reminding Denise of a baby bird. What she'd give to be in a warm bed right now with someone waiting on her hand and foot. Lucky old crow.

'Ruby!' she called, too loudly.

Ruby's eyes scrunched tighter but her tiny body remained still. Denise grabbed the end of the frilly doona and whipped it off. Her frail body started the way a baby does in its sleep, both arms flinching outwards.

'Come on, you lazy thing. I've got work to do.' She knew she shouldn't talk like that, but Ruby wouldn't tell anyone. She was too polite, too shy. Most of them were.

The old woman's grey eyes peeled open, disorientation turning into recognition. 'Oh, hello, Denise love. How are you?' Her voice was soft and croaky, like an old engine needing to warm up.

'Fine,' lied Denise. 'Come on, get a wriggle on!'

'Oh, I'm sorry, my hip has been playing up a bit,' she said, attempting to shuffle her meagre frame to the edge of the bed.

Denise grabbed her arm, a little harder than she should have, and pulled her to a seated position. 'Hands up!'

Ruby slowly lifted her twiglike limbs and Denise yanked her nightie and undergarments off. Ruby flinched again. Denise led her to the shower chair and turned on the water. Shit – she'd forgotten to check the temperature.

'Ooooh!' Ruby yelped. 'I'm so sorry, love, I hate to complain . . . it's just a bit cold.' Her pruny skin shrivelled further, like lips tasting lemon.

'Don't be fussy, Ruby, we're already running behind.' The words spluttered out like boiling water, burning her mouth with guilt. Even so, Denise felt unable to turn them off. Just like the packet of bickies she'd demolished in one sitting last night, each Tim Tam creating a bigger hole than the one it filled. She closed her eyes, her head spinning.

'Oh, I'm so sorry, love. I didn't mean to make you late.' Ruby bowed her head.

Her small, thin body shivered on the shower chair. The old woman's skin was practically transparent; Denise could see every ancient vein. She looked away and swallowed, pushing down the ball of guilt that was rising in her throat. Yet part of her found some sort of warped satisfaction in seeing someone else suffer the way she did. God, what sort of sicko was she becoming?

Denise grudgingly adjusted the temperature, grabbed the soap and lathered the woman's back, the face washer rubbing over her protruding spine like an old-fashioned washboard she'd seen on a period drama on the ABC.

When Ruby was showered and dressed, Denise told her to wait in the bathroom while she put clean sheets on the bed. As she removed the pillowcase, she paused. There was a near-full bottle of pear liqueur on the bedside table. Ruby's grandchildren must have visited; they always gave her the good stuff. She picked it up, studying the label as bad thoughts stewed in her mind. This would be a new low, even for her. Images of her suffering daughter and of her husband with another woman suffocated her mind.

'Can I come out now, love?' Ruby's voice warbled from the bathroom.

'Just a minute, almost done,' Denise shouted back, checking to see if the coast was clear. Then, without further thought, she expertly unscrewed the lid and took a long swig straight from the bottle. It burned her throat and a numbing warmth crept up the length of her body. She inhaled slowly, allowing the feeling to wash over her before topping up the bottle with the big glass of apple juice that Ruby always had by her bed.

'All right, in you come. Looks like you've run out of apple juice, Ruby. I'll just nip out and get you some more.'

Ruby shuffled back into the room. 'Thanks, love, that's very kind, my mouth gets so dry as you —'

Denise was already walking away. This would get her through. Something had to.

Chapter 17

Hannah's left leg was asleep and her bum was totally numb. The cold concrete step sent a shiver up her spine. Dad should've been home an hour ago. The automatic porch light clicked on as the last bit of sunshine disappeared. She glanced up at Sadie's window. She'd already gone to bed, exhausted as always. Hannah had often wished for a later bedtime than her big sister, but not like this.

She looked down at the birdhouse she'd finished at school that day and rubbed its shiny wooden surface. She almost hadn't made it for him, but then she'd thought about what Aunty Jane had always told her: 'You'll never regret being kind even when people aren't kind to you.' It was red and white, his favourite colours. She closed her eyes and pictured his face lighting up when she gave it to him.

Maybe, just maybe, she'd get a glimpse of the dad she used to know.

She stamped her foot on the ground, pins and needles sizzling in her toes. Maybe, if he was in a *really* good mood, they could even get a pet magpie. It could sleep in her bed at night (or Mum and Dad's bed if Dad wanted it as his own pet) and it could use the birdhouse during the day. Could you train magpies to use the toilet?

She'd ask Dad about that when he got home. If he was in a better mood than this morning, that is. He was probably just extra grumpy as he'd slept on the couch last night. Mum had said it was because she was coming down with a cold and didn't want Dad to get sick. Hannah thought she'd smelt cough syrup when Mum had driven her to school.

Headlights lit up the garage roller door as the engine stopped and the car door opened.

'Dad!' Her singsong voice rose as her eyes met his. But he stared straight through her.

'Not now, Hannah.'

A tiny piece of her heart chipped off. If not now, when? He pushed past her through the screen door, stinking of cigarette smoke. Tossing his leather briefcase to the floor, he bounded up the steps to his bedroom. She followed, holding the birdhouse in front of her as carefully as if it were a puppy.

'But, Dad, I made —'

'I said not now, Hannah!'

He had the look in his eye, his jaw clenched, his lips pulled tight. She should probably leave him be, but surely if he just saw it . . .

'Look what I made you, Daddy!' She tugged at his shirt and lifted her heartfelt creation up for him to see.

'I said, LEAVE ME ALONE!'

Hannah couldn't tell if she heard the shouted words before or after she felt the birdhouse being ripped from her hands and thrown against the wall. The pieces fell to the floor faster than her tears, which stayed hovering in her tear ducts. Letting them fall would make it feel more real. He slammed the door to his room.

To his heart.

She couldn't breathe.

'Hannah?' Mum's voice came from the kitchen, followed by footsteps up the stairs. Hannah covered her face. Mum shouldn't see her upset. She had to be strong. Things were bad enough as it was.

Mum's face fell as she stared at the shattered birdhouse.

'Oh . . . I'm so sorry, love,' she said, bending down to pick up the pieces. 'He's just . . . just . . .' She opened her mouth as if to say something, but nothing came. She stared in silence at the jagged wooden fragments.

What word was Mum searching for? Angry? Sad? Stressed? Very busy at work? Fallen out of love with us? That last thought opened the tear gates. She stood up and lunged into her mother's warm, soft embrace.

'I love you so much, Han.'

'Love you too, Mum.'

'Let's get you off to bed. Sadie fell asleep straight after dinner again, poor love. I've got an early shift tomorrow and I can't be late again, so we'll need to keep moving in the morning.'

Hannah nodded, rubbing her eyes with her sleeve as she headed to bed. There'd definitely be no magpie. Her hope for a pet and her father's love lay shattered along with the birdhouse.

Hannah was unable to sleep on her soggy, tear-stained pillow. A crash echoed from somewhere. She bounded down the stairs into the kitchen to see her dad bent over, picking up pieces of broken purple porcelain. She clapped her hand over her mouth. It was Sadie's most treasured possession: the beautiful bone-china teacup from Aunty Jane. Sadie drank *everything* from that cup – water, juice, tea . . . even vinegar! Mum always took it to the hospital for her.

Her father hissed as he brought his hand up to his face, drops of blood dripping from his thumb. He'd sliced it on one of the broken pieces. Serves him right! Something tickled Hannah's nostrils and before she could stop it a big sneeze burst out. He looked up and saw her, his face all twisted.

'Hannah, this was an accident. I knocked it —'

'I HATE YOU!' she screamed and bolted back upstairs, slamming her bedroom door behind her.

Breaking her birdhouse was one thing, but this was unforgivable.

Chapter 18

Denise stared at the computer monitor, the words on the screen melding into a blurry black-and-white blob as the horrible events of last night clawed at her brain. She tried to add up all the calories she had consumed after, so she'd know just how much self-loathing to take with her today.

'Denise . . . Denise?'

The voice sounded like it was coming from far away.

'Denise!'

It was louder now, snapping her back to the present. She blinked hard and looked up to see Kevin, his eyes pooled with concern.

'You okay there?'

'I'm fine.' It was the lie she told herself day in and day out. She grabbed the mouse and pretended to look busy. The action caused a stab of pain to slice through her right thumb.

'Ouch! That looks like a nasty splinter!' Kevin knelt down beside her.

She hadn't even noticed it last night. 'It's fine,' her robot reply came again.

'Here, let me get the tweezers for you and help get it out.'

Too exhausted to protest, she plonked her hand palm upwards on the desk in front of him.

'I'll just get the Betadine.' His thick New Zealand accent brimmed with a kindness that crept under her skin and made her want to cry at the same time.

'How did you get that? Gardening, was it?' he said, gently inching the tip of the tweezers under the skin.

She found herself nodding, then looked away. Just shut up, Kevin. Please, shut up.

'I'm a bit of a green thumb myself. Had a tussle with a cactus the other day. Hazard of the trade, isn't it?'

She didn't answer, barely feeling the removal of the splinter, her hand now as numb as her brain.

'There we go, that's much better.' He dabbed on the antiseptic and reached for a bandaid.

She swooped in before he could grab it. 'I'm quite capable of doing that myself, thank you very much.'

Kevin flinched. 'Oh, all right . . . Well, you take care, Denise. Are you sure you're okay?'

'I'm fine.'

Maybe if she said it enough, she would be.

Chapter 19

With a yelp of pain, Fred plucked an unruly hair from his left nostril that had cheekily tried to join his moustache. He smiled at his reflection in the mirror. He'd slept better the last two nights than he had all week and it showed: the rings under his eyes had faded, and his eyes looked clearer, brighter. A delicious feeling bubbled inside him as he spritzed himself with Bernard's sandalwood cologne, a luxury he'd gone without for years.

After the body had been found and he'd officially decided to stay on as Bernard, a great weight had been lifted off his shoulders. Fred was dead, but he'd been able to make peace with that as it wouldn't hurt anyone. He was confident that there would be no one grieving him and doubted that anyone would have turned up to his funeral, if one had even been held for him. A trickle of guilt about the money and lying still oozed out of the box in his mind, but he promptly stuffed it back in.

As an added bonus, he'd found some glasses in the lost-and-found that had a much milder prescription. He could wear them quite comfortably; in fact, they actually improved his vision. He'd hidden Bernard's eye-crossing pair deep in one of the pansy pots, telling Denise that Patricia had gifted him the new frames.

Fortunately, she seemed to believe him. From what he could piece together from Ruby and her silver-haired gossip queens, Bernard and Patricia had partaken in the occasional spicy midnight fling before the stroke and, alarmingly, even after. Although he was now committed to playing the role of Bernard, he definitely wasn't prepared to act out *those* particular scenes.

He popped his slippers on – yes, his now – and opened the curtains. Sunshine poured in like a dam had broken, warming his already happy heart. What would be for breakfast today? Dare he hope for bacon two days in a row? There was a knock at the door, and he rubbed his hands together in anticipation. Perhaps he was about to find out!

'Okay, Bernard! Time for some medicine!' It was Denise, not with his breakfast but a clear-plastic cup containing a capsule inside.

His calm disappeared quicker than a man escaping a prostate exam. This morning's heart medication was long gone. He'd become quite the expert at hiding the tablets under his tongue after practising in the mirror a few times with some Tic Tacs Ruby had given him. Fred would then throw them into the courtyard where, without fail, the same scruffy seagull would gobble them up. To his great surprise, they hadn't knocked the poor bird off – if anything, it seemed to be a bit more sprightly.

Fred's hair stood on end as he stared at the gigantic translucent pill Denise was now holding up. The size and shape reminded him of the chocolate Clinkers that Dawn had loved to devour, guessing which colour she'd get before biting into them. How was he going to hide *that* under his tongue? Blast! He might really have to take this one. Would it knock him off? His life in the home might be over before it had begun. Should he try confessing again?

'I'm so sorry, but I'm not sure I'll be able to swallow that,' he said, backing away.

'Oh, no, love,' she chortled. 'This one is not the kind you swallow, remember?'

A high-pitched nervous laugh that Fred didn't recognise escaped his mouth. As the penny dropped so did Fred's pants, courtesy of an efficient Denise, in a moment that could only be described as sheer horror. Yet Fred's desire to stay at the home was now marginally greater than the reluctance of his sphincter. The words 'grin and bear it' (or 'bare it', as it were) had never been more pertinent.

'There we go, that should get your bowels moving.' She exited, leaving Fred sitting on the bed, like a doomsday prophet awaiting the Armageddon that would inevitably unfold. He grimaced. Why on earth had he mentioned to her that he'd been a bit blocked up of late (likely because he got so much more to eat here than he had at home)?

The next two hours were rather unpleasant, to say the least. He couldn't even sit long enough to tuck into the breakfast Linh brought (which was a travesty because it was indeed bacon). He tried to distract himself by watching *To Kill a Mockingbird*, which was playing on the telly, but to little avail. He dashed to the toilet multiple times, sometimes with Denise's mortifying assistance. As he sat on there for the umpteenth time, he was struck by the wisdom of Atticus Finch: you can't begin to understand another person until you climb inside his skin.

Or until you take his wretched suppository.

Finally, when the worst had passed, he collapsed onto the bed, accidentally knocking his cup of water over as he did so. Bother. With a great deal of difficulty and several alarming creaking noises, he knelt to retrieve it. The little brute had rolled right under the bed. He got as low as he thought he could go without needing to involve an ambulance. As he fumbled for the cup, his fingers touched something smooth. He pulled it out, revealing an old red shoebox with *Bernard Greer* written on the lid in permanent marker. A tingle crept up his spine. Should he open it? Maybe it would contain something useful for the new role he was taking on? Some homework, per se?

A wet patch expanded on his knee as his pants absorbed the spilt water. He ignored it, his mind drawn to the box.

Taking a deep breath, he opened the lid. Sitting at the very top of a pile of papers was an old envelope, the words *RETURN TO SENDER – I DON'T EVER WANT TO SEE YOU AGAIN* written in bold red pen above the recipient's name and address.

A heaviness descended in Fred's stomach as he turned the envelope over. It had been torn open and resealed with sticky tape. Curiosity got the better of him and before he knew it, he had ripped it open and removed the letter it contained. It was dated five months earlier.

> *To my darling daughter,*
>
> *I know that it's been over thirty years and you probably don't want to speak to me, let alone see me. I just wanted to let you know that I have just moved to a nursing home. I may not have much time left and I wanted a chance to talk to you even though I know I've done nothing to deserve it. But you should know that I did try to get to your mother's funeral.*
>
> *Please consider a visit.*
> *Love from your father,*
> *Bernard Greer*

Fred gripped the bed, a chill expanding across his core. Bernard has a daughter.

Chapter 20

After miraculously getting up from the ground without the help of a forklift, Fred sat himself on the bed and reread the letter from Bernard to his daughter.

With his hands still shaking, he poured himself a long-overdue drink of water to replace some of what he had lost during the horse pill ordeal, gulping it down. It did little to quell the fire inside. He sifted through what remained in the shoebox: receipts, odds and ends and a few old photographs. Even when they were younger, although they had hair differing in colour and style, Bernard and Fred had shared a striking resemblance. Now that their hair was grey and they'd both grown moustaches and wrinkles, there was almost no distinguishable difference between them to the unsuspecting eye, especially with the glasses. It was the strangest thing to look at a photo of what you thought must be yourself, yet have no memory of it. Perhaps that's what having dementia was like.

As he replaced the photos in the box, his hand recoiled as it touched something sharp that lay camouflaged against the red cardboard. He picked it up and turned it over, noting the name written on the back. Along with a couple of other items, it looked as though it belonged in the bin, not in a keepsake box, but who was he to judge what had been precious to Bernard? He put each item back carefully, with the letter on top.

Fred gripped the side of the bed, questions flooding his mind. A daughter! What was she like? How old would she be? What had caused the rift?

He gazed out the window. The pansies bowed to a gust of wind.

Would it be worse to have never had a child or to be estranged from one?

The pain of mourning something you'd never truly had was all too familiar to him. Surely it must hurt even more to be rejected by someone you'd once known, once held. The red scrawl across the envelope glared up at him, the anger of the writer palpable.

His stomach rumbled and he glanced at the clock. Almost time for lunch. Putting the lid on the shoebox, he pushed it back under the bed as a fresh wave of guilt rose to the surface. It tasted different to the other guilt.

Bernard had a daughter. What did this mean? Was it a deal-breaker? Would it lead to him being found out?

He waved to Kevin as he walked past and thought of Albert and Val who would be waiting for him in the dining room. He clenched his jaw. He couldn't leave now. And Bernard's daughter obviously wanted nothing to do with her father anyway, so he guessed that was that. He straightened his shirt, exited his room and shut the door, trying to shut his thoughts in with it.

But his mind remained ajar.

Minutes later, Fred's nostrils were in a state of ecstasy courtesy of a beef casserole that had just been placed in front of him for lunch. Val and Albert sat opposite holding hands, and he managed to restrain himself just long enough for them to be served their meals before he gobbled a big mouthful with glee. This morning's evacuation had made a great deal of extra room, so he had a lot of catching-up to do.

It was such a delight to eat in the dining room with company – far better than eating a Vegemite sandwich in front of the telly alone, which would have been his usual state of affairs.

Albert stared down at his plate, his eyebrows knitted together creating a monobrow. 'I can't remember where I've parked the car, love. Can't seem to find my keys.' His eyes searched Val's face nervously, his hand patting his shirt even though it had no pockets.

Val placed her hand on his shoulder and leaned in close, making eye contact. 'That's okay, sweetheart. I know exactly where the car is.'

'You do?'

'I do.'

Albert turned to wink at Fred. '*This* is why I'm marrying her!' He took a bite of his meal and stopped again. 'My mum's coming over tomorrow, isn't she?'

'No, not tomorrow, sweetheart,' said Val. It wasn't a lie.

'Oh, okay. You know I wish I didn't have to go to work this afternoon, Val. I'd rather spend the day with you.'

Val put down her fork and smiled. 'Well, lucky for you there's no work today, so you can.'

'Really?' Albert's face glowed. 'Can I take you out? On a date? To the pictures, maybe?'

Val glanced at the activities schedule beside her. Fred followed her gaze. The Movie Matinee was on this afternoon and *Forrest Gump* was showing.

'I'd love that.'

'Great, well, I can organise tickets.' He frowned. 'Only I seem to have forgotten where the cinema is. I'm also not sure where I've parked the car.'

'It's okay, Albie, I know where the car is, and I'll organise the tickets, too. Okay?'

A grin erupted on his face and his bushy eyebrows took on a life of their own, jumping up and down like an excited fox terrier. 'And they tell me I'm too young to get married! Pfffft,' said Albert, making a face at Fred. 'Just look at her, Freddy! Even more beautiful than when I met her seven years ago. We were high school sweethearts, you know. What would I do without her?'

What indeed. Albert went back to staring at his plate, like an electronic toy that had suddenly shut down. Val gently scooped up some rice and offered it to him.

'Sometimes he forgets to eat.'

Fred never had that problem.

'Sorry guys, I forgot your lunchtime music.' A staff member with peroxide blonde hair turned on the radio and Louis Armstrong's velvety voice came gliding through the speakers.

The music brought Albert to life again, like a jumper lead firing up a car. 'Val! Val! It's our song! "It Had to Be You"! To your feet, my darling!'

'Oh, Albert . . .' Val laughed, glancing around the full dining room. 'I don't think we can dance here, sweetheart.'

'Nonsense – we can dance anywhere our feet take us, my love.'

Everyone watched as Albert took Val's hand and teetered to a clear space in the centre of the room. He put his arms around his wife of over sixty years, looking at her with the giddy love of a teenage boy. She blushed but soon gave in to his gaze, seeing only him, as she rested her head on his chest, her eyes closed, her face glowing with a peace usually only found in sleep. Fred wondered if for a second she could forget that Albert forgot, and just be in the moment, absorbing the love that not even the cruellest of diseases could snatch away. Fred's foot tapped in time to the music while his heart ached so badly for Dawn that he almost couldn't breathe.

As the song finished the room thundered with applause. Albert gave a proud little bow before he and Val resumed their seats and hastily tucked into the tinned fruit and custard that had magically appeared.

Fred sighed, unable to wipe the grin from his face. He leaned closer to Val and spoke softly, 'Can I ask another question, love? It's sort of personal . . .'

'Of course,' she said, smoothing down her pastel-pink skirt.

'He's head over heels for you, it's like you are on your honeymoon. Did the dementia, did it . . . make him like that again?'

Val's eyes lit up as she gazed at Albert, who was now sporting a custard moustache. 'No, that's not the dementia. He's always been like that.' She patted Albert's hand and he looked up at her with a delighted custardy grin. 'It's one thing the dementia hasn't stolen from us. When memory goes, you see, all that's left is emotion. What we have for breakfast or where we parked the car or what year it is doesn't matter, but we still feel who we love – and we love each other very, very much.'

She leaned in closer to Fred. 'People always say that the magnificent love you see in movies doesn't exist,' she whispered. 'It actually does.'

But Fred already knew that.

Chapter 21

Later that afternoon, Fred adjusted Bernard's elastic-waisted trousers. If only he'd discovered these years ago: they were the epitome of comfort. Wearing someone else's clothes really wasn't too bad – but the underpants, in all their stained glory, were another kettle of fish.

Bingo had just finished and he'd really cleaned up, winning two Freddo frogs and a lavender potpourri bag that he intended to put in his underwear drawer. At least then they would smell good.

He walked back along the hall, tearing open one of the Freddos on the way. The sweet smell brought a memory of Dawn, a self-confessed chocoholic.

He pictured her sitting in the white hospice bed in their lounge room. Thankfully, they'd been able to get a double – the thought of sleeping apart had been too much for either of them to bear.

'We know I'm dying, Fred, and I've made a very important decision, darling,' she'd said one day.

Fred's heart had sunk with dread.

'There's no use trying to talk me out of it. I've given it a great deal of thought and I truly feel it's the best thing to do.'

He'd waited with bated breath. Surely she wasn't considering stopping the pain meds?

'From now on, I am only going to eat chocolate and nothing else!' She'd winked at him, the twinkle in her eye a stark contrast to her pale, sunken face. How he had lived for that twinkle, spending countless days lost in it like a child in a magical forest.

They'd burst out laughing and joked that she was living the dream. But it had been a short dream. She'd died six days later. Despite the cancer, Dawn had always said she was the lucky one as she would never have to face life without him. Was she right? Was cancer less painful than grief?

Fred closed his eyes and brought the chocolate to his lips, savouring the sweet creaminess, the last thing she had ever tasted apart from their final kiss.

A yell thundered down the hall, derailing his thoughts. It was coming from Albert's room. Reluctantly putting the barely nibbled chocolate in his pocket, he picked up speed and popped his head in the door. A red-faced Albert paced around the bed, shouting and waving his hands.

'It's not true! Don't say that to me!' He threw a jug onto the floor, water spilling everywhere. A fire Fred hadn't seen before ignited his friend's eyes.

Val stood in the corner, dabbing her eyes with a crinkled Kleenex.

'Oh, love. Can I help?'

'We're having a bad afternoon,' she said quietly, wringing the tissue in her hands. 'Albert, my love, you have to have your dinner and take your pills.'

'No! No! NO!' shouted Albert. 'I've already eaten and those are *not* my pills!' His normally meek eyes flashed. Was it with anger or fear? Maybe both.

'Why don't we listen to some of your Christmas music, darling?' asked Val. 'Albert loves Christmas,' she whispered to Fred.

'I said *no!*' Albert snarled.

'Hey, mate,' tried Fred, 'it's me.'

'Leave me alone!' he yelled, waving Fred away with a whip of his arm.

'Now, let's just hang on a minute. I wanted to ask you about Launceston, you see.'

Albert narrowed his eyes, looking Fred up and down.

'I've been needing to ask someone the best place to go for a beer if I'm there.'

'I don't want to talk to you!' Albert fumed, turning his face away.

'Oh, please, mate, I really need your help. What's the best pub there?'

Albert stopped pacing and sat down on his armchair, his demeanour softening. 'That's easy, the Royal Oak. Best watering hole around.'

'Ah, I knew you'd be the right person to ask!' Fred took a seat on the bed near him. 'Tell me more about this Royal Oak. Can you get a decent meal there, too?'

'Oh, yes, best steak and chips in Tassie.'

'Oooh, I love a good steak. Now tell me, please, how does this meal compare?' Fred pointed at the shepherd's pie on Albert's dinner tray. 'Taste-wise, I mean?'

Albert picked up the fork and began eating. 'This is actually pretty good. Do you want some?' he said, waggling the fork towards Fred.

'Oh, no, mate, you eat that up. I'll save myself for the steak and chips. Here, better take these while you're at it. Gotta keep us fellas fit and healthy, right?' He placed the pills in Albert's hand and flexed his biceps.

Albert smiled, swallowing the pills without question or water. Impressive.

Val sighed, shooting a grateful look to Fred. 'I can normally work around anything, but I'm just so tired today and I didn't have the . . .' Her voice trailed off as she wiped her cheeks.

Fred walked over, took both her hands in his and looked deep into her eyes. 'You need to hear this, Val. You are doing an *extraordinary* job, you hear me? A job that no one should ever have to face. Why don't you go and get a cuppa, love – have a pause?' He turned to Albert. 'We'll be right here when you get back, won't we, mate? Gosh that carrot cake looks good . . .'

Albert grabbed the carrot cake like a young child who was worried his brother would get to it first.

Val wrapped her arms around her husband. 'I love you so, so much, my darling. Always have and always will.'

Albert patted her arm, his face lighting up. 'I'm so lucky, aren't I?' he mumbled to Fred, through a mouthful of cream-cheese icing.

'You sure are, mate, you sure are.'

Albert finished his dinner and fell asleep in his armchair, a solitary nostril hair curling in and out of his nose like a party blower. Val returned shortly after, noticeably calmer although her eyes were still blotchy. She gave Fred a thumbs up and took a seat next to her sleeping husband.

'You're very good at this, you know, Bernard. I suspect it's not your first time. Was it your wife?' she asked, placing a fleecy rug from the bed across Albert's lap.

'My mum,' he said softly. 'Early-onset dementia.'

Fred had never forgotten the first time his mother didn't recognise him. It was the day after his thirtieth birthday. He and Dawn had driven over to visit his parents for lunch. His dear old dad had done his best to cook a nice meal but had burned the chicken rather badly and the taste of ash lingered on Fred's tongue. Mum sat in the sun-drenched garden on her favourite wicker chair, the sweet perfume of her rose bushes brightening the air. She'd managed the gardening well despite her diagnosis, and the backyard was a sea of colour.

'Hi, Mum! Lovely out here, isn't it?'

She gave no response, staring vacantly at something beyond him. Perhaps she hadn't heard.

'Hi, Mum, how's it going?' he said louder.

'You've stolen it. I know it was you,' she said, pulling her lips into a thin line – a look foreign to her face.

'Sorry, what's that?'

'You're a thief! My pearl earrings are missing, and I know it was you. We should never have hired you! You're a bad plumber and a dirty little man.'

Fred stepped back, recoiling from the sharp words. 'Mum, I didn't take anything, I'm not the plumber. I'm Fred, your son Fred.'

'Liar!' she hissed, baring her teeth.

Bile rose in Fred's throat, more bitter than the burnt chicken. The screen door squeaked as his dad backed out, a stubby in each hand. He passed one to Fred, his muscular shoulders slumped.

'Sorry, son, she's having a bad day. We've had a few of those lately.' His voice was quiet, almost apologetic. Had Dad always looked this old?

'Aw, Dad.' Fred put down his beer and took the older man in his arms, holding him tight.

Dad rubbed his eyes with the base of his hand. 'Jolly hay fever!' he sniffed.

Fred nodded. Poor Dad. Poor Mum. Fred knew the signs had been there for a while, but to forget your own son – it was as if she had died, or he had. Like one of them no longer existed. From that day on he realised it was possible to grieve a living person.

The next time they visited, at Christmas, she had remembered him again and he savoured her warm hug, not knowing when, or if, he'd get another. Mum wouldn't hug a stranger, after all. Over the next few months, her remembering him became rarer. Every visit, he wondered if it would be the last day she'd know him. It was like watching someone slowly disappear. Cruelly the body remained, a taunting illusion, making you believe they were right in front of you when in fact they were possessed by an imposter, filled with rage, grief or panic. A torturous show for the audience of loved ones.

Fred had learnt all the tips and tricks over the years: never argue, go with the flow; never shame, instead distract; never condescend, always encourage. All the while, his heart was breaking.

'Did she have it for long?' Val's voice pulled him back to the present.

'Eight years.' Fred shifted in his chair. 'Took a while before the doctors worked it out. Started with little things. Becoming agitated and forgetful – like putting her purse in the freezer or getting lost. Mum's sense of direction was never great to begin with, though, so that hadn't stood out.'

Val nodded in recognition, tears coating her grey-green eyes. 'I had Albert call me from the local shops. He couldn't remember how to get home. He was so embarrassed, so shaken up. That terri-fied me, as directions were always his strong suit.' She looked out the window as if watching a memory. 'I knew I would never be lost when Albert was around, but now . . . Well, he's lost without me, I guess.' Her eyes glistened, a lingering tear swiftly dabbed before it had the chance to fall. 'I cried myself to sleep the night he called me. I knew even then what was coming.'

Albert snored loudly and let out a chuckle. What a blessing sleep could be sometimes, a merciful relief from dementia, from pain, from grief. A brief holiday where there were no suitcases full of burdens to carry. In dreams you could forget that you didn't remember, and remember those who were no longer there.

Fred often met Dawn in his dreams. Never anything fancy – sometimes they'd be chatting as she brushed her long silvery hair before bed, or standing side by side doing the dishes. Sometimes they would even be holding the lovely giggling baby they had lost. Those mornings, as he drifted into consciousness, his foot would seek hers in the bed only to be met by a cold emptiness that spread to his heart. The pain of waking was still worth that delectable dream, though, and he occasionally napped on purpose to escape the grief, on the off-chance he might spend a bit more time with her, blissfully unaware of reality.

Albert snorted as a big grin spread over his face.

'I often wonder what he dreams about,' said Val, tucking a white strand of hair back behind her husband's ear.

'Well, if I had to take a guess, I'd say he's dreaming of you, Val. Probably dreaming of marrying you. He talks about it all the time, you know.'

She blushed.

A guttural howl escaped Albert's lips, causing Fred to jump.

'No! No!' Albert winced violently in his sleep before relaxing again, his breathing steadying.

Val squeezed Albert's hand. 'Maybe he was dreaming of the wedding,' she said brokenly, 'and just now he's found out about Freddy.'

Fred bowed his head. And then, of course, there were the nightmares. How could he forget? Not the Dolly Parton ones, but the ones where he relived the miscarriage and her death all over again, waking up in a pool of sweat and tears.

'He was never the same after Freddy's death,' said Val. 'I guess you never could be after something like that.' She pressed her lips together. 'We didn't even go on our honeymoon. How could we? Don't get me wrong – we had so many happy times, but I always saw a sadness in his eyes after he'd had a big laugh, or at Christmas and birthdays. I suppose he was wishing Freddy was there to share it with.' She patted Albert's chest.

'He felt so guilty,' she continued, not taking her eyes off Albert. 'Guilty that he was still alive. But we did our best, we moved on as best we could. He promised to cherish me in our wedding vows, no matter what came.' She gently stroked his head. 'It's a funny word, isn't it? Cherish? I never fully understood what it meant, not until Albert lived it out.' She paused, her eyes distant, like they were inside the memory. 'It was the little things, you know – always giving me the biggest slice of anything, checking if I needed something before bed, bringing me cups of tea. Do you know he complimented me for every meal I ever made, even when it was a barbecued chicken from Woolworths and microwaved frozen peas?' She chuckled. 'You know, Bernard, I get the feeling that you and Albert are cut from the same cloth.'

A warmth spread across Fred's cheeks. 'Well, that might be the biggest compliment I've ever received.' He gazed over at the mighty man he was glad to call a friend.

'He was – is, I mean – the most wonderful dad, too. He'd move mountains for our Sarah. As thick as thieves, they are, and she thinks the world of him. She's in Melbourne now for her wife's work, but they FaceTime every day. That's her,' she said, motioning to the pair of framed photos on the wall Fred had seen the other day. Sarah had her arms wrapped around her dad. They smiled at the camera in one photo and pulled funny faces in the other. Fred beamed back at them.

'Do you have any children, Bernard?'

The familiar ache tugged at Fred's heart. 'I, um, well, we had a, we couldn't. Oh, I mean I, um, have a —'

A loud snort erupted from Albert's nose, waking the sleeping giant with a start. He blinked slowly as if he had just learnt how. When his eyes finally came to focus on Val his face transformed, like someone who was finally home after a long journey.

'So,' he said, clapping his hands and rubbing them together, 'what's for breakfast, folks?'

They all laughed, and Fred exhaled slowly. That was a close one.

A torrent of loneliness surged through him. How nice it would have been to be himself even just for a minute, to tell a kind, listening ear about his Dawn, about the miscarriage, about their inability to have kids. Memories were lonely on their own.

Instead, he stood and turned towards the door. 'Well, I'll leave you two lovebirds to it.'

'Thanks again.' Val shot him another grateful smile.

He walked out, pausing to take a closer look at the pictures of Albert and his daughter, the love between them almost palpable. The photo of Bernard on the nightstand with his birthday cake flickered in his mind. No daughter to share *his* birthday with.

What could have been so terrible to cause such a fracture between father and daughter? What was she like? Did she look like Bernard – like *him*? The thought made him giddy. He put his hand in his pocket, his fingers meeting the sticky, abandoned Freddo.

Most importantly, did she like chocolate?

Chapter 22

'**M**um, what happens if it doesn't work? If it doesn't cure me, I mean?'

It was 10 p.m. and Hannah stood frozen in the hallway outside her sister's bedroom, eavesdropping on Sadie and Mum's conversation. She was meant to be in bed, but, like most nights, she was having trouble getting to sleep. Mum had come home dead tired from work. It was happening so often that Hannah couldn't remember her mum's eyes without those big bags under them.

Why did they call them bags? Did they carry the tiredness? They weren't doing a great job.

'Oh love, don't think like that. I'm sure it's going to work.' Mum was using the same tone of voice as when she'd said Hannah's flu shot wouldn't hurt. It *had*. A lot.

'Is there a heaven, Mum?' Sadie's voice sounded strange, like a much younger kid's.

'Well . . . yes, love, I think there is. Your grandma always told me there was.'

'Is it like a second life? Like how in video games the characters get more than one if the first life is cut short? If they get defeated by the big monster at the end?'

Mum paused. 'Yes, I suppose it could be. But don't worry about any of that, Sadie girl. It's going to be okay. You're a fighter and I'm so proud of you. Get some rest now; you'll need a good sleep before the hospital tomorrow. Love you.'

'Love you, too, Mum. Goodnight.' The sound of a kiss on the cheek, the rustle of a doona.

'Mumma?' Her sister's voice was so quiet now that Hannah had to strain to hear it. 'I don't think I can beat my monster. Is that okay? Will you still be proud of me?'

Mum was quiet for a long time, and when she spoke again her voice sounded crackly, like when the vacuum cleaner sucked up the Christmas tinsel. 'Yes darling, of course.'

Hannah's tummy felt yuck. Probably the two helpings of pav for sweets.

The strip of light from under the door disappeared and Hannah tiptoed back to her room and slid under her covers. Mum's footsteps came closer, and the door creaked open. Hannah pretended to be asleep. It was Mum's nightly ritual to check on her before going to bed herself. Normally she could tell if Hannah was faking it, but she mustn't have this time because she began to sob softly in the doorway.

Hannah's body stiffened. Should she jump out of bed and give Mum a hug, or keep playing possum? Mum hated people seeing her cry, though, so Hannah chose to stay still, each sob tearing at her heart. Why wouldn't Mum just talk to her about it, about everything, the good and the bad? She wasn't stupid. She knew Sadie wasn't doing great and they were going to try another round of treatment, but she never got any details.

She hugged her pink teddy tighter. Sadie's skin had become almost see-through and she was so thin now that Hannah worried she might snap if she hugged her too tight. Sayd had missed so much school, including her school camp, which Hannah knew she'd been counting down to. She'd snuck into her room a few weeks back and seen Sadie's calendar on the wall. The camp dates had been crossed out in permanent marker. A month later, as Hannah sat on the bus going to her own camp, she'd felt sick to her stomach. Why did she get to go? To keep her hair? To feel well?

At least Sadie's birthday was coming up and they could plan something special for her, even if it was small. Hannah turned over, still faking sleep. Her pillow was soggy from her own tears, but she didn't dare flip it over and risk Mum knowing she was awake. The sobs in the doorway grew louder.

'You shouldn't have told her that.' Her dad's voice came in a sudden sharp whisper.

'Told her what? Please lower your voice – you'll wake Hannah.'

'I heard you from the next room. What you said to Sadie about heaven. We don't know that. There are no second chances when you die. This is it!'

'How do you know?' Her mother sniffed. 'How can we know? Did you just get home? Where have you been? I . . . I had to do everything myself again tonight, and I'm just not bloody coping. I'm trying to, but —'

'Leave it alone. I have to work longer hours, to make enough money to support us all, to cover the treatment costs.'

'I have things going on at work, too, you know . . .' Her mother's usually strong voice sounded weak. 'You're still minding the girls on Friday, aren't you? I'm working a double shift.'

'What? No, I never agreed to that!'

'You did! What am I supposed to do?'

'You'll just have to bring them in with you.'

'Sadie is so frail! You can't be that heartless . . .' Mum gasped.

'They have beds there, don't they? Just stop, will you? Don't you think I'm under enough stress already? Without you . . . without this . . .' His voice trailed off.

Hannah scrunched her eyes tight as heavy footsteps sounded down the stairs, followed by the slam of the front door and the familiar sound of his car driving away.

He'd left, and she was terrified Sadie was going to leave, too. Just not through the front door.

Chapter 23

Fred sat on the toilet, his heart pounding. What he wouldn't do for a tad more privacy. Denise was waiting in his room and all that separated him (and the challenge ahead) from her was the thin plywood sliding door of the ensuite. Ironically, since the god-awful suppository, he had found that his back pipe was a bit blocked up again. Surely it was too soon to become 'laxative dependent', a horrifying term he had heard one of the doctors use about poor Albert. The memory of the giant horse pill being shoved up his derrière sent a shudder down his spine. He looked at the piece of luxurious three-ply toilet paper in his hand, a dangling reward at the end of a hard task. Even in his glory days he'd only ever spotted for two-ply.

Fred's ears pricked up as muffled sobs sounded through the door; it was Denise. Poor love. Should he call out to ask if she was okay? Before he had a chance to decide, the door to his room creaked open. He froze mid-business.

'Hey, Denise, did they deliver the extra-large incontinence pants yet?' He recognised the voice. It was one of the other carers, Sally.

Denise gave a loud sniff. 'Yeah, just before – they're in the supply closet.'

'You okay?' asked Sal.

'Yeah, yeah – all good. Just got a bit of hand sanitizer in my eye. Hey, actually, before you go, do you know what's really odd, Sal? Bernard here doesn't seem incontinent at night anymore. Every time I've gone to get him dressed in the morning his pants have been bone dry. Been happening for some time now. You had him on the weekend, yeah? Was it the same then?'

'Come to think of it, yes. He's been a lot friendlier too, don't you reckon? Maybe the doc's given him an anti-grumpy pill?' Sal laughed.

'Nah,' said Denise dryly, 'I checked and nothing's changed. His hearing and comprehension seem to be a bit better as well, though. He's even been remembering my name.'

'Yeah, that's a bit odd. Maybe speak to Sharon about it.'

'Okay, will do. Ta.'

Fred went over the conversation in his mind as he finished his business, releasing the captive and trying to time the offending splash with the closing of the door as Sal exited. It wasn't as perfect as he'd hoped.

'Sounds like you've finished in there, Bernard?'

He winced. 'Almost . . .' said Fred, louder than necessary. There was one more thing he had to do.

It was normal for him to do a bit of wee in this part of the proceedings, but he held it in just long enough to pull up the wretched incontinence pants then let it flow like a high-pressure hose. Well, a low-pressure hose. Okay, a leaky tap. Regardless of how it came out, his goal had been met. Fred had successfully wet his pants on purpose. He wasn't taking any chances.

He climbed into bed, the pad squishing against his skin. Blast! This wouldn't do. He asked Denise for a fresh one, unwilling to face a night in a soggy nappy.

She rolled her bloodshot eyes. Had she really gotten sanitiser in them? The way she was glaring at him made Fred a little afraid to ask. She muttered something under her breath and helped him change into fresh bottoms. He'd grown accustomed to the lack of dignity now. First thing in the morning, he'd have to wet his pants again. Better set an alarm. And write a reminder just in case he forgot what the alarm was for, which, let's face it, was very likely. But he also couldn't risk Denise seeing what he wrote down. He'd have to get creative.

The next morning, Denise stood in front of the staff bathroom mirror and tried for the umpteenth time to pin back her stupid hair. She sighed and pinched the bridge of her nose. Damn it. It was no use; she was destined to look like she'd been electrocuted. What did any of it matter anymore? After bingeing a whole tin of Milo she'd made herself vomit last night, hoping that she could expel her daughter's unbearable words. It hadn't worked. If she couldn't throw them up, then she would drown them.

She removed a tiny bottle from the pocket of her pants and popped the top, brought it to her lips and drank. The vodka slid down her throat, igniting a blissful, foggy warmth that diluted her mind. How she longed to be rescued like one of the princesses in the Disney movies her girls loved so much. Why couldn't a strong, handsome man break her out of this prison, free her from her rotten husband and a world where even kids got dealt an unfair hand? None of the strapping heroes ever visited nursing homes though and it would take an absolute saint of a man to rescue someone as stupid and ugly as her. She replaced the bottle, finished washing her hands and headed in to wake up Bernard. The old man was bunched up in a little ball, eyes closed tight, his wrinkly skin camouflaged against the beige doona.

'Bernard! Wakey-wakey! Time to get up.'

He let out a snore so loud it almost sounded fake, like when one of her girls played possum.

She poked him. 'C'mon, lazybones!'

He stirred and slowly opened his eyes. 'Oh, good morning, Doreen, love! Sorry, was in a bit of a deep sleep there. How are you?'

Doreen? He'd never called her that before.

'Fine,' she lied, helping him to his feet.

'Wine? No, it's a bit too early for me, thanks, love.' His words were quick and loud.

She narrowed her eyes at him then removed his pyjamas and incontinence pants. Her nose registered something.

Huh. They were wet.

'Well, I'll be damned.'

'Tanned?' he asked. 'Yes, I do probably look a bit tanned, got some sun in the garden yesterday.'

She pressed her lips together and scowled. His hearing seemed to have worsened overnight.

After Bernard was showered and dressed, she straightened up his bed. On his bedside table lay a scrawled note: *Remember to get ants.*

Looked like his dementia was back as well.

Chapter 24

Days dribbled into weeks, and Fred found his rhythm in the home. Guilt and worry were less frequent visitors. When they did appear, he locked them away with the lie. Having lots of distractions helped; he enjoyed catching up with Val and Albert a few times a week and exercising daily. His regular afternoon chats with Kevin made him feel young again.

Fred attended most of the activities that were on offer, even the choir, where he and Albert, both baritones, would grin at each other while they belted out melodies from their youth with gusto. Albert recalled every word, which never ceased to amaze Fred. Being surrounded by people who had lost a few marbles made him more determined than ever to hold onto his, and to that end he did the crossword each day without fail.

He glanced at today's clue for seven across: 'To clear out'.

E-X-C-A-V-A-T-E? His bowel spasmed as he began pencilling in the letters. As he got to V, the lead snapped. Blast. He rummaged in the bedside-table drawer where he recalled having seen a small, grey pencil case. He soon found it and emptied the contents on the wheelie table. But instead of stationery, a handful of cards fell out. A faded driver's licence (Bernard's had a much better picture than his), a Medicare card, a Sydney Swans membership card (expired) and a Visa debit card from the Commonwealth Bank. A prickling unease clawed at Fred as he held it, a physical reminder that he was living on Bernard's dime. He tried to ignore it. If Bernard had lost his money as Denise had said, and was estranged from his family, then his fees must be covered by the government. Fred had always paid his taxes, so it was all right, wasn't it? His stomach let out a disagreeable noise as if speaking on behalf of his conscience.

'Bugger it,' he said aloud to his gut. If he couldn't live on the edge in his eighties, then he never would. He returned all the cards except for the debit card. Curious to see Bernard's signature, he turned it over. Taped to the back of the yellow plastic was a tiny piece of paper with the numbers 2-6-0-4. Surely it couldn't be the PIN? Dad had done something similar with Mum's credit card when her memory started to fail, which he'd soon realised was a mistake when she returned from the supermarket one day with enough cat food to feed a feline army. Shame they hadn't had a cat.

Fred's mouth watered as he thought about the jubes and spearmint leaves he could buy from the lolly trolley that Linh tantalisingly wheeled around every Thursday. If there was any money on the card, that is. 'Probably best not to get your hopes up, boys,' he quietly cautioned his tastebuds.

Footsteps approached and he glanced up to see Albert ambling past without his walker. Within seconds, he was back again.

'You right there, mate?' called Fred.

Albert's watery eyes searched for where the sound was coming from and finally rested on a now-waving Fred.

'It's you! Wonderful you!' Albert's weathered face lit up with such delight that Fred's whole being was flushed with love. He'd forgotten what it felt like to be important to someone.

'I'm so glad I've found you, my lovely Fred.'

'What's up, my friend?'

'Well, it's this!' Albert tugged on his porridge-stained shirt and grimaced. 'I cannot in good conscience get married in this! What would Val say? Her mum already thinks I'm a bit of a bludger.'

Fred chuckled, placing the crossword down. Though Albert would likely forget in a few minutes, it would cost Fred nothing to humour him. 'We can't have that now, can we? How about we take a look at what else you've got?'

Albert pointed to Fred with both index fingers. 'I knew you'd know what to do! I keep telling everybody. Simply marvellous you are, my brother. I need to look like a million bucks for my beautiful Vally!'

A few minutes later, the two men stood in front of Albert's brown laminate closet. Fred flicked through the small row of hanging shirts, each one shabbier and more stained than the one before it – not exactly wedding material. He pulled out the least offensive option (a pale-grey number that only had stains on the back) but Albert gave it a double thumbs down, blowing a raspberry.

'I'd lend you something, but I'm afraid mine aren't much chop either,' said Fred, picturing the meagre contents of Bernard's wardrobe. 'Plus, they'd be far too short on you.' He eyed his friend's elongated appendages. Albert let out a woeful sigh, the wrinkly skin above his mouth cascading like melting candle wax over his down-turned lips.

Fred scratched his head, cogs turning. He put his hand in his pocket and felt the plastic debit card. There was only one way to find out if it had any funds.

Parkmore shopping centre was fairly close to the nursing home but definitely too far to walk for two old codgers. They needed wheels.

'Loverooo!' Patricia crooned, her warbling voice breaking his train of thought. Fred looked to see the avocado-squeezer gliding past on a two-seater maroon mobility scooter encrusted with stick-on jewels. Albert pointed, mesmerised by the sparkle.

'Fred! It's Santa's sleigh!'

Patricia's front basket was laden with bananas and kiwifruit. She came to a stop in front of the two men and smiled, revealing her pearly dentures.

'You gave me quite the run-around last time, Bernie!' she pouted as she adjusted her hearing aid.

He laughed nervously and shifted his weight. 'Nice set of wheels. I've never seen one that big before.'

'I recall saying the same thing to you,' she winked.

Fred's eyebrows shot up. Good for you, Bernard, old mate.

Patricia laughed. 'I like having the extra seat for my *companions*.'

'I see. So, where are you off to?' he asked, desperate to change the subject.

'Just come back from the greengrocers. I *must* have my fresh fruit, you know. The stuff they give us here tastes worse than my colonoscopy preparation.'

Fred shuddered, remembering the laundry-detergent-like liquid he, too, had had to endure a few years back. It had cleared him out faster than dodgy prawns.

He paused for a moment then pointed at the scooter. 'Hang on a tick – you're allowed out? On your own?'

She frowned, tilting her head to the side. 'I'm in low care, sweetheart. I can do as I please. Not like you high-care lot. Anyway, poodums, I must love you and leave you. They're showing *Dirty Dancing*

today at the Movie Matinee and I must eat these ripe bananas first!'
She circled her sluglike tongue slowly around her lips and winked,
cackling as she launched the scooter into full gear. That thing could
motor. He glanced from the scooter back to his friend, who was
studying a light switch with great intensity. 'Come on, Albert, I've got
an idea.'

The two men plodded down the hall to Patricia's room, where
she sat in a pink velvet armchair, meticulously peeling a banana.
Fred pulled Albert back before she spotted them. They stumbled
into the room next door, startling a large man in an electric
wheelchair.

'Oh, I'm so sorry, mate. We were just . . . um . . .'

'Playing hide and seek,' said Albert, unusually helpfully.

'Is it okay if we, er, hide here for a bit?' Fred asked.

The gentleman nodded. Albert didn't seem to know what they
were waiting for but looked excited nonetheless. He took a seat on
the bed, grinning and winking repeatedly at the man in the wheelchair while Fred kept a lookout, waiting for Patricia to leave for the
movie. Like clockwork, at 1.50 p.m. she hobbled out of her room in
the direction of the theatre lounge.

'Now's our chance!' Fred led Albert into Patricia's abode, where
the scent of musk lay heavy in the air. He approached the scooter –
he'd never seen a two-seater before. The controls didn't seem too
complicated. The real question was how they'd get past reception.
He was already listed as a known escapee, and Albert would never
be allowed out without Val . . .

Bugger it. You only live once (or twice, in Bernard's case).

'Well, no time like the present, old boy,' he said, turning to
Albert who was rummaging around in Patricia's wardrobe wearing
one of her floppy straw hats.

Fred's jaw dropped. 'Oh, Albert, you're a genius, mate!'

Twenty minutes later, a very peculiar-looking figure exited Patricia's room on the mobility scooter, a lumpy moving bundle seated alongside, covered with a large rainbow crocheted blanket.

'You've got to keep still, mate!' whispered Fred, who was sporting Patricia's fuchsia overcoat and a floral silk scarf, which he'd draped over his head. To finish off his ensemble, he'd camouflaged his moustache as best he could with her concealer, borrowed her big sixties sunglasses and painted his lips with her signature bright-red lipstick. He hoped to high heaven that no one would see them.

He zoomed into the large foyer, which was fortunately empty apart from the receptionist, Christine, who was on an animated phone call at her desk in the far corner. She barely glanced up as she put her palm over the handset.

'Stepping out again, are you, Pat? Forget something?'

Fred managed a quick nod, before turning his head so she couldn't see his face.

'Okay, I'm just heading to the laundry.' Christine returned to her call, exiting down the hall.

Jeepers, that was close!

All he needed now was for someone to enter or exit so the doors would open. He still didn't know the blasted code.

Without warning, the bundle began to sing, a vivacious voice springing out. 'Jingle bells! Jingle bells! Jingle all the way!'

Fred's palms became slippery on the handles. 'Shhhh!' he hissed, but Albert was singing too loudly to hear him.

A young couple with two small children exited one of the rooms into the foyer.

'Oh what fun it is to ride in a one-horse open sleigh! HEY! Jingle Bells! Jingle Bells . . .'

Fred coughed loudly, trying to mask the sound, beads of sweat now dripping down his forehead. It wasn't even anywhere near Christmas!

The couple turned to look. It was do or die. Fred cleared his throat and tried to channel his best female impersonation. What came out sounded like the breaking voice of a teenage boy. 'Jingle all the way! Oh what fun it is to ride in a one-horse open sleighhhhhh!' Fred sang, waving his arms melodiously to the imaginary music to add to the distraction. Probably looked like he was having some kind of seizure.

The dad raised his eyebrows as the little girl took a step closer to her mum. Fred paused and, mercifully hearing nothing more from the bundle, stopped singing. The couple began to clap slowly, and Fred smiled as widely as possible. 'It's um, never too early to celebrate the festive season,' he spluttered.

The woman took a step closer. His pulse quickened. Was the jig up?

'Merry Christmas, darl. You've got a bit of lippie on your teeth.'

Fred's cheeks pooled with blood. 'Oh! Happens all the time,' he replied, in a voice that resembled an Australian Julia Child.

'Mum, why does that lady have a moustache?' The small girl's voice was innocent.

'Shh, it's just old age, darling.'

The family gave him one last look before typing in the code for the door and exiting. Fred didn't waste his chance.

'Hold on, mate,' he whispered to the bundle as he accelerated and shot out, leaving the startled family behind.

Once they were safely a couple of blocks away, Fred pulled over and uncovered poor Albert, who had valiantly followed his instructions of adopting the brace position. Fred removed Patricia's clothes and tucked them in the basket on the front of the scooter.

'You okay there, old boy?' he asked Albert.

'Yes. Reminds me of all those times I used to dink on your bike, Freddy!' Albert crooned, tousling Fred's hair.

Fred smiled. The earlier embarrassment was worth finally having a brother to dink.

Parkmore shopping centre was bigger than Fred remembered. Fluorescent lights glared down while bossa nova music pulsed in the background. The sweet smell of cinnamon from a donut shop called out to his nostrils. If Bernard's card worked, he could treat Albert after their shopping expedition.

Thankfully, the department store Fred had in mind was right near the entrance. As they zipped past the perfume counter, Albert grabbed a bottle of Chanel No. 5 and, before Fred could stop him, sprayed it into his mouth like breath freshener. The subsequent cough sounded like his poor friend was trying to exorcise a demon.

They soon reached the menswear section and disembarked.

'Hello, my name is Nigel. Can I help you gentlemen with anything?' said a thin, well-dressed man with a name tag.

'Yes. My tongue tastes like a baboon's bottom. Got anything for that?' said Albert, sticking out the offending appendage within an inch of Nigel's widening eyes.

'We need wedding suits —' interjected Fred, stepping forward.

A look of surprise flashed across Nigel's face as he saw Fred.

'I'm the groom!' beamed Albert.

'Ah, I see now. Good for you.' Nigel surveyed some options from a rack of suits. 'How long have the two of you been engaged?'

Fred furrowed his brow, then caught a glimpse of himself in the mirror on the counter. His mouth fell open – he'd forgotten to remove Patricia's bright-red lipstick and the concealer!

'He's the best man,' said Albert, helpfully, as Fred tried to rub away the make-up, 'and I mean that quite literally, not just for the wedding.' He stared at Fred, his eyes filled with so much admiration that Fred could barely hold his gaze.

'Oh, my apologies,' said Nigel, pointing them towards the changing rooms. 'Well, let's try on some options, shall we?'

Fred's wedding to Dawn had been a simple affair. There hadn't been a lot of money then, either, and Fred had borrowed a suit from a mate. Fashion wasn't of any real significance to him, but deep down he had wished that just once he could dress like his silver-screen hero, James Bond.

Nigel handed a charcoal suit to Albert, who began patting it like it was a fluffy kitten. Fred ushered him into the nearest cubicle. 'Deck the halls with boughs of holly, fa la la la la la la la la!' Albert sang, as he dropped his tracksuit pants. Fred slapped his palm to his forehead as he saw that his friend had succumbed to the same fate as him and was wearing large incontinence pants.

'Oh dear. I think we are going to need a bigger size in the trousers, please!' he called out. Nigel quickly obliged and popped a larger pair over the changing-room door.

Minutes later, having just managed to get the trousers over the plasticky white monstrosity and the swinging hips, Albert's bottom now resembled a latin dancer's rather than a gangly nonagen-arian's. Fred put the finishing touches on Albert's bow tie. The suit didn't quite look like a million bucks, but Albert's glorious smile as he gazed upon his reflection was absolutely priceless, washing away any guilt Fred felt about the price tag, which exceeded Fred's monthly rent on his old flat.

'Fred, do you think Val will like the look of me?' asked Albert, his happy expression slipping away. 'Sometimes I worry I'm punching above my weight, and that she might realise it one day and leave me.' The corners of his lips turned down.

'Mate,' said Fred, placing his hands on Albert's shoulders. 'If there is one thing I know for sure, she is going to love you forever. Stand by you no matter what comes. You, my friend, are an absolute catch, whether you're in a fancy suit or your trackie daks!'

Albert's lips trembled, his eyes moistening. 'You always know just what to say. I really don't know what I'd do without you.'

Fred saw himself glow in the mirror. 'Okay, mate, let's get you back into your clothes.'

'I'm right to get changed on my own,' Albert replied. Fred shrugged, and popped into the cubicle next door.

Five minutes later, he looked in the mirror and James Bond looked back. Well, maybe James Bond's father – or grandfather. Close enough. He smiled. If only Dawn could see him now. An unexpected flash of envy prickled his skin. Albert still had the love of his life, even if he had forgotten most of the life they'd shared. Fred remembered every detail of his life with Dawn: the stolen kiss in the bookstore, the first time he touched her hair, the softness of her earlobes, the joy in her voice as she sang while vacuuming, their many camping trips. He stared at his reflection. Unlike the suave jacket and pants, jealousy didn't suit him, so he took it off.

'How are you going, Albert?' he called, as he changed back into his clothes.

'All is excellent,' replied Albert, passing his suit over the door.

Time to put his money where his mouth was. Or, rather, Bernard's money. He whipped out the card and placed the two suits on the counter where Nigel was waiting.

'We'll take them, thank you!'

His heart raced as he typed 2-6-0-4 into the keypad, silently praying that the PIN was correct and Bernard's card would withstand the force.

Beep.

'You little ripper!' he accidentally said aloud as he punched the air. Nigel offered a thin smile.

'We're all good, Albert. Ready to go?'

Albert exited the changing room wearing only the incontinence pants and a grin – Fred couldn't tell which was larger.

'I'm afraid the lav in that cubicle is broken, good sir,' the near-naked man said to Nigel. 'Might want to take a look at it. No toilet paper left either, but don't worry, I made do.'

Fred gasped as an unquenchable giggle rose in his throat. The colour left Nigel's face faster than a toupee in a tornado.

'But, sir, there's not a toilet in —'

Fred wasn't sure which he noticed first: Nigel's mortified glare or the smell of Albert's unmentionable. Whichever it was, it was clearly time to leave. No time for donuts. He grabbed the suit bags and hurriedly ushered Albert back onto their getaway vehicle. They zoomed away, Nigel's exasperated groans echoing behind them.

Chapter 25

To Fred's great relief, returning home was surprisingly easy. He expertly re-disguised the almost-naked Albert as the bundle and himself as Patricia in her colourful garb. Ruby's daughter arrived just as they were driving in, allowing them to slip straight inside the doors. Fred dropped Albert back to his room, then returned the scooter and clothes to Patricia's minutes before the Movie Matinee finished. As he snuck the suit bags into his wardrobe, he pictured the two of them strutting their stuff down the hall. Wouldn't it be marvellous if they had a chance to wear them?

As soon as he'd removed the remaining red lipstick (with a great deal of difficulty and enough toilet paper to wipe the bums of a chamber orchestra), Val appeared in the doorway carrying a white parcel.

'Hello, Bernard, I've brought Albert in some fish and chips and wondered if you'd like some, too?'

'Gee thanks, Val! I'd love that, but only if there is enough, of course.' His pulse quickened as he looked from her to the door. 'Did you just get here?'

'Yes, just now.'

'Oh, phew! I mean, that's nice.' Thank heavens she hadn't noticed her husband's absence. 'So how, um, is Albert?' he asked, doubtful that Albert would have had the time or inclination to get dressed.

'He's in extremely good spirits, but he's naked again, I'm afraid,' she said, tossing back her grey bob with a chuckle. 'It's not the first time I've found him in a state of undress, but he didn't try any funny business this time.' She winked and Fred felt his cheeks colour. 'Anyhow, I'd better go to him. Enjoy, Bernard!' She passed him the glorious-smelling package.

Fred stared at it in delight, its white wrapping paper turning translucent from the grease. His real lunch would be here soon, but who was counting? He could easily manage both. Tearing it open, he inhaled the salty aroma. There was even a lovely sachet of vinegar, which he splashed liberally over eveything. He tucked in, the tangy taste instantly transporting him to the old pier in Newcastle where he had taken Dawn all those years ago. It was there, after this very same meal, that he'd asked her to marry him against an apricot sunset. He closed his eyes and allowed himself to give in to the memory, to fall into its warm embrace.

His love for her had been instantaneous, faster than two-minute noodles. It was the dizzy kind of love, the bright, new and shiny sixteen-year-old, jumping-into-the-ocean kind of love. Like the first sip of a cold beer, the first warm day of spring, like opening the door of a holiday house for the first time. He loved her on that pier when he asked her the easiest question he had ever asked. Her yes meant they would delight in growing old together. When she walked down the aisle towards him, he knew he'd never be homeless, as she was his home. She was his everything. She saw every single one of his flaws and loved him regardless. Her patience, kindness and selflessness were as limitless as the horizon. She was his biggest advocate and encouraged him to chase his dreams, no matter how far away they seemed.

He wiped his eyes, popping an extra salty and soggy bit of fish into his mouth. How far away those dreams seemed now.

'Bernard!' Denise's sharp voice made him jump, popping his balloon of memories. 'What the hell are you eating? Who gave you that?'

He froze like a naughty schoolboy. Was it really such a sin to have food from the outside?

'I . . . I . . .'

'YOU'RE ALLERGIC TO FISH, YOU IDIOT!' she yelled, yanking the box from him.

Fred's jaw dropped. 'Oh . . . oh, dear. I forgot. I —'

He stuck his hands up as though he was being arrested. He'd have to play along to cover himself. What were the symptoms of a fish allergy? He tried a guttural cough and rolled his eyes backwards.

'Oh, god!' Denise yelled, and dashed out of the room, a red pen falling from her pocket. He grabbed it and quickly drew some dots on his face and then rubbed them in vigorously.

Denise charged back in like a rhino, her eyes ablaze, looking as though she belonged more in an action movie than a nursing home. 'Don't worry! I've got the EpiPen!'

Fred let out a little drop of wee as his lips formed the word 'Wait!' but no sound came out. She pulled down his trousers just enough to reveal his shaking thigh, then plunged the pen in.

If he'd ever wondered what being raised from the dead felt like, he was sure this was it. An almighty, throaty gasp sprung from his mouth. The sharp sting in his thigh was soon overtaken by a demonic force enveloping every inch of his being. His heart punched violently against his sternum, like a lead frog trying to escape his chest. Sweat seemed to be forming on the outside *and* inside of his body. Was this what having a heart attack felt like?

'Just breathe, Bernard, breathe through it,' Denise said, still red in the face. 'You'll be right soon. The doctor is on his way.'

He didn't want the doctor. He just wanted his ruddy flake and potato scallop.

An hour later, after the doctor had visited, Fred lay on his bed feeling something resembling normal again. His stomach growled at him. So much for his two-lunch plan – they hadn't even brought his normal one. He eyed the top of the potato scallop now taunting him from the bin and considered it a moment. But he wasn't that desperate, not anymore. Opening the bedside-table drawer, he removed an individually wrapped Scotch Finger biscuit he'd been saving for emergencies. Snapping it in two, he popped both halves in his mouth, the crumbly sugar rush brightening his whole body.

He picked up the red pen and opened the newspaper to the sudoku section – a new hobby that Val had recommended to keep the old melon sharp. He went to write his first number, but no ink came out. Blast, must have used it all for the rash.

Swallowing the last of his meagre biscuit lunch, he got up and wandered over to the oak bureau in a corner of Bernard's room to find another pen. As he moved some old magazines and papers around his eyes settled on a long, narrow drawer he hadn't noticed before. Admiring the ornate brass handle, he slid it open. Sitting at the very top was Queen Elizabeth, smiling at him from a postage stamp on a beige envelope.

Fred's breath caught in his chest. He recognised the recipient's name in the same spidery writing as before. He flipped it over. *Sender: Bernard Greer, Wattle River Nursing Home.* The air thickened.

Another letter from Bernard to his daughter, this time unsent. Fred plonked down in his armchair, tracing his finger over the smooth envelope, his heart once again pounding. It was really none of his beeswax. Let sleeping dogs (and dead old men) lie.

Returning the envelope to the drawer, he took a black biro that was next to it and went back to his sudoku. But before he could even finish one row, the magnetic pull of the letter drew him back to the desk. Removing it once more he opened the courtyard door and settled into the seat beside the pansies. The enveloped fluttered in the breeze. The air was crisp, but the sun was trying hard to make a break from the feathery clouds, caressing the tops of the sage-coloured gum trees beyond the fence. Fred sat with the letter for some time, as though he and it were two strangers sitting politely, each too shy to say anything.

Thoughts ricocheted through his mind. Should he just post it? Would that help Bernard? There was a stamp on it, so he'd most likely intended to send it. But what if it was bad? Surely he'd better read it first. His mother had taught him never to pry, but the idea of opening it didn't seem terribly wrong, given its author was dead and buried.

Finally, Fred's curiosity got the better of him and before he knew it he was ripping open the envelope.

Scrawled across the top was the date: *25th December 2022*. Christmas of last year. A whisper of recognition tickled his brain. Why was it significant? Wasn't that the date Bernard had had the stroke? Yes, he'd overheard Denise mention it to Kevin the day he arrived. Bernard must have written the letter and had the stroke the same day! Never had the chance to post it. The minor kick Fred got out of his detective work was soon replaced with a deep sadness in the pit of his stomach.

The poor, poor bugger.

It was a much longer letter than the first. Fred read it quickly, and then a second time slowly, absorbing every word. A drop of water fell onto the page, and he looked up, expecting rain. But it was coming from his eyes. Again.

'Oh, Bernard,' he whispered, and he sat and wept for a very long time.

Chapter 26

'*Xin chào*,' said Fred, as he pointed to the words on the paper. 'It's X-I-N C-H-A-O, but the X is pronounced as "sh" like when you're trying tell someone to be quiet. Give it another try – you'll get there.'

It was Thursday morning and Kevin was taking Fred's vitals in the lounge. Patricia strutted in wearing a fire-engine-red pantsuit. She waved at Fred, taking a seat opposite and fishing out her iPad from a matching handbag. She held the tablet to face him. The word 'Tinder' flashed on the screen. What would Patricia want tinder for? The home didn't have any fireplaces.

'You really think she'd like it if I spoke some Vietnamese to her?' asked Kevin, recapturing Fred's attention.

'It can't hurt, mate.'

'Shing chow?'

'*Xin chào*.' Fred mouthed the words as if his lips were moving in slow motion.

'*Xing chào*,' repeated Kevin, his ginger eyebrows furrowed in deep concentration.

'You've got it!' Fred gave Kevin a high five. 'You can now say hello!'

'So how do you know all this stuff?' Kevin's boyish face was eager and earnest. A heaviness settled in Fred's tummy.

'The war – I was in the army.'

'Wow. I mean, I can't even imagine.' Kevin shook his head.

'I'm glad you don't have to, mate. I was about your age when I went.'

'Gosh.'

'Met some beautiful people there, I did . . .' A succession of images struck Fred's memory. Rice paddies, the thrum of mosquitos, sticky wet boots . . . He closed his eyes.

'You okay there, Bernard?' Kevin placed his hand on Fred's shoulder.

'Yep,' said Fred, shaking it off. 'Anyway, she's a splendid girl. Linh, I mean.'

Kevin let out a long, dreamy sigh. 'She's the most beautiful girl I've ever seen, Bernard. I don't just mean how she looks – I mean like the way she is with residents and all that. She's so kind.'

'Just like you, mate. You're one of the good ones.' Fred patted him on the back. 'I don't take it for granted, you know.'

Kevin beamed, two dimples appearing on his freckled face. 'Aww, shucks. You know, Bernard, they told me when I came that you were a bit of a grumpy-bum, but it couldn't be further from the truth. You're ace, mate! And as sharp as a tack – I can't help but wonder if you need to be reassessed. Anyway, I'd better get back to my rounds. Another lesson tomorrow?'

'Thanks, buddy, and *dúng*,' said Fred.

Kevin cocked his head to the side.

'It means yes.'

The young man smiled as he turned to leave. 'Bernard?'

'Yes?'

'I'm probably not meant to say this, but you – you're one of the good ones, too.'

Fred offered a smile. But it came with a side of guilt. If only Kevin knew just how bad he really was.

'Ah, Patricia,' said Kevin, spotting the older woman. 'I was just headed to your room. You've saved me a trip.'

Patricia gave a half-hearted wave, her eyes still glued to her screen.

'Now, Patricia, I counted your pills and one is missing. We only have five,' he said. The older woman barely looked up as she took a big gulp of tea from her thermos, her eyes wide, acrylic glitter nails tapping at the screen.

The young nurse shook his head at Fred. 'She's forgotten her hearing aids.'

'Patricia!' Kevin stepped closer, his thick Kiwi accent brimming with an urgency that commanded her attention. She met his gaze. 'Patricia, I was just saying that we should have *six*.'

Patricia promptly spat out her tea along with her false teeth, which landed with Tiger Woods-like accuracy in Fred's water glass. She frowned, her mouth agape.

'Absolutely not! Good Lord! You should be ashamed of yourself for even suggesting it, young man!'

Fred buried his face in his hands, unable to stop his snorts of laughter. Not wanting to cause offence, he made a rapid exit, giving the trembling Kevin an apologetic wave as he headed back to his room. He had an hour to kill before Crossword Club. For better or worse, his bladder always had a suggestion of what to do. He headed into the toilet, sending an urgent message to his prostate to relinquish its hostage. Like clockwork, the second he pulled down his trousers there was a knock at the door. 'Just a second,' he yelled, as he zipped up and exited the ensuite. 'Come in!'

A tall, beautiful woman stood in the doorway, her long brown curly hair framing green eyes so striking that Fred found himself unable to look away. There was a sadness in them that drew him in. She must be one of the visiting doctors, although she had no stethoscope and her attire – a flowing white skirt and ripped denim jacket – was not the usual garb of the medicos. Denise stuck her head around the door, her eyes wide.

'Bernard, it's your daughter here to see you. It's Hannah!'

Chapter 27

Fred stared at the woman in the doorway and blinked hard, checking if she was an illusion. She was not. His jaw dropped as a flush of adrenaline fizzed through his body. Bernard's daughter!

Denise patted Hannah's arm. 'He's had a bit of mental deterioration after the stroke. He might be a bit confused, so go easy on him.' Hannah's eyes remained transfixed on Fred, like she'd seen a ghost. If only she knew the half of it.

'When did you last see him?' Denise asked.

'When I was nine years old.' Hannah's voice was even.

'Gosh, you can see the family resemblance, can't you?' Denise said, glancing from Hannah to Fred. 'We didn't even know he had any family on the scene . . . Anyway, I'll leave you to it. I'm sure you've got lots of catching up to do!'

Fred's chest tightened, the air in the room so thick you could scoop it into a waffle cone. Was the jig up? Would she know he wasn't her father? Dare he speak? Could his voice be the same as Bernard's too?

'Hannah . . .?' It was both a statement and a question.

Hannah, the name on the letters.

Hannah, Bernard's daughter.

Hannah, who wanted nothing to do with her dad.

He had imagined this moment, even dreamt of it, but his dreams had left him grossly unprepared. She'd made it crystal clear she wanted nothing to do with her father, so he'd never thought she'd actually show up. A wash of nausea came over Fred, or was it guilt? His body shook with a curiosity and a nervousness that was foreign to him. He *had* to tell her the truth – didn't he? This was a different game altogether now, one he wasn't equipped to play.

'So, you recognise me then?' Her nostrils flared as she fired the short, clipped words.

Fred smiled, uncertain of what to do or say, like a foreigner in a land where he didn't know the customs. Almost without him realising it, his trembling hand reached into the drawer next to him and removed a faded photo he'd found in the shoebox.

'This . . . this is you, isn't it? You were so adorable,' he said, pointing at the smiling girl holding a butterfly net. 'I can see you've grown into a beautiful woman.'

A solitary tear ran down Hannah's cheek. She sniffed and flicked it away with her finger like it was a fly.

'I don't know how you can even *talk* to me,' she said, her voice dripping with rage, 'after what you did, to me, to Mum . . .' She looked out the window. 'To Sadie.' She swallowed hard, flicking away another tear.

Fred stared into her eyes: among the anger and sadness was fear. Great big chunks of it. The poor woman. He took a deep breath, trying to suck in air or bravery, or maybe both. After many trips around the sun, he'd learnt that when someone was angry, it was best just to let them talk. And frankly, he hadn't the foggiest idea what to say anyway.

Her voice got louder, her eyes flashing. 'You just left! You left us with nothing, you ruined everything. You didn't even go to Sadie's funeral, for god's sake!' She stared out at the grey clouds that had begun forming in the sky, as heavy as her soul seemed to be.

A teapot of grief poured sadness into Fred's heart. Although she was a stranger, his arms longed to reach for her.

'I got your letter asking me to come,' she said, spitting out the words as if they tasted bad.

His heart picked up pace as a cold sweat broke out all over his body. This would not be a good time to have a heart attack, although it may be less painful than this. 'Oh, yes, I was, er, wondering if you received that.' The scribbled red 'Return to Sender' blushed in his mind.

'I know it was a few months ago, but I couldn't come then. Wasn't going to come at all, actually, so I sent it back. But now I am pr— Now I'm . . . well, I'm here. You don't seem to be that sick to me.' Her eyes flashed again, looking him up and down like he was something a cat had thrown up.

Fred took out his handkerchief and offered it, his hand still shaking.

She shook her head, her breathing becoming shallow. 'So, you're dying, are you? Want to wipe your conscience clean before you go? Try to gain my forgiveness? Well, you won't get it, that's for sure. What do you even have to say to me?'

The pain beneath her eyes was palpable, its jagged edge stabbed at Fred's tummy. He was not cut out for this. Should he just come clean? But what possible way was there to explain to someone that you were pretending to be her father and that her real father had in fact died and been buried as you? She'd think he was a fruitcake, probably put it down to dementia and not believe him. How could he tell the truth? How could he *not* tell it? He was too far in to go back, but he couldn't move forward either. Dishonesty looked about as good on Fred as Patricia's lipstick, but maybe he needed to try.

He cleared his throat in hope that the act itself might spur him into saying something appropriate or even profound, but his mouth was empty. His gaze met Hannah's. She didn't look crash hot. The colour drained from her face and she swayed for a moment before slumping to the ground.

'Hannah!' Fred leapt to his feet with the nimbleness of a seventy-year-old. 'Someone help!' Kevin ran into the room and bent down to examine Hannah. She was conscious, but her milky forehead was beaded with sweat.

'Oh, I'm sorry.' Hannah placed a hand on her stomach. 'I just got really dizzy there for a second.'

'Has this happened before?' Kevin asked, taking her pulse.

'Well, yes.' Her eyes met Fred's for a second before looking away. 'I'm twelve weeks' pregnant.'

Fred's heart skipped a beat as the words sunk in. A *baby*! Bernard's grandchild! Kevin assisted Hannah to her feet and led her to the armchair.

'No, please, she can lie on my bed,' Fred insisted, clearing the newspaper off his crumpled doona. 'Let her put her feet up.'

'Oh, I really don't need to.' Hannah shook her head.

'Please,' said Fred.

'Well, okay.'

Kevin helped her onto the bed and poured a cup of water while Fred fetched some lamingtons from his cupboard that Val had made the day before. He'd been saving them for a special occasion. This certainly qualified.

'For you,' he said gently to Hannah. 'And your passenger,' he added, glancing at her stomach. She wasn't showing yet. 'Might help to get your blood sugar back up?'

She hesitated a moment before taking a piece. 'I do love coconut.

I'm surprised you remembered.' Her voice was flat, but not as cold as it had been before.

'Um, yes. Coconut. I don't suppose we could get a cup of tea, please, Kevin, mate?' In Fred's experience, a cuppa was a good idea in any situation.

'Sure thing, Bernard. How do you both take it?'

'White, no sugar, please,' Fred and Hannah said simultaneously. They locked eyes and Hannah's face flashed with what seemed like the beginning of a smile, but it was gone before Fred was sure. She examined the lamington then took a small bite off the corner.

'So . . . when, um, when is the baby due?' Fred fidgeted with the button on his sleeve.

'January.' Hannah wiped a bit of coconut from her lips.

'Is it . . . your first?' Fred swallowed. This was far more terrifying than filling in for Dolly Parton.

She nodded. 'I wasn't planning on telling you, to be honest.'

The words hurt, but why? He was a complete stranger, after all, but as the closest thing Bernard had left to a soul, perhaps Fred felt sad on his behalf. He pretended to clean his glasses. The thought of telling her the truth once again pulled at his mind, but he pushed it away. She didn't need any extra stress right now, especially in her condition. He would lie low for the time being and hope for the best.

Kevin returned with the tea. The good lad had used the nice china instead of those awful insulated mugs. Fred blew on the hot liquid and took a long, slow sip. 'I hope you didn't have to travel too far to come here today?'

'I actually live just down the road. I didn't even know if you were still in Wattle River. How did you get my address?'

Fred frowned, scratching his head.

'To write the letter.' Hannah crossed her arms.

'Oh, yes, the letter. I don't actually recall. Maybe one of the staff looked you up?' He fumbled with a stray bit of wool on his jumper.

'Anyway, it doesn't matter now. I can't stay. I don't feel dizzy anymore.' Hannah stood up slowly, picking up her handbag and her anger along with it. 'This was a mistake. I don't even know why I came. I can see you aren't going to give me any answers, let alone an apology.' She marched for the door, the heat of her fury making Fred sweat again.

His stomach knotted; he couldn't leave things like this. This couldn't be her last interaction with her 'father'.

'Never let the sun go down on your anger.' Dawn's voice echoed the rule that had seen him through fifty years of marriage. He had to say something, do something, but he didn't know what. His eyes searched the room and settled on the desk drawer.

'Hannah,' he said, choosing his words carefully, 'I *am* sorry. I'm so sorry you've been so badly hurt. But before you go . . .'

She stopped and turned around as he opened the drawer to retrieve Bernard's second unsent letter. 'Please take this, it's for you. You don't have to read it now. But it contains information you need to know.'

She narrowed her eyes, studying his face carefully. Could she tell he wasn't her dad? Was she taking a mental measurement of his ears?

'Please?'

'Fine, whatever.' Her sharp words sliced the silence. As she took the letter from his hands he felt a weight lift, as though it had been made of lead. He couldn't do much for poor Bernard, but he could at least do this. She scrunched it up, stuffed it into her handbag and turned again to leave.

'I won't see you again, so, yeah, have a good life. Or a bad one. Whatever.' Her voice was shaky.

'Hannah. Thank you. I'm so glad you came. And I'm so glad you told me.' He motioned to her belly. 'About the passenger, that is. I think it's truly marvellous. I'm sure you'll be a terrific mum.'

She sniffed and, without a word, walked out, slamming the door behind her.

Chapter 28

Hannah held her tears until she was inside her front door and then let them drop to the floor like a pile of heavy parcels she could no longer carry. She tossed the scrunched-up letter on the wooden coffee table and buried her head in her hands. Her dog yapped from the courtyard, but she didn't let him in. Seeing her this mad would only upset the little guy.

Sucking in shaky breaths, she gripped the back of the couch for support. Confronting her father was never going to be easy, but it shouldn't have been this hard. She didn't give a rat's arse about him. She was over him. So why did he still have this power over her? She'd cried the last time she'd seen him, too.

The memory of that day played as clear in her mind as a movie she'd seen a thousand times. It had been a sunny, warm September Tuesday. She'd felt cross at the sun for shining so brightly on a day when all light had been lost.

Only the week before they'd been planning a little party for Sadie's thirteenth birthday and voyage into teenage years, though she'd been sick for so long she was largely bedridden by that stage. When Mum's friends rang to ask how Sadie was, Mum would put on her bright voice and say they had high hopes for the third round of chemo, but she'd always cry after hanging up the phone.

Mum had taken Hannah shopping to choose a special present for Sadie. After looking carefully at every piece the jewellery shop had to offer, she'd chosen a gold chain with a heart-shaped locket, classic and beautiful. Hannah had put a photo of her and Sadie inside and wrapped it in pretty blue paper with stars on it.

Sadie had never got to open it.

Hannah caught a glimpse of herself in the hall mirror, the gold heart catching the light and winking at her. Mum had given it to her a few months after Sadie's death. 'She would have wanted you to have it, love,' she'd said.

Hannah opened the locket and gazed at two sisters who had once been happy. She closed her eyes and breathed deeply. The salty taste of tears summoned bile to rise up her throat.

Uncle Simon had driven her and Mum to the funeral. As they were leaving the house, Dad had said that he'd meet them there. Standing around the wrongly small coffin, her eyes had searched for him among the sea of mourners, certain he must just be behind one of them.

But he wasn't.

He never showed up.

She could almost forget about all the other stuff – the mood swings, the emotional distance, never being there for important events – but this . . . This was unimaginable. When they got home, all of Dad's things, including his car, were gone, leaving Mum and her with broken hearts that now had not one but two people to grieve.

Hannah grabbed the letter, fury and nausea bubbling up inside her. She ran to the bathroom, her knees giving way to the cold white tiles just in time to vomit into the toilet. She wiped her mouth and squeezed the letter hard as if trying to squash the life out of it. Her hand cramped and she threw the letter in the direction of the small bathroom bin.

She rose slowly, flushed the toilet and rinsed her face, the cold water sending a shiver down her spine. Pulling on her tie-dyed Oodie, she opened the door to the small courtyard, staring out at the dark, ominous sky.

The bastard didn't deserve a second chance.

'Where were you that day?' she shouted to the clouds, or her father, or both. A countless list of things she wished she'd said to him scrolled through her mind: how much she hated him, how she would never become the shitty parent he was, how Sadie would have *never* forgiven him. Why was it you always thought of the best things to say after the chance to say them was gone?

She grabbed a red pen and notebook from the coffee table and started jotting down her furious thoughts, as repulsive as the bile. She'd go back as soon as she could and tell the monster to his face.

As she put the pen down, her frustration finally easing, she paused. A thought tugged at the back of her mind. She recalled the meeting, everything her father had said and done. Something didn't quite add up, yet she couldn't quite put her finger on it.

Then it hit her. It was his eyes. They weren't the cruel, angry eyes she remembered.

They were kind.

Chapter 29

The melodious voice of Elton John swept through the room as Fred and Albert played chess in the Linton Lounge – if you could call it playing, that is. Albert moved a pawn sideways six squares then plucked his own king from the board, popped it in his shirt pocket and declared checkmate, his signature toothy grin illuminating the room. Fred chuckled. If you could manufacture that smile, lighting shops would go broke. He didn't have the heart to say anything – the company was far more valuable than the rules.

'Good game, mate,' he said, shaking Albert's hand enthusiastically.

'Don't tell anyone, but I stole this for you, Freddy!' whispered Albert loudly, producing a large, rather squashed chocolate bar from his trouser pocket. Fred raised his eyebrows. But who was he to judge? He had stolen a whole identity, which was slightly larger than a Violet Crumble, even the maxi size.

'Whacko. Let's split it, old boy,' suggested Fred, licking his lips.

'No way, José! I got this all for you. You eat up every last crumble.'

Touched by his generosity, Fred opened the wrapper and took a bite, the sweet honeycomb melting in his mouth while Albert looked on in delight. Fred's gaze wandered to the window beyond.

Hannah and her passenger had been constant visitors to his thoughts. Had she read the letter? How would she respond? Would he ever see her again? What would he say if he did? Did she like honeycomb? The questions played on repeat, like a stuck record.

'So, how are you, Freddy?' Albert's voice snapped him back. Aside from his unconventional chess moves, the old boy seemed particularly astute today. Fred studied his friend's face and the deep wrinkles surrounding his mouth, which had no doubt supported many a laugh.

'Oh, Albert, if only you knew the half of what was going on . . .'

'I'm all ears!' Albert said, wiggling his ears up and down masterfully, something Fred had never been able to do despite hours of practice in the mirror. 'Feelings are like flatulence: better out than in, that's what I always say.' Albert leaned closer.

Fred chortled and glanced around the room. There was no one else there. Maybe it would be good to get it off his chest – and who better to confess his sins to than a confidant who wouldn't remember? Perhaps having dementia should be a prerequisite for all priests?

He took a deep breath. Where to begin? 'Well, you see, mate, there was an accident, a mix-up . . .'

'Oh, no, not an accident!' Fear spread over his friend's face.

'No, no, mate, nothing bad!' Fred took Albert's hands, instantly regretting his choice of words. 'No one died. Well, I mean, someone died, but he was already dead.'

Another deep breath. 'You see, I'm not meant to be here. I was taking a walk and I saw a dead man in a wheelchair. I tried to get him back to the group he was with but then the darn seagulls attacked us, and I tripped . . . and, well, his body got flung into the water and the river just took him away.'

Albert burst into singing 'Old Man River' with great gusto, then gave Fred a wink. 'You keep on talking, Freddy.'

'Well, then it all just happened so quickly. He looked exactly like me! Everyone just assumed that I was him, and I got taken back in his place. But I'm not him, I'm not Bernard. I'm Fred.'

'I know who you are!' said Albert. 'The most wonderful one there is. Simply marvellous.' He gave Fred's shoulder a playful nudge.

'Thanks, Albert, but I don't feel marvellous. I don't know if I can go on living this lie. It gets worse . . .' The words were now spurting out of him uncontrollably, like water from a bung hose. 'Bernard has a daughter! And a grandchild on the way! She turned up out of the blue and made it clear she doesn't want anything to do with me – I mean, him. It's all getting rather confusing. But gee, I do feel better telling someone about it. I feel like my life is full of shadows at the moment.'

'You know what they say,' Albert clasped Fred's hand. 'You can't have shadows without light.' He tapped his nose and pointed at Fred, who couldn't help but smile.

'You know what I say, mate?'

His friend shrugged.

'You're the biggest light I've got.'

Albert's face shone with a joy so pure that Fred feared his heart may burst from it.

'I just don't know if I should stay or go, or *where* I should be. I feel like I don't belong anywhere . . .' Fred's voice trailed off.

Albert placed his big hands on Fred's shoulders, his often-distant eyes now focused firmly on his. 'You, sir, are exactly where you need to be,' he said slowly. 'Right here with me is where you belong. It's where you were always meant to be. When we were little, you promised you'd always be here for me, and that's what you are doing.'

Albert couldn't possibly have understood his confession, yet his words enveloped Fred in a calming hug. And maybe in some strange way he was right. Maybe Fred wasn't just borrowing Bernard's unlived life, but Albert's brother's too? He exhaled. 'Thanks, old man.'

Albert smiled. 'Whenever I'm in a pickle, do you know what I do? I dance it out,' said Albert, licking a pawn like it was a lolly pop. He stood and, although the music had stopped, began shaking his bottom to a silent melody.

'Come on!' he said, pulling Fred to his feet.

'There's never a dull moment with you, mate,' Fred chuckled, joining in the jig. The two friends danced around the room, swinging their hips and punching the air. At one point they took hold of each other and did a little tango strut. Albert was a bit unsteady on his feet but a better dancer than Kevin nonetheless. A giggle began to form in Fred's belly working its way up his whole body, like an eraser rubbing away all the stress as it went. Soon the pair were belly-laughing, gasping for air amid their chortles.

This was certainly good for his soul, not to mention the old ticker.

'You're a good man,' said Albert, catching his breath as he sat back down. 'Don't ever forget that. Have I told you how grateful I am that you found me, Fred?' Albert closed his watery eyes, resting his head on Fred's shoulder. Fred put his arm around him.

'Me too, mate. Me too.'

Denise stood at the edge of the doorway of the Linton Lounge, her mind suitably numbed from the new bottle of sherry she'd snuck from Ruby's cupboard after she'd changed her. The pear liqueur bottle was all apple juice now, although Ruby didn't seem to notice.

She rubbed her temples, trying to make sense of the conversation she was eavesdropping on.

'But I'm not him, I'm not Bernard – I'm Fred.'

She narrowed her eyes, taking in the scene. Bernard seemed dead set on convincing poor Albert that he was his brother. She shrugged. What harm could it do? Denise knew that you shouldn't correct someone with dementia, although sometimes she did so on purpose to create a stir that would distract from the turmoil raging within her.

Something niggled at the back of her mind, a thought she couldn't quite reach. What had they just said about the river? She never offered to take Albert on the bus outings to the river and gardens – he was too much bother.

The two men were now dancing. Crazy old things. Despite herself, a smile forced its way to her mouth as a memory of Kostas, one of the first residents she had cared for, appeared. His dancing to his Greek music had always made her smile. Hell, she even used to join in when 'Zorba the Greek' came on. The memory stung her eyes. She closed them, digging her fingernails into her palm.

When had she stopped loving this job? Begun loathing it? Begun loathing herself? How had she got here? To this shitty desert of a place? Where had the joy gone?

She quietly eased herself through the doorway and sat down at the back of the lounge, where the men couldn't see her. A heaviness came over her, pushing her further into the chair. Truth be told, she hadn't felt happy in years.

It had all happened gradually: the stress of becoming a working mum with a fussy baby who didn't sleep; the kilos piling on from the copious amounts of Nutella she would opt for instead of attempting to sleep when the baby napped briefly; Greg's work

hours getting longer and longer. She'd barely had time for gardening, the one thing she loved. Hell, even that had turned against her
last time, culminating in a big splinter from a rosebush.

The first time Jacqui had slept through was at three-and-a-half.
Ella was born the next day. More Nutella, more weight, more self-
loathing. She'd completely lost herself then. Greg's criticisms of her
became harsher and more frequent. And she started to believe every
single one of them. She was too fat, too lazy, would never cook like
his mother. His mother would know how to get the baby to sleep –
why didn't Denise learn from her? Why didn't she make more effort
like his colleagues' wives did? Why? Why? Why?

Then had come Jacqui's diagnosis of severe anxiety and sensory
processing disorder earlier this year, both a relief and a curse. At last
there was a reason behind the violent tantrums, the refusal to put
on a school uniform, the picky eating, the hours Denise had spent
trying to get her to sleep while Jacqui screamed insults at her, all of
which no doubt had an effect on placid Ella. But it was with a deep
sadness that Denise had learnt the condition wouldn't be something
Jacqui would grow out of – she would have it for life. And worst
of all, Greg blamed Jacqui's behaviour on Denise's bad mothering,
despite what the paediatrician and psychologist said. His saint of a
mother would *never* have raised a daughter like Jacqui.

'Yeah, well, she raised a pig like you!' she'd wanted to yell at
him, but never did, as deep down she'd begun to believe him too.

And of course, the worse Jacqui was, the more distant Greg had
become. He'd given up on his own daughter, put her in the too-hard
basket. He'd put Denise in the too-hard basket too. Too hard to
talk to, too hard to parent with, too hard to love. Their sex life was
extinct. The medication had helped Jacqui's behaviour immensely,
though Greg had accused Denise of taking the easy way out.

But it was too late by then: he'd already checked out emotionally, and she suspected the worst. He was a wanker just like her own dad had been.

Two hearty laughs snapped her back to the present and she was hit with a bolt of raging jealousy. She clenched her jaw. Why did they get to be happy, even with dementia and old age and incontinence?

She pushed herself to stand. Her knees ached – and no wonder. They had to carry her stupid, fat, useless body.

Denise approached the men, who were now seated again, panting after their exertion, the smell of sweat in the air. 'C'mon, you two, that's enough! We don't want any broken hips around here. Albert, you know you have to use your walker, stupid!'

Bernard's face fell. The words were awful, but Denise didn't care.

'Right you are! You're doing a great job, love,' said Albert, seemingly unfazed by her cruel comment.

She glared at the two men, then turned and left them there, along with her desire to do anything other than give in to her self-destruction.

Chapter 30

Fred, flitting between consciousness and sleep, felt himself being poked. He willed it to stop so he could catch a few more winks before his alarm went off to remind him to 'get ants', but it was no use. He opened one eye to the blurry outline of a lopsided grin an inch from his nose, the owner's milky breath warm on his face. Fred sat up quickly, hoping to avoid the string of saliva that was heading towards his left cheek. Missed it just in time.

'C'mon, Fred! We'll be late!' insisted the intruder, an urgency in his voice. Fred startled. The mention of his name sparked a pang of confusion and a dash of panic until he computed who was speaking.

'Today is the day! It's my wedding day, Freddy!'

He blinked, and Albert's face came into focus, his eyes sparkling with an excitement and anticipation befitting a groom. An old man with a young man's zeal trapped inside him, bursting to get out. His enthusiasm was contagious, and Fred couldn't help but give in to the smile creeping across his face. He peered at the clock and the little dachshunds covering Albert's pyjamas. A synchronised gurgle erupted from both of their tummies.

'All right, all right, Albert! First things first, mate. It's still early and we need to have brekkie and showers, et cetera, okay?'

Albert winked. 'Okey-dokey. I'm just going to post that letter to Aunty Joyce. Mum said she can't come to the wedding, but I promised I'd write to her on my wedding day.'

His friend's hand clasped a coffee – *hopefully* coffee – stained envelope with an indecipherable scribble on it. Fred watched from his open door as Albert dashed out to the central courtyard and posted the letter in the dog-poo bin that was there for visiting canine friends, giving Fred a double thumbs up. Fred gave him one back.

After breakfast, Fred wiped a stray dab of Vegemite off his moustache before checking the activities schedule. Albert would likely have already forgotten about his wedding day. But as Fred went to stand, the old boy had reappeared in the doorway, his voice more urgent than before. 'Is everything ready for the big day? Don't forget you're my best man!'

The words hugged his heart. Might he finally get to be a best man at the ripe old age of eighty-two? An inkling of an idea twitched in his brain. 'Things aren't ready yet, but they will be. You have a rest and I'll get you when it's time, okay?'

'Okay!' Albert practically skipped down the hall, almost bowling over a startled Patricia, who nevertheless retained enough balance to turn and stare at Albert's rear end as he left. Fred shook his head. Relentless.

He glanced at his watch, his idea taking hold. Happy Hour was at 3.30 p.m. It seemed like the perfect setting for a wedding. He had six hours, four if he included meal, nap and prostate breaks. He was going to need help. Denise had called in sick, but he wouldn't want to bother her anyway; she seemed to have enough on her plate these days. He found Kevin and Linh in the Linton Lounge chatting to each other, their faces glowing.

Fred smiled at the sight. 'I'm sorry to interrupt, but would you two mind terribly helping me with something?'

Six hours, two cappuccinos, ten trips to the toilet, a roast beef sandwich, a nanna nap and a fortifying blueberry muffin later, Fred sat dressed in his new suit at the entrance of the nursing home, waiting for Val. She always came to Happy Hour unless she was sick. How he hoped she wasn't sick today.

He caught his reflection in the automatic glass doors and pictured his Dawn sitting next to him. She would have worn her signature cornflower blue, and the pearls he'd given her for her fiftieth birthday. The vision split in two as the doors opened and Val stepped through, almost walking past him but catching his eye just in time.

'Oh, hello, Bernard! What are you doing out here?' she said, looking him up and down. 'Wow! Don't you scrub up nicely? Are you going out somewhere?'

He smiled, busting to share his delicious news. 'Hi, Val. I'm actually just heading to Happy Hour, but it's a bit of a different Happy Hour today . . .'

He produced a bouquet of pink roses that Linh had picked from the garden and a white veil that Ruby had kindly fashioned for him from some leftover material in the craft box. Val looked from the flowers to the veil and then to Fred, her eyes quizzically putting the pieces together.

'It's your wedding day, Val.'

The words transformed her, appearing to conjure both a memory and the delight of a surprise yet to come. Her eyes moistened as a chuckle sprung from deep within, so free and joyful that Fred couldn't help but join in.

'I can't believe this. What have you planned?' she asked, a twinkle in her eye.

'You'll see, love. You don't need to worry about a thing.'

'I knew there was a reason I wore white today!' she said, removing her tan overcoat to reveal a smart cream pantsuit.

He clapped his hands. 'That's just perfect! You look beautiful.'

'Do you think so? I look so old!'

'Not to Albert you don't, love.' To the beholder, dementia was the world's strongest anti-ageing cream.

'Bernard, I hope you haven't gone to too much trouble. You're a cheeky fellow doing all this, you know!'

'Trust me, you're going to love it.'

After helping Val pin the veil on, Fred signalled to Christine at reception, who was in on the plan, too. She pressed a button and a string arrangement of Pachelbel's *Canon* flowed through the speakers. 'I just need your ring,' said Fred, motioning to the silver band on her ring finger. She gave it to him, and he placed it inside his suit pocket alongside Albert's.

Fred offered his arm and Val took it, squeezing his hand. Grinning from ear to ear, they made their way down the long corridor to the Wentworth Room, stepping in time to the music.

'I think I'm even more nervous than on my wedding day!' Val whispered. 'I'm so glad I've got you to steady me, Bernard.'

Fred patted her arm as they approached the door where Linh was standing, a rose pinned to her yellow uniform.

'Ready?' he asked Val.

'Ready,' she said.

Linh opened the door and a delightful warmth spread through Fred's whole body as he took in the sight before him. The round tables had been split into two groups, an aisle forming between them. Battery-operated candles cast a welcoming glow around the room. A sea of fifty or sixty smiling residents looked on, some with flowers pinned to their outfits, others wearing the hats they had made for the Easter-bonnet parade. And there, at the end of the aisle, stood Albert in his new charcoal suit, a pink rose pinned to his buttonhole, looking like the million bucks he'd hoped for.

Fred recognised the look in his friend's eyes when Albert saw Val enter the room. It was the same one he'd had when he'd laid eyes on his own blushing bride, Dawn: a potpourri of joy, excitement, anticipation and adoration. The expression of a man who saw a future that exceeded his wildest hopes and dreams. When the tears began streaming down Albert's face and over his gargantuan grin, a lump formed in Fred's throat as his own tears fell. He cried for Albert, he cried for Val, and most of all he cried for his Dawn.

'Oh dear, will you look at me! What a duffer,' he said. He glanced at Val, whose face was equally wet.

'If you're a duffer, I'm a double duffer!' Linh passed them tissues and they composed themselves before Fred handed Val over to Albert, who gave a giant sniff and wiped his nose on his sleeve.

Kevin stood between them, shifting his weight, his hands trembling as he held the piece of paper he'd printed off the internet. Linh winked at him from the sidelines, which seemed to give the lad courage.

He cleared his throat. 'We are gathered here today to celebrate the marriage of Valerie and Albert.'

Albert nodded enthusiastically.

'Do you, Albert, take this woman to be your lawfully wedded wife, to have and to hold, to honour and to cherish in sickness and in health from this day forward?'

'Oh, do I ever! Will you just look at her?' Albert beamed out at the audience like a chuffed little boy showing off his brand-new whiz-bang toy.

Kevin smiled. 'And do you, Valerie, take Albert as your lawfully wedded husband, to have and to hold from this day forth, to honour and to cherish in sickness and in health as long as you both shall live?'

Val gazed into the eyes of her husband of sixty-four years. 'Definitely, and without hesitation,' she said, confirming a promise she had already kept so faithfully.

Fred handed them their rings and the couple exchanged them, eyes locked.

'Well then, you may now kiss the bride,' said Kevin, shooting a furtive glance at Linh. Albert, quite the showman, turned around and gave the audience an exaggerated wink as his eyebrows bounced up and down. Then, in an unusually sprightly move, he turned back to Val and dipped her, planting an almighty smooch on her pink lips.

The delighted onlookers burst into applause, a jovial buzz tingling throughout the room.

The bride and groom took their seats at the nearest table, where Linh had glasses of champagne ready. Fred sat opposite them, not wasting a minute to tuck into the mini hotdogs that appeared in front of him.

'Delicious! Aren't they?' said a guttural voice from behind him. 'I do love me a little boy – or a big boy, for that matter!' He jumped as Patricia's bony fingers crept up his spine. Fred's stomach convulsed as he dropped the shrivelled hotdog, now as appetising as raw chicken.

'I never got married, you know. Not that I didn't want to, but no one ever asked,' said Patricia, her eyes unusually dim. 'I guess I found other things to fill the void . . .'

'Oh, Albie, it's okay, it's okay . . .' Val's voice rose from the other side of the table, grabbing Fred's attention.

Albert was wringing his hands and shaking his head, the joy of earlier replaced by fear. Val tried to comfort him.

'He's not here! He'll miss the speech. He's got to give a speech! He promised he would. He promised!' The old man rocked back and forth, his eyes darting nervously around the room, searching yet unfocused.

If unchecked, his friend's distress would rapidly get worse. 'It's okay, Albert, I'm here,' said Fred, reaching across the table, but his words didn't register.

Albert's breathing quickened. 'No! No! No! It's not right! IT'S NOT RIGHT!' His shouts got louder and the rocking more violent. Val was on the verge of tears. The entire bespectacled room was staring.

Before Fred knew what his legs were doing, he had stood up, taken a spoon and dinged it against his glass. A tank full of goldfish swirled in his stomach. At least he wasn't wearing a Dolly Parton wig like in his dream. With a shaking hand, he tapped the glass again and the room quietened.

He cleared his throat, taking a large swig of champagne for courage. 'Good evening, or should I say afternoon? As you know, we are here to celebrate the wedding of Val and Albert and I'd like to say a few words if I may, as, um, the best man.' He flushed with pride. Would this work?

Val nudged Albert. 'Look, Albie, look! He's giving a speech.' Albert's wandering eyes rested on Fred.

Fred continued. 'My name is . . . My name is Fred.' The same words he'd said at the river now filled him with relief and terror in equal measure. He winked at Kevin just to cover his bases.

Albert stopped rocking and stared, mesmerised, like a child watching live theatre for the first time.

'You see, we aren't just here for a wedding. We all know what a wedding is, and most people know what romance is. The lucky ones even know what being in love is. But love that lasts a lifetime – well, that's something very few get to experience. Love is . . . about picking someone up and never, ever putting them down again, no matter how heavy things become.' Fred took another quick sip of champagne before continuing.

'Sometimes in life we wish we had a crystal ball to see the future. Where will we be? What will we be doing? Well, I don't have a crystal ball, but I strongly suspect that sixty or more years from their wedding day, these two here will still be just as much in love. But it will be an even stronger love, strengthened by the daily exercise of choosing each other. Not just a love that loves when things are easy, when you're feeling happy. No, it will be an unbreakable love that continues loving when things are hard. One that loves through bad times, through loss, in health, and in sickness.'

'Sometimes terrible sickness.' He looked knowingly at Val.

'Their promise today is to make that decision to love every day, to care for each other no matter what. And I know for a fact that Val – that they – will keep that promise faithfully for the rest of their lives.'

At that moment an image of his beloved Dawn, asleep for the last time, illuminated his mind. Sometimes 'until death do us part' just wasn't long enough.

Fred turned and locked eyes with Albert. 'And, well, as far as Albert goes, a man couldn't wish for a better brother than him. Albert here, he sees the good in everyone and in every situation, finds the light where there are shadows. He is as generous as he is tall. He always has a song in his heart, a dance in his feet, a chocolate bar in his pocket. He makes people feel like they matter. He makes *me* feel like I matter. He is the best encourager I know. I, well, I love you, Albert, and I can honestly say my life is so much richer for having you in it. So without further ado, let's raise a glass to Albert and Val!'

'To Albert and Val,' chorused the residents as they raised their glasses, some with champagne, others with thickened apple juice.

Albert jumped to his feet in a standing ovation, tears slipping unabashedly down his cheek. He smiled and decades slipped from his face as he embraced Fred in a big bear hug.

'Thank you, Fred. Thank you so much. I was waiting for you for such a long time. I knew you would get here, no matter how long it took. I love you. Have I told you that today?'

'I love you too, cobber.' And Fred meant it from the bottom of his heart.

Hannah stood at the back of the large room, her mouth agape. It was as though she were watching a movie, because it sure as hell wasn't any reality she knew. She'd come here today to blast her father. Her hand scrunched the piece of paper she had doused with her fury, scribbling all the things she should have said to him the other day about Mum, about Sadie, about her. She blinked. Even more bizarre than the fact she found herself at some kind of wedding for old people was seeing her father standing there and talking about love in a way that seemed almost impossible. Like watching someone suddenly speak a language they had never learnt.

Something definitely didn't add up. It was as though she had two fathers: one who lived in her memory, flaky and full of anger, and another who showed beautiful emotion and was obviously admired by those around him. Her wobbly legs carried her to the nearest seat. She didn't know whether to laugh or cry or yell. Where had this devotion, this passion, been when she was growing up? *He* hadn't chosen to love when things were hard – he'd just bloody given up! What a hypocrite. She took a slow, shaky breath in, her nerve to confront him dissipating from shock.

Taking one last look at him – and she was determined it *would* be the last – she stood up and left.

The wedding lasted longer than Fred could have envisioned. Linh floated around taking photos and the DON arranged for dinner to be served a bit later so that the residents could continue to enjoy the festivities. Val was even allowed to stay the night, much to the groom's delight. Fred sat back, shandy in hand, cherishing the scene before him. The scent of roses from Val's bouquet gladdened his nostrils as the silky tones of Louis Armstrong wafted through the air. He watched as Val and Albert slow-danced, their eyes closed, Val's head resting peacefully on her husband's tall frame, Fred's heart a metronome to the loving scene.

Linh, who normally left at 5 p.m., stayed on chatting with Kevin, who was also off the clock. Fred looked on like a birdwatcher as his two young friends exchanged shy conversation. Kevin caught Fred's eye and he responded with an encouraging gesture.

C'mon, mate, now's your chance.

He willed his thoughts to be telepathic. And perhaps it worked, because Kevin asked Linh a question and pointed to the makeshift dance floor. You little ripper, Kev! Linh nodded enthusiastically and soon the two of them were dancing next to Val and Albert. Fred let out an unintentionally audible cheer, which he quickly stifled when everyone, including a glaring Kevin, spun around to stare at him. Linh hadn't been joking about her ballroom dancing skills. Even in her uniform, she was graceful as she swayed to the music. Kevin tried his hardest to show some of the moves Fred had pointed out in Astaire's video, but the poor lad looked like he was stomping on grapes in a wine barrel. If a sweet vintage came out of it, what did it matter?

As Fred gazed upon young love and old love side by side, his heart felt fuller than it had in a very long time. If only he had a loved one to share it with. Yet to his surprise, this time, instead of Dawn, it was Hannah who popped into his mind.

Chapter 31

F red grinned at his reflection in the bathroom mirror as memories of the previous night and the delightful – albeit unusual – wedding danced in his mind. He couldn't wait to see Albert. It was almost impossible that he would remember the events of last night, but Fred wanted to be in his friend's company anyway.

He wet his nappy and waited for Denise to dress him. Small prices to pay for roast dinners and, more importantly, to be with Albert. He ate his breakfast quickly before heading down the hall towards his mate's room.

'Bernard! Did you hear what happened to Mabel?' Patricia, drunk on gossip, almost sideswiped him as he passed her room.

'Hi, Patricia. No, I didn't. I must keep moving, I'm afraid.'

He kept walking, but she scampered alongside. She evidently hadn't brushed her teeth yet. Or worse, maybe she had.

'*So* embarrassing for her to be found like that!' Patricia blurted.

'Excuse me, please, sir.' Fred looked over his shoulder, then stepped aside as two ambulance officers came up behind him wheeling a stretcher. Poor Mabel. He hoped she hadn't had another fall, recalling the last time the ambos had been there. She really needed to hang up those tap shoes.

But they walked straight past Mabel's room. He glanced inside. Two carers were wiping away a rainbow of various shades of lipstick from all over her face.

'It's okay, love, we'll get it off. We know you didn't mean to do it.' Poor Mabel. Parkinson's was sadly not conducive to giving oneself a makeover.

He turned the corner. The ambulance officers were out of sight now. They must have gone into one of the other rooms.

The moment he saw Val standing in her dressing gown outside Albert's room, he knew. He recognised her expression; he had seen it on his own face in the bathroom mirror on Dawn's last day. The look of someone whose light has been switched off.

Every one of Fred's eighty-two years came crashing down upon him, each weighing a tonne. His body was unable to take the force and he gripped the handrail, an ache pervading his whole being – his head, his bones, but mainly his heart.

Val stared ahead, her eyes wide, holding a hanky in her trembling hands. The air was like knee-deep mud as he trudged towards her, reaching the poor woman just in time for her to collapse into his arms. How he remained standing, he didn't know.

'He's gone, Bernard, he's really gone.' Her fractured words tumbled out through rapid gasps.

Fred held her for a long time, the grief heavy between them. At least there were two people to shoulder it now.

A kindly young ambulance officer came out of Albert's room. 'I'm so very sorry for your loss, madam. Would you like to say a final goodbye before we take him to the funeral home?'

She squeezed Fred's hand tightly. 'Come with me?'

'Of course.' His chest tightened and for a moment his feet stalled, unwilling to take him to what was ahead.

'We'll give you a moment,' the officer said, leaving.

They took a deep breath and walked hand-in-hand into Albert's room. Albert lay pale on the bed in his dark-green flannel pyjamas, his remaining hair a wisp of cloud around his head.

The complete stillness of a dead body had always disturbed Fred. He remembered Bruno, lying there in his best suit at his open-casket funeral, and his dear, dear Dawn after she'd breathed her last. It never got any easier.

Val sat on the edge of the bed and bent down to hug Albert, burying her face into his still chest. 'Oh, Albie, my love, my beautiful, beautiful husband. I never dreamt that my life could have been this good. That I could ever have felt so cherished. It's all because of you. I will love you until the day I die, my darling, my sweetheart.'

As she stroked her husband's cheek, Fred gazed upon Albert's face. He couldn't quite name the expression; it was one he hadn't seen on the old boy before.

'May we take him now?' the ambo with the kind eyes asked as he gently approached Val.

'Yes . . . Just one more thing, please.' Val removed the black-and-white picture of Albert and his brother from the wall and placed it in Albert's hands as they transferred him to the gurney.

'You go be with Freddy now, my darling.' Her voice shattered into gentle sobs. None of her tomorrows would be the same. They would always be just that little bit worse.

Fred took one last look at the man who had brightened so many of his days over the last three months.

'Goodbye, mate,' he said, grasping Albert's shoulder. 'You really were like a brother to me.' His voice broke, mirroring his cracked heart.

And as Albert left his room for the last time, Fred realised what the expression on his friend's face was: pure tranquillity. The cruel clasps of dementia had finally been released, and his mind and heart were now at peace.

Val's mobile rang, and she excused herself. 'It's my daughter,' she said, stepping out of the room.

Fred allowed his legs to give way and plonked onto the bed, the lingering scent of his friend's musky aftershave stinging his eyes. A lone white hair clung to Albert's pillow, refusing to let go. He knew how it felt.

The sea of photos on the wall now gazed over a bed that was as empty as Fred's heart. How much grief could a body handle in a lifetime?

He didn't want to be here without Albert.

Perhaps it was finally time to leave.

Chapter 32

Sadie's grave was overgrown with daisies. Hannah had planted her sister's favourite flower there almost a decade ago and they'd flourished ever since. Taking her secateurs, she knelt down and gently trimmed around the headstone, Sadie's death date coming into view. She'd seen it a hundred times, but it still hurt her eyes. It would always be too early.

She held the gold heart locket around her neck, wishing it was her sister's hand. 'You're going to be an aunty, Sayd,' she whispered, splashes of tears watering the daisies. 'Gee, you'd have made a great aunty. If only I still had you, I wouldn't need anyone else. Not Mike, and certainly not *him*!' She pressed her hand to her chest, trying to still her shaking heart. 'I saw him, Sadie,' she said softly, a pulse of guilt shooting through her veins. 'I saw Dad.'

The last time Sadie had seen Dad was the day she died. Hannah closed her eyes. Her sister's hospital-room door came into view, sights, smells and sounds echoing in her mind. Her mother's animal-like howls, the stench of hospital disinfectant. Her father's wide-eyed stare and robotic movements.

Hannah had been told to wait outside. That was fine with her, as what was inside the room was the unthinkable, the impossible, the unbearable. She'd sat in the plastic hospital chair, face buried in her sister's fluffy yellow jumper, singing over and over again in her head 'You're the One that I Want' from their favourite movie, *Grease*, to block out the pain. Sadie was the only one she wanted, but could never have again.

'I'm so bloody angry, Sayd!' said Hannah, forcefully yanking out a clump of weeds near the grave. 'Sorry, you've never heard me swear before but I am bloody furious. What an arsehole! He can rot in hell!'

An elderly woman a few graves down shot Hannah a dirty look. Shit. She'd been yelling like a crazy person.

She bowed her head closer to the tombstone, her shaky voice dropping to a whisper again. 'You needed him. *We* needed him when we lost you. Where the hell did he go? *Apparently* he's sorry now. *Apparently* he has emotions now and kind, bloody eyes. He's written me a letter, but I threw it out. Don't worry, I'm not going to forgive him. I'll *never* forgive him. Not for your sake, or Mum's or mine.'

She rubbed the backs of her hands up her tear-stained cheeks as a memory floated to the surface. It was that awful day when he'd broken Hannah's birdhouse and Sadie's teacup, painful images that were frequent visitors to her mind over the years. She'd run upstairs after screaming that she hated him. The recollection always ended there.

But today there was more, like an extra scene at the end of a movie, shown after the credits. Hannah picked a daisy and twirled it in her fingers. She closed her eyes, concentrating on the distant memory as it rematerialised.

After crying herself to sleep she'd woken around midnight, passing Sadie's room on her way to the toilet, her bunny slippers silent on the beige carpet. The door was ajar, and her sister's soft reading light gave a warm glow.

Sadie was gently putting a pink bandaid on Dad's sliced thumb, patting his brown hair, like a mother comforting a young child. He was looking at his feet and weeping, a piece of the shattered teacup in his lap. Sadie placed a finger under their dad's chin and tilted his face up to meet her gaze. 'It's okay, Daddy,' she said. 'I forgive you.'

Chapter 33

A violent wind rattled the windowpanes in Fred's room, as grief rattled his heart. He wasn't sure which would break first. It had been twelve days since Albert's death and the world seemed to have shrunk. Fred had been invited to the funeral the week before but had come down with a nasty cold and couldn't go. He'd lain in bed that day, staring at the photo Linh had taken of the two of them in their wedding suits flexing their biceps. He doubted he would ever feel strong again.

Fred poked at the untouched eggs and bacon on his breakfast tray. He could count on one hand the number of times he'd refused food: the time he got food poisoning from risking some rissoles he'd left out overnight, the day Dawn was diagnosed, and the day she died.

His sleep had been crowded, splintered with nightmares of telling the truth: to the police, to the staff, to Hannah . . . He'd woken in a foggy sweat, only to remember Albert. Fred's blood had been replaced by grief, which his heart pumped relentlessly around his body, delivering no sustenance to his weary cells. His throat constricted as he thought of the pain Val would be in. At least Sarah, Cassie and the girls would be up from Melbourne now to be with her. What would it have been like for him to have had a child to share the grief with when Dawn died?

He looked out the window, his thoughts drifting to Hannah and her passenger as familiar questions circled his mind. Had she read the letter? Perhaps she'd thrown it away? A chill crept over him and he reached for the brown cardigan on the bed. The inside of the collar sported a neatly sewn label: *Bernard Greer*. He ran his finger over the name of the poor bugger who'd died before he'd had the chance to say sorry, the chance to be forgiven. His limbs tingled with gratitude towards Bernard. If only he could somehow set things right with Hannah, would it possibly be a way of reimbursing the man for the last few years of his life? If so, how? He pushed his plate aside, the smell of bacon falling on a deaf nose.

'I'm worried about you, Mr Bernard.' Linh's slight frame appeared at the door. She took a seat and placed her small arm around him. 'You haven't been coming to anything, not even exercises. You're going to lose your strong muscles – and why aren't you eating your bacon? You told me it's the food of life!'

Her voice was soft and gentle, and Fred offered a weak smile. 'Thanks for caring about me, love, I just . . . haven't felt up to it, you know.'

'I know, you miss your friend Mr Albert. I miss him, too. He was such a cheeky fellow, like you.' She patted his arm. 'I hear your daughter came to see you. That must've been nice? Perhaps you can give her a call. When is she coming in again?'

'Oh, I . . . She did come to see me, yes. I hadn't seen her . . . in a long time,' *or ever*, 'but she doesn't want to see me again. She doesn't need me in her life, you see.'

Linh's face softened. 'My dad still lives in Vietnam. We had a big fight when I wanted to leave to move to Australia. He wanted me to stay. I didn't want to listen, so I pushed him away – I told him biến đi! It means "get lost". And he did, Mr Bernard.' Her deep brown eyes looked at him intently. 'We didn't talk for weeks. It was really awful.'

'I'm sorry to hear that, love.' Fred patted her hand.

'You know what, though, Mr Bernard? It was then, when I was pushing him away, that I needed him most. I needed him to show up and say that he loves me no matter what I do or where I live – which he does, of course.'

Fred nodded.

'Kids always need their parents, even if they don't know it. And maybe you need her now, too. I don't want you to be lonely, Mr Bernard. You've got too much love and kindness in that big heart,' she said, tapping his chest. 'I've got to go set up for exercises this afternoon. Please come?'

'I'll think about it, love.' But he knew he couldn't face it without his marvellous workout buddy.

A memory of Albert doing his strong-man's pose stung his eyes. He did need to get some form of exercise nonetheless; his avocados were feeling like porridge again. Maybe he could manage a walk. The river would be ideal, but the courtyard would have to do. He stretched his aching joints and made his way down the hall. A cackle of laughter sprang from the craft room as he walked by. Knitting Group must have already started. Patricia, sporting a magenta blouse with big shoulder pads, spotted him and called out in a singsong voice, 'Bernard! Do say hello!'

Fred stuck his head around the door. 'G'day, ladies, how do you do?'

A dozen crinkled faces looked up and beamed flirtatiously at him in what looked like a synchronised smiling routine, causing warmth to flood his cheeks. The craft room with its large wooden table was the most colourful place in the entire nursing home, with residents' paintings (executed with varying degrees of talent) adorning every wall. There were several paintings of pink and beige mushrooms of varying lengths and widths, the letter P painted in the corner of each, leaving little doubt who was responsible for them.

'We were so very sorry to hear about Albert, dear,' said Ruby, the kindness in her eyes still visible through her thick glasses. 'I know you two were friends. It was a lovely thing you did for him, a beautiful wedding. You know, most people seem to get grumpier as they get older – you are the opposite, you just get kinder.'

'Thanks, love, I appreciate that.'

'Join us, Bernie!' Patricia beckoned with a long, bony finger.

'Oh, well, I, um . . .'

Ruby patted an empty seat beside her. 'Please?'

How could he say no to dear, sweet Ruby? The oldest resident in the home at a grand 101, with the zest of a sixty-year-old. He sighed. Perhaps it would be a good distraction.

'What, you afraid we aren't cool enough for you?' Patricia's pencilled-on eyebrows arched upwards.

'We are known as the hip crowd around here, you know!' said Lorraine, a vivacious woman with a pink bob.

'Hip-replacement crowd, more like it,' chortled Patricia.

'Ha ha. Well, I can't knit, you know,' Fred said, his feet still parked at the door.

'That's okay, we'll teach you,' said Ruby as he took the seat beside her. 'I'm so glad you've come out again, Bernard. When you first moved here I never once saw you smile, you barely spoke and you rarely came to any activities. I was afraid you'd become a hermit again after losing dear Albert.'

Fred patted her hand. 'Pretty hard to resist company like yours, Ruby dear.'

Ruby blushed and rummaged in a box for some spare needles. Dawn had been a magnificent knitter. He pictured the pale-yellow booties she had created expectantly for their unborn baby, each stitch made with love and gleaming eyes. They had remained unworn and were still in a shoebox in his flat. A pain stabbed at his side – they would likely be in the ruddy bin now, along with everything else he owned. His heart sank. They'd done so much to prepare for parenthood, as much as you could back then. Nowadays there were even books that told you everything, like *What to Expect When You're Expecting*. Sadly, no one had written *What to Expect When You Are No Longer and Never Will Be Expecting*.

Ruby took out a pair of big grey needles and some orange wool, and showed him how to cast on. He was surprised at how quickly he picked it up despite his 'sausage fingers', as Dawn used to call them. Thankfully the doc here had put him on a ripper arthritis med that was truly life-changing.

'You're probably best to start with something easy, like a scarf,' explained Ruby. 'Then you can move on to something more complicated, like booties. We sometimes donate blankets and booties to the local maternity hospital. Or give them to our grandchildren or great-grandchildren. I've got seven.' She grinned, two well-worn dimples coming into view.

Grandchildren.

The word hit him, and slowly a genuine smile broke through for the first time since Albert's passing.

'Ruby, I don't suppose you have any yellow wool?'

Chapter 34

The numbers on Greg's phone bill blurred into one as Denise's stomach plummeted to the floor. One number appeared multiple times each day. She studied the digits, which were somehow familiar. Bile rose in her throat, and she quickly swallowed it. What a bloody cliché. She collapsed onto her bed.

Normally the bill went straight to Greg's email, but she hadn't been able to guess his password so she'd rung the phone company and requested to switch to paper bills, in a desperate attempt to find clues. She shuddered at the memory of putting on a man's voice, pretending to be Greg so she could be authorised to make the change.

Another new low.

Her life was set to recirculate, leaving her breathing in the same disappointing air again and again. She was ridiculous, pitiful, stupid. Stupid, stupid, stupid. She pushed the backs of her hands into her forehead. The silver-framed wedding picture taunted her from the bedside table. Her eyes flicked over her youthful face. The hairdresser had worked a miracle that day and her unruly locks were somehow tamed and smooth, beautiful even. Greg, of course, was as handsome as ever, with his blond hair and grey eyes. And the way he was looking at her. She'd lost two decades to that look. The picture went fuzzy as her eyes filled with tears.

Concentrate, you idiot!

Her mobile was dead so she picked up the landline phone and began dialling the first four digits, hands trembling, bile resurfacing.

'Mum!' Jacqui burst into the room holding a jar of strawberry jam, startling Denise. Shit. She'd forgotten for a split second that the girls were home. She dropped the phone.

'Can you please help me open this? Ella wants it instead of honey.'

'Sure, love. Thanks for helping your sister.' It was amazing how far Jacqui had come with her behaviour.

Denise gripped the sticky jar lid and took in her daughter: her expectant brown eyes, her signature strawberry-blonde ringlet in the middle of her forehead. She averted her gaze. Her girls deserved better than this, yet she was incapable of being stronger. It was one thing to have an absent dad whose emotions could flip like a switch, but now a mum who couldn't get through the day without booze? Pathetic. Absolutely pathetic.

She promised herself, not for the first time, that she would stop, wouldn't drink again, would do better, would be a better mum regardless of what, *or who*, her husband did.

The jar clicked open and Jacqui took it, her small fingers twitching with anticipation.

'Ta!' Jacqui flashed her mum a toothy smile before skipping down the hall.

Denise picked up the phone again, unable to resist the temptation of finding out more. Her stomach quivered and before she was sure what she was doing she dialled. It rang. Her knuckles whitened as they gripped the receiver.

'Hello?' A woman's voice answered, muffled by loud music in the background.

Denise slammed the phone down as the woman's ocker accent sliced through her heart. She grabbed the bin next to her bed, ready to vomit. Instead, the nausea passed and she unlocked her bedside-table drawer, removed a bottle and broke her silent promise to her daughters.

Chapter 35

Weeks passed, and Fred practised his knitting every day. Ruby had kindly given him a pair of needles to take back to his room, and Linh said he could help himself to the large tub of colourful wool in the craft room. Some days, despite the meds, his arthritic hands ached from the new workload, but he pushed through determinedly, starting with a couple of scarves then graduating to a small blanket. He asked Linh to print out some patterns from the internet. Fred was good with patterns, with following instructions.

He'd found a few more photos tucked away at the back of Bernard's cupboard, including one of Hannah and her sister. As he knitted, he would often wonder whether his own daughters would have borne a resemblance to them. The rhythmic clack of needles became a metronome for his thoughts. His mind would drift to Albert and Val – and, of course, to Dawn and their lost baby. He let the memories sneak out of his tear ducts and roll down his cheeks. He thought about the weeks after Dawn had died and those shattering mornings when he would wake up and suddenly remember he was alone. The grief would ooze into him like a prick of paralysing poison filling every crack. Some days it had been hard to get out of bed, but he knew Dawn would have wanted him to keep going. So he got up. He got dressed. He read the newspaper. Normal things on the outside masking emptiness on the inside. Dawn had once described to him a similar feeling, one she'd experienced in the weeks and months after that dreadful appointment where she'd been told that following the miscarriage, it was unlikely she'd ever conceive a child again. She'd put on a brave face and continued to do normal things, all the while feeling about as far from normal as you could be.

Now that she was gone, Fred carried that grief for her.

With his remaining friends having moved or passed away in the months and years after losing Dawn, and the death of their beloved cocker spaniel Lulu soon afterwards, he was the only one left – an astronaut alone in space, impossibly far from home. Who'd have thought that wool, of all things, would pull him slightly closer to earth? Yet with each stitch he had more purpose, more connection.

After several dodgy, unidentifiable, scraggly creations he'd been too embarrassed to show even to Ruby, he had at long last been able to complete his goal. He held up his handiwork, a warmth spreading over his face and body. They were rough, granted, and nowhere near as delicate as Dawn's, but he was proud of his re-creation of the pale-yellow booties – and knew she would have been, too.

He wrapped them in yellow tissue paper from the craft room with a matching ribbon. The Scrapbooking Group made all kinds of cards, which were displayed for visitors to buy at the cafe but were free to residents; he selected a light-blue one with a picture of a seagull. Seemed only fitting.

He stared at the card for some time. Should he sign it 'from Bernard', or even 'from Dad'? He couldn't quite get his hands to put down either name, so he kept it simple, writing just three words.

Fred copied the address carefully from the old letter, took some stamps from the oak bureau and gave the parcel to Linh to post.

Maybe, just maybe, he had one last chance to be a dad.

Chapter 36

Smeagol the chihuahua was getting on in years. Several unidentifiable lumps and bumps had appeared underneath his translucent skin with its thinning white hair, and it took him an increasingly long time to go to the bathroom.

Hannah tugged gently on his lead. 'Come on, buddy, I need the toilet myself and I can't get away with doing it here like you can. The last thing I need now is to be arrested.'

As if comprehending perfectly, Smeagol let out a raspy cough and mercifully did his business, allowing Hannah just enough time to make it back home to do hers. This pregnancy thing had really messed up her entire system, and she still felt faint most days. She winced at the memory of her collapse at the nursing home a few weeks back. How mortifying! Just when she had wanted to appear strong and together, like she didn't need him. Or anyone.

Every day since she'd seen her father he appeared in her mind without fail, with those stupid kind blue eyes. She had zero regrets about throwing the letter away without reading it. There was no way she was going to give him a foothold to climb back into her life. The old bastard probably just wanted money, anyway.

The doorbell rang and Smeagol sprang to life, yapping like he'd just had new batteries put in.

'Got a package for you, love. I'll leave it on the step,' called the postie.

Hannah went to the door and retrieved a small, neatly wrapped parcel addressed in beautiful cursive writing, but with no sender address. She sat on her bed and unwrapped the delicate paper to reveal a roughly knitted pair of yellow booties. She frowned. Who could they be from? Not many people knew she was pregnant. She hadn't yet summoned the energy to tell most of her blissfully married girlfriends as this would invariably involve telling them about Mike – yet another failed relationship.

She lifted the booties to reveal a card with a seagull on it. Inside it read: *For the passenger.*

The words burned her fingers and she let the card drop to the floor. It was from *him*. How dare he! A manipulation, no doubt. He'd probably conned one of the old ladies into making them for him. They should be put straight in the bin.

Yet instead of chucking them she found herself holding them again, rubbing the soft merino wool between her fingers, unable to let go. She blinked back hot tears. She'd always imagined receiving booties from her mum if she ever got pregnant, thinking fondly of all the slightly quirky jumpers Mum had knitted for her and Sadie as kids.

God, she missed her. Just talking to her father had felt like a betrayal of her mother, and of Sadie. Mum's death had left a rip that not even Mike or the baby could mend.

Pregnancy had never been part of the plan, not at this age, anyway. Maybe if she'd been younger and married to someone who wanted to be a dad, things would have been different. Mike had told her he didn't want kids on their third date. He'd grown up in a physically abusive home, so she couldn't blame him. It hadn't been a deal-breaker at all. She'd been pushing forty and, if she was honest, she'd always been petrified by the idea of becoming a mother. She was happy enough to hold her friends' kids, but it was a relief to hand them back, knowing they weren't in her company long enough that she could do any actual damage. Not like her father had done.

On her forty-second birthday Mike had taken her out for a big Mexican feast at Mamasita, their favourite restaurant. The next day she'd had her head over the toilet thinking she'd been struck with food poisoning from the prawn tacos, which Mike, hating seafood, had avoided. A week later, when she wasn't any better, she'd gone to the doctor, who told her it was a little more than a crustacean making her feel sick.

When she'd shared the news with Mike, he looked like he'd received a cancer diagnosis. In his head there was only one solution: to visit the family planning clinic and get an abortion. Hannah had always been pro-choice but never thought she'd have to make such a decision herself. It was a week later, when she heard the thrum of the baby's heartbeat in the cold white ultrasound room, that she knew she could never get rid of it. She went home and showed Mike the photo the sonographer had taken, hoping against hope it would change his mind.

'Don't bloody manipulate me, Hannah!' he'd yelled when he saw it. 'You knew I never wanted kids! I couldn't have made it any clearer. You've obviously made your choice – but I'll be damned if I'm going to hang around to be a father!'

His words rang in her ears for days. She could have possibly forgiven him for not being able to stay, though it hurt like hell. But when he blatantly told her later that he'd turned to a prostitute that night, it was the nail in the coffin of their relationship. To make matters worse, he'd admitted it wasn't the first time; it was apparently his way of dealing with stress. A sickening weight had settled in her stomach at the thought of how little she'd known him.

She looked at the now-soggy booties, and then to the right side of the wardrobe. Although it was empty, she could almost smell Mike's citrus cologne on the soft polo shirts that had once hung there.

How the hell was she going to do this alone?

She sniffed, wiping her nose. Better alone than with the wrong man, a man who would no doubt hurt her again. She wasn't just thinking of Mike. She crumpled the yellow wool in her hands and headed for the door.

'Right. You've sorted your crap out, Smeagol. Now it's time for me to sort out mine!'

The booties felt illogically heavy in Hannah's coat pocket. Her purple Merry People boots trod the wet footpath robotically. The pathetic pricks of rain that had started to fall couldn't deter her – she was used to dealing with pathetic pricks. She would return the booties and not let her father have the satisfaction of giving her a present. Let *him* feel what it was like to have a handmade gift rejected. She'd take them to reception so she wouldn't have to see him and his bloody kind eyes.

Striding through the automatic doors, she approached the front desk. Damn it, no one was there. A young black-haired woman in a yellow uniform walked past carrying craft supplies. Hannah tried to catch her attention.

'Excuse me, please . . .'

'Yes, can I help you?'

Hannah cleared her throat. 'I need to return these to Bernard Greer.' She pulled the booties from her pocket.

'Oh! Mr Bernard!' The name swiped happiness across the woman's face.

'Er, yes. Please give these back to him. I don't want them.'

The woman cocked her head to one side and frowned at the booties. 'Oh, you must be Hannah! He made them for you! You're having a baby, right?' she said, outlining an imaginary semi-circle on her own belly.

'Yes. But I don't want them. He got one of the ladies to make them. He should give them back to her – I won't use them.' An uncontrollable heat simmered in her voice.

Just take the bloody booties.

'Oh, no, Mr Bernard made these himself!'

Hannah narrowed her eyes. 'No, he wouldn't have. You must be mistaken.' Her father had never seen any value in homemade presents. The shattered birdhouse pieces grazed her thoughts with their splintered edges.

'I saw it myself. He practised every day. He learnt to knit for you, for the baby.' The woman pointed at Hannah's tummy.

'But,' Hannah's voice choked, 'he . . . he never . . .'

'Do you want to come and see him now? It's almost time for morning tea.'

'No, no. I have to . . . I have to go. I'm sorry.'

She thrust the booties into the startled woman's hands and ran back outside into the storm. She wanted to scream.

Why was he doing this? Why couldn't he have been like this before?

Damn you, Bernard!

She couldn't even call him 'Dad' in her mind. He didn't deserve that.

The wind whipped her hair as she pushed forward – if only it would blow out the crap in her head. Tears and raindrops slid down her face, now indecipherable from each other. Soaked to the bone, she reached her front door. Her hands shook as she tried to get the key in the lock. Damn it. As it finally gave way, she made a beeline for the bathroom and ran a bath, her cold hands stinging as the warm water washed over them. She grabbed a wad of Kleenex and blew her nose. As she went to put them in the bin, she caught sight of the scrunched-up letter hiding behind it. Adrenaline and curiosity coursed through her.

'Fine, then!' she yelled. 'What do you have to say?'

She grabbed it and tore it open, sliding to the floor as she read.

Chapter 37

25th December 2022

Dear Hannah,

    I know you sent my first letter back and that you don't want to see me. I want you to know that I understand and hold no ill feeling as I've done nothing to deserve a visit from you.

    I'm writing this from the nursing home I moved to six weeks ago. The doctor here told me that my heart isn't so good, so I am writing this now, while I still can. I want to try and explain things to you.

    I don't expect you to believe me, but I wasn't always a bad dad. Our family had some happy years when you were little, before all the problems started. I remember the day you were born, bringing you home from the hospital to meet your big sister. I used to take you for long walks in a baby carrier so your mum could get some sleep. I felt so proud, like a kangaroo with my precious baby joey in my pouch. Later, I used to take you and Sadie to catch butterflies in the park. Those were happy times. We used to laugh a lot. How I miss your laugh, Hannah.

The day we heard that Sadie had leukaemia was the second-worst day of my life. The following evening after work, I couldn't bring myself to go home. I couldn't face your mum – seeing her sadness made it all too real. So, I went to the track with a colleague. I won a lot of money that night. I often think about what would have happened if I hadn't. The win made me feel better, stronger. It got me thinking that maybe having a flutter wasn't so bad – maybe if I could keep winning, we could afford to see the best doctors, find the best overseas treatments, save Sadie somehow. That was the lie that started it all, and how I justified things to myself.

So, I kept going. The bets got bigger, more daring. After a while, little bets no longer satisfied the growing urge in me. I didn't know at the time that I was becoming addicted to gambling. Those sorts of things weren't talked about back then like they are now.

Seeing Sadie suffer was unbearable. I became a monster of a man. I sank into deep bouts of depression and rage, and I didn't know how to get out of them. I come from a generation in which men never talked about their feelings or problems. It was a different era, and I wouldn't have known where to find help even if I'd been brave enough to seek it.

I don't know if you remember the day you tried to give me a birdhouse, but I fear that you do. I can see it now: it was red and white – just like my team, the Swans. I want to explain why I did what I did, though it is no excuse. That night, I'd bet more than ever before. I'd lost our house, Hannah. I'd lost everything we had, and I was utterly disgusted with myself. And for no good reason, I took my anger and shame out on you. To make matters worse I accidently broke Sadie's purple teacup too.

I cried myself to sleep that night. I never told anyone what I'd lost, not even your mum. The guilt was so crippling, I couldn't even bring myself to apologise. I felt so ashamed, so useless, so despicable – and then soon after Sadie died, and my world felt like it had ended. I wanted to kill myself, Hannah, but I was too much of a coward to even follow through on that. So I did the next best thing. I left, believing that you'd all be much better off without me. I rang your mum's boss, Harry, and begged him to give her the assistant manager job at the hotel. I wanted to be sure you'd be okay, at least in some way. And then I packed my bags.

I couldn't bring myself to go to Sadie's funeral and see my sweet little girl being put into the ground. And, knowing what I had done and what I was about to do, I was too ashamed to look your mum or you in the eyes. I chose to slink away, a decision I have regretted for the rest of my life.

It wasn't until I was in my mid-sixties that a colleague finally insisted I get help. Eventually, after a lot of setbacks, I stopped gambling. I haven't placed a single bet in over ten years.

So many times, I wanted to reconnect with you and your mum. I even picked up the phone to call, but I could never face owning up to my mistakes. I never remarried or had any other kids; you were always my only family. I forgave myself for ruining my own life – I came to terms with that – but I could never forgive myself for ruining yours and your mother's. How I hope I haven't ruined your life, Hannah . . .

It's Christmas today and I wish I could wind back the clock to when you were little and still believed in Santa, and in me. But I can't.

I'm sorry you got stuck with me as a father.

I'm sorry I never knew how to love you like you should have been loved.

I'm sorry I broke your birdhouse. So, so sorry.

And I'm sorry I never said goodbye.

I hope you get to live a good life, Hannah, a happier one than I did. Make the most of every opportunity life gives you, and please stay kind. You and Sadie were the kindest people I ever met. Goodbye, Han, I love you so much.

Love,

Dad

The sobs came violently, fiercely. Hannah howled like Mum had after losing Sadie. Her body shook and gasped for air. The past forty-two years scrambled around in her head like ill-fitting puzzle pieces rearranging themselves, trying to click together. She gave into it all with reckless abandon. Decades of tears flowed, her grief manifesting in liquid form. She had mourned the loss of her father decades ago. The letter brought him back to life.

Was the pain he had inflicted on himself as bad as what he had inflicted on others?

A ringing sounded in her ears as a slide show of memories played in her mind. Chasing butterflies, Mum's hugs, the hospital waiting room, Mum crying, broken wood, Sadie's shattered teacup, Sadie forgiving Dad, Sadie vomiting, a coffin that looked too small, the gold heart necklace. Dad's face livid with anger again and again and again.

But was it anger? Or had it been fear, or even shame, this whole time?

Hannah scrunched her eyes tight. Another image came into her mind: a wrinkled face, kind blue eyes, a genuine smile.

Her heart splintered.

She was tired of being so alone, of swimming upstream, of holding on to bitterness and regret. Her shoulders sagged. She'd been carrying this weight for so long. What might it feel like to let it go?

To forgive, even?

It was hard to imagine.

The sound of running water spurted into her thoughts, and she turned off the tap just before the bath overflowed. She let some water out before peeling off her wet clothes and climbing in, fully immersing herself in the warm water.

Maybe it wasn't too late.

She placed her hands on her belly. She had a decision to make – not only for herself, but for her baby. After all, the man was the only family she had left.

'Shall we find out what you look like in yellow, little one?'

Chapter 38

'You did so well today, Mr Bernard! You're getting stronger!' Linh pummelled an invisible punching bag and smiled at Fred.

He'd finally returned to his regular exercise classes – it's what Albert would have wanted. He was amazed that someone his age could make improvements to their health. If only there was balloon tennis for the prostate.

'So, Linh, do you think I should hold on to my dream of becoming an Olympian?' Fred said with a wink.

'Absolutely!' Linh went to pack up and then paused. 'Oh, Mr Bernard, before I forget, these came back for you. Your daughter, she doesn't want them. I'm sorry.' Linh made an exaggerated sad face, reminding Fred of an emoji Kevin had shown him on his phone. He recognised the glimpse of yellow she produced from her pocket but was unable to focus on it. Tears coated his eyes, masquerading as cataracts.

'I see.'

She placed them in his hands, the wool weighed a tonne.

Fred worked as hard as the elastic on his underpants to keep things together. He caressed the tiny knitted shoes and brought them up to his nose. He knew they couldn't smell like a baby but his nose hoped, nonetheless. Their scent was of dashed dreams and of getting home too late. His whole posture slumped and he no longer cared to correct it. Like a stereotypical old man, Fred trundled back to his room, shoulders hunched, and plonked into his armchair.

'I've failed you,' he said aloud to Bernard, and perhaps to Dawn, too. He closed his eyes and pictured her amber irises with the gold rim. 'They weren't perfect like the ones you made, sweetheart. Maybe if they had been she would have accepted them. I'm sorry. About this baby. About our baby, that I wasn't home sooner. Dawnie, I don't know what to do. I'm so lost without you.' His chest tightened and for once he wished it was a heart attack so he could be with his wife and unborn child.

He opened his eyes. The Father's Day lunch flyer that Linh had given him mocked him from the bedside table. He crumpled it up along with his hopes of being a father. What would he have done anyway? How could he pretend to be Hannah's father? The very thought was absurd.

'Bernard! Are you talking to yourself again?' Fred looked up to see Denise. 'Cheer up – there is someone here you can talk to instead.'

His eyes widened as Denise stepped aside and left.

Hannah!

She was standing in the doorway, a vision in a lavender dress, tears trickling from her beautiful green eyes. Unable to speak or move, Fred was unsure if he was in a dream or having a stroke. Filled with sudden motivation to live, this would not be the most opportune time for the latter.

'I-I read it. I read the letter.' Her voice sounded like that of a girl, not a woman. 'I didn't know, I didn't think —'

'You don't need to say anything, sweetheart,' said Fred,

miraculously finding his tongue, relieved that he hadn't in fact had a medical episode.

Her gaze locked on the booties still sitting in his lap. 'I know I sent them back, but I *do* want them. To try them, at least. For the passenger.' She patted her tummy, now sporting the slightest of bumps.

Fred couldn't wipe the smile off his face. He found himself standing, being drawn to her like a magnet, her soft scent of peaches and vanilla lowering his raging blood pressure. He went to embrace her, but she put a hand up to stop him.

'I'm . . . I'm not quite there yet, sorry,' she said softly. 'And I'm not sure that I'll ever be. But I'm here and I'm willing to give things a chance.'

Fred nodded and placed the booties gently in her hand, clasping his own hands over the top.

'Thank you,' she said.

'I've got some lamingtons if you can stay for a cuppa. They aren't as good as Val's, but . . .'

'I'd like that.'

Two cups of tea and four lamingtons later, they sat opposite each other for what seemed like an eternity, neither speaking, an occasional beep from the nurses' station filling the awkward space between them. Where to begin?

'So, how are you feeling?' he finally offered. 'Not too dizzy, I hope?'

'The little one sure is brewing up a storm in there. It's a bit of pot luck what I can keep down, but lamingtons never seem to be a problem.'

Her smile was divine. Fred beamed, making a mental note to ask the kitchen staff for the recipe.

'I remember Mum saying she was really sick with us.' Her eyes drifted. 'With Sadie and me, I mean.'

Fred paused, trying to find the most truthful words he could in the jumble of lies he'd constructed.

'I found a photo of you both,' he said, getting up and rummaging in the bedside-table drawer. 'Here it is.' He turned it over and read the back. 'Sadie and Hannah at Phillip Island, 1984. How old would you have been then? Four, five?'

'Three,' she replied. 'I remember that trip, actually. You and Mum took us to see the fairy penguins. I loved those little guys.'

'I love penguins, too,' he said earnestly, picturing the tuxedoed birds he and Dawn had seen at Manly beach.

She nodded, tucking a curly lock behind her ear. 'So, um, what's it been like living here? Big change?'

'Yes, it's been . . . interesting.' Fred looked around the room that had become his home. 'A big change, huge change, I'd say – but good. I've put on weight.' He laughed as he patted his happy tummy. 'The food here is just great. Budget was tight at home, you see, so tea and toast were a regular dinner. The best part is I'm not as lonely as I've made some friends.' A hit of grief pulsed through his veins as he pictured Albert.

Her face reddened. 'I'm sorry I didn't visit sooner.'

'Please, you have nothing to apologise for.'

'And you really learnt to knit?' asked Hannah, picking up the booties.

'Yes,' laughed Fred, relieved at the change of topic. 'I really did. I've still got a long way to go, though!'

'Mum loved to knit. Remember all those Christmas jumpers she'd make us wear?'

Fred looked away, wishing he shared the memory. 'I'll bet she would have loved to make something for the little one, but I'm afraid you'll have to make do with old fat fingers here.' Fred crossed his eyes, pointing to himself with both thumbs.

A flicker of a smile appeared on her face, unveiling a brief glimpse of a different, happier person.

Heat radiated from the scrunched-up flyer on the table. His heartbeat roared through his ears.

Just ask her.

'Hannah, they're, um, having a Father's Day event here at the home and I, um . . .' He looked at his feet. 'I don't suppose you'd want to . . . Sorry, I shouldn't even . . .' His words tapered off.

Her lips parted as she studied the booties in her hands, her green eyes flickering with an expression he couldn't read. Fred held his breath.

'I think I could do that,' she said finally, her gaze meeting his.

Despite the tidal wave of gratitude almost flooring him, Fred managed to stand. His clammy hands couldn't stop shaking as they fumbled to smooth out the flyer and pass it to her.

Fred, having received a terminal diagnosis of a never-dad, miraculously had been given a clean bill of health. Any hope of ever celebrating Father's Day had evaporated long ago. All those apologetic glances Dawn gave him when a Father's Day ad came on the telly played in his mind. They were always met by a suffocating blanket of guilt. *I should have come home sooner.* He would smile at Dawn and shake his head dismissively, as if it didn't matter or hurt that he wasn't a dad. He knew that for her the loss must have been worse, but the fact was it did matter to him, and it did hurt. They had looked into fostering or adopting and had even begun filling out paperwork, but the process was long and unpredictable, and Dawn simply didn't have it in her to put her heart out there once more.

He read through the flyer with Hannah.

WATTLE RIVER NURSING HOME
FATHER'S DAY LUNCH
Join us for a delicious sausage sizzle lunch
and some fun games!
Sunday 3rd September 2023
12.30 p.m. to 2.00 p.m.
Rear courtyard (weather permitting)

'I'll be there,' she said, meeting his eyes.

Fred grinned. The last time the corners of his mouth had been stretched this wide had been at the dentist.

'Thank you for believing in second chances.'

The rest of the visit was pleasant and relaxed. Thank goodness she hadn't asked anything too direct, too hard to answer. Being in her company was like sitting by a fire on a cold day eating toasted marshmallows. He soaked in her sweet warmth.

When she had gone, a familiar heaviness settled upon him. The deposit box of guilt had cracked open: he would either have to come clean or get a bigger box. He tried burying the feeling with more lamingtons. It didn't help. He turned on the telly for some distraction. It was a news report on the increase in homelessness this year.

'Hundreds will struggle to cope with the coldest September predicted in thirty-one years,' said the solemn news reporter.

Fred shivered and took the Mylanta packet from the bathroom cabinet. Perhaps antacids worked on guilt, too.

Chapter 39

Hannah sighed as her internet banking password finally came back to her. Was this baby brain already? She arched her back, the cheap plastic desk chair exacerbating her already aching hips. Her stomach sank as the account balance flashed up on the screen: $307. She glanced at the car insurance bill in her hand.

'You are going to have to start eating home-brand, mate – no more Pedigree for you,' she told a wide-eyed Smeagol. Thankfully, the horrendous morning sickness had mostly settled; she'd lost far too many bookings over the past few months. All her savings had gone into opening her own business last year. Her hairdressing studio, 'Hair by Hannah', had racked up a steady base of customers but still hadn't broken even. Without Mike's income, it had been hard to make ends meet lately. When the baby came it would be almost impossible.

She tossed the insurance bill onto the couch. The armrest still had the stain where Mike had spilt his fancy coffee. Even now she could smell the extra-strong latte. Was he thinking of her? Of them? Probably not. He'd likely be in class, giving an economics lecture in the grey suit she'd bought him for Christmas. He looked so good in that suit, handsome bloody bastard. Yes, she could ask him for money, for child support, but after finding out about the way he'd been dealing with stress, the idea of talking to him repulsed her. She didn't even want to see his nauseating name on a bank statement again.

Logically, she could tell herself she'd dodged a bullet: she knew he wouldn't have been a good dad. 'So why does it still hurt so much?' she asked Smeagol, who, disappointingly, had a very waggy tail but no answers.

She rubbed her belly and logged onto Centrelink (mercifully using the same password as for her banking, even though Mike told her never to do that). She clicked through multiple links. Surely there was some sort of government assistance she could get? She did some quick sums on the computer's calculator. With rent, the business loan and baby costs, it still wouldn't be enough. She'd have to keep working after she'd had the baby. Maybe she could see clients in the evening when the little one was asleep? But weren't you meant to sleep when the baby slept?

Hannah stretched again, catching her reflection in the framed photo on the desk. She picked it up, taking in her mother's thick wavy hair that framed her gentle, round face. What she wouldn't do to talk to her now. To get her advice, to vent her feelings. To ask more about her father, about Bernard. What would Mum have thought of his supposed change of heart? Would *she* ever have forgiven him?

Bubbles ran under her tummy and she shifted in her chair. Mum had been a single mother for so many years: she'd never remarried. Bernard had left them with next to nothing, apart from a tonne of medical debt and a mortgage. Mum had only been working part-time as a cleaner but her promotion at the hotel the month after Dad left meant they survived, albeit barely, and hung onto the house.

She never mentioned their financial troubles, but Hannah knew things were tight. The second-hand uniforms, homemade gifts, holidays camping in the backyard. Mum was always run down with frequent colds and headaches from lack of sleep, but she'd held it together for Hannah. A task that in retrospect seemed impossible. The grief of Dad leaving would have been bad enough, but the grief of losing a child?

Hannah placed her hands under her striped T-shirt and onto her taut, bare belly. Even if she lost this baby now, before she'd ever met them, she didn't think she'd be able to bounce back. She blinked away hot tears. How superhuman her mum must have been.

Could Hannah hold it together for her child, too?

Mum had never spoken much about Dad after he left, though Hannah had asked time and time again where he'd gone. At first, Mum had told her he'd gone away for work; maybe she'd genuinely thought he was coming back. Then, a couple of months after Sadie's funeral, there'd been no more pretending, and she'd sat Hannah down and told her that Dad wasn't ever coming back, just like Sadie wasn't. No, Dad didn't have cancer, he just couldn't live with them anymore. There were no details, just a black void that gave space for her mind to invent worst-case scenarios.

Hannah cried herself to sleep for months. Though her father had been distant and moody for as long as she could remember, she still loved him and missed him despite herself. But her heartache soon turned to anger. How could a man just give up on his family? Leave his wife and remaining child when they needed him the most? There was no reasonable excuse, although she'd built up many assumptions about him over the years. She frowned at her reflection. How much of it all was actually based on fact? As a teenager, she'd tried to broach the topic again, but even the mention of his name dug up the ever-present sadness in Mum's eyes, pulling the grief right to the surface. It was an almost unbearable sight. After a time, Hannah couldn't do it anymore and stopped asking.

She'd been distrustful of men ever since. How many failed relationships had she clocked up now? She always left them before they had a chance to leave her.

Smeagol yapped and gazed lovingly at her with his beady eyes. She lifted him onto her lap. Mike was the longest relationship she'd ever had, apart from this little furball.

Another bubble rippled under her fingers, jolting her back to the present and the frighteningly low number on the computer screen. Could she possibly ask Bernard for money? She chewed on the thought for a minute before spitting it out. Who was she kidding? Firstly, he didn't have any; he'd let slip how tight things had been in recent years. He would have lost it all with the gambling. Secondly, as with Mike, she didn't want to be indebted to her father in any way. She still didn't fully trust that he was the man he said he was.

Chapter 40

Fred was only a couple of feet away from Hannah, but they may as well have been in different cities. She'd arrived early for the Father's Day lunch and now sat on his bed staring at her brown ankle boots. The small talk had evaporated like a puddle on a 42-degree day, leaving an awkwardness as palpable as his enlarged prostate. He took in a breath of thick air and fiddled with a button on his sleeve. It was like a first date that was hard to get started – not that he'd had one of those for well over sixty years. If only he'd been able to buy some flowers for her like he'd wanted to. He'd asked Denise about it, but she'd glared at him suspiciously and told him he had to watch his spending.

Hannah cleared her throat and Fred looked at her expectantly. Gosh, she was lovely with her long hair cascading over a blue cotton dress, not dissimilar to one Dawn used to have when she was younger. His stomach fluttered. She was a stranger and yet loving her was easier than eating a chocolate cake that had been placed in front of him. How could you already love someone you barely knew? Someone you hadn't even hugged? Is this what it felt like to be pregnant?

She dug out a tube of lip balm from her leather handbag and opened her mouth as if to speak, but then applied the balm and turned away again. Perhaps she wanted to ask him something that was too painful? His mind was chock-full of thoughts of what it might be and how he could possibly answer. Those same thoughts had kept him up most of the night. He shifted in his seat; the armchair was soft but his guilt was hard. It dug into him, impossible to escape.

She looked at him once more, taking a long, deep breath, as if courage were air.

'Did you . . .' Her voice trailed off. 'Did you ever think about coming back?' Her eyes were steady now, holding his gaze.

Fred's stomach plunged to the floor like a bungee jumper without a cord. This was it. Do or die. Bernard had done the dying, so it was up to him to do the doing.

'I . . . I . . .'

'Time to go, Mr Bernard!' Linh's timing was impeccable.

Fred looked Hannah in the eyes, searching for permission to leave without answering. She gave it. 'Come on,' she said. 'Let's go.'

The beautifully manicured garden at the back of the home was an array of colour against the backdrop of ashen sky. A cherry-blossom tree displayed its first blooms like a guest who had arrived early. The unbeatable smell of fried sausages and onions crept from the barbecue into Fred's nostrils. He and Hannah took a seat on the wrought-iron garden chairs that had been placed around the neatly trimmed lawn area decorated with blue and white helium balloons.

'Would you like a snag, B . . . Bernard?' she said hesitantly. She hadn't said 'Dad', but he suspected either name would be foreign and awkward to her.

He smiled. 'Oh, yes, please, that would be delightful. Thanks, love.'

'Onions and sauce?'

'You betcha. Lovely. Thanks, Hannah.'

She soon returned with two sausages in white bread. Fred closed his eyes as his teeth pierced the hot skin of the sausage, savouring the pop of meaty delight and the smokiness of the onions. He'd come so close to getting one last year at Bunnings but was fifty cents short; he'd needed to prioritise buying a washer for the leaking tap over his rumbly tummy.

He turned to Hannah. 'Gosh, these onions are good, aren't they?'

'I've always hated onions,' said Hannah evenly, showing him her onion-less sausage. 'You probably forgot.'

'Oh, yes, um, sorry about that.' Fred looked down at his loafers. 'The old noggin isn't all that it used to be,' he said, tapping his forehead and going cross-eyed. This was going to be harder than he thought.

'That's okay, it's been a minute. I still love tomato sauce, though!' The corners of her lips turned upwards.

She had a gentleness about her, a grace he'd also recognised in Dawn. He smiled and took another bite of his sausage, looking over to where Linh was busy unloading an oversized game of Connect Four, one of a selection of games varying in difficulty that had been laid out: playing cards, mahjong, Scrabble, Hungry Hungry Hippos. His eyes rested upon an old favourite.

'I don't, um, suppose you play chess by any chance?' he said, turning to Hannah.

'I never have,' she replied, 'but I remember seeing your old set at home and always wanting to learn. You . . . you didn't seem to have the time to teach me, though. I mean, you didn't even really play yourself after she . . . after Sadie got sick.'

Fred's tummy churned, his sausage sanga suddenly looking less appealing than it had moments ago. How he wished he could fish the pain out of her eyes, even if he had to take it on himself. He couldn't change the past. He couldn't undo what Bernard had done. But he could love Hannah, love her fiercely, and by George he was going to do that with everything he had.

Fred took a deep breath, trying to harness all the kindness and tenderness he could in his voice. 'Well, I'd love to teach you now. If it's not too late, that is?'

She tapped her lips with her finger, glancing at the chessboard then back at him. A smile crept across her face.

'It's not too late.'

They took their seats at the table and set up the wooden board with tan and dark-brown pieces. He smiled as he picked up the brown knight, rubbing his finger over the small indentations – Albert's bite marks from the time he'd thought it was chocolate. His friend would have loved Hannah.

She was a fast learner and had a logical mind, much like Fred had, and he enjoyed their game immensely. Playing with Albert had been fun, but it was never a proper game.

'I believe that's checkmate?' she ventured, raising a solitary eyebrow and pointing to his king.

He smiled, taking far more pleasure in her winning than if he had won himself. Was this what it felt like to be a dad?

'Hang on a second!' she said, studying his face. 'You let me win, didn't you?' He tried to look very serious, not wanting to give the truth away.

'Well . . .' He shrugged.

'You ratbag!' A joyful laugh erupted from within her. 'Let's play another round, but this time don't go easy on me, okay?'

They played again, but he couldn't resist letting her win. Not one to be fooled, she caught him out a second time.

'You cheeky old bugger,' she said, giving him a gentle push on the shoulder. His heart sang.

Linh arrived and declared it was time for the balloon volleyball championship.

'Any volunteers?' she asked, her eager face searching the sea of people before her. Hannah and Fred locked eyes.

'I'm game if you are,' whispered Hannah.

Fred didn't need to be asked twice. He raised his hand and Linh escorted them to two plastic chairs on one side of a low net that had been set up.

'Who will play against Bernard and Hannah?'

Fred looked over the net to see Patricia and a middle-aged woman he assumed to be her daughter taking up the challenge. They looked unnervingly alike, with dark sultry eyes, both dressed in colours that belonged in a packet of highlighters and skirts that were too short for any age. The younger woman gave him a sugges-tive wink. Yes, definitely the fruit of Patricia's loins.

Linh produced the biggest balloon that Fred had ever seen, its shiny blue surface blocking her tiny face. She stuck her head out from behind it. 'First team to get five points wins a prize. No cheating!' Linh raised an eyebrow at Patricia.

She tossed the balloon high in the air and Fred punched it over the net with his right fist. It hit poor Patricia on the nose, and she recoiled like a startled pug dog.

'Oh, I'm terribly sorry!' said Fred, trying to stifle a chuckle. He looked at Hannah, who hadn't been able to hide a giggle, which set him off even more.

Patricia shook it off as her daughter served the balloon back across the net and Hannah gave it an almighty slam. Their oppo-nents couldn't get to it before it hit the ground.

'Huzzah!' shouted Fred. 'Good one, Hannah!'

She beamed at him. The game continued until it was four points all. Patricia put up a good fight with her quick reflexes and a powerful right hook. Fred and Hannah worked well together, finding a natural rhythm. His heart palpitated from the excitement. He'd never been particularly good at sport and their success was rather thrilling.

Fred served the ball, Patricia went for it but popped it with one of her long acrylic nails, the sound causing everyone to jump in fright then break into laughter. Patricia blushed, her cheeks now matching her fuchsia eye shadow.

'Sorrrrryy! They don't call me a ball-buster for nothing!' she said.

'I think that's a point for team Bernard,' announced Linh. 'Bernard and Hannah are the winners!'

Everyone clapped. Hannah raised her hand to Fred for a high five, which he gladly gave. He reached for his pocket handkerchief and mopped his brow, now beaded with sweat from the exertion. Linh skipped over and presented them with their prize: a $25 voucher for the cafe.

'You make a good team,' she said, shaking both their hands. Fred flooded with pride.

'Is it too early for afternoon tea?' He turned to Hannah with a hopeful stomach.

'I'm always hungry!' she said.

Like father, like daughter, thought Fred. How he wished it were true. Guilt momentarily gnashed at his guts, yet he found he had a new weapon to combat it: love. Paternal love. For he had totally, inexplicably fallen head over heels for his 'daughter', Hannah.

Chapter 41

Well, that had been more fun than she'd expected. Hannah looked over at her dad as they walked along the corridor to the cafe, his moustache a silver roof over his chuffed little grin. It felt strange to call him 'Dad', even if only in her head.

She'd tried a new lavender tea that morning, to prepare for the meeting, that was supposed to provoke a sense of calm and well-being. Instead it had provoked indigestion and reflux.

There was no handbook for this kind of thing. There were so many questions she wanted to ask him, but for now she was relieved not to have had to deal with the heavy stuff. She'd been carrying so much lately and needed a break. Hopefully all the answers she was seeking would come in time.

Hannah smiled at the image of them winning. She loved games, but struggled to recall the last time she'd actually played one. Mike hated them, so she'd put that part of herself into hibernation. It had been ages since she'd laughed so hard. So hard that she'd almost cracked a rib when the lady popped the balloon. Letting her hair down might have been just what the doctor ordered – no lavender tea required.

The ragged clouds that had persisted all day finally cleared, allowing streams of golden sunlight through the cafe windows. They ordered coffee and carrot cake and sat at a table in the corner. Hannah looked across at the man she had always wanted to look up to. He didn't seem scary now.

He took a long sip of his cappuccino, placing the cup down to reveal a milk moustache covering his actual moustache. She chuckled and tapped her upper lip. 'You've got a bit of a moustache.'

He grinned, his eyes studying her quizzically. 'Why, yes – I do!'

She giggled. 'Sorry, I mean a milk moustache, as well as the regular.'

He threw back his head and laughed, and a wisp of a memory from early childhood flickered before her as he dabbed the froth away with a paper serviette.

'I like it, the regular moustache. Is it new? You never had it when I was little.'

He stared down at his cup. 'Oh, I've had this old fella a while,' he said, smoothing his mo with his fingers.

'Suits you.'

'Thank you. So, tell me a bit about yourself, Hannah. What do you do? Are you working at the moment?'

'I'm a hairdresser. I opened my salon about a year ago.'

'How marvellous! I've always admired hairdressers, you know. I try to cut my own hair to save a bit of money, but more often than not it looks like a whipper snipper has got the better of me.' He pulled his face into a dramatic grimace.

Hannah smiled. 'You wouldn't be the first person.'

'Do you like your job?'

'I do. It's been great having my own business – no boss around, although no sick pay either.' Her measly bank balance flashed in her mind. She didn't want to talk about her financial issues, though. Not yet, anyway. She took a bite of carrot cake, the creamy, tangy icing was just like her mum's. What would she think now, seeing the two of them together?

'What do you like best about your job?' he asked.

She licked a dab of stray icing from the corner of her mouth. 'Making people happy, I guess. I know it's only hair and all that, but a new haircut can turn a person's day around, bring them a smile, give them confidence.' She scooped the froth off her cappuccino and into her mouth, allowing the milky bubbles and chocolate powder to blend into a delicious mouthful. She paused – Bernard was staring at her, transfixed. Were those tears she could see?

He blinked and took a sip of coffee. 'I bet you'd be just great at that!' he said with a smile that lit up his eyes.

His kindness was blinding, and she couldn't look directly into it. How she longed to surrender herself to its allure, to fall into it like a warm, comforting bed, but it felt impossible. A shield flicked on deep within her gut bringing on a wave of nausea. She rested her hand on her stomach.

Bernard adjusted his chair. 'So, the baby's dad, is he . . .?'

'He's not around. Didn't want kids.' Her voice was now clipped.

'Oh, love, I'm so sorry. Were you together long? Sorry if that's too personal, you don't have to answer . . .' His eyes were overflowing with that alien compassion again.

'Almost two years. I never thought I wanted to be a mum.'

'Why is that . . . if you don't mind me asking?'

She tore open a sugar packet and tipped it into her cup. If only she could be one of the white grains disappearing into the liquid.

'I was scared. Scared of the damage I could do to a child, that I might not be a good parent . . .' She stared at him, her cold gaze unwavering. Would he make the link?

At first, his face showed nothing. Then, as he connected the dots, she saw the words wound him, a stab of pain flashing in his eyes. Surprisingly, it gave her no satisfaction.

'You deserved a better dad, Hannah.'

She looked away, though she wanted to run away.

'You'll never be like him . . . I mean, er, like me. I want you to know, Hannah, I'm a completely different person now.' The old man's face blushed as his eyes darted from her to the floor.

Aunty Jane had always told her that people never change as they get older, they only become more like themselves. Yet he seemed to be breaking the mould. Or trying to, at least.

They sat in silence for a while, finishing their cake, before Bernard spoke again. 'I don't suppose you'd, uh, consider cutting my hair, would you? I mean, there is a hairdresser here on site but everyone who goes in there comes out with blue hair, and I'm too scared to make an appointment.'

A smile nudged itself on to her face. 'It's called a "blue rinse", and if it's done right, it's actually meant to brighten the grey.'

As if on cue, Ruby hobbled past them, with baby-blue hair that wouldn't have been out of place at a circus.

They burst into a peal of giggles.

'Yes, I'll do your hair. I can bring my things in tomorrow.'

Maybe it was a good thing she hadn't disappeared with the sugar after all. She wasn't ready to. Not yet, anyway.

᪣

The following morning Fred sat in the shower chair in his bathroom cloaked in a red cape. His reflection returned a steely gaze. Could he pass as a superhero? Spiderman? Spider-vein-man, more likely! He hadn't had a proper hairy in years, even the pensioner special at the local salon would have used the money he needed for food.

Hannah ran her fingers through his silver hair, the touch carrying a memory that made his eyes sting. No one had done that since Dawn. Until he was widowed, Fred never realised he'd taken physical touch for granted – yet it meant so much. How many millions of other people were going without hugs?

'So, who cut this last?' Hannah raised an eyebrow.

'Uh, that old brute there,' he said sheepishly, pointing to his blushing reflection.

'I see.' Hannah pulled her lips into a tight smile.

'That bad?'

'No, no . . . it's just a little, um, uneven at the back.' She showed him a section of hair from the back of his head that was much longer than the others.

Fred chuckled. 'Oh dear, people must think I was going for a rat's tail!'

Her reflection grinned behind him. She really was lovely when she let her guard down.

'Don't worry, I'll get you sorted, old man.' She winked at him in the mirror and sprayed something onto his hair.

'That's not the blue stuff, is it?' he said, his eyes wide.

'No – no blue today, I promise. Maybe next time.' Her relaxed smile made everything feel right in the world.

Hannah was a magician with the scissors, moving deftly and confidently.

'What about that moustache? Looks like it could do with a trim.'

'Well, if you don't mind, love, that'd be fabulous.'

She moved in front of him and knelt down, gently taking his moustache between her fingers. 'Hold still.'

A few seconds later she was done and rubbed a fruity-smelling cream into his hair.

He admired her handiwork in the mirror, turning his head from side to side. Had he ever looked this suave? Even Dawn, who was good with the scissors, wasn't this good.

'Wow. You have a real gift, Hannah.'

'Oh, I don't know about that.' She shook her head dismissively, sweeping up the cut strands of hair, which resembled the mesh scourer he'd used to clean his pots and pans.

'No, you really, really do. If you can make an old codger like me look half decent, then that's proof!'

'You look more than half decent. Maybe three-quarters, even!' Hannah crinkled her nose in just the way Dawn used to when she made a joke. His heart overflowed.

'I'd definitely like to pay you,' he said, as she packed up her equipment.

'No, no, this one is on me.'

'Well, I shall pay you in lemon slice then. I saw the cafe putting it out this morning. Will you join me?'

She glanced at her watch. 'Sure. My next client isn't for another hour.'

They headed down the hall, where they ran into a flustered Denise.

'Hi, Denise! Hannah here cut my hair. Isn't it marvellous?'

'Fine,' said Denise unsmiling, rubbing her temples. She hurried away without saying anything more.

Fred frowned. She didn't look too good. He hoped she was okay.

Patricia rounded the corner, her lilac sequined top casting spots of dancing light as they reflected the sun from the window. Spying Fred, she stopped and did a double take.

'Do you like my new haircut, Patricia? Hannah here did it – she's so talented!'

'Very, very suave,' she said, her raven eyes absorbing his frame. Fred felt his face flush, yet he couldn't help feeling a bit chuffed – it had been forty years since he'd turned heads. Except Dawn's head, that is. She was always telling him how handsome he was, even in his seventies when his nostril hair had declared independence and begun taking on a life of its own.

'Well we'd best be going, Patricia. Trying to catch some of the lemon slice before it runs out.'

'Oh, yes, I've just had some. It's very, very . . . tangy.'

Hannah looked from Patricia to Fred in smiling horror, then looped her arm through his and marched briskly away. He glanced over his shoulder to see Patricia staring at his avocados.

'I think I'm going to have to protect you!' said Hannah, laughing. 'Who is that? We played volleyball with her, didn't we? The ball-buster?'

'Yes, that would be the one and only Patricia.'

'Is she like that with all the men?'

'Probably, but it seems she has a soft spot for me. She's harmless enough – well, most of the time, anyway.' Their bedroom encounter flashed briefly in his mind.

The line at the cafe counter was thankfully short, with only one woman in front of them. She turned, and Fred flooded with joy when he saw who it was.

'Val! Oh it's so good to see you, love!' He embraced her with a peck on the cheek.

'Bernard, how lovely to see *you*!' Her neat veneer smile was on full display. 'I hoped I'd run into you. They found Albert's watch in the laundry and asked if I wanted to pick it up. I also had some little gifts and thankyou cards to give to the staff.'

'Oh, well, you must join us! Would you mind, Hannah?'

6d

Hannah smiled at the well-dressed woman who seemed vaguely familiar. Her soulful eyes were lit from within by a gentleness, just as her mother's had been. 'This is my dear friend, Val,' Bernard said, his face flushed with delight.

'I'm Hannah. Pleased to meet you.' The trio took their seats at a window table.

'Are you a friend of Bernard's?' Val asked.

'Oh no, I'm . . . I'm his daughter.' The word was unnatural on her lips. If Val was trying to hide her surprise, she was unsuccessful.

'Oh, how lovely. I must say I didn't know you had a daughter, Bernard.'

Bernard reddened and straightened his shirt. 'Albert knew – well, as much as he could – and we've only just recently connected.'

'Who's Albert?' Hannah asked brightly.

Val smoothed her paper serviette on the table. 'He was my husband. He passed away about six weeks ago.'

'Oh, I'm so sorry.' Hannah paused, taking a sip of water. 'How long were you married for?' Couples with long marriages always intrigued her. Was it that they were a better match than others, or they just worked harder at it?

'Well, that depends on whether you count from our first or second wedding.' She winked at Bernard.

Of course! Val had been the bride in that bizarre wedding she'd observed the day she'd come back to blast her dad.

'You must miss him.'

Val sipped her coffee. 'Every moment. He was a very special man, not unlike your dad here.' Her voice cracked, and she reached for Bernard's hand.

Hannah's jaw tightened. Why had she got the bum end of the deal with her dad and missed all the good stuff?

'Albert was the cream of the crop, no doubt about it.' Bernard passed Val a generous chunk of his lemon slice. 'Here, get this into you, Val, it's delicious.'

'Thanks.' Val dabbed her eyes with the serviette. 'What a goose I am.'

'Not at all.' Hannah shook her head as an image of Mike's deep hazel eyes appeared. Would she even cry now if he died? She wasn't sure.

A loud gurgle erupted from the direction of Bernard's stomach. 'I'm so sorry, ladies, I need to visit the little boys' room. Won't be a moment.' He took a few steps then looked back sheepishly. 'Who am I kidding? I'll be more than a moment, but I know you girls will be just fine.'

Val gave him a wave.

'So do you come to see your dad much, Hannah?'

'No, we haven't actually seen each other for a very long time – decades, in fact. We were estranged.'

'Oh, I see. That sounds terribly difficult.' The softness in her voice eased the tension in Hannah's shoulders.

'Yes, it has been. There's been many hard years. He hurt me. He hurt me a lot.'

Val's eyes widened, her shapely brows knitting together. It was her turn to pat Hannah's hand now. 'It's funny, but I can't imagine Bernard harming a fly.'

She had to agree. The sweet, wrinkly old man she was getting to know looked more like a Pixar character than someone who had caused so much destruction. She stirred her coffee. 'Yes, I don't see any of that side of him now. He wrote me a letter of apology explaining his behaviour. I found out he was a gambling addict; it was his way of coping with the stress of my sister getting cancer and dying.' Hannah hesitated. She was oversharing, telling things to Bernard's friend that he might not want her to know, but she felt safe with Val and the words kept flowing.

The older woman's face was awash with sympathy. 'I'm so sorry about your sister. Was she young when she passed?'

'She died just before her thirteenth birthday. I was nine.'

'Oh, sweetheart.' Her eyes moistened as she squeezed Hannah's hand. 'What was her name, if you don't mind me asking?'

'Sadie. Her name was Sadie.' She picked at some loose flakes of coconut that had come off the lemon slice. 'She'd have loved this. It was her favourite.'

'Albert's, too,' said Val warmly. 'Although he enjoyed just about anything that was put in front of him. I don't know about you, but I think it helps to talk about people who have passed, to say their name. I love talking about Albert – it keeps his memory alive. When my brother-in-law Fred died in a car accident, people wouldn't talk about it. They were afraid to say his name. But not talking about it is worse, I find. Almost like pretending the grief doesn't exist, which only makes the person who's grieving feel more alone.'

Hannah thought about the weeks and months after Sadie was gone. 'Yes, I know what you mean. The kids at school, they sort of just avoided me. I don't think they meant anything by it, but it didn't help. I'm so sorry to hear about your brother-in-law. Was that recent?'

'No, love. It was almost sixty-five years ago. He died on our wedding day, as it happened, on his way to the ceremony.' Val turned to look out the window, where the sun had gone into hiding.

'Oh, how awful. I'm so sorry. Gosh, life can be shit.' She flushed. 'I mean, sorry, it can be rough.'

Val smiled. 'No, I believe "shit" is the correct word, darling!'

Hannah returned a sheepish grin as Val continued: 'When Albert's dementia started, he would always look for Fred. He forgot that his brother had died. It was so hard. At first I would remind him what had happened, but every time I did, his heart broke all over again, and I just couldn't do it anymore. Do you know, when he met your dad he believed *he* was his brother? Bernard brought out a joy in Albie that I hadn't seen since the accident.'

Hannah gripped her cup tightly.

'Your dad, well, he was just brilliant. He was so kind to Albert and me. He watched out for us. He knew how to calm Albert down, too, when he hit a bad patch, even when I couldn't. He once mentioned that his mother – your grandmother – had early-onset dementia, so he knew what to do.'

Hannah pictured Grandma Mary with her perfect bun, rose perfume and strict rules. She hadn't seen her since her father left. She tried to sift through the few memories she had of her. Dementia didn't feature in any of them. Hannah frowned.

'I hope I haven't upset you, dear?' Val leaned forward.

'Oh, it's just that Mum and Dad never mentioned that to me. I guess I don't remember her too well.'

Val nodded. 'Just marvellous he was, your dad. Do you know he even arranged a second wedding for us?'

'I thought I recognised you – I actually saw part of it.'

Two dimples appeared in Val's cheeks. 'Albie woke up one day convinced it was his wedding day. His brother Freddy was the best man, you see, and was meant to give a speech. Bernard got the staff involved and organised the whole thing! And the speech he gave . . . Hannah, that is something I will never, ever forget. I don't think I ever saw Albert so happy. And do you know what? He passed away that night. It was as though the act of finally seeing his brother give that speech allowed him to let go. It was his "unfinished business", so to speak.' Val wiped her eyes.

Hannah passed her a clean serviette, her thoughts in a knot once more.

The wedding speech. The birdhouse. The puzzle pieces just didn't fit. The staff had told her that Bernard had early signs of dementia, though she hadn't seen it yet. Could it cause a complete personality change? Or was she witnessing a true and full transformational repentance, the kind you saw in the movies?

Bernard returned from the bathroom, a huge, lopsided grin on his face. She couldn't help but smile.

'Sorry about that, ladies! So, have you been talking about me?'

'Of course!' Val said with a wink.

'All good things, I hope?'

Val glanced at Hannah.

Hannah chewed on the words a while in her mind. 'Yes,' she said, studying his face. 'All good things.'

Unexpectedly good things.

Chapter 42

Denise grabbed a tray of food off the stainless-steel meal trolley and headed into Tony's room. She glanced at her watch. Dinner was late because of Patricia's elaborate birthday party, which had included many questionably shaped balloons Denise had had to pop and dispose of.

Crap! It was Greg's birthday this Sunday. She hadn't arranged anything for him. He didn't even deserve a bloody card. The wanker was probably having dinner with that woman. Or more than dinner. Her stomach heaved. The vitamised blobs of brown, orange and green on Tony's dinner plate didn't help; nor did the slight stench of human waste.

Tony sat in his big brown La-Z-Boy chair, staring vacantly ahead. She took a seat on his bed and fastened a giant bib around his tree-trunk neck.

'Here's ya slop, Tony,' she said to the large, bald man. He opened his mouth, revealing crooked grey teeth flecked with gold fillings. Tony had dementia, spoke little English and was quite deaf, so he always had the TV blaring. Denise would often change it to *Bondi Vet* and fantasise that she was married to Dr Chris Brown rather than her dipshit of a husband. She'd feed Tony very slowly so she could see the whole episode. He didn't seem to care if the food was cold by the end, and she always blamed him if anyone mentioned she was taking too long. But the sexy vet wasn't on tonight, so she left the telly on the news. They were showing the yearly marathon at Wattle River Reserve. She sighed. Even looking at people exercising made her tired.

She spooned the porridge-like unidentified meat into Tony's mouth as the news anchor's overly dramatic voice blared from the screen. 'As viewers may recall, this is the same river where the body of an 82-year-old man was found by a jogger in April.'

The spoon clattered to the floor. She squinted at the TV, the anchor's words repeating in her head. How had she not heard about this? She was often at Wattle River Reserve on the bus outings. Granted, she usually avoided the news – she had enough in her life to be depressed about without hearing about the latest wars or road tolls – but she loved a good true-crime podcast or murder story, if that is what this was. Unusual for murder victims to be eighty-two, though . . .

Something tugged at the corner of her mind. She pushed it away, but it grabbed harder, rearranging the shapes in her head. An image of the river appeared before her. The outing. Bernard's fall. He had tried to tell her something. Hadn't that been in April?

She picked up the spoon from the floor and quickly finished feeding Tony, much faster than she should have. A decent person would have got a new spoon, but who would even know? Wasn't worth the effort. Her temperature rose, her stomach knotting with guilt and self-hatred, two perfect companions. Wiping Tony's mouth roughly with the bib, she rose, leaving the confused-looking man without a word.

She ran to the nurses' station. Thank god no one else was there.

She plopped down in front of the computer and opened a web browser.

Why was the internet here so bloody slow! It would have been quicker to grab her phone from her locker, even though she wasn't meant to use it during work time.

Her mind turned again to the outing. Yes, it had definitely been April as it was a couple of days before Jacqui's diagnosis.

The screen came to life. She typed 'Wattle River body' into Google and hit enter. Perhaps there was a juicy story here.

After a few painful seconds, an article came up. She read it twice, glaring at the screen. *'The body has been identified as Frederick Fife, aged 82.'*

Frederick Fife . . . Where had she heard that name?

She clicked on the second article in the Google search. As it began to load, she tried to replay the events of the Wattle River outing in her head. Bernard had a fall . . . and then she had helped him up, and she . . . she . . . The article flashed up with a photo of a smiling older man.

An icy terror gripped her body as the room began to spin.

OH. MY. GOD! What the hell?

She stared at the face on the screen. It was bloody *Bernard*! Or Fred! She couldn't tell – the two looked identical.

Her breathing quickened as her brain tumbled through the unexplained improvement in Bernard's dementia, his better physical health.

His change in personality.

Then it struck her. The name. Fred! When Bernard was talking to Albert. He wasn't pretending to be Albert's brother: he'd been confessing who he was! But there was something else . . . before that . . . it wasn't the first time she'd heard that name. A recollection appeared in her mind, the edges blurry. He *had* said something to her that day, but what? Her memory was shot.

Her eyes tore through the second article – Fred had been on the verge of homelessness when he had died. Denise clenched her jaw. Had he done this on purpose? To get food and accommodation? How far back did it go? Had he spotted his doppelganger and planned every move? Was it an accident, or . . . could it be *murder*?

She hit print, the sound of the old Epson grating on her nerves. The second it was finished she grabbed Bernard's file from the shelf and took out his resident photo, taken the day he was admitted. She placed it next to the printed article. It was like a spot the difference, only there was no bloody difference aside from the glasses!

This must be reported immediately. The sneaky bugger had been living on Bernard's dime the whole time. *The whole time!* She shuddered. He probably didn't even need help in the shower!

She rubbed her chin, an uneasy feeling swelling in her stomach.

The thing was, he didn't seem like a dodgy bugger. Had he been trying to tell her the truth at the river? And afterwards? Her memory was so foggy these days.

The alcohol hasn't helped with that, you stupid cow.

She had to admit she never took anything he or any of the other residents said very seriously. Especially with the dementia. But he probably didn't really have that!

Her head throbbed. Well, even if he'd tried to say something, it didn't matter: he'd had plenty of chances since and hadn't admitted anything! Rules were rules and they had to be followed. One too many men in her life had thought they could flout the rules – of marriage, of life. There wasn't much she could do about her philandering husband, but she'd be damned if she wasn't going to do something about Bernard – Fred – whatever the bastard's name was.

She chucked the articles and resident photo into a manila folder and marched to the DON's office.

Damn. The door was locked. Sharon had already left for the day.

Denise stormed into the staffroom, shoving everything into her metal locker. She sent Sharon a quick email on her phone, saying she needed to talk to her ASAP about Bernard Greer. She'd present all the evidence to her as soon as she was next in. The small plastic mirror on the locker door caught her good angle and she smiled at herself. Denise the detective, uncovering the truth, just like on *CSI*. Maybe this would be the work win she needed, and her other minor indiscretions would be overlooked? She was walking on thin ice with her tardiness, and there was that time Linh had seen her looking through a resident's drawers. Denise had made an excuse but wasn't sure if she'd bought it. This could change things.

The heating in her Honda was broken, but Denise didn't care. The adrenaline coursing through her veins was keeping her warm. She pulled into the driveway. Greg's black Mazda was on the street, not in the garage as normal. Strange. Opening the front door, she found him sitting straight-backed at the glass dining table, still in his work suit. Her pulse quickened.

'My mum just picked up the girls,' he said, brushing his sandy fringe from his face. He hadn't taken her hint to get a haircut. His new woman probably liked it long.

'Hello to you, too.' She placed her handbag tentatively on the stone kitchen bench.

'We need to talk, Denise.' Greg's grey eyes stared coldly ahead.

Could he not even look at her? She tensed her tummy, bracing herself for the dagger that was coming. She wasn't going to give the prick the chance to confess.

'I know what's been going on.' Her voice came out shakier than she wanted. Was he going to beg her forgiveness? Could she, would she, even consider forgiving him? Possibly, if he was repentant. Not for her sake but for the girls'.

'Well, then, you should know I'm in love with someone else.' He said it without emotion, like it meant nothing, like *she* meant nothing.

Love?? The word screamed in her mind. Her legs gave way and she fumbled for a kitchen bar stool. Sticks and stones may break my bones, but words will never hurt me. My arse they won't. His words felt all too physical, piercing through her skin to her heart.

'I . . . I . . .' She hadn't expected this. Sex was one thing. Love hurt more.

'I'm leaving you, Denise,' he said evenly, still not making eye contact.

'But, but . . . what about the girls?'

He was standing up. 'We'll tell them we're getting divorced. It happens. They'll deal with it. They're old enough.'

She gasped for the thickened air, polluted with betrayal. 'But I . . . we can't just . . . We need to talk about this!' She was shouting involuntarily.

'I don't want to talk about it with you. I've made up my mind. Things between us haven't been good for years, you know that. Look, I asked my mum to take the girls for a couple of nights because I knew you'd be on night shift tomorrow. It'll give you time to get used to the idea.'

What an arsehole. Did he think she should be grateful that he was being so considerate? Her teeth clenched, sending an ache through her jaw.

Greg's mobile rang from the table, the name and photo of the caller blinking on the screen. Her heart stopped.

He lunged for the phone, his face reddening as he killed the call.

'Greg! Tell me it's not *her*. Tell me you're not sleeping with *my friend*!'

He looked at his shoes. 'Well, you would have found out at some point.'

The blood plummeted from Denise's face at the same speed as her dignity. How could he do this to her? How could *Alexis* do this to her?

'I'll call you later to discuss telling the girls,' he said, moving towards the door. 'I'm thinking we should do it the weekend after Jacqui's party.'

'Greg —'

'My bags are already in the car. I'm staying with . . . I'm staying elsewhere for a while.' His eyes darted to the side.

Her breath caught in her throat. It was obvious who he was staying with: Alexis. Who, by the way, was as ugly as she was. Well done, Greg. At least you avoided the skinny, blonde cliché.

But that hurt even more.

She watched in disbelief as he turned and left, taking his briefcase and seventeen years of marriage with him.

Denise slammed the front door behind him, ran to Jacqui's bedroom and dove into her bed, an avalanche of teddy bears falling to the ground as she pulled the polka-dot doona over her head. The girls already knew things weren't rosy between her and their dad. How could they not? As hard as she'd tried, Denise couldn't be like other mums who left their worries at the door. She couldn't mask her pain from her kids. Instead, disappointment came in on the soles of her feet and she walked it through the house like dog poo, trampling it into the carpet and across the tiles.

The cabinet above the kitchen sink called to her. She got out of the bed.

'Don't look at me like that,' she said to the row of Beanie Boos judging her from the bookshelf. She stopped as she caught a glance of herself in Jacqui's heart-shaped mirror. Had she become instantly fatter, or had the world just become smaller? She pressed her fingers hard into her temples, trying to shut her brain down as she would a computer. It didn't work.

Don't do it. Not this time. You are stronger than this. You have to be. You are the only grown-up here now. You must do better for them.

She scowled at her reflection, her mind was already made up. Her final plea to herself dripped off her like water off a duck's back. She sighed, squared her shoulders, and tried to swallow the ball of hate in her throat. Taking a small key from a chain around her neck, she went to the kitchen and unlocked the cabinet.

Chapter 43

The man weed into his water bottle with astonishing accuracy then took a long drink. Fred grimaced. He shouldn't look, but it was like watching a train wreck and he couldn't avert his eyes. It was Saturday evening and Fred sat comfortably in his armchair, his tummy practically purring with content from a dinner of chicken pie with flaky pastry, followed by tinned peaches with custard. How lucky was he to have good meals like this turning up night after night! He must remember to tell the cook how grateful he was. *Man vs. Wild* was on telly, a show that Hannah had recommended, where a guy was put into the middle of nowhere and had to survive off the land. On screen, the bloke continued drinking his own wee. Hopefully, Fred would never have to face that situation as he wasn't sure his bladder could produce the necessary amounts of liquid for survival. And aiming into a bottle, as this guy did, would be like using a sprinkler to fill a glass of water.

He took out his latest woodwork project that he'd made in the men's group. He was about to give it a final polish when the sound of breaking glass made him jump. A loud thump followed. It was coming from Ruby's room next door!

Fred immediately jumped to his feet – well, as immediately as possible at his age – and went to investigate. Ruby sat half-dressed on her armchair like a shrivelled baby wombat. She was attempting to stoop down to help Denise, who'd collapsed onto the floor. Fragments of a glass vase and the gerberas it had contained lay scattered around her head, an empty bottle of brandy sat lidless on the carpet nearby.

'Oh, Bernard, she's not good. I didn't know what to do.' Ruby's frail body was shivering.

'Oh, dear. Careful there, Ruby. You just stay where you are. I'll deal with this.' He took a blanket from Ruby's bed and wrapped it around her shoulders.

'I don't think she's very well at all. I'll call for help, shall I?' she said, reaching towards the call button.

Fred eyed the brandy bottle and paused. 'No, no. We needn't bother anyone. I'll get her sorted.'

With great effort he got down on his knees next to Denise's head, being careful to avoid the broken glass. A bead of sweat trickled over her forehead, joining her freckles like a dot-to-dot puzzle.

'Denise? Denise, love? Are you okay?' He squeezed her hand.

'He's sssshuch a bastard . . . I don't think he eber luffed me.' The slurred words poured out of her slack jaw. Her glassy eyes darted around the room before she broke into blubbery sobs.

'Oh . . . It's okay. I'm here now, Denise,' Fred offered, before turning to Ruby. 'Do you have a newspaper, please love?'

She passed him one from her side table. He opened it and carefully picked up the pieces of glass. The ache he should have been feeling in his knees was overcome by adrenaline. Disposing of the shards in Ruby's bin, Fred returned to Denise, who was smacking her lips like there was a nasty taste in her mouth.

'I'm going to help you stand up now, Denise, okay?'

'Nooooo. You shouldn't be doing that, maaaaate,' she blurted before letting out an almighty belch, the fumes of which would have been enough to light a bonfire. He waited for the air to clear before taking a deep breath.

'I'm going to help you up, just like you've helped me up so many times. Have to even the score a bit, don't we?'

She nodded, her lips curling upwards into a smile that quickly came crashing down into another violent sob.

'There, there. Let's get you sitting first,' he said, helping her up slowly. Then, tucking his arm under hers, he got her to her feet, surprised at his own strength. Perhaps the balloon tennis was paying off after all.

He surveyed her damp body, carefully checking that no glass had landed in her hair, reminded of the time Bruno's kids had caught head lice and he'd been on babysitting duty. He caught another whiff of her breath. Woof. It had more brandy fumes than a Christmas pud.

'You'd better come to my room, okay, Denise?'

She swayed, blinking slowly.

'I'll be back in a minute, Ruby love.'

Ruby sat still in her chair, goosebumps covering her pale skin like an uncooked chook. He instructed Denise to hold onto the wall while he took off his woollen cardigan and placed it over the old woman's shoulders.

'Thanks, Bernard, I'll be here if you need anything.'

Fred nodded. Darling Ruby and her 101-year-old kindness.

He assisted Denise to his bed, her wobbly legs just making it before she sprang up and ran to his ensuite to vomit into the toilet.

'Oh, love.' Fred held her hair back as another attack came on, just like he'd done for Dawn during the chemo.

'He doeshent, he doeshent lub me . . .'

'Never mind about that now. It'll all be okay. We'll work it out.'

'My poor guhrls! They need better. They're at my mobber-in-law's, ya know? She probably knows everything, the witch, what a shlit show. I don't—' Her words were cut short by another round of vomiting.

After a few minutes the worst was over, and she rested her sweat-drenched face on the floor. Fred flushed the toilet and wiped her mouth gently with a damp face washer. Her eye make-up had run, leaving blackened silhouettes of all the tears she had shed. He tried as best he could to erase those, too.

'Come on now, let's get you up.' Fred linked his arms under hers and somehow – with gargantuan strength again (rattling knees be damned) – pulled her up and tucked her into his bed. He poured a large glass of water into a plastic mug. 'I want you to drink all of this, please.'

Denise obeyed, her slurps dotted with jerky hiccups. She made quick work of it and slammed the cup on the table, admitting another almighty, foul-smelling burp. Her mouth retaliated as if she'd just tasted sunscreen.

'Ugh, these mugs are terrible – so chunky,' she spluttered, licking her chapped lips.

Was it the first time she'd drunk from one?

'Thank you,' she mumbled, trying unsuccessfully to smooth her wayward hair. 'I cahhn't thank you enough, Fred.'

Fred.

The name caught in his chest, snatching his breath. Was she just too drunk to remember who he was, or keeping up the pretence that he was Albert's brother? The third alternative was too scary to think about. He mustn't dwell on it now. There was no point talking to her when she was this sloshed: he must focus on the task at hand. He busied himself by tidying up the bathroom.

'I'm gunna looshe my job. I've still gotta dress Ruhhhby and feed Tony,' she wailed from the bed, followed by another juicy belch.

Oh dear. He'd almost forgotten about Ruby.

'You let me worry about that, love,' he said, exiting the bathroom. 'You just sleep for a bit.' He pulled the doona over her. She grunted, rolled over and went to sleep, a loud snore sounding almost instantly. Definitely genuine, unlike his morning routine of wetting his pants.

Content she was settled, he returned to Ruby's room, shutting the door behind him.

'Is Denise okay?' she asked as Fred untied her shoes.

'She will be. She's had a hard day.'

'I think she's been having a lot of hard days lately.' Ruby's eyes filled with sympathy. 'I've been a bit worried about her, Bernard, to be honest.'

He nodded. Denise *had* seemed very stressed of late.

'Would you be able to help me into my nightie, Bernard? I'm so sorry to ask.'

Fred hesitated. 'Would you like me to get one of the other carers?'

'No, no, I don't want them to know about Denise, and believe me, at 101 and after having six kids, I'm not shy!' She giggled.

It was funny to think how older people were often clumped together regardless of age. Many folks would consider nursing home residents to be of the same generation; yet Ruby was old enough to be his mother.

'I tried to undo my bra, but I just can't. Isn't that ridiculous? Something I took for granted for so many years.'

'I can relate – well, not about the bra thing!' He chuckled. 'But I mean about taking things for granted. I'll be damned if I can undo a jar of pickles now.'

'At least we can laugh at ourselves. People often ask me about the secret to living a long, happy life. I think that's it – not taking things too seriously.'

Fred smiled in agreement. He handed Ruby the blanket so she could cover herself, averting his eyes to preserve her dignity. With some difficulty and a bit of laughter from them both, he helped remove her top and bra and slip on her nightie.

'You're the perfect gentleman, Bernard, thanks so much. You could get a job here, you know. You're much gentler than most of the carers.'

He beamed at the compliment, but his heart sank. How was it okay to be rough with anyone, let alone someone as vulnerable as Ruby?

'It's a pleasure. Can I get you anything else?'

'No, dear. I'll pop the telly on and I'll be as right as rain. The finale of *The Bachelor* is on tonight, and I can't wait to see who gets the final rose!'

Fred grinned, and crossed the hall to help Tony, a non-verbal resident who barely registered Fred's warm greeting. A tray of dinner lay untouched on the wheelie table. Denise hadn't even started to feed the poor guy.

Feeling that the meal was now stone cold, Fred popped to the visitors lounge to reheat it in the microwave. He returned to the room, then put a tiny bit of the mashed potato on his wrist to check it wasn't too hot. He knew from Bruno's babies that this was what you did to test milk, so assumed it would work for food, too. Satisfied, he fed Tony, dabbing his mouth gently after each spoonful.

Fred looked into his eyes and smiled, but could see only brown irises and black pupils – no spark, no soul. He was grateful that Albert had never seen the end stages of the cruel disease.

Behind Tony sat a bookshelf where a dusty pile of records rested against a turntable. He hadn't seen one of those in yonks.

'Would you like some dinner music, Tony?'

There was no response, so Fred took the initiative and removed the top record, *Italian Opera Greats*, from its faded sleeve and popped it on. He put the arm down, but no sound came out. After a quick survey, he saw the tone arm hadn't been reset and the belt was loose.

'Not to worry, I'll fix this in a jiffy, mate.' Fred worked deftly and in a couple of minutes the record player was playing perfectly, the Big P belting out 'O Sole Mio'.

Nothing could have prepared Fred for what happened next. The music was like an EpiPen to Tony, bringing him to life in a spectacular transformation. It was his eyebrows that woke first, shooting up like they were being pulled by a string. His fingers joined in next, tapping on his armrests, soon followed by his feet. A smile spread slowly across Tony's lips and up to his eyes, which sparked to life. Then, without warning, a voice sprang from deep within the old man's chest as he sang along with Pavarotti, emitting the same enthusiasm as the master. Tony knew the song word for word, the beautiful Italian lyrics sliding effortlessly off his once-mute tongue in a polished bass voice. Fred could almost see the music's notes as the sound wrapped around him.

'My god, what's happening here? Tony, my man, you sound amazing!' Geraldine, one of the nurses, stuck her head in, her spellbound eyes brimming with delight. 'Did maintenance fix your record player, finally?'

'Hi, Geraldine. Um, I fixed it,' said Fred, quickly putting the cover back on the half-eaten meal to protect Denise.

'Oh, hey there, Bernard! Wow! Didn't know you were handy! It hasn't worked since he moved here last year.' She walked over to Tony and rubbed his back. His face was still plastered with the joy of the song. 'Who would have thought it? Our very own Tony, who never speaks but sings like an angel! Wait until his daughters hear about this, Bernard. Thank you so much.'

Fred grinned. 'It's amazing what the brain can hold on to, and the power of music.' He pictured his dear mum at the piano playing 'Für Elise' by heart, when she couldn't recognise her own husband. If only there was a way of making loved ones into melodies so they, too, could be remembered.

Forty-five minutes later, after miraculously getting Tony to bed, Fred returned to his room where Denise was still asleep, snoring loudly. Thank goodness no one had found her. No sooner had he taken a seat next to her than there was a knock at the door.

'Hey, Bernard, just Kevin here. Can I come in?'

Yikes. Fred's heart quickened. 'Er . . . could you please come back a bit later, cobber? I'm just on the phone,' he said, picking up the receiver so it wasn't a complete falsehood.

'No worries, mate. It can wait until tomorrow. Night!'

'Goodnight,' Fred called, as quietly as possible.

He replaced the phone and removed Denise's shoes, pulling the doona higher up so she wouldn't get cold. She was in a deep sleep now. Good. The poor girl definitely needed it.

He paused. What if someone looked in overnight? Better not take any chances. He pushed the armchair against the door, covered himself with a spare blanket and settled down to keep watch.

Chapter 44

A dreadful ache hammered Denise's skull. Why was it so bloody dark in here? She struggled to make sense of what was happening until she realised her eyes were closed. With great difficulty, she prised them open, light shooting in like razor blades. Shit! She quickly closed them again. A muffled voice in the distance was asking someone a question.

'Denise? Denise, love? Are you okay?'

Could it be Greg? She peeled open one eye and saw Bernard sitting next to her bed. She sat up slowly, surveying the spinning room. Shit. Shit. *Shit!* She was in his room, in his bed. Like a bucket of ice water being thrown on her, it all came back: Ruby's room, the bottle of brandy, her arse-wipe of a husband and her shitty, shitty friend.

Pain slashed the pit of her stomach. She was going to be sick. She glanced at her watch: 5.02 a.m.! Bloody hell, she'd been here all night.

'The girls!' she yelled, panic taking hold.

'They're sleeping over at your mother-in-law's. You told me last night.'

She exhaled loudly. He was right – they wouldn't be home until after lunch.

'Here, have this, love, I've made it extra strong, three scoops.' Fred handed her a cup of instant coffee. 'And I saved my Teddy Bear biscuits from last night's supper in case you want them, though I'm not sure if you'll feel up to eating,' he added, offering her the small packet of treats.

The kind and considerate gesture jolted her memory. This wasn't Bernard. It was Fred.

She brought the cup to her lips and winced as her tastebuds met the bitter liquid, but the caffeine felt good. She forced a swallow, dreading the conversation that would come next.

'Have this, too – you need it,' he said, offering her a mug of water. She downed it gratefully, her heart and her head in stiff competition for which one could throb the loudest.

'I'm so sorry,' she began. 'I'm just . . . I'm absolutely mortified.' She searched his eyes, expecting judgement but found only compassion.

'We are all entitled to a bit of a wobble, love. Please don't be embarrassed. I'm not here to judge.' The old man's voice was soft and warm, so unlike her father's or Greg's.

She looked over at the armchair, where a crumpled rug lay. 'You didn't sleep there, did you?' Bloody hell, she was going to lose her job for sure.

He nodded. 'I slept well, actually. When you get to my age, you can fall asleep on the toilet!'

She attempted a smile, but her lips felt glued together. She sat forward in horror. 'Oh, no, what about Ruby . . . and Tony?'

'Don't worry, I took care of them. They're tucked up in their beds.'

Her mouth fell open. 'I . . . I don't know what to say. Thank you. Thanks so much.' Oh, to have been a fly on the wall last night!

Talk about the blind leading the blind. Although she realised now that this man was caring for her far more competently than she had ever cared for him. Shame flushed through her.

She checked her watch again – her shift had ended hours ago. Shit.

Her heart punched against her sternum, beads of sweat budding from the surface of her skin. 'You didn't . . . tell anyone, did you? I mean, I'd totally understand if you did. Did anyone else see me?'

Please, please say no!

'Don't worry, your secret is safe with me. Only Ruby knows, and she won't tell a soul. She just thinks you were unwell. I got rid of the . . . bottle.' He glanced at the floor.

She felt her cheeks flush, but her shoulders relaxed. No one else had seen. Maybe she could still keep her job.

'I, um, I don't usually drink. I mean, not that much at once, not like that.' She looked at Fred, whose eyes still offered an unwavering stream of empathy.

'It's my husband, you see. I've been having trouble at home. He just confessed to what I've already suspected for a long time. He's been having an affair . . . with my friend.' Her aching brain felt too big for her skull.

'You don't need to explain to me,' said Fred. 'Although you can if you want to.'

She sniffed. 'Actually, it's quite nice to have someone to talk to, to say things out loud.'

He nodded, with a knowing smile.

'My friend, she looks, well, pretty much like me. I could under-stand it more if she was like a Barbie, but this means that Greg . . . he doesn't like *me*.' She broke into sobs, each one driving a nail into her head. 'Like, I've met some pricks in my life but . . . but . . .'

'He sounds like the full cactus, if you ask me.' Fred took a seat beside her. 'I think you've got more going on than you realise. It sounds like it's been hard for you for a very, very long time.'

Denise gasped in snotty breaths. 'Yes, yes, it has. He became distant a couple of years ago. Not just to me but to our daughters, especially Jacqui. She hasn't been an easy child. She was diagnosed with anxiety and severe sensory processing disorder this year.'

Fred looked at her blankly.

'She used to have big mood swings. Bedtimes and getting her to school were a nightmare. It was hard on us all. But Greg, he just pulled away even more, couldn't deal with her. He blamed me for everything. He lost his temper all the time and checked out emotionally.' Denise sighed. 'I used to just have a glass of wine at night, to help me sleep, you know? Then it got worse. Much worse.'

Fred passed her another wad of Kleenex.

'Even though we're on top of Jacqui's condition now, it's all too late. Greg moved out the day before yesterday – had already packed his bags when I got home from work. Turned out to be exactly like my dad. He was only there for the good times and left when things got bad.'

Fred stared at the bureau desk. 'I'm afraid it's a common story.'

'How could I have been so stupid? I'm such an idiot!' Denise wrung the tissues in her hand.

'Hey now, don't talk to my friend Denise that way.' Fred placed a hand on her shoulder. She recoiled, the kindness so unfamiliar it was almost painful.

'Sounds like he didn't hold up his end of the bargain – "in sickness and in health"?' he continued.

'No, no, he didn't, not at all. Anyway, it's no excuse for what happened last night. I'm so sorry. Thanks for looking after me, Fred.'

And there it was. In that one word. The elephant in the room had been released, ready to trample everything in its path. The old man froze, his mouth agape.

Fred.

She'd said it naturally, without meaning to broach the topic. But she locked eyes with him, and just like that his secret was out and they both knew it. He shrank before her like a small, frightened child.

'So, you know then?' His quivering lips tried to form a smile.

'I-I do. I've suspected for a while now that something was amiss, but I couldn't put my finger on it.'

He rubbed his eyebrow. 'How did you work it out, if you don't mind me asking?'

'Well, I guess there were a few things that didn't add up. There were the physical things – your dementia seemed to be different, or even gone.'

'I'll take that as a compliment,' he said, winking.

'Your hearing was better, of course. Then I overheard a snippet of a conversation you had with Albert. But it wasn't until I saw the news a couple of days ago. There was a mention of that body found by the river. I googled it out of curiosity, then I saw an article with your photo. That was when all the pieces fell into place. The body they found was Bernard, wasn't it?'

Fred nodded slowly. Denise couldn't tell if it was weariness or relief she saw on his face – maybe both.

'I did try to tell the truth, several times actually – it's just that no one listened. You'd be surprised how people treat you differently when you're older. You don't feel any different, but it's as though you fade away, like a Polaroid picture in reverse.' He rubbed his wrinkly hands and she bit her lip as she saw for the first time how arthritic they were.

'I'm sorry, I was probably a big part of the problem. I just assumed, you know. The chances of you being anyone other than Bernard, well . . .'

'One in a million, hey?' They laughed, melting some of the tension.

'What about your daughter? I mean . . . Bernard's daughter. Does she know?'

Fred's face reddened as his eyes welled with tears. He shook his head, looking out the window at the blackened sky.

'No. I didn't know she existed at first. And then she turned up. She hadn't seen her real dad for over thirty years and I . . . I . . .' A tear broke free and dripped onto his trousers. 'My wife and I, we couldn't have kids. I've always wanted a child. I was going to say something at first but then I didn't . . . and then I couldn't . . . It's despicable, I know.'

'Hey, I'm not one to judge despicable.' She sighed and gazed at him through narrowed eyes as the wheels began turning in her mind. 'Hang on . . . the fish. You aren't allergic to fish, are you?'

Fred turned an even darker shade of red, busted like a naughty schoolboy. 'Ah, well, about that . . .'

Denise let out an incredulous laugh. You had to give the old bloke some credit.

'I thought your "rash" was a bit dodgy. You cheeky beggar! Well, then, I'm sorry for stabbing you with an EpiPen unnecessarily – that can't have been a walk in the park.'

'Please don't be, you did exactly what you needed to do. You are good at your job, Denise.'

The kind words brought fresh, warm tears to her eyes. 'No, no, I'm really not, and I haven't been for some time.' She dabbed her sweaty forehead with a tissue. If only it would absorb her guilt, too.

'I reckon there's more good in you than you know, love. You've had a hard time with your daughter, and you've done so well in getting help for her. None of us are perfect – I mean, strewth, look what I've done! We're all human, love, and I've yet to meet a person in my eighty-two years who is irredeemable.'

Denise studied his face. She'd heard that wisdom came with age, but it had never seemed more true than now. Compassion like this was alien to her, but it felt good. It was like an air purifier, making the air more breathable.

'Thanks, Fred. My shift finished ages ago. I'd better get home.'

He shook his head. 'I can't let you drive. Sorry, love, I'd be too worried about you. Let me call you a taxi.'

She closed her eyes, her brain lurching from side to side. Granted, she still felt slightly tipsy. If it was just her, she wouldn't care about driving or even crashing, perhaps. But for her girls? She had to start stepping up.

'Okay, thank you.'

He poured her another glass of water before picking up the phone and dialling. She pulled herself out of bed, her head spinning.

'Taxi will be here in ten minutes.' Fred replaced the receiver before helping her to her feet.

'This is so wrong,' she laughed. 'I'm meant to be helping you!'

Fred began to laugh, too, and soon they couldn't stop.

Busting for a wee, Denise hurried into the ensuite.

A moment later, a knock sounded on Fred's door outside. She froze.

'Hi, Bernard! It's just Linh here with the Halloween Day flyer. Did you enjoy Happy Hour yesterday?' Her colleague's voice was extra chirpy this morning.

'Yes, yes, I did, thank you,' said Fred. 'Gosh you're in very early today?'

'Yes, I finish early today so I started early, too. Kevin is taking me to see the ballet in the city!'

Denise reached for some toilet paper, accidentally knocking over the toilet brush. Shit!

'Is someone else here, Bernard?'

'Oh, um, yes, well, it's . . . um, it's . . . it's . . . Patricia.' He said her name like it was a dirty word. Denise's eyebrows shot up and she clapped her hand over her mouth, stifling a laugh. Had Fred 'pretended' with Patricia, too? Far out!

'Ohhhhhhh! I see,' laughed Linh. 'Hey, Mr Bernard, I think someone took a full bottle of brandy out of the drinks cabinet last night. There was one missing when I went to put things away after Happy Hour. I thought it might be cheeky Miss Carmel, but I already checked and she doesn't have it. Did you happen to see anyone take it?'

Denise froze. Shit! Linh knew about the bottle. Carmel *was* known to throw a few back and to steal food, grog and medication, but if Linh knew it wasn't her . . .?

'Oh,' said Fred. There was a long pause. Denise could almost hear her rampant pulse.

'I'm terribly sorry, but that was me. I took it.' Fred's voice was clear.

'You?' Linh sounded shocked.

'Yes, well, I was missing Albert, you see, and I thought I'd toast him. We used to have a glass together. But I'm afraid I spilt most of it and the bottle is now empty. I'll happily buy another one to replace it. Or wash dishes to earn my keep.'

'Oh! No, no. Don't you worry about that, Mr Bernard. I won't tell anyone. I miss Mr Albert, too, and Mrs Valerie, you know. Such lovely people, like you. I'm here to talk anytime you need, okay?'

'Thanks, love.'

Denise stood, gripping the washbasin in disbelief, unable to stop shaking. What she'd done last night should have ended her career. This man whom she had treated abominably *and* pegged as a criminal had shown her nothing but kindness. She couldn't get her head around it. Maybe he'd try to blackmail her into keeping quiet about his little secret?

She heard the door to Fred's room close, then exited the ensuite cautiously.

'Who was that?' she said, testing the waters. It seemed easier to pretend she hadn't heard.

'Oh, just Linh with the Halloween Day flyer – nothing to worry about. I still can't understand why people in Australia celebrate Halloween, although I am partial to the lollies,' he added with a smile. His silver eyebrows met as his tone changed. 'Denise, I need to know that you are going to get some help, love, some real help. There are people you can call.'

She blinked at him. Her shaky legs made her sit again as she tried to order her muddled thoughts. She wasn't used to someone caring about her.

'I guess you're right. I just feel like such a failure, though.'

'Asking for help isn't failing, you know – it's refusing to fail.'

The words struck a chord in the pit of her stomach. 'It's just so hard. I feel so alone . . .'

'Not alone now.' He clasped both his hands over hers. 'How about we make a call together soon?'

She nodded, unable to form words.

'Taxi will be here now,' said Fred, glancing at his watch. 'I asked them to come to the side street, no explanation needed.'

'I don't know what to say. Thank you, Fred.' Her eyes pricked with tears.

'Denise?' The old man's voice was wobbly.

'Yes?'

'Before you go, I want you to know that your secret is totally safe with me, regardless of what you do or who you need to tell about me. I completely understand and I hold nothing against you. My secrecy is unconditional.'

Blinded by his earnestness, she had to look away, managing only a slight nod as she left. She collected her things from her locker, and staggered into the waiting taxi outside.

The alcohol had made her shaky, but grace had absolutely floored her.

Chapter 45

After Denise had left, Fred returned to bed for a cat nap. His alarm woke him all too soon. A smile spread across his face: Hannah was taking him out for lunch today. The joy he felt was soon whipped away as the memories of last night sent a chill down his spine.

She knew. Denise knew.

He pictured Hannah's glowing face. He couldn't lose her. Would Denise report him? Would it be this afternoon? He gripped the edge of the bed, and forced himself to take some slow, deep breaths. Most likely he had until Tuesday at least, when she was working again. She would sleep it off today.

He must push it out of his mind until then. Being present for Hannah was his top priority, and if it was his last day with her, he wanted every second to count. Screwing up the Post-it note on the bedside table, he rose to his feet. No point 'getting his ants' anymore. Ah, well, at least his backside would be the happier for it; he'd begun developing a bit of nappy rash. If only the silver lining extended beyond his bum.

6∂

The cafe was delightful. It was a mild day and they took their seats outside at a small round table among pear trees in shiny terracotta pots. Evidently, it was much easier to break free when you had a getaway car and driver.

Though Fred and Hannah had spent a lot of time together at the home over the past few weeks, this was the first time they'd been out. The warm, fresh air invigorated his lungs. For a moment his heart felt bouyant, but his brain soon caught up and sank it. Anxiety took hold and he mustered his very best poker face, determined to keep it from Hannah. He watched as her bemused eyes followed a sparrow eating crumbs from the adjacent table. Gosh, she was picture perfect. If he had just come home sooner that night, would Dawn and he have produced a daughter like her? His tummy churned. His relationship with Hannah was blossoming into something so precious that the thought of having it ripped away was simply unbearable.

A short, stocky waiter approached, handing them two laminated menu cards.

'This is my shout.' Hannah smiled warmly. 'I insist,' she added, before he could protest.

'That's so kind, love. Thank you.' Guess he wouldn't have to test Bernard's card again.

The menu was extensive, with more choices than there were moles on his body. 'Chia' must be a misprint of 'cheese', though it sounded odd to have cheese with yoghurt and muesli.

'What looks good to you, Han?' The nickname was new for him, and he tried it out cautiously.

Her shiny lips pulled into a smile. 'You used to call me Han. I always liked that.'

Fred beamed.

'Oooh, the smashed avo looks good!' Her eyes sparkled as she perused the menu.

'Smashed what?'

'Avo – avocado. You've never tried it?'

'Can't say I have.'

'They mash the avo up with lemon and capers and spread it on toasted sourdough. It's delicious.' She kissed her fingers like a chef.

'Well then, I'll definitely have to try that.'

The waiter arrived with some water. 'Have you decided what you'd like?'

'Two bashed avos, please,' Fred said, with as much gusto as he could muster.

'Smashed,' giggled Hannah. 'It's *smashed*.'

'Ahh . . . I'm afraid my brain is a bit smashed,' laughed Fred, crossing his eyes.

The waiter gave a thin smile. 'And are we having coffees this morning?'

'A cappuccino, please,' they said simultaneously, locking eyes. The waiter scribbled down their order as Hannah's phone rang, its vibrations causing her green handbag to almost fall off the table. She fished it out just in time.

'Hello? Yes . . . Oh . . . Oh, I see.' Her face fell.

Oh no! Was it Denise telling her the truth?

'Can't you just tell me now? Yes, I understand. Okay. Yes, tomorrow at 10.30. Thanks, bye.' Hannah placed her phone on the table and stared at it, two lines appearing between her brows.

'Everything all right?' Fred tried to keep his voice steady.

'It was my obstetrician's clinic. They said they need to discuss some test results that came in today.'

His pulse quickened. All thoughts of himself disappeared as he pictured the passenger. 'Is something wrong?'

'She didn't say. Told me they want to do another scan, as well.' She reached for a serviette, her hand trembling.

Fred took a sip from his glass, hoping it contained bravery as well as water. 'I don't suppose you'd, um . . . like me to go with you?'

She looked up, her eyes wide. 'Would you?'

'I'd love nothing more.' He placed his wrinkly hands over her perfectly smooth ones, his sunken heart swelling.

She exhaled. 'I feel better already. This single-mum thing, I knew it would be hard when the baby was born, but I didn't realise it would be this hard now, too. I've felt so alone. Mike made it very clear he wants nothing to do with the baby.'

'Sounds like an absolute prawn, if you ask me. It's totally his loss, Hannah. Any fella who can't see that, and walks out on you, is a fool in my books.'

Her face flashed with an emotion Fred couldn't quite read. He rubbed his cheeks, the irony of his words slapping him in the face. 'I mean, I was a fool. I *am* a fool.'

'You're here now,' she said, squeezing his hand, 'and I'm so, so grateful for that.'

Thoughts of Denise reporting him darkened his mind. He just hoped that 'now' would be a long, long time.

The waiter returned carrying two plates of toast piled high with a bright-green mash topped with seeds, capers and . . . were they flowers? Fred had never seen anything like it.

'You can eat these, can you?' he said, eyeing a bright-purple flower and trying to recall a book he'd once read on poisonous plants.

'You sure can!' Hannah selected a yellow one from the top of hers and popped it into her mouth.

He raised his eyebrows. 'Well, there you go! I haven't been to a cafe in a very long time – not a real one like this, anyway.'

'Oh, since you've been in the nursing home?'

'No, even long before that. Money was tight, you see.'

He stared at his fork. He was speaking for himself of course; he really had no idea about Bernard's precise financial situation other than he'd lost most of his money but had enough for two men's suits. Thankfully, she didn't ask anything else.

'Anyway, this is such a treat – just delightful, Hannah. Thank you.'

She flashed that smile that made him feel as if all was right in the world, even if only for a moment, just as Dawn's had done.

He surveyed his technicolor plate and took a big mouthful. His tastebuds zinged with tangy flavours and new textures.

'What do you think?'

'Mmmm,' he said, giving her a double thumbs up as he swallowed the delicious bite. 'Just glorious!'

After they had licked their plates clean (quite literally, as no one but themselves was looking), Hannah asked if he'd like anything else. 'Dessert, maybe?'

'Have I ever said no to dessert?' he said, with a wink.

After some superb vanilla slice and equally delightful conversation, they went to the register to pay.

'That will be $65 please. On card?' said the young, blond server.

Hannah nodded, and tapped her pink credit card. The machine gave a double beep.

'Sorry, it says the card is declined,' the server said, averting her eyes.

'Oh, that's funny!' Hannah blushed. 'Can I try it again, please?'

'Of course, not a problem.'

Another double beep. 'Oh, I must have the wrong card.' A light sweat appeared on her forehead as she pulled out another from her purse. She tapped for a third time but the double beep sounded again.

Fred could feel the embarrassment radiating off her. He was no stranger to having a card declined – he'd had to abandon his groceries at the check-out on more than one occasion. It was one of the most undignified feelings there was. The server glanced from Hannah to Fred.

'Please let me,' said Fred, reaching into his jacket pocket for Bernard's card, willing it to have at least $65. The idea of an arthritic codger and a pregnant woman washing dishes to earn their meal wouldn't appeal to anyone.

He stuck the card into the machine and typed in the PIN. A single beep and a few seconds later a receipt started printing. Phew!

'That's all good, thank you. Enjoy your afternoon,' said the server, turning to the next customer.

Hannah stared at Fred, her lower lip quivering. 'Your PIN. I'm sorry, but I couldn't help noticing. It's my birthday, two-six-zero-four, the twenty-sixth of April. I can't believe you remembered . . .'

Fred's face flushed and he forced his lips into a smile.

Hannah rubbed her forehead, her cheeks still pink. 'Anyway, thanks so much for paying. I'm sorry – I'm absolutely mortified. I just need to move some money around the accounts, you know.'

Fred knew, all right. 'Please don't worry about it, love, it's my absolute pleasure. It's happened to me many times before.' He tried to keep his tone light, despite the fiery ball of worry that was forming in his stomach. Was she having money trouble? He flicked the thought away. She had said her business was going well; hopefully today's problem was nothing more than a banking error.

'Thank you, I really do appreciate it. I know you don't have much to spare.' Hannah patted his shoulder.

'It's totally fine, Han. That bashed avo was worth every cent.' He winked, eliciting a small smile.

They didn't speak much on the drive home. Hannah turned on the radio and stared straight ahead.

'You sure about coming tomorrow? You don't have any plans?' she asked, as they pulled into the carpark.

He laughed. 'Love, I haven't had plans for ten years! My calendar is all clear.' Unless I'm flung into jail tonight, that is.

'Great, well, I'll pick you up at ten?'

'Perfect,' he said, offering a silent prayer that he would have at least one more day of being Bernard.

Chapter 46

Hannah pulled up to the nursing home fifteen minutes early. Thank goodness there hadn't been any traffic. Her heart had been pumping on overdrive since this morning and showed no sign of letting up. Was there a problem with the baby? With her? Her chest tightened. The call from the clinic, alongside her rapidly diminishing funds, had caused a sleepless night, which wasn't helping anything.

As she steered the car into the pick-up space she caught a glimpse of her dad sitting at the entrance. He hadn't seen her yet. How sweet he looked in his knitted khaki vest, his blue eyes scanning the doors eagerly, smiling even though no one else was nearby. She watched as a male staff member gave him a high five. Her dad said something that made them both laugh. Everyone seemed to love him – and who could blame them?

The image summoned a hazy memory from the back of her mind. A kindergarten fete, the taste of fairy floss, an egg and spoon race and that same laughing face. He used to laugh. Quite a lot. At least before Sadie's diagnosis, that is.

She'd forgotten that.

She looked back at him and he spotted her, his face billowing out into a gigantic grin.

This.

This was the look she had always longed for as a child, that she had been waiting to see that night as she sat on the cold, concrete step holding the birdhouse. It was over thirty years late, but better late than never.

His smile calmed her racing heart.

Perhaps everything was going to be okay.

'Hello, Han! How are you feeling?' he said, rising to his feet as she entered.

'Hi. I'm okay – a bit nervous, to be honest.'

'Of course you are, love, that's totally understandable.' He stretched out his arms and pulled her into a warm embrace. She stiffened at first but then surrendered to it, suddenly feeling like a small child again. How different her life could have been with regular hugs like these. Déjà vu washed over her, his familiar sandalwood cologne conjuring the scent of his long-forgotten cuddles.

'I'm glad you're here,' she said.

He took her hand in his. Her skin, which she had often thought looked old, seemed as smooth as a baby's against his prune-like crevices.

'Whatever it is, we will get through it together.' His eyes gazed deeply into hers, bringing her another wave of calm, of safety.

She had once feared those same eyes, but they had a clarity and peace in them now. A glimmer of something else appeared in his face, but it was gone before Hannah could read it.

'Sorry to have kept you waiting, Hannah,' the obstetrician said as she entered the overly airconditioned exam room.

'That's okay. Dr Rajesh, I'd like you to meet Bernard,' said Hannah, as her dad shook the doctor's hand.

'Lovely to meet you. Okay, Hannah, I realise you'll want to know straightaway why we called you in, so I won't beat around the bush. Your glucose tolerance test has come back showing you have what we call gestational diabetes.'

Hannah's throat tightened.

'Diabetes? How can that be? I don't eat a lot of sugar,' she said, pushing yesterday's snot block to the back of her mind. She reached for Bernard's hand and squeezed it. He squeezed back.

'No, no, it doesn't come from eating sugar. It's a specific type of diabetes that occurs in pregnancy and will go away after you deliver. Please rest assured that the disease is treatable, and when well managed it won't harm you or the baby.'

Hannah took a deep breath. 'Okay. So what do I do?'

'Well, you're going to have to keep a close eye on your diet and engage in regular physical activity. We'll see how we go with that as a first port of call and then, if we need to, we can introduce medication.'

Bernard patted her hand. 'It's going to be okay, love. We'll do it together.'

'Have I done something to cause it?' asked Hannah, guilt hovering in her chest.

'No. I know you lead a fairly active lifestyle, and you aren't overweight. It can happen more frequently in geriatric pregnancies, though.'

Hannah and Bernard looked at each other in alarm, seeming to have the same thought.

'Oh, no! I'm not the father!' said Bernard, turning the colour of beetroot.

'He's my *dad*!' Hannah quickly interjected.

Dr Rajesh chuckled and shook her head. 'Don't worry, I assumed that. Any pregnancy where the mother is over forty is considered a geriatric pregnancy. It's a terrible term, I know.'

Hannah and her dad burst out laughing.

'And I thought that *I* was the only geriatric in the room,' said Bernard, giving Hannah a nudge.

Dr Rajesh smiled. 'Now then, as you know, I'd also like to do an extra scan just to be sure everything else is okay. Hannah, would you like to show your dad the baby?' She motioned to the ultrasound machine.

Bernard's face sparkled like a child about to be taken on an amusement-park ride.

'Yes, I think we'd better, don't you?' she said brightly, hopping onto the table and pulling up her top.

The doctor smeared gel across Hannah's belly and pressed the probe against her skin, and a pixelated image appeared on the screen. A fast beat galloped through the room, making her own heart slow as relief washed over her. She stared at Bernard, whose tear-streaked face could not have been more joyous if it was his own baby on the screen.

Back at the home, Hannah smiled at the ultrasound picture Bernard had proudly tacked to the wall above his bedside table.

'Han, before you go, I have something for you,' he said quietly, handing her a crumpled paper bag from his wardrobe.

'You didn't need to get me any —' She stopped as she saw what was inside, a wave of emotion and recognition passing over her.

'I made it. They have a woodworking group here,' he said, as she removed the red-and-white birdhouse from the bag.

'It's the same colours as the one I made . . .'

'Sydney Swans,' they said simultaneously.

She ran her fingers over the polished surface. There was a
jagged line where a faded broken piece had been inlaid in the wood.
Something was written on it. She brought it closer. Her heart skipped
a beat. It was her name, written in her own childhood handwriting.
Surely it couldn't be . . .

'This . . . this isn't . . .'

Her dad smiled. 'A piece of the original? Yes, it is. Been in the
shoebox under the bed the whole time.'

Her jaw dropped. 'You kept it?' She blinked, warm tears starting
to fall.

'I thought you could put it in your garden. You and the passenger might like to watch the birds.'

She squeezed his hand, unable to form words.

'There's this, too.' Bernard reached into his pocket and pulled
out a piece of broken purple porcelain.

Hannah gasped, and clasped the gold heart locket around her
neck. Sadie's teacup.

Bernard blushed. 'I really wanted to fix it too, but I'm afraid they
don't do pottery here, not that I'd know how. But Ruby was telling
me about a type of art called mosaics, where you stick pieces of china
next to each other to make a picture . . . make something beautiful and new out of things that were once broken. I thought . . .' his
eyes glistened with hope, 'I thought maybe we could do that . . .
together?'

'I can't think of anything I'd like more.'

After Hannah had left, Fred lowered his shaky body into his
armchair and let out a long breath, and an even longer bit of wind
that he'd been holding in for most of the morning.

What a day. Hannah had loved the birdhouse. He'd had many doubts when making it, that he was somehow crossing a line that he could never uncross. Yet he felt confident that Bernard would have done the same if he were able. Piece by piece he was mending this broken life. He just needed more time.

Happy tears pricked the back of his eyes as he touched the ultrasound picture. He and Dawn had never had the chance to see their baby. It wasn't an option back then.

'Please,' he said to no one in particular, 'please keep this little one safe, even if I'm not around to.'

For almost sixty years he'd lived with the guilt of not being there in time. Now he feared he wouldn't have enough time to be there.

Chapter 47

Denise shifted uncomfortably in the unpadded chair in Sharon's office. You'd think her arse would be an ample cushion, but no. Her head pounded, presumably from the alcohol withdrawal. Last night she'd emptied every last bottle down the sink, apart from a new bottle of pear liqueur, which she'd slipped into Ruby's cupboard this morning, and a bottle of brandy she'd snuck into the nursing home supply room.

The manila folder weighed heavily in her hand as she grappled with her conscience. Inside lay the power to change a man's life – the articles and photo that could prove Fred's identity. She couldn't stand it when other people got away with things. And what about Bernard's poor daughter? Didn't she deserve to know the truth?

'So, Denise, sorry we couldn't do this earlier. You said in your email you had something important to discuss about one of the residents. Bernard, was it?' Sharon peered over the top of her trendy red glasses.

Denise swallowed hard and placed the folder on the desk, her hand hovering over it. 'Yes. I just wanted to say that he . . . he . . .' She pictured the kind eyes that had brought her coffee, that had taken the rap for her, that had brought joy to Bernard's daughter.

Bernard's pregnant daughter. She glanced at Sharon, then out the window. 'That he isn't . . .'

Her stomach flipped. She couldn't do it. Not to this man.

'That he actually helped me to realise that I should take some leave. I have some personal health issues I need to deal with.'

'I see.' Sharon nodded. 'I have to admit, I thought something wasn't quite right. Nothing serious, I hope? Is there anything we can do to help?' The DON's eyes pooled with concern.

She was lucky to have a boss like Sharon.

'No, thank you,' she said, her shoulders relaxing.

'Well, I can see you've got a lot of sick leave and personal leave stored up, so there's no problem there. Do you think you'd be able to do one last night shift for me, though? Sorry, normally I wouldn't ask but we've got both Sally and Geraldine out with this dreadful flu, and I haven't been able to get a locum for Saturday night.'

'No problem at all. Thanks, Sharon.'

As Denise walked back to her locker, her feet felt light for the first time since she could remember, like she was going in the right direction. She would get help. She would get stronger and be a better mum for her girls. She would give the residents the care they deserved. And she'd be kinder to 'Fred's friend Denise' and finally stop believing Greg's lies.

Fred's secret would be safe with her just as hers would be safe with him. Ironic that he was the first man ever to have shown her any real grace. She paused, a smile sneaking onto her lips. Her prince had showed up after all. Shame he was eighty-two years old.

Denise took a long sip of water from her drink bottle. This would be her only clear substance now, thanks to him. She must tell him.

'Hello, hope I'm not disturbing?' she said, reaching his room.

The old man looked up from his newspaper. A smile crossed his face that didn't quite reach his eyes. 'Denise, love, I've been thinking about you. How are you?' He fidgeted with the biro he was holding.

She closed the door behind her.

'I'm good, Fred. For the first time in a long while, I'm good. I wanted to let you know I spoke to Sharon,' she said, then paused, taken aback by the sudden terror that had gripped his face. 'No, no, please don't worry. I only told her that I need to take some personal leave. Fred, I'm not going to report you. Not today, not ever.'

She placed the manila folder on his table. 'So, I think this better stay with you.'

Fred opened the folder, his hands shaking. He bit his trembling lip and burst into tears, relief flooding his face. It was a full minute before he could form any words.

'Oh, Denise! Thank you. Thank you so much.'

'No, thank *you*, *Bernard*.'

After Denise left, Fred made himself an extra-strong cup of tea and sat outside his room next to the pansies. He gulped in the fresh air like a drowning man who'd finally come up for oxygen. The body had been accounted for. The one person who knew was now an ally and would never tell. He only had to deal with the ball of guilt that still bounced inside him. But he could do that – couldn't he? He drop-kicked it out of his mind. He was a free man! A celebration was in order.

Fred wanted nothing for himself, but maybe he could buy Hannah and the baby a gift. Going to the mall again was out of the question. Who had he overheard talking about her online shopping spree the other day? Was it Ruby? He grimaced. No, it was Patricia.

Did he dare ask her? He was well aware that any help she gave him might have strings attached. But Linh and Kevin weren't working today, so he didn't have a choice.

Fred found the Twistie grabber in her room watching a soap opera on TV, her dark eyes transfixed by the screen. She was wearing what looked like a cross between a polar-fleece blanket and a hooded jumper, with pictures of eggplants on it. Her face lit up when she saw him.

'Good timing, Bernie! Show has just finished; you shut the door and get comfy. My Oodie is so warm and fluffy, you'll love it. It's so loose there is even room for two!'

Fred stumbled backwards, not liking to think what the devil an 'Oodie' was. Perhaps it wasn't worth it.

'Oh, no, no. I actually want you to teach me how to buy something online. A present.'

She raised her raven eyebrows. 'And I thought you'd forgotten our anniversary!'

'Oh, I . . . actually need to buy something for my daughter. As you know, she's expecting a baby.'

Patricia pouted. 'Well, okay. I'll teach you how, but then you can buy me a surprise! Don't get any lingerie though, I'm already stocked up.'

Fred gulped.

'Got your credit card, Bernie? My iPad is out of juice so it will have to be the computer lounge, I'm afraid.'

Twenty clicks later, Fred spotted the most delightful wooden change table, hand painted with smiling kangaroos and their joeys. At $250, it was a hefty price tag, but it was the perfect gift. He had no idea how much money was left on the card, but there was no harm in finding out.

Patricia helped him to type Bernard's card details into the website, along with Hannah's address for delivery. They checked it all over and then clicked 'Complete purchase'.

The page went blank for a minute, then displayed the words 'Your transaction was unsuccessful. Please try a different payment method.'

Patricia suggested trying again in case they'd entered the number incorrectly, but the same message appeared. She scrunched up her nose and scowled at his debit card as though it was a piece of dog poo.

'Sorry, no chop, old man. Looks like you've run out of dough. I suppose I'll have to buy my own anniversary present.' And with a roll of her eyes she left.

Fred stared at the words still on the screen. So Bernard was low on funds too – another thing they had in common. At least, between the two of them, they'd given Hannah the birdhouse.

A deliciously serene feeling settled upon him as Denise's words reverberated in his head: 'I'm not going to report you. Not today, not ever.' But a moment later, agitating his new-found calm, came that ever-present niggle.

The one hurdle remaining was his own conscience.

He glanced at the ultrasound photo of the passenger on the wall: another human to love, and to be loved by. Shame seeped through his bones. It was also another person he'd have to lie to, who would be pulled into his deception while their real grandfather lay in his grave. If only he could rid himself of his wretched morals that constantly itched like pinworms up his bum.

Bruno, Dawn and his parents had often described him as honest to a fault, but he didn't want to be this time. He wanted to be selfish, damn it!

But *was* this even being selfish?

Didn't Hannah need him as much as he needed her? Wasn't it better for Bernard to be remembered as a loving dad? Didn't Fred owe that to him? What good could it possibly do to confess now? No, he was going to take this chance. Now that the fear of Denise reporting him was gone, he wasn't going to let anything stand in his way. Dawn had been his lighthouse, casting meaning on the shapes that were his life. Albert, Val, Kevin and Linh were all candles and lanterns helping him to find his way again.

But Hannah, darling Han . . . she was the sun. His sun. And he couldn't step back into the darkness.

The more his heart swelled, the less room there was for guilt. It was finally getting easier to normalise his big, fat lie. It was a heavy weight, yes, but an increasingly bearable one, carried by his love for Hannah and the baby.

Guilt could bugger off.

Chapter 48

Fred, doing his best Elvis impersonation, belted along to the car radio, shaking his hips as well as he could in a seated position.

Hannah raised an eyebrow and chuckled. 'Don't give up your day job, old man!' Then she joined in with reckless abandon and for a moment he saw Dawn, singing in her Corolla.

The song had almost ended when she pulled the car into a tired-looking apartment block. The dated brown bricks stood in stark contrast to the more modern rendered houses nearby. Patches of scraggly brown grass and overflowing recycling bins were all that was left of a front garden.

'I'm sorry I haven't had you over sooner,' she said, unlocking the door to apartment 1C, 'and that things aren't tidier. I still haven't had the chance to unpack much since the move.' She scrambled to pick up some piles of papers from a plastic hall table. A yapping white rat of a dog zoomed out, running circles around Fred before rapidly exiting.

'I didn't know you had a dog.'

'Oh, don't mind Smeagol! He's a sweetheart once you get to know him.'

The tiny apartment wasn't much bigger than his room at the nursing home. The walls had seen better days and the yellowing paint seemed to know it as it tried to peel away. His eyes followed the cracks up the wall to the ceiling where they met patches of damp. He rubbed his eyebrow and forced a smile, trying to hide the creeping shock in his belly.

'Please come in. I'll put the kettle on,' she said, motioning to the lounge room, which was also the dining area and kitchen.

Fred's knees protested as he took a seat on the astonishingly low brown couch. Getting up again would not be guaranteed. Smeagol jumped onto his lap and began giving his left ear cavity a thorough cleaning with his wet, pink tongue.

'Ha ha ha! Who's a cheeky varmint?' Fred's heart panged for old Lulu, who'd also been an expert ear cleaner.

'Oh, sorry! I totally forgot you are allergic to dogs. Here, let me get him off you.'

'Oh, no, no. Please leave him,' he said, patting the now-placid canine, who was loving him with beady eyes the way only a dog can. 'I love him.'

'You sure you don't mind him? He's a geriatric too, you know!' Hannah poked out her tongue.

'He's lovely. I've grown out of my allergy.' Was that as lame as it sounded?

She opened her mouth then shrugged, returning to the bench.

A tiny kitchenette stood in one corner, with what looked like its original orange and brown seventies lino floor. Its prime had long gone, if it had ever existed. A damp smell concerned his nostrils. The scratched wooden coffee table was strewn with mail, including some envelopes with 'final notice' in big red letters. It was an all too familiar sight. He shifted uneasily.

'So where did you live before this?'

'Oh, I had a lovely townhouse a few suburbs over,' said Hannah, removing mismatched cups and saucers.

'Did you like it there?'

'I loved it. Three bedrooms with a nice garden. Very modern. Mike and I moved in together about twelve months ago and then, well, he moved out, as you know.'

Fred furrowed his brow, staring at the peeling paint again. 'So, if you don't mind me asking, why did you move to this . . . um . . .'

'Shithole?' She laughed. 'You can say it.'

'Well, not quite the word I would have used.'

'After Mike left, I was down to one income and then I lost a lot of work being so sick with the pregnancy and all. I couldn't make the rent, in the end. All my money went into setting up the salon. I'm lucky to be able to hold on to that for now.'

So she *did* have money problems.

'This place is small and old, but we'll make do. I mean, some families with loads of kids live in tiny places, right?' She removed two teabags from a bulk packet of home-brand tea, the same as he used to buy.

'That's true.' He nodded as his eyes returned to the damp patch on the ceiling, his mind flooding with worry. 'Have you got the things you need? For the baby, I mean?'

'Well, someone made me a magnificent pair of booties.' She smiled, her eyes twinkling. 'Not much else yet, though. I've heard there's a great second-hand kids' market in the city on the first Sunday of the month – was thinking about checking it out soon. I might be able to pick up a cot and car seat there.'

'You've got to be careful with used car seats, I hear – make sure they haven't been in any accidents and so on.' Fred had read about that in a 'Preparing for baby' article in a *Women's Weekly* magazine Ruby had saved for him.

'I know. I'd love to buy new, but I'm afraid I can't just now.' She poured boiling water in the cups, added UHT milk and brought them over.

The words 'your transaction was unsuccessful' blinked in Fred's mind as they had on the screen at the cafe. He hadn't had enough for the fancy change table, but did he at least have enough to buy her a new car seat? He knew Bernard would have wanted to. Maybe the old guy was on the pension and had money coming in weekly? He really needed to find out once and for all.

Hannah placed the drinks on the coffee table, flushing red when she saw the bills.

'Sorry again about the mess!' she said, chucking them hastily in a nearby cardboard box. 'Oh, I almost forgot. I have to show you something.'

She reached into the box and pulled out some kind of book. Fred's pulse quickened as he registered what it was.

'When I moved, I found this photo album of when me and Sayd were little.' Hannah rubbed her hand over the faded green cover.

He tensed his tummy as she opened it to the first page to show a slightly out-of-focus photo of a pretty young woman in a crimson dress, a mane of wavy brown hair surrounding her gentle face.

Hannah's mum.

'She's lovely,' he said.

'Wasn't she just?'

He ran a finger over the newborn baby she cradled in her arms.

'And you were so cute.'

'That's Sadie,' she corrected, but there was no agitation in her voice. She flipped the page. 'There I am, with you and Mum.'

This time there was a photo of Bernard with his arm around Hannah's mum, holding another baby dressed in purple outside a white weatherboard house.

'Gorgeous baby girl,' he smiled, determined to avoid directly lying as much as possible.

Hannah turned the page and smoothed down the curled corner of the protective plastic over the next photo. A family of four: mother, father, two smiling young girls with short curly hair, now primary-school aged, Fred guessed from their checked school dresses. Their joy radiated from the image. His heart sank. Where had it all gone so wrong?

'That was my first day of Grade 1, a few months before Sadie's diagnosis.' Hannah's voice was quiet.

He nodded. Of course.

'You must have been so scared when it happened – when you heard about your sister, I mean?' Fred's stomach began eating itself.

She paused, her brow slightly furrowed. 'I don't think I really understood – not at first, anyway.' Her voice trailed off as she gently touched the picture. 'You and Mum didn't go into a lot of details. In a way, I wish you had. Sometimes the uncertainty of not knowing is worse than knowing, even if it's bad – does that make any sense?'

He nodded again. Dawn's cancer diagnosis had been world-shattering, but it had been a relief to find out what was going on. To understand why she had been having such terrible symptoms and to be told there was something they could do about it – or try to do about it, at least. His core tensed as a hot, grief-fuelled rage erupted inside him. 'Cancer is a bloody bastard!' he blurted.

Hannah's mouth dropped open. 'I'm surprised to hear you use such strong language. I haven't heard you swear since . . .' She looked down at her hands. 'Well, not for a very long time, anyway.'

He smiled grimly. 'Cancer deserves the strongest language we've got, I reckon.'

'Well, I can't believe the "bloody bastard" took Mum, too,' she said, matching his intensity.

Though he didn't know the details of her mother's passing, Fred had suspected this may have been the case.

He took her hand. 'You've dealt with so much, Hannah, and on your own for all this time. I'm so sorry. Did your mother suffer much?'

'Thankfully, no. It was quick, unlike poor Sadie who was so sick for so long. But to be honest, I don't know what's worse. "Bloody bastard" is right.'

'Here's to no more bloody bastards!' Fred raised his cup of tea and clinked it against Hannah's. They clinked mugs, their laughter turning into tears for all the wonderful women they had lost too soon.

After they had finished their tea, he took the dishes to the sink.

'You can just leave them there,' she called from the couch. 'There's no dishwasher.'

'Nonsense, you've got a top-of-the-range dishwasher right here,' he said, pointing to himself with his thumbs. He turned on the tap and startled as a cockroach scurried across the floor.

Strewth. This was not good at all. The kitchen sink looked out to the tiny concrete courtyard featuring a rotten wooden garden bed filled with weeds. Hardly the place he'd imagined for the birdhouse. He must find out more about Bernard's finances. He wasn't computer-savvy enough to try online banking, and he somehow doubted Bernard had been either. The Commonwealth Bank logo on Bernard's debit card popped into his head. From memory, there was a branch in the strip of shops not too far from here. He patted his pants pocket. Fortuitously, he'd brought Bernard's wallet. Surely he'd just need to show the ID and no questions would be asked? It was worth a shot.

'Hannah love, on the way home do you think we could go via the bank, please?'

The long strip of shops was a hive of activity. They finally found a park in a nearby side street and walked arm in arm towards the bank, the sweet scent of roses filling the air from the technicolor florist next door.

'Do you want me to go in with you?' asked Hannah.

'No, I'll be fine, love, thanks,' said Fred quickly, straightening his shirt.

'Okay, I might pop to the newsagent down there. I need to buy a card for a friend's wedding.' And with a wave she was gone.

Sweat trickled down the backs of Fred's knees as he ran over in his head what he needed to say.

The bank was modern, neat and air-conditioned. Two security cameras watched him from the ceiling, bringing to mind the many heist movies he'd seen on late-night television. He always appreciated a meticulously planned bank robbery.

He frowned, his eyes darting from side to side. Hang on a sec. Crikey! Was he, in fact, committing a robbery? Technically yes, as this was not his money. The thought caused the sweat to flow on full-bore. Regrettably, he'd chosen to wear a white polo shirt.

Just think of Hannah and the baby. It's for them.

He made his way to one of three tellers who stood at tall white desks behind Perspex screens.

'How can I help you, sir?' A blond-haired man who looked all of fifteen offered a textbook greeting. A black-and-white name tag told Fred his name was Ivan.

'I'd like to, er, check my bank balance, please. I've got my debit card right here,' he said, a little too loudly.

'No problem, I'll just need some photo ID, please, sir.'

Breathe, just breathe. Remember you're doing it for Hannah.

'Absolutely.' Fred was unable to lower the volume of his voice. He slipped Bernard's driver's licence under the screen.

The man-boy glanced briefly at the photo and then at Fred. 'Perfect,' he said without hesitation.

Fred exhaled. He was over the first hurdle.

'So, were you just wanting the balance for your main everyday account?'

'Er . . . yes, please.'

'Your balance is sixty-two dollars.'

Fred's shoulders slumped. 'That's the account linked to this card, is it?'

'Yes, sir.'

Fred sighed. Rats. That was loads of jubes from the lolly trolley, but no car seat. He scratched his moustache. How were the nursing-home fees being covered? Was he about to be made homeless a second time? He was lucky to have managed the wedding suits and the bashed avos.

He retrieved his card and was about to walk away when Ivan said, 'Did you want to know the balance of your other account, sir?'

'My other account?'

'Yes, I can see you have a joint term deposit account here, too. It's not a carded account.'

'Oh, yes. Yes, of course. Might as well check that too while I'm here, I guess.' Fred tried to appear nonchalant with a casual tone and wave of his hands but feared he more closely resembled a drunk octopus.

A click on his screen brought a flash of surprise on Ivan's face, though he quickly tried to hide it. 'That would be showing a balance of one million, seven hundred thousand and forty-eight dollars. And fifty cents.'

The saliva in Fred's mouth evaporated. The room froze, as if someone had pressed a pause button. 'I'm sorry, could you say that again?' he stammered, adding quickly, 'I'm a bit hard of hearing.'

'One million, seven hundred thousand and forty-eight dollars. And fifty cents,' said the teller, louder.

Fred's legs turned to mush, and he grabbed the counter for support.

'Are you okay, sir?' The man-boy leaned forward.

'Yes, yes, quite okay, thank you,' he said, finding his tongue. 'I just, um, well, I wasn't expecting that fifty cents, you see. It threw me. Must be the interest.'

'Riiight,' said Ivan slowly.

'So can I withdraw some of that money or transfer it to someone, please?'

'I'm afraid you'd need the signature from the other party to do that, as it's a joint account.'

His stomach sank. 'Oh, of course, the other party . . .' Could it be Bernard's dead ex-wife?

Ivan glanced at the screen. 'Mr Andrew Mora?'

The name drew a complete blank, which was no surprise, but he wasn't going to let Ivan know that.

'Oh, right. Yes, of course, Andrew. Andy. I'll have a chat with Andy. Thank you, you've been most helpful.'

He left quickly, stumbling out the door, his brain exploding. Bernard was a ruddy millionaire! You little ripper! That kind of money would set Hannah and the baby up for life. Forget renting, she could buy a house, a glorious house! The passenger could have the safest car seat on the market!

Hannah was waiting outside the door, holding a small paper bag, her pregnant silhouette illuminated by the afternoon sun.

'Are you okay?' she asked. 'You look flustered.'

'Yes, thanks, love, I'm super! Just a bit hot in there, that's all.'

'Come on, let's find the car,' she said, looping her arm in his.

He nodded. First the car and then Andrew Mora.

Chapter 49

Hannah dropped Fred back to the home and stayed for a quick cuppa. As soon as she left he put on his detective hat and got to work. His knees burned as he knelt at Bernard's bureau. Opening the ornate oak door, he surveyed the contents. Old books, a few bird magazines, a pile of manila folders and another box of old photos. He took the latter out, flinching as a disgruntled daddy-long-legs crept away over the lid. The photos were all helpfully labelled on the back in biro, but most were of birds. He searched for any sign of an Andrew. Could he be a brother, a best friend perhaps? The only one he could see of a man other than Bernard was 'Bernard and cousin Stephen'. No Andrew in sight.

He moved on to the manila folders labelled in small, scrawled writing: *Certificates*, *Miscellaneous*, *Legal* and *Bank*.

Opening the first folder, he found Bernard's birth certificate, brown and faded in a crimpled plastic sleeve. Bernard Phillip Greer had been exactly eight months older than him to the day, also born in Sydney but at a different hospital. A wave of sadness passed over him as he read the next piece of paper, a marriage certificate. Bernard had married Mary Grace Porter seven years after Fred had wed his Dawn. The following document showed their divorce.

Hannah must have been only ten. Poor little mite.

The pain from his knees was now shooting down his legs and he attempted to shift his weight onto his bottom. The patch of damp in Hannah's apartment seeped into his mind, willing him to persist. He moved on to the folder marked 'Legal'.

Paperclipped to the inside was a beige business card:

MORA & DAVIDSON
Estate Lawyers
Andrew Mora

'Bingo!' he shouted aloud to no one in particular. Andrew was Bernard's lawyer! Sherlock Holmes could eat his heart out: a new detective was on the scene! He smirked, placing the card in his shirt pocket.

As he went to return the other items, he spied a small black-velvet box in the back corner. Fishing it out, he paused a moment before opening it. Inside sat a man's wedding ring, not unlike his own: a simple white-gold band.

He picked it up and ran his finger over the inside. Engraved in a beautiful cursive script were the names Mary and Bernard. Had they been in love, at least at the start? He hoped that poor Bernard had felt what it was to be loved at some point in his lifetime. Everyone deserved that. A stab of pain shot into his left knee, slicing through his thoughts. What a drongo to think he could kneel for this long. He needed to sit.

The armchair across the room may as well have been Everest. Fred tried pushing himself to his feet, but his knees wouldn't budge.

He startled as a silk-bathrobe-clad Patricia entered, quickly closing the door behind her.

'Shhhh! No one knows I'm here,' she oozed, going to undo the tie around her waist.

The hairs on Fred's arms stood on end. 'No! Wait, please don't, I need to . . .' He scrambled, desperately trying to get up again, but could only get one leg out from under him, leaving him kneeling on one knee.

Patricia's jaw dropped to the floor. 'And they said why buy the cow if you can get the milk for free! Yes, yes, of course I'll marry you, Bernard!'

Fred felt weak all over, his body temperature rising. 'I . . . uh . . .' He fumbled with whatever it was he was holding.

It was the blasted ring.

Good grief! He slapped his hand to his forehead.

Patricia approached, like a fly drawn to honey, her flapping gown showing flashes of unidentifiable fleshy objects bobbing about. He tried to avert his eyes as she plucked the ring from his hand, her brow furrowing as she examined it.

'Hmmm . . . Bernard, you do know that diamonds are a girl's best friend, don't you? And really, what size do you think I am!' She placed the giant ring on her bony finger – like a hula hoop on a sausage. She narrowed her eyes. 'Well, I'm going to have to think about this. I thought you knew me better,' she said, turning to leave in a huff.

Fred grimaced. He knew he shouldn't look a gift horse in the mouth and should let her leave, but his knees could bear it no longer.

'Patricia . . . Could you just help me up before you go, please?'

She flashed a devilish smile. 'Well, I *am* the expert at helping you up, aren't I?'

Fred winced as she helped him to his feet, relieved that was all she did.

'I'll get back to you on this,' she said, waving the ring in his face.

She walked away, swinging her hips from side to side. Just when Fred thought he was safe, she lifted her robe and flashed a bum cheek, bringing to mind a two-month-old apricot he had once retrieved from the back of his fridge.

He sat on his bed and distracted himself from his aching knees and traumatised mind by removing the business card from his pocket. It would be better to get it over and done with, like ripping off a bandaid. Grabbing a pen and paper from the bedside table, he jotted down a few notes in case his nerves caused a brain fart. He cleared his throat and dialled the number on the card.

A chirpy voice answered. 'Hello, Mora and Davidson, this is Louella speaking.'

'Why, hello, Louella. My name is Frer-nard Grife . . .' He coughed. 'Sorry, I mean Bernard Fear – or rather, *Bernard Greer*.' Saying your own name for eighty-two years was a hard habit to shake. 'I'm a client of Andrew Mora. I'd like to speak to him, please.' He plucked a tissue from the box next to the phone to mop his brow. Fingers crossed Andrew still worked there.

'Certainly, just one moment, please.'

Classical music played through the receiver. Every note of it crawled under his skin. He clicked the pen in his hand until his thumb went numb.

Finally, Louella spoke again. 'Good timing, Andrew is between clients. I'll transfer your call now, Mr Greer.'

His whitening knuckles clenched the receiver, now slippery with sweat.

'Hello, Bernard!' A deep voice boomed through the phone.

'Hi, Andy . . . Andrew . . . Yes, it's Bernard here. Bernard Greer,' he said in an accent that didn't sound like his own. But maybe that was a good thing? He rubbed his forehead.

'Yes, Lou told me. How are you? You sound different, mate. It's been a while, I guess.'

Fred coughed. Should he try to speak lower or higher? He went for higher. 'Ah, well, I can't remember if I told you, but I've moved into a nursing home,' he said, glancing at his notes.

'Yeah, Richard actually told me about that. Sorry, I haven't had a chance to call. You feeling okay?'

Who the devil was Richard? Never mind, he'd have to deal with that later. 'Yes, I'm fine, thanks. Look, I wanted to talk about our joint account. I'm hoping to withdraw some money, you see. And I also wanted to look at my will.' With any luck Andrew had taken care of that, too.

'Right. Look, if it's anything significant, we really need to do it in person, mate. I'm guessing it might be a bit hard for you to come here?'

Patricia's scooter flashed into his mind. 'Yes, it would, I'm afraid.'

'No worries, I can come to see you. Actually just had a cancellation for Friday morning, if that'd suit?'

'Perfect. Thanks, Andy.'

After providing the address of the home and a brief goodbye, Fred replaced the receiver, heart still racing. He rubbed his aching knees. Come to think of it, his bottom hurt, too, like there was something sticking into it. He lifted his left bum cheek to see a peach-coloured object wedged behind the seat cushion. Hannah's purse. Must have slipped out of her pocket when she was here. He opened it and saw her kind green eyes looking back at him from her driver's licence, along with the pink credit card that had been declined at the cafe.

He pressed his lips together. The phone call had been cringe-worthy, but he would do absolutely anything to help Hannah and the passenger to be financially secure.

Anything at all.

Chapter 50

Hannah watched the little grey car with hawklike intensity as it made its way from Tommy's Noodles to her house, as if the act of watching it would make Santosh go faster. Rain fell without apology from the charcoal clouds now shrouding the sky.

The car stopped at the railway tracks.

Damn you, level-crossing works! Uber Eats was a luxury she couldn't really afford, but she had an insatiable desire for chicken-and-sweet-corn soup, something she'd always detested pre-pregnancy. Ironically, it had been Mike's favourite. Is that why she was craving it now? Could the baby share its father's tastebuds? Bloody Mike.

She grabbed a handful of salt-and-vinegar chips and stuffed them into her mouth. How was it possible to feel starving and nauseated at the same time?

The vinegar burned her tongue. To this day it reminded her of Sadie, who had loved the stuff, even by itself, but especially on fish and chips. She'd always ask for five sachets from the fish-and-chip shop and sometimes even drink one on the way home. Until she got sick, that is, and then she couldn't eat much of anything.

A memory flickered in her mind. The two of them at the beach, sprawled on old beach towels, with a box of flake and greasy chips between them. Dad with his burger with the lot, of course, as he was allergic to seafood. Mum must have been at work.

Hannah tried to piece the memory together. It was a heatwave. The girls had desperately wanted to swim but Sadie hadn't had the energy, her limp body wrapped up in the towel they'd given Dad for Father's Day, the one with the seagulls on it. Dad had lifted her waif of a sister like a fireman and carried her into the ocean, where he gently rocked her in the water. If Hannah tried hard enough, she could still hear Sadie's giggles echoing over the sand as he carried her. The three of them had made a sandcastle together, their feet lapped by the salty waves.

The memory had been buried deep and pricked her with emotion as it rose to the surface. Hannah chewed on it as if trying to deduce what flavour it was. She placed her hand on her bump, reconsidering her father's erratic behaviour in light of losing Sadie, of losing a child. It had been unforgivable, yet not incomprehensible.

Finally, the little car got over the tracks. Four minutes later there was a knock at the door, and she sprang to answer in hangry anticipation.

But it wasn't Santosh, it was Bernard.

He was rugged up in a jacket and what looked like striped flannel pyjama bottoms, drips of water falling from his shivering body. Smeagol greeted the old man, his wagging tail a blur.

'Bernard! You're soaked through! How did you get here?'

'I walked,' he said, bending down to pat the dog. 'Did a little runner and slipped out with a visitor. You left your purse, and I didn't want you to be without it, in case you needed anything.'

'Oh, gosh, so I did,' she said, taking it from him. 'Here, come on in, let's get you dry.'

She fetched a towel from the bathroom, wrapping it around his shoulders. 'Silly duffer, you didn't have to do that! You could have just called me, you know.'

'I know, but I really wanted to see you again,' he said from chattering lips.

'You don't need an excuse for that. Let's get you out of these wet clothes. Are these your pyjamas? Ah, crap, I don't even have any of Mike's clothes to offer you. Don't worry, I'll find something.'

She returned with her fleecy lilac maternity dressing gown embroidered with pink flowers.

He raised his eyebrows.

'I'm sorry.' She laughed. 'It will have to do!'

'I'm very grateful,' he said, taking the robe into the bathroom.

She took his wet clothes, running her hand over the shirt and pants meticulously labelled with her father's name, and popped them in the dryer.

A few minutes later he emerged dressed in the maternity gown, silver hair still dripping, giggling like a schoolboy. He had tucked a pillow under the stomach area so he too had a baby bump.

'You dag!' she chortled, as the baby kung-fu-kicked her bladder, prompting an urgent dash to the toilet.

'Someone's knocking at the door,' he called from the lounge. 'Should I answer it?'

'Yes, please. It'll be the food.'

As she washed her hands, loud chuckling erupted through the wall. She stepped out and raised an eyebrow.

'I forgot I had the gown on when I answered the door,' he cried through tears of laughter, 'not to mention the baby bump! I think that poor delivery chap deserves a tip next time; probably scarred the bugger for life.'

They erupted into fits of laughter.

Once the giggles had finally subsided, she placed the bag of food on the coffee table.

'So, won't they know you're missing?'

'Hopefully not. I ate my tea and told the carer I needed an early night. They helped me into my PJs and I pretended to go to sleep. Then when the coast was clear I put some giant nappies under my doona to make it look like I was there, and snuck out.'

Hannah shook her head incredulously. The oldest trick in the book. Well, apart from the nappies – that was a new twist. She recalled pulling the same stunt, sneaking over to a friend's house across the road. She'd needed to get away. Dad had been furious when he found out. Did he remember? Not likely – look at him now! The cheeky bugger. Her tummy growled as she eyed the Uber Eats bag.

'Please stay and help me eat this. I'm supposedly eating for two, but I think I've ordered for six.' She opened the bag and the delicious scent of garlic and ginger wafted out.

'Oh, smells divine, but I wouldn't want to put you out, love, and I've already had dinner, you know.'

'And your point is? We both know you can manage it, old man. I won't tell if you won't!' She smirked. 'Please, you'd really be doing me a favour. Your clothes will take a while to dry, anyway.'

'Challenge accepted! I guess you could say I'm eating for two also,' he grinned, patting his padded tummy.

They sat on the couch and tucked into the soup, spring rolls, lemon chicken and fried rice. It was obvious that eating wasn't just a necessity for them, it was a passion.

'It's so nice to have proper company for dinner,' he said, dipping another spring roll into the plastic tub of sweet chilli sauce. 'Apart from Albert and Val, I haven't had that since Dawn – I mean, since what feels like the dawn of time.' He blushed and turned away.

'I understand. I miss Mike the most at dinnertime, funnily enough. Just means we'll have to do this more often. Wanna watch a movie and eat ice cream? I found a low-sugar one that isn't terrible.'

His eyes lit up. 'That would be glorious!'

She picked up the remote and scrolled through Netflix. She'd had to actively unsubscribe from the other streaming services, having forgotten to cancel after the free trial. More fees that had started to add up. They settled on a romantic comedy called *About Time* and were soon snuggled under a fluffy blanket with two generous bowls of diabetic-friendly salted-caramel ice cream. They laughed and they cried. When the credits rolled, Hannah went to grab a tissue and saw she was holding his hand. It felt like the most natural thing in the world.

Fred put on the toasty PJs that Hannah had just taken out of the dryer, the delicious heat enveloping him like a hug. When he'd snuck out, he hadn't dreamt he'd have the gift of a whole evening with her. How lucky was he? The film they'd watched was brilliant, about a man who could go back and relive any part of his life. Would he have done anything differently over the last few months? Unlikely. Despite the guilt, he knew he could never backtrack on any path that had led him here, to Hannah. Although perhaps he would've told Patricia he was gay – but she'd probably have taken that as a challenge.

'You all set?' called Hannah.

'Good as gold!' he said, putting on his jacket and exiting the bathroom.

Despite his protests, she insisted on driving him back to the home, and even chaperoned him inside to ensure he didn't get caught. They giggled like naughty schoolchildren as they crept past reception and down the hall, arm-in-arm.

'Thanks for such a great night. I haven't had that much fun in years. I wish you could have stayed!' she whispered in the hall outside his bedroom.

'Me too. Although I guess it would have been only so long before they discovered the nappies pretending to be me,' he laughed.

Hopefully it would be much, much longer before anyone discovered the man pretending to be Bernard.

Chapter 51

On Friday morning, the sun shone brightly through the window like a spotlight on Fred's guilty conscience. He glanced at the clock. Andrew Mora would arrive any minute. He pushed his boiled eggs and mutinous toast soldiers aside; they tasted like betrayal. Passively being Bernard was something he could handle, but the upcoming active portrayal sat as well in his stomach as week-old oysters.

A knock sounded at the door, followed by the deep voice from the phone.

'Bernard?' A short man with an olive complexion Fred guessed to be in his late sixties entered.

Fred injected his smile with all the gusto he could muster. 'G'day, Andy! So good to see you.' He stood and shook the man's hand firmly with what he hoped was the same confidence he had practised in the mirror that morning. 'How long has it been?' It was a genuine question.

'Oh, at least six, maybe seven years, I'd say, mate! How've ya been? They treating you okay in here?'

Fred exhaled, relieved to have passed the Bernard test.

'Can't complain. And you? How's the family?' he said, silently praying that Andrew had a family.

'I'm divorced myself now, sadly. Didn't work out with Charmaine in the end – she never did believe me about that toilet-brush incident.'

Fred tried to look serious. 'Oh, I'm so sorry to hear that. Please take a seat, Andy. Would you like a tea or coffee or something to eat?'

'I won't say no to one of those.' Andrew settled into the armchair, motioning to the stockpile of biscuits on the table. Fred had kept his word to Hannah and resisted all sweets in solidarity with her. He handed Andy a couple of Tim Tams.

'Thanks. Look, I don't have heaps of time, mate, so let's get straight to it, shall we?' He bit into the biscuit, crumbs raining onto the lid of his brown briefcase as he popped it open.

'Yes, absolutely.' No more small talk suited him just fine. He sat on the bed and cleared his throat. 'Well, I went to the bank the other day and I wanted to withdraw some cash . . .'

'Yes, and you have your everyday account if you need money,' mumbled Andy through narrowed eyes and a mouthful of food.

'Well, the thing is, that's quite low. To be honest, I'm not even sure how we're paying my fees here . . .' Fred ventured, testing the waters.

'Now if I remember correctly,' Andy said, flipping through some papers, 'we agreed that if you ever needed care, it would all come out of your super. This other account was more for essential spending money. Yep, your fees here are coming out of your super, so all good there.' He pointed to a particular paragraph.

'Right, well. I'd still like to withdraw money from my term deposit. It is my money, isn't it?' Fred was asking a genuine question, but Andy seemed to think he was having a go, and swallowed the remaining biscuit with a frown.

'Yes, Bernard, of course it's your money.' His voice was now hard. 'It was your jackpot win. You won it fair and square, but I swore I would never release the funds, no matter what you said. It's for Hannah, mate, remember?'

Adrenaline coursed through Fred's veins, his words coming louder and faster. He leaned closer. 'Yes! Yes! Exactly – it's for Hannah! I've reached out and I've met her, I mean, reconnected with her! I want her to have all the money.'

Andy ran his hands through his salt-and-pepper hair and sighed. 'Mate, I've known you for forty years, remember? You've tried that one before. We've been through this. We discussed it with your sponsor. The deal was it cannot be touched until —'

'My sponsor?'

'Richard. From Gamblers Anonymous? I mentioned to you that we'd talked. I didn't want to say anything, mate, but he said you called him back in November as you'd had a slip-up, you'd called a bookie. You said you'd tried to reach out to Hannah but she wanted nothing to do with you. So your call earlier this week wasn't exactly a surprise. I knew you'd want the money.'

Fred hung his head. 'Oh, I see.' The return-to-sender letter had a November date.

'It's probably why you are low in your spending account, mate – that was meant to last you for a few years. Look, you'll still get everything you need here, that's all from your super. You don't really want anything else, do you? I know you like your bird magazines, but . . .'

Fred grimaced, shaking his head. 'I . . . I don't need anything. I want to give it all to her. She needs it now, she's having a baby. What if you met her?' he said, wringing his hands.

'I'm sorry, mate. Congrats on the grandkid and all but this isn't the first time you've tried that one, remember? I wish I could help.

I assure you she will get the money, though. She'll get all of it, plus whatever is left of your super. It's all drawn up rock solid. She'll get it when you . . .' Andy paused, suddenly taking a great interest in his shoes.

'When I what?'

'Well, it automatically goes to her when you . . . pass away. Just like we discussed.'

A great weight pushed down on Fred's shoulders. 'I see,' he said quietly.

'I'm sorry, mate. I want to help, I really do. I hope you can understand.'

'I understand. But she really can't have it now? Why not?'

'You told me you never wanted her to feel like she owed you anything, and if you gave the money to her when you were still alive she might reject it or feel obliged to see you. Look, if I'm entirely honest, even if I believed you, you might not have the legal capacity to make any changes.' Andy leaned closer, his expression softening. 'I had a chat to the nurse on the way in and the fact is, you've been diagnosed with the early stages of dementia. Have they told you?'

Fred's heart dropped, his eyes stinging with tears. He could only nod.

'I'm sorry, mate. I guess that explains you not remembering what we agreed upon.' Andy stood up. 'Well, it's been great seeing you, Bernard. I'm afraid I have to dash to another appointment. Thanks for the bickies. Hope there are no hard feelings, cobber?'

Fred shook his head and offered a feeble handshake before Andrew left.

He moved over to his armchair, suddenly feeling like a much, much older man. The sun was still out but its light couldn't reach him. Grief seeped into his veins, spreading like poison. He already knew in his heart what had to happen. It would not be easy, but there was no other option if Hannah and the baby were to be taken care of. And it would have to happen as soon as possible.

Bernard had to die.

For the second time.

Chapter 52

'Checkmate!' Hannah smiled broadly at her dad.

'What? Noooo! C'mon! Really? Ha ha, clever girl! I didn't even let you win that time!'

'I have a good teacher.' She winked.

Bernard surrendered his king with a mock pout, his kind eyes twinkling.

The nursing-home courtyard was heavy with the scent of jasmine as the spring flowers came out of hibernation. Hannah stretched, inhaling the warm breeze. So this was what happiness smelt like. It was like rediscovering a treat that she hadn't had since child-hood. Who would have ever thought this could be possible? This reconnection, this change of pace. She should be more stressed than ever with single parenthood on the horizon. Yet for the first time in decades she felt a deep security.

She took a sip of cold water from her drink bottle and repos-itioned herself in the chair. For a moment she'd even forgotten her money troubles, which, along with the abhorrent heartburn, were keeping her up most nights. It was going to be tight. Very tight. And on top of everything she needed a new car. Her old Camry was living on borrowed time.

Her father reset the chessboard, trying to free a pawn that had got stuck in a gap in the wrought-iron table, his hands shaking ever so slightly. Sometimes a wave of anger and resentment towards him would rise up like reflux, but she only had to take one look at his dear sweet face and earnest eyes to know that he was a totally different person now. Mum had always told her that forgiveness had to be complete: 'You can remember, but you can't forgive halfway, Hannah darling.'

It was good advice.

Her stomach rumbled and she glanced at her watch. It was almost morning-tea time and they often served scones on Saturdays. Early (and frequent) meals suited her pregnancy appetite very well. The nursing home was like her second home now. She would visit most days and take walks with her dad, go to the cafe, play chess or cards. They'd been making their way through a list of rom-coms they both loved. She'd miss their usual Saturday dinner and Sunday brunch this weekend but was looking forward to Lucy's wedding in the mountains this evening. At least they had the morning together before she had to head off.

'Han.' His voice interrupted her thoughts. He'd finished resetting the board and was now staring at her intently, his bottom lip quivering.

'I want you to know that I'm so glad you came into my life.' He coughed. 'Back into my life, that is.' His hand reached across the table for her, his eyes damp.

What an old softie he had become! She took his hand and gave it a gentle squeeze. 'Thanks. I know. But I'm only going away for the night, you duffer. I'll be back tomorrow afternoon.'

'Yes,' he said, squeezing back, 'but if there is one thing I've learnt in life, it's to not wait to say things. As we both know, life is short, sometimes unexpectedly short.' His voice cracked as he reached out his other hand and placed it on top of hers. 'I love you, Hannah. I love you with my whole heart. I feel like I have a lifetime of "I love yous" to catch up on. No matter what happens, know that. I think you are going to be an expert mother and I'm so very proud of you, my darling girl.'

Her eyes brimmed with tears, unprepared for the intensity of his statement. Her heart trembled. Had it healed enough? Could she say the words? Could she put courage before fear?

'Well, in the spirit of not waiting, I . . . I love you, too . . . Dad.' The words she hadn't uttered since she was nine years old came easily and without reservation or resentment. His eyes widened as he reached for her, his hug even tighter than normal. She closed her eyes, his familiar sandalwood scent enveloping her in comfort. After a long moment they let go.

'Now then, how about letting *me* win?' He smiled.

Dad. She had called him Dad! The word flicked on a light inside him, illuminating the drab room. His old heart had long given up hope of this title and now it was here. Yet the moment had been bittersweet, like tasting a Tim Tam for the first time only to be told you can never have another.

He had reached the pinnacle, and just in time. Without it, he mightn't have the strength to do what he needed to next, for it was only the love of a parent that could so willingly give up their life for their child.

This was his last day.

He looked to the walls as if he might find support for his breaking heart. He wanted to stay. He wanted to stay so badly.

But he couldn't withhold this gift from her. Withhold the gift that Bernard, her actual dad, had wanted her to have, had made sure she *would* have. The gift that would take care of her and the baby for longer than he ever could. He owed it to her and to Bernard to get out of the way. Yes, this would be his first and last day as 'Dad'.

Linh brought him his dinner. Ironically, it was his favourite: roast lamb with all the trimmings. A fitting last meal, exactly what he would have chosen if on death row. A chill crept up his spine at the thought. He ate slowly, savouring every bite. Dessert was a coconut cake, Hannah's favourite. He didn't bother to stop the tears now. They splashed freely onto the icing, but he didn't care. Perhaps if he ate up all his tears he would hurt less.

The wet moral cement he'd been trudging through for so long had finally set and he could go no further. He could never look her in the face and confess what he had done. He must take the coward's way out. Fred shut his eyes, aching for Dawn, longing to be with her, with Bruno, with Albert.

He'd at least leave a note. He owed her that. Taking a pen and paper from the bureau, he began to write, a flood of tears making his last words to her bleed like his heart.

He had placed what he required in the bedside-table drawer. It was all he needed for this whole charade finally to be over.

Denise yawned and sipped her strong black tea, grateful for the kick of caffeine. Night shift was never her favourite, but this would be the last for a long time. Sharon had been surprisingly gracious and not asked any questions. Thank god.

Denise had kept her promise to Fred and worked up the courage (thanks to an ironic shot of tequila) to call Alcoholics Anonymous, and had attended her first meeting. It wasn't nearly as awful as she'd feared. In fact, being surrounded by others in a similar situation had planted a seed of hope that things could get better. Though the daily numbers on her bathroom scale hadn't changed, she felt light for the first time in decades.

She placed her teacup in the sink and caught a glance of herself in the mirrored cabinet. She didn't see someone she liked yet, but felt no hate, either. The eyes of her younger self were still in there and they were actually quite pretty.

Denise checked her watch. It was time to give Kathleen her sleeping tablet. She took the little white bottle from the trolley and frowned. It only had one tablet left.

According to the chart, it had been full two nights ago.

Chapter 53

Hannah turned off the car radio as yet another love song taunted from the speakers. The wedding in the Blue Mountains had been spectacular, but also painful. How many times had she fantasised about her and Mike getting married there? Her dream A-line ivory dress glowing in beautiful contrast to the backdrop of the deep greens, blues and greys of the mountains.

She sighed and rubbed her growing bump. 'We don't need him, kiddo – we've got my dad instead, and he isn't going to let us down this time.' A big smile swept across her face as she pictured him. She couldn't wait to show him the photos, so much so that she'd come home half a day early to surprise him.

She pulled up in front of the nursing home and paused. Red and blue lights illuminated the beige brick. An ambulance wasn't an uncommon sight at the home, so its presence didn't faze her. Another death or fall, most likely. It wasn't until she got out of her car that she saw the police car parked out the front, too. Maybe one of the residents with dementia had escaped, which wasn't unheard of.

She entered the glass doors and signed the visitors log, turning to hear someone crying loudly. Patricia was sitting near the reception desk sobbing, her tears plopping onto her pink parachute tracksuit.

'I just can't . . . I just can't believe it.' Her voice was loud and dramatic.

'Patricia? What's happened? Are you okay?'

'He-he-he's *gone*. I've just been to his room and the cleaner told me.'

'Who's gone?' asked Hannah, placing her hand on the old woman's shoulder pad. It was no secret that Patricia had several men on rotation.

She clutched Hannah's hand and looked up at her with panda eyes. 'I'm so sorry, darling. He gave this to me, but I think you should have it now.' Patricia handed her a white-gold ring.

Hannah frowned, examining the engraving. What the hell? It was Dad's wedding ring! Her eyes darted across the foyer to where Kevin was consoling Linh. Hannah's numb legs bolted into action. She sprinted to Bernard's room, almost knocking over a tea trolley on her way. Arriving breathless at the door, her worst fear was realised: his bed was empty, stripped of all linen. Bile rose in her throat, and she barged into the ensuite and threw up her breakfast.

She had barely sat up when she felt a gentle tap on her shoulder.

'Hannah, I'm so sorry. He left this letter for you, I found it this morning after he departed.'

A male cleaner whose name Hannah couldn't recall handed her an envelope. She stared at her name written in spidery writing.

Her hands couldn't feel the paper but somehow, she tore it open.

To my dearest Hannah,

I am so sorry that I had to leave you in this way, but I had no other choice . . .

For a split second her heart stopped beating before launching into a gallop. She couldn't read on. 'I don't . . . I don't understand. In what way?' she wept, but the cleaner had already gone.

Hannah rushed back to the entrance to see a gurney being loaded into the ambulance, a white sheet draped over what could only be a body. She tried to run outside to it, but her stupid legs had stopped working. Motionless, she watched on in horror as the paramedics shut the door and drove away. Her lungs grasped desperately for oxygen that didn't seem to be there. She gripped the envelope, her mind whirling in confusion. Had he known he was going to die? He wasn't sick, though! Was he? Then the horrible thought slammed into her gut like a freight train, as cold terror trickled down her spine. Surely not. Surely it couldn't be a suicide note? She tried to quieten her screaming heart, but a deeply stitched trauma was ripping open.

He was leaving her all over again.

She searched for something nearby to be sick into, when the DON's office door opened. Two young police officers walked out, one of them holding a newspaper article and a photo. Hannah tilted her head to see it.

What the hell?

It was of her dad.

A moment later Sharon emerged, her usual pantsuit replaced by jeans and a T-shirt. Before Hannah could process what was happening, another person exited the office and spoke. 'Sharon, love, I'm so sorry you had to come in on a Sunday on account of me.'

Hannah's mouth went dry. She knew that voice like her own.

'Dad?' There was no volume behind the word. 'You're . . . you're alive?' Her body flushed with relief.

He gasped as he saw her, his eyes flooding with pain. He didn't have a chance to speak before one of the officers turned to him. 'Frederick Fife, you are under arrest for obtaining property by deception. You do not have to say or do anything but anything you say or do may be recorded and given in evidence. Do you understand?' The policeman placed a pair of handcuffs on the old man's wrinkled wrists.

'I'm sorry!' her dad cried, his eyes now heavy with tears. 'I'm so, so sorry, Hannah. I didn't think you'd be here for this.'

They began leading him away. 'Wait! Wait a second! What are you doing? What has he done? That's my father!'

Sharon whispered something to the officer and he gave Hannah a sympathetic look. 'I'm afraid he's not your father, madam.'

What on earth? She glared at him. His words sounded distant, like they were coming from a television, like they weren't happening.

'We'll be in touch.'

'It's all in the letter, Hannah – read the letter . . .' said Bernard, his voice cracking as he tried to wipe away a tear with his cuffed hands.

His voice trailed off and she watched in disbelief as they escorted him into the police car and drove away.

Hannah flinched as Sharon placed a hand on her shoulder.

'This must be an awful shock, Hannah. Would you like to take a seat in my office and we can talk things over? It's been a crazy morning. We found Carmel's stockpile of meds and poor Kathleen passed overnight. First the ambulance, now the police . . .'

'No, no. Sorry, I . . . I have to go,' she said, already walking away, her brain in overdrive. She needed to be alone.

Hannah collapsed on her bed, unable to remember the drive home. She wanted to clasp her knees to her chest, like she used to when she was little, but her baby bump was in the way. Had the cop actually said that Bernard wasn't her father? Had her mother had an affair? But why on earth would *he* be arrested for that? Her thoughts spiralled.

She clutched the envelope from her handbag and removed the letter with shaking hands.

Chapter 54

The decrepit plastic chair groaned as Fred shifted his weight. It was doing little for his aching rear end, though the pain in his bum was nothing compared to the pain in his heart. He placed his elbows on the scratched wooden table, etched with initials and sketches of certain things that Patricia could have drawn. What hardened criminals had sat here before him? Had their bottoms hurt as much as his? He rubbed his wrists, now mercifully uncuffed, and took a cautious sip of the lukewarm water he'd been offered, hoping his prostate would behave itself.

The hands of a cheap clock moved at what seemed like a snail's pace. A fluorescent light hung overhead, emitting an irritating buzz like a fly zapper. The opposite wall was one long mirror, but Fred had watched enough police shows to know that behind it there was likely an audience watching his every move. His heart skipped a beat. Had they heard him pass wind just before? Better not risk it a second time. On the other hand, what could they do? Sentence him extra for flatulence? He let one rip seconds before two police officers entered. Bugger. Not enough time for the room to clear. His face was on fire, probably making him look even more guilty.

He tried to make eye contact with the officers so he wouldn't look shifty. They were different to the young cops who had arrested him. A middle-aged brunette woman offered him a stern smile. She had what Hannah had taught him was called a 'pixie cut'. Next to her was a bald man around sixty, sporting a beard but no moustache. Fred tried to hide his disdain. To him, that was like choosing vanilla ice cream when you could have had chocolate. At least have both, mate.

The offending gas still lingered and he saw their nostrils twitching. He considered apologising but thought better of it and decided instead to play dumb. 'Those who smelt it dealt it' was one of the first English phrases Fred had taught Bruno.

'Hello, Mr Fife, I'm Senior Constable Shepherd, and this is Sergeant Walsh. We need to ask you a few questions today, please,' said the moustacheless man, sitting on one of the chairs opposite. 'Firstly, as my colleague said before, we do apologise about the handcuffs. They weren't necessary. A new officer on the job, bit overzealous.'

'No problem, I know they were just trying to do the right thing.'

'Right, let's begin then.' He switched on a recording device and stated the time and the names of everyone present before reading Fred his rights again.

'Can you please confirm that you are Frederick John Fife, born on the twenty-eighth of November 1940?'

'Yes, that's correct.'

'Do you understand that you have the right to have a lawyer present here today?'

'Yes. I'm okay on my own, thanks.'

'Is there anyone else you'd like to call?'

His mind drifted to Dawn, to Albert and to Hannah.

'My daughter . . . Sorry, I mean Hannah knows where I am. I don't have any other friends or family.' The truth of his words sliced deep. He didn't even have anyone to list as an emergency contact, so he'd just written '000' on the arrest paperwork.

'Do you understand why you've been arrested today?'

'Yes, I do. I was pretending to be someone else.' The words tasted ridiculous.

'I understand that you found the deceased, Mr Bernard Greer, on the fourteenth of April this year. Can you tell us in your own words what happened, please?'

Fred's eighty-two years hung heavily on his bones, his mind tired. He shut his eyes and could almost hear the river with its peaceful babble. Would he have done anything differently?

'Mr Fife? Are you okay? Do you need me to repeat the question?' Senior Constable Shepherd's deep voice reverberated through his thoughts.

'No, I'm okay. You are doing a great job, mate.'

Shepherd's unruly eyebrows furrowed for a moment before he cleared his throat.

Fred took a slow breath and explained his first meeting with Bernard at the river.

'Why did you try to wheel him back to the group rather than ask someone for assistance?'

The thought had never occurred to Fred. How different would his life have been if he'd done that?

'Mr Fife?'

'I don't know,' he said honestly. 'I guess I thought it was the fastest way to get help. I don't like to put people out.'

He told them about the seagulls and the fall, about the current taking the body and his wallet.

'And you said that is when the staff member,' Shepherd glanced down at his file, 'Denise Simms, saw you?'

'Yes, she must have seen me just after the body was out of sight. She thought I – well, Bernard – had fallen. She thought I was him from the start. As you know, we look remarkably alike.'

The constable pulled two photos out of the file, one of Fred, one of Bernard. His eyebrows shot up briefly as he compared them. 'I see.'

'And here's the thing, officers,' Fred continued. 'I did try to explain who I was, more than once. I . . . I . . .' Fatigue crashed over him.

'Denise meant well, I'm certain of that. She's a great carer. Please make sure you write that down.' He motioned to the officer's pen. 'She didn't listen to me at the river, but who can blame her? I gather Bernard had the beginnings of dementia towards the end. My head was also throbbing from the fall, so it was all a bit blurry.'

'So, you were taken back to Wattle River Nursing Home?'

'Yes. I nodded off on the bus and when I woke up, I was in Bernard's room.'

The interview dragged on as they went through every excruciating detail. He had to be excused for the toilet four times, and his bottom screamed for a cushion. Halfway through they offered him a stale cheese sandwich and some instant coffee, which he gratefully accepted.

He told them about trying to speak to the DON, about his attempt to leave, about Albert and Val and Denise. Talking about Hannah was the hardest. Fred could smell the shame emanating from his body, a charred ashy odour. The more he inhaled it, the harder it became to breathe. He told them about Dawn, about his dreams of the children that were never born. He spared them the details of Denise's drunken incident. That was her story to tell.

Finally, when Fred thought his bottom and hoarse throat could take no more, they said he could leave. He walked past another interview room and flinched as he saw Denise sitting at a table in tracksuit pants and a T-shirt. He'd never seen her in anything but her uniform. Fred caught her gaze and smiled but she didn't smile back, her eyes staring straight through him. His tummy twisted. What was she saying about him? Poor thing. He hoped she was finally getting the help she needed, and that this incident wouldn't affect her job in any way. She had enough to deal with.

'Don't leave the country now, will you?' Constable Shepherd placed a gentle hand on Fred's shoulder.

'Well, I had been planning to go to Las Vegas. Shall I put that off for a bit?' He tried to lift his lips into a smile, but they, like the rest of him, had the energy of a dead budgerigar. Like Bernard, he had gambled everything and lost.

Shepherd chuckled, then his face went serious. 'Do you have anywhere to go tonight, mate? Anyone you can call?'

Fred looked down at his feet, his cheeks flushing. 'Well . . . I haven't exactly figured that out.' The truth was he didn't have anyone. No friends or family to call upon. He'd considered trying to get in touch with Val, but he was too ashamed. She didn't need to be burdened with all this after what she'd been through. At least her last memory of him could remain intact. Hannah's laugh echoed in his ears, sending shrapnel through his body. He'd found yet another way of grieving a living person.

Shepherd shot Fred a sympathetic look. 'Take a seat here and we'll make a few phone calls, okay? I'll get you a cuppa.'

Tears pricked Fred's eyes, and he could only manage a grateful nod. He stared at the blank brick wall opposite him and breathed in the truth. It sat there now, big and full. The lie was gone, set free from the deep dark box he had kept it in. But the box hadn't disappeared, and it couldn't stay empty. It now filled rapidly with an even heavier and all-too-familiar grief and guilt, and he feared he might drown in it. He had imagined this moment many times. Of course, he'd known it would be awful, but he'd expected some relief, too. Yet the pain he was now causing Hannah was far worse than the shame of the lie, and his head ached with the rottenness of it.

'Mr Bernard?'

Fred looked up to see a wide-eyed Linh holding the hand of an equally wide-eyed Kevin.

The shame was suffocating, and he could barely make eye contact.

'It's Mr Fred, as it turns out,' he said quietly to his shoes.

'We heard,' said Kevin. 'They've brought us in for questioning. I don't really know what to say . . .'

'I'm sorry, I'm so sorry,' said Fred, wishing his stream of tears could wash him away. 'I never meant to hurt anyone.'

Constable Shepherd returned with a styrofoam cup of dark tea. 'You guys can go in now,' he said to Kevin and Linh.

The young couple began walking down the hall before Linh stopped, breaking free from Kevin's hand. She ran back and without a word ploughed into Fred, enveloping him in her small arms before rejoining Kevin. The gesture absolutely broke him. Would it be the last hug he'd ever receive? Kevin shot Fred a sympathetic wave before the two exited around the corner.

'Hey, Fred.' Constable Shepherd handed Fred the tea and a wad of tissues from a nearby side table. 'I've spoken to the Salvos, mate, and we've managed to find you a bed. You'll be able to stay there for a while, at least until we sort this out. I'll take you there now.'

Embarrassment pummelled his guts. Fred swallowed the lump in his throat, along with his pride. So this is what it had come to. Still, he didn't regret a single penny he'd spent trying to save his darling Dawn, even if it meant he would have to live on the street for the rest of his days.

Fred sculled the tea and took a seat in a police car for the second time that day. It was dark outside now and the black road glistened from the rain. They pulled up at a run-down building, yellow paint peeling off the brick facade. A man with bushy white sideburns wearing a crucifix around his neck was waiting outside. His tall frame and broad smile reminded Fred of Albert, providing him with some comfort.

The man stretched out a big, hairy hand. 'You must be Fred. I'm Brian. We'll look after you, mate.'

Fred shook his hand then turned to Constable Shepherd. 'Thank you for your time. I'm so sorry to have created this extra work for you.'

'Not a problem, mate. We'll be in touch soon.'

Brian ushered him inside down a long grey hallway to his room. It was better than a prison cell, but not by much. A narrow bed with a patchwork quilt stood in one corner next to a wooden chair and faded green card table. The scent of lavender air freshener lay heavy in the air. Fred tried not to think about what it might be covering up.

'Dinner was a couple of hours ago, but I'm sure I can rustle something up for you,' Brian said.

Fred's tummy growled on cue. 'Thank you, I'd really appreciate that, mate.'

Brian returned minutes later with a bowl of soup, toothbrush, jocks and some second-hand PJs.

'These might be a bit big, I'm afraid, but they'll keep you warm. Bathroom is down the hall to the right. Do you need anything else?'

'I'm fine. Thank you so much for your kindness. I'm ever so grateful.'

Brian nodded, closing the door behind him.

Fred placed the soup on the table. Its back leg was as wobbly as he was; he removed some of the tissues from his pocket and tucked them underneath to stabilise it. If only he could do the same for himself. The soup was watery but hot, and it warmed his aching bones.

He ate quickly and undressed. The pair of new, bright-white jocks was not unappreciated, but he would gladly have worn Bernard's old, stained ones for the rest of his life if it meant having more time with Hannah. Unfortunately, he hadn't received his dose of arthritis meds before he'd left, so his hands ached as he buttoned up the faded off-white PJs. They were more Albert's size than his, the pilled sleeves dangling well past his hands, like a child in a Halloween ghost costume. Bernard's pyjamas had been a perfect fit. His life, in many ways, had been a perfect fit; it had given Fred the daughter of his dreams.

He sighed and picked up the toothbrush, wandering down the creaky hall to the communal bathroom. It was small and old, much like the rest of the building. Cream tiles with yellowing grout covered the floor and walls. The smell of urine was unmistakably present, though that was nothing new. One of the three stalls was occupied. Fred hesitated. He didn't feel like being seen by anyone right now. But the door flew open, removing his opportunity to leave. A young man with a bleached mullet, eyebrow ring and blotchy skin emerged.

'Hello,' said Fred, offering a polite smile.

The young man sniffed loudly and threw him a dirty look before abruptly pushing past him, causing Fred to lose his balance. Tears nipped at his eyes as he gripped the basin for support, pleading with his reflection in the mirror to somehow take him away. But the mirror showed only a tired, useless and silly old man whose eyes had lost their spark, like those of someone with dementia. Losing his memory now would be a blessed relief – if he couldn't remember, he wouldn't know that he had once held the world and lost it. His mind searched in vain for the bright side, like his dear mum would have done, yet he couldn't seem to grasp it as darkness swallowed him whole.

He missed Dawn. He missed Albert. He missed Val. But most of all he missed Hannah. She had become his everything, and now she and the passenger were lost for good. Just like Dawn. Just like their baby.

Fred could barely bring himself to clean his teeth before wandering back to his room and burrowing underneath the thin patchwork quilt on the hard mattress. He shivered, unable to even warm up his side of the bed. The heat of the soup had worn off, leaving him exposed to the cold, lifeless room. A lifeless room for a lifeless soul.

And for the first time since the weeks after Dawn had passed away, Fred cried himself to sleep.

Chapter 55

To my dearest Hannah,

I am so sorry that I had to leave you in this way, but I had no other choice.

There is no easy way to say this, but I am not your father. I am not Bernard Greer. My real name is Frederick Fife.

The following is going to sound crazy, but every word of it is true.

I'm very sorry to say that your real dad died in April while on a nursing home outing. I was the first to find him in his wheelchair, just after he had passed, while I was out walking by Wattle River. I tried to wheel him back to the staff but there was an accident — I tripped and your dad's body, along with my wallet and ID, ended up falling in the water. He was taken away by the current.

Denise found me on the ground next to your dad's wheelchair, woozy from a bump on the head. She hadn't seen what had happened, so she assumed I was Bernard. She bundled me up and shortly after I ended up at the home.

Wasn't her fault, though. You might realise by now that my resemblance to your father is quite uncanny.

*I tried to tell everyone at the home that I was not him.
I tried many times. But no one would listen. Your old man had
early signs of dementia, so they thought I wasn't in my right
mind. I even tried to escape, to go back to my flat to get my ID,
but I was caught and returned to the home. Back then, even the
police didn't believe that I wasn't Bernard.*

*The thing is, when I found your father I was on the brink
of becoming homeless. My darling departed wife Dawn (she
would have loved you, Hannah) had a long battle with cancer,
and we poured all our money into her care, into experimental
treatments that sadly didn't work. When she died, I lost our
home and was forced to move into a rental. Things became
increasingly tight over the years with the medical debt, and the
day I found your dad, I had been told by my landlord I had to
be out of my flat that night.*

*So, after several attempts of setting the record straight
I just gave in, let people think I was Bernard. I was relieved
and thankful to have a place to stay and lovely food to eat
but, more than that, I was so grateful for the company. I'd
been so very lonely after Dawn passed. I am an only child
and all my friends have died too, so I had no one. When I met
Albert, he became such a great mate to me, as did Val. They
became my family, and I felt they needed me to keep an eye
out for them.*

*Even so, I constantly worried about what would happen
when your dad was found. But when he was, the police
identified him as me! They thought I was the one who had
died. It seemed like a miracle, a sign that maybe it was okay for
me to take his place, to borrow his life as it were. All the loose
ends had been tied up, or so I thought.*

Please believe me when I say that during that time, I didn't know you existed. I didn't know Bernard had any family. I kept up the charade because I assumed I wasn't hurting anyone.

Then I found your dad's last letter to you. Hannah, it's important that you know that it was ALL from him; he wrote every word of it but never got to post it because of his stroke later that same day. He also kept the pieces of the birdhouse and teacup this whole time. His letter broke my heart, and I felt in some way that I owed it to him to make sure you got his message.

Then you, darling Hannah, you came. While I never directly said I was your dad, I didn't try to correct anyone. I lied by omission. I thought about telling you so many times, but your company was such a gift to me that I selfishly kept the truth to myself. Dawn and I could never have children of our own, despite how much we desperately wanted to. When I met you, and got to know you – well, I just felt an inexpressible desire to be a good father to you, especially given what you went through in your early life.

Quickly, you became the most precious thing in the world to me. My love for you is as real as the ocean, and I will cherish every second we spent together for the rest of my life. You have no idea what I wouldn't give to be your real father, Hannah.

I know that none of this is an excuse for what I have done. I did an abominable thing, and I will live with the guilt of it until my dying day. While I never met your father when he was alive, I feel that over the past few months I have come to understand him a little. I know he was a troubled man with so many regrets. And I know his biggest regret was not reaching out to you sooner.

You will find out about this in his will, but some years ago your father won some very decent money, just before finally getting help with his gambling. He didn't trust himself so placed the money in an account that he couldn't access, to ensure it would all go to you when he passed. Please contact Andrew Mora (his lawyer) who will tell you everything – I've included his details below.

When I learnt this, I realised that I was in the way of you receiving your rightful inheritance, one that your dad desperately wanted you to have and that you so desperately need now with the baby coming. The guilt of my terrible cover-up has also become too great for me to bear. So, I have decided to make a full confession to the police. Thanks to a news article, I now have evidence that I am not Bernard, which I'll present to the police and Sharon in the morning.

I'm not sure what will happen to me now, but it doesn't matter. I am just so happy that I got to meet you, Hannah, and that for a brief time I got to be your dad. I don't expect you to ever forgive me. I know that by lying to you and leaving you, like Bernard did all those years ago, I have left you so much to deal with. Things will be terribly difficult for you, but I hope you can get the support you need. I know Kevin's sister is a great psychologist and I'm leaving her number in here for you, too.

You are so kind and gentle, and I think you'll make the loveliest of mums. With me gone, you won't ever have to worry about money again – you'll be able to buy a nice house for you and the passenger and be set up for life.

Before I say goodbye, please know that I love you and I never, ever meant to hurt you. I am truly so sorry.

Love from Fred x

Hannah barely made it to the toilet before violently throwing up whatever remained in her stomach. It was as if the shock was literally pouring out of her, yet the act brought no relief. She lay on the cold tiles and closed her eyes, but couldn't pretend she was dreaming: vomit didn't smell in dreams. She lay there for a long time, goose-bumps prickling her clammy skin.

Her belly ached with that hollowed-out sick feeling she'd had when Mum and Sadie died. Which made sense, because someone *had* died. In fact, it was almost like two people had died: her dad, whom she now realised with great sadness she had never truly known, and a man, a stranger, whom she had come to love and depend upon.

He was as good as dead, too.

Betrayal gripped her body, anger rising like hot air. How could he have done this? Did this mean that her real father had never changed? She remembered the day she had read his first letter, barely giving it a second glance as she stuffed it back into the envelope and scrawled 'Return to Sender' on the front. Why hadn't she gone to see him straightaway when he had reached out?

Was her forgiveness of Bernard even real? He had, according to Fred, written the apology letter. Rummaging in her bedside drawer, she pulled it out and read it again with the knowledge that her real father, the actual author of the letter, was dead. She wept and shook, gasping for breath as the room spun around her.

'Oh, Dad,' she said softly. 'I'm sorry. I'm so sorry you never had a chance to be forgiven.'

Chapter 56

Denise felt like scratching her eyes out. The hay fever combined with the alcohol withdrawal were a match made in hell. Her head throbbed in time to her foot, which nervously tapped the cracked ground.

'Mrs Simms, did you hear me?'

The officer's gaze bore into her. She scrunched her eyes tight and opened them again. 'Can you repeat the question, please?' Her concentration was shot.

'Did Frederick Fife try to identify himself at the time?'

Denise closed her eyes. Memories came in and out of focus, just out of reach.

'Yes,' she said slowly. 'It's a bit blurry now, but yes, he tried to tell me something. I didn't think anything of it as Bernard was always going on about one thing or another. Often didn't make sense. Never in my wildest dreams could I have imagined it was anyone other than him, though. I mean, what are the chances?'

If the officer thought anything, he didn't reveal it.

'He tried to tell me again at the home, but I thought he was just talking about himself in the third person. Dementia can do funny things to the mind.' She clasped her hands together, trying to still her shaking fingers.

'Did you ever notice anything to make you suspect he wasn't the same person?'

She'd been dreading this question.

'Yes, I did.'

'Such as?'

'Little things that didn't really add up.'

'What sort of things?'

'Well, he became sort of nicer, and continent again at night. Which is very unusual. I checked with the doctor if any meds had changed, but they hadn't.'

'Did you think of telling someone?'

'Well, I was about to but then he went back to . . .' she paused and narrowed her eyes, 'back to being incontinent.' An incredulous smile spread across her face as the penny dropped. Cheeky ratbag!

'In your opinion, did Frederick Fife actively set out to try and deceive people?'

She breathed deeply, ignoring her pounding skull. Had she been asked this question a few weeks ago, she knew her answer would have been different. But now . . .

'No, he did not. I believe that Fred tried to tell the truth but gave up after so many of us didn't believe him. He didn't know about Hannah or the money at the start. I don't think he intended any harm by befriending her, or anyone else. In fact, he went out of his way to help other people. So no, I don't think he set out to deceive.'

The officer nodded. 'In your own words, how would you describe Frederick Fife?'

Denise had not expected the wave of emotion that came next.

'He . . .' She choked on her words. 'He's the most decent man I've ever met.'

Chapter 57

The damp, scrunched tissues formed a halo around Hannah's pillow. She must have cried herself to sleep. She reached for Fred's letter and read it again slowly, her disbelief still unshakable.

Her eyes came to focus on the red-and-white object glaring at her from the open-mirrored wardrobe. The birdhouse. They'd never got around to hanging it. She climbed out of bed and picked it up, rubbing her hands over the surface as she had done all those years ago. How could he think that leaving was the answer? That his absence would make things better?

That money meant more than love?

She frowned at her reflection. Was she talking about Bernard or Fred? How was it that two men, so different, had ended up doing the same thing to her?

She shut the birdhouse in the cupboard and returned to the letter, glancing at the lawyer's phone number written across the bottom. May as well get it over and done with.

After a strong coffee, several trips to the bathroom and a lot of pacing, she called the number and was asked by a perky secretary to come in later that morning.

👓

The modern black-leather couch in Andrew Mora's office had obviously been chosen for style, not comfort. Hannah shifted uneasily, the bubbly mineral water the receptionist had given her doing little to settle her churning stomach.

A short, greying man who had gone a tad too heavy on the aftershave that morning entered the room.

'You must be Hannah. Andy Mora,' he said, extending his hand. 'We've actually met before, but a very long time ago when you were about yea high.' He motioned to his waist, which was not high, flashing a smile flecked with gold fillings.

'Hi. I can't say I remember, sorry. So you knew my father?' She swallowed a burp just before it escaped.

'Yeah, for over forty years, in fact. And I've just been brought up to speed on what's happened,' he said, running his hands through his once-black hair. 'I cancelled all my other appointments this morning, of course. Talk about a plot twist! Strewth. You just wouldn't read about it, would you?' He stared out the window at the city street below like he was looking at a mystical creature. Exhaling loudly, he turned back to Hannah. 'Anyway, how are *you*?'

'Numb. Confused. Angry. All of the above.' She'd promised she wasn't going to let herself cry.

'No wonder. I was gobsmacked when I found out this morning.' He shook his head, pacing the room. 'The resemblance is uncanny! The other bloke – Fred, isn't it? – I saw him just last week, but I didn't think for a second he wasn't Bernard. I mean, something about his vibe was a bit off, but I just put it down to the dementia. When he rang to tell me the truth this morning, I thought he had a few kangaroos loose in the top paddock, gone troppo, if you know what I mean. But the manager of the home called me straight after and said it was all true.'

Andrew's tummy let out a loud gurgle. 'Sorry, I haven't had breakfast. Do you mind?' He motioned to a couple of sausage rolls on his desk.

Hannah shook her head.

'You know, it was pretty decent of Fred to call me himself,' he said, popping a squeezy pack of tomato sauce on a sausage roll and taking a big bite. 'He wanted to double-check you would be looked after. It's all just unbelievable, really, like a movie plot or something!'

Hannah sighed, taking little solace from the fact that she wasn't the only one who had been fooled.

'Anyway, I suppose you are wanting to hear about the will and whatnot?'

She nodded, wishing Fred was there to hold her hand and hating him at the same time.

'Right, well, it's a pretty simple one. As you probably know by now, your dad had a history of gambling.' Andrew sat down at his desk and removed some papers from a file.

She nodded again.

'Well, about twenty years ago, he had a massive win. And some-how, despite his addiction, he had the strength to arrange that the money – every cent of it, mind you – be put into a trust account that could only be accessed with my consent. The poor bugger abso-lutely hated himself by this point. Hated what he did to you and your mum after your sister died. I'm sorry about that, by the way.'

He paused, a flake of pastry falling from his downturned mouth.

'At the time, I asked him why he didn't just track you down and give you the money straightaway, but he couldn't bring himself to contact you back then. And besides, he doubted you'd even accept it. So he made me swear on my life, and even put in writing, that I wasn't to release the money to him no matter what. He wanted it all to go to you, and only after he died.' He wiped a stray dab of tomato sauce from his already stained green tie.

'Then, back in November, I got a call from Bernard's sponsor saying that your old man had been trying to gamble again.'

Hannah bowed her head. 'That's when he first tried to contact me. And I sent his letter back.'

Andy grimaced and shrugged his shoulders. 'Yeah. He did mention something about that, actually. I think he'd lost all hope of reconnecting with you by then. But don't feel bad, love. I wouldn't have wanted to see him either, after the number he pulled on you.'

She rubbed her neck. Was the guilt she was feeling now even an iota of what Fred was feeling?

'Anyway, so when he, I mean Fred, reached out to me last week saying he'd met you and wanted the money, I didn't believe him. I genuinely thought he was having me on so he could gamble. Addiction is a horrible thing; it can turn good blokes into monsters.' He looked apologetically at her. 'Sorry, I know you know that.'

'It's okay,' she said, as an image of her real father's pained eyes crashed over her.

'So, let's get down to it. You inherit the rest of his super, which is just over two hundred grand.'

Her heart skipped a beat. She drank the last of her water, but it did little to quench her dry mouth. Two hundred grand! That would help a lot. 'Wow!'

'Oh, no, that's nothing,' Andy said, shaking his head and pulling out another document. 'The term deposit account is also entirely for you. Including the interest it has accrued over twenty years, it comes to one million seven hundred thousand and forty-eight dollars. And fifty cents.'

The room began to spin. Had she heard right?

'Sure you don't want a sausage roll?' Andy asked.

She shook her head, grasping the arm of the couch so hard that her knuckles turned white.

He filled a glass from the water cooler and handed it to her. 'It's a lot to take in.'

She sculled the cool water, grateful it was still. She didn't need any more bubbles in her rapidly boiling mind. Had she really just been told she was going to be a millionaire?

'If I may, Hannah,' said Andy, taking a seat beside her, 'I want to tell you a bit about your old man. He was a friend as well as a client, you see, a golf buddy of mine. Even though we weren't as close recently, I knew him well back in the day.'

She took a tissue from the coffee table, pre-empting her need for it.

'He wasn't a bad bloke, Hannah. Just a very broken one who ended up on a rotten path. He couldn't deal with your sister's illness or her death, and rather than getting help, as I tried to persuade him to do, he buried himself in his addiction.' Andy gazed out the window. 'His old man was an alcoholic – did you know that?'

She shook her head, frowning. She'd never met Grandpa Leonard; he'd died before she was born.

'Bernard did finally get help in the end, though. Before his sponsor called me recently, he'd been clean for ten years. He could have easily spent that jackpot on himself, but he didn't. Do you know he lived very meagrely after he left you? Had a dingy little flat near the freeway and would eat spaghetti on toast and that god-awful tinned meat.' He shuddered as if tasting it now.

'He wouldn't spend anything on himself. Felt too guilty, I think. It was like he was punishing himself. One time he came to see me and the soles were literally falling off his shoes, but he refused to get new ones. To be honest I reckon he stopped buying deodorant in the end, too.' He scrunched his nose, smelling the memory. 'The only places he couldn't resist spending were at the track and the slots, but whenever he could be strong enough, he'd put his winnings straight into that term deposit account. He'd send me the cheques directly with little Post-it notes on them that said, "For Hannah". In fact, I've still got one of them here.' He removed a yellow square and handed it to her.

Hannah brought it up to her face, a tear falling onto her name in her father's handwriting. She closed her eyes, information swirling in her brain. Almost two million freakin' dollars! It was life-changing. Her money troubles were over not just for now, but forever. The baby kicked and she placed her hand on her belly. The little one was going to be okay now, too. Financially, at least.

'He loved you, you know. Your dad . . . I wish he'd had the balls to reach out to you before it was too late.' Andy passed her another tissue.

Hannah tried to catch her breath in between the sobs. 'He wrote me a letter, explaining it all. I-I thought he was alive at the time, of course. I forgave him . . . not just because of the letter, but also because he seemed so different, so kind. That kindness was just Fred, I guess. If I had only got the letter in the mail and not seen him, not met him again, I-I don't know that I would have forgiven him.'

'Maybe you needed Fred to help you forgive your father?' Andy suggested gently.

The thought hung in the air, too surreal to grasp.

'I don't know. I really don't know. And now . . . well, now I'm just so hurt, and I feel so betrayed – again! I mean, what kind of person pretends to be someone else? Pretends to be your father?' The anger rose again, warming her face.

'A desperately lonely man, perhaps? The thing is, Fred didn't come off as a con artist to me. He seemed like a genuine, decent bloke who wanted the best for you.'

Hannah pinched the bridge of her nose. 'I just don't know what to believe anymore. I need some time to get my head around all of this.' She wiped her eyes. 'Anyway, thank you so much for your time today, Andy.'

'You're welcome, love. Don't forget to leave your details with Louella at reception. And look, I apologise if I've overstepped. I am very sorry for your loss . . . for both of them.'

She sighed. 'No, I appreciate it. It's kind of nice to talk to someone who knew my real dad, seeing as I never did.' She rose to leave.

'I'm glad I had a chance to tell you how much he loved you. And do you know what?' Andy said, as she reached the door. 'I don't know Fred, but I really got the feeling he adores you as well.'

She bit her lip and walked out. How could she respond to that? The elevator ride down was slower than her thoughts, which zipped along at lightning speed. She was now a millionaire – she should be happy, right? But she couldn't shake the feeling that she had lost much more than she had gained.

The money was a fortune, but having a dad was priceless.

Chapter 58

The hot-pink umbrella was useless. Hannah couldn't feel the rain on her numb skin. She threw it down, unopened, next to the daisies around Sadie's grave, and knelt on the damp grass. Ignoring the water seeping into her maternity jeans, she opened the gold heart locket that hung around her neck so she could see her sister's face. Removing her father's final letter from her pocket, she read it for the twelfth time, knowing now it was his last words to her.

> . . . *I'm sorry you got stuck with me as a father. I'm sorry I never knew how to love you like you should have been loved. I'm sorry I broke your birdhouse. So, so sorry. And I'm sorry I never said goodbye.*
>
> *I hope you get to live a good life, Hannah, a happier one than I did. Make the most of every opportunity life gives you, and please stay kind. You and Sadie were the kindest people I ever met. Goodbye, Han, I love you so much.*
>
> *Love,*
>
> *Dad*

She rested her fingers on his name and placed her other hand on the grass in front of the tombstone where Sadie lay six feet below, buried with her favourite teddy and a piece of the purple teacup.

With shaking breath, she said the words that had been trapped deep inside her for so long: 'I forgive you too, Daddy.'

Chapter 59

Fred picked a stray crumb of toast out of his teeth, the bitterness from this morning's cup of Nescafé lingering in his mouth. After three nights at the shelter he was lonelier than ever. He'd tried to initiate small talk with some of the other men, but they had all been abrupt and closed off.

He sighed, flipping through an old magazine he'd found in the common room. The crossword had already been done and he had no interest in reading about celebrities, so he shut it, burying his face in his hands. He couldn't make any plans until he heard the outcome of the investigation. It was obvious he couldn't pay a fine, so he supposed that prison was his only option. Would they let him do the crossword there? They probably didn't do roast dinners in jail, let alone dessert.

'Fred?' Brian stood at the doorway, wearing a fluoro T-shirt and an even brighter smile.

'G'day, Brian.'

'I just got a call from the police station – they want you to go down there this morning. I'll drive you.'

Fred's stomach tightened. 'Oh, okay. Thank you. I don't suppose they gave you any inkling of what's happening, did they?'

''Fraid not, mate. You must be nervous, hey?' Brian placed a big hand on Fred's shoulder.

Nervous was an understatement. He'd never expected to be facing prison at his age. 'Well, let's get it over and done with, hey?'

The bum-numbing chair was even less comfortable than last time. Two sirens blared outside, competing for which could be the most irritating. Crikey! Was one of them there to take him away?

Constable Shepherd and the other one, whose name Fred couldn't recall, appeared at the door.

'Mr Fife. Thanks for coming in. How are you?'

'Oh, a little anxious, if I'm honest,' he said, forgetting about the pain in his bottom.

'Well, I've got some very good news. Hannah has been in contact with us, and she doesn't plan to press charges. Although the money you spent living at the home was rightfully hers, she doesn't wish to take things any further. We know that you didn't have the intent to steal or deceive. All the staff put in a very good word for you. You were quite popular there, it seems.'

A gush of oxygen filled Fred's lungs as his mouth scrambled to find words.

'So . . . so, I'm not going to jail?'

'No, mate, you're not.'

He exhaled and accidentally passed wind simultaneously.

'Oh, goodness, I'm so sorry. I'm just so relieved.'

They both laughed, and even the stern female officer cracked a smile.

'So, we are going to take you back to Brian and he's going to get the social worker to figure out your next steps, okay?'

Fred couldn't stop nodding. 'Yes. Gosh. Thank you, thank

you so much.' He stood up, shaking both of their hands with his clammy palm.

'Oh, and you might want this back.' He handed Fred a faded, brown leather object.

'My wallet!' Fred exclaimed.

'We found it, you know, with Bernard. Seems like he looked after it for you. Anyway, good luck, Fred. You're one of the nicest criminals we've met.' And with a wink the constable turned and left.

Fred's hands trembled as he opened the warped, leather wallet, discoloured from water damage. Dare he hope to find what he was looking for? Would it be intact? After a minute of searching through odd coins and cards, he found his driver's licence, and there behind it was his Dawn, her beauty radiating through the laminated photo, undisturbed by her journey down the river. Bernard had taken care of her then, and perhaps he was now too. He brought the photo to his lips and kissed it, his voice cracking as the tears fell. 'Oh, my Dawnie, what am I supposed to do now?'

Soon Fred was in the back of a police car again, siren blissfully off. As they came to a stop at some traffic lights, he stared out the window at a young father and daughter who sat on a bench eating ice cream. The little girl was speaking animatedly to her dad, waving her hands about. The look in her eyes said that he was her everything.

How he wished that things could have been different. That Hannah could have been his and Dawn's from the start. That she could have existed as that baby in Dawn's womb, that he could have come home in time to stop the miscarriage, and that Dawn could have held Hannah in her arms. That they could have seen her first steps, been there when she fell over at the playground, when she woke up on Christmas morning. That he'd been there to guide her, to love her, to tell bad boyfriends where they could shove it.

That he'd never had to pretend he was her dad.

Hannah dropping the charges had come as a relief, but not as a surprise. He knew her well enough now to know that despite any anger she felt towards him, she would get no joy from sending him to jail. He acknowledged, though, that it didn't mean forgiveness.

The little girl's ice-cream scoop fell to the ground and, without missing a beat, the dad transferred his scoop to her cone.

Fred sighed. If only he had one more opportunity to do the same for Hannah.

Back in his room at the shelter, Brian came to see him.

'I just heard the good news. It's been a big day for you, Fred. I've made an appointment with the social worker for tomorrow. Just take it easy today, okay? I've got some morning tea and the paper for you, mate.' He handed over a cup of coffee with two Choc Ripple biscuits and a copy of the newspaper.

'Yes, it's amazing news. Thanks, Brian, I'm ever so grateful.'

He downed the frothless coffee but left the biscuits untouched, keeping his promise to Hannah that he'd lay off sugar with her before the birth. Perhaps it was silly in light of the destruction he'd caused, but this was one small thing that could remain intact, that didn't have to be broken. Though she'd never know, it was a tiny scrap of integrity to which he could cling. And that meant something to Fred. He flipped through the paper to find the crossword and instead found a notice in a small, neat box.

FUNERALS

Bernard Greer

28/03/1940 – 14/4/2023

Father of Hannah and Sadie Greer.

Funeral to be held at St. Luke's Church

Tuesday 21st November at 10 a.m.

A ball of sadness clumped in his gut. The surrounding notices said 'loving father' or 'devoted mother'. The lack of an adjective for Bernard stuck out like a sore thumb. Surely he deserved an adjective? Fred sighed. What would *his* adjective be when he died? Not that there would be anyone in his life now who cared to write one.

He glanced back at the paper, wondering if anyone would notice the gap between Bernard's death and funeral. His stomach flipped as he thought about the body. Poor Bernard Greer had already been buried as Frederick Fife; he hoped they wouldn't dig the poor bugger up and rebury him. The old boy deserved to rest in peace.

Perhaps his story would make the news? The shame of it all was lessening now. He was past the point of caring what people thought of him. That was like a stubbed toe, completely overridden by the burst appendix of losing Hannah. It wasn't just the loss of their relatively brief past but the loss of their future. He reached into his pocket and removed a woollen item, the only thing he'd taken with him from the home: a pale-yellow beanie he'd made for the grandchild he would never meet. He brought it to his nose and inhaled. He could almost smell the future he had lost. Its scent made him struggle to breathe.

Fred's own ice-cream scoop had fallen, and there was no one to comfort him, or replace it for him.

Chapter 60

The day of the funeral rained solidly, just as it should have for Sadie's. The wooden pew beneath Hannah was just as uncomfortable as it had been thirty-three years ago when they'd laid her sister to rest. The scent of white lilies from the front of the small church would normally be pleasant, but today it was nauseating. She glanced out at the inky clouds, heavy with sorrow, trying to sift through her tangled emotions. She was racked with grief, that was for sure. The problem was she didn't really know whom she was grieving.

Someone coughed, and she turned around, taking in the pathetic smattering of people who had shown up. A couple of old colleagues, the lawyer and some of her father's cousins whom she barely recognised. It had, after all, been decades since she'd seen them, though she had made contact this week over the phone.

'Hi, Hannah.' A tall man with white hair and dark eyes waved at her from the pew behind. 'You probably don't remember me. I'm Stephen, your dad's cousin. We spoke on the phone last week? This is my wife, Marjorie,' he said, motioning to the well-dressed woman beside him.

Hannah forced her lips into a smile. 'Hi. Thanks for coming.'

'You know, I was just trying to remember when I last saw your dad. At least ten years ago, I think.'

Hannah blinked as a bit of spit flew from his mouth.

'I didn't realise he'd moved to a nursing home. I feel bad; I would've visited if I'd known. I was just telling Marj that I actually borrowed some money from him that last time, if I recall correctly. He always used to joke he'd come back to haunt me if I didn't pay him back. Hope that isn't true!'

He smirked as Hannah wiped another flick of saliva from her cheek.

'He was a funny guy, your dad.'

Her fake smile slid away. How the hell would she know? Organ music filled the room, giving her an excuse to turn back around. Thank god.

'Anyway, we'll chat after,' whispered Stephen.

The music swept over her, the notes carrying a painful memory of Sadie's funeral. Hannah opened the gold locket and gazed into her sister's eyes. She held the order of service with her young father's photo next to it, so her sister and dad were side by side. At least in some way he could be here now for Sadie, even though he was over three decades late.

It seemed strange that she was the one to organise the funeral, to give the eulogy, seeing that her father had practically been a stranger to her. She'd doubted her decision to hold it in a church, but it seemed like the obvious choice. And who knew what he believed in the end, about heaven and second chances? There was no coffin; he'd already been buried in one, as Fred. It was easier to just change the tombstone.

Hannah frowned. Had anyone gone to "Fred's" funeral? Had he even had one?

She looked over at the large, more recent photo of her father that had been placed on a stand next to the beautiful white floral arrangement. Her heart fluttered. The resemblance between the two men she'd called 'Dad' was indeed astounding.

A priest stepped up to the pulpit. After an initial welcome and a hymn that Hannah pretended to sing along to, it was time for her to speak.

Writing the eulogy had not been easy – there was so much about her father that she didn't know. She'd tried to piece something together from the scraps she'd learnt from his cousins, the lawyer and old photo albums.

She walked to the microphone, feeling even more uncomfortable than she'd been on the hard pew. Looking out at the small congregation, she cleared her throat.

'Thank you all for coming today to mourn the loss of my father. Bernard Phillip Greer was born on the twenty-eighth of March, 1940, in Sydney, to parents Leonard and Mary. An only child, he grew up in Beecroft and attended the local primary and secondary schools there, before moving to Wattle River. He got a job in advertising and worked at Birch and Hargraves for nearly fifty years.' How he'd been able to keep his job, Hannah didn't know.

'He married my mum, Mary Morris, in 1970, and they had two daughters, Sadie and myself.' She lowered her head. 'Sadie passed away from leukaemia when she was twelve. The loss hit Dad hard and, sadly, he and Mum separated. Dad lived in a nursing home for the last few months of his life.' She'd decided to spare the meagre crowd the sordid details of the more unsavoury chapters of her father's life. What was the point in sharing them now?

'So, what can I say about my dad . . .?'

She looked at her note cards. The internet had told her that a good eulogy doesn't just give a life history, but also talks about what the person was like. But Hannah hadn't been able to formulate any words for this part of the speech. Her decision to wing it didn't seem like such a good idea now.

'My dad . . .' she said, her heart beating through her chest. Her mind was blank. 'My dad . . .' she tried again, hoping that starting the sentence would help her finish it. She sighed, her face getting hotter by the minute. Should she fake labour? Someone coughed again as the tiny sea of eyes stared at her.

The rear door of the church creaked open, and she glanced up to see who the latecomer was. Her heart skipped a beat.

It was *him*.

It was *Fred*.

He slunk quickly into the back pew with an apologetic look on his face. A fresh wave of emotion erupted within her, an odd concoction of anger and longing. What on earth was he doing here? She cleared her throat, flipping through her notecards with trembling hands. She had to keep going.

'My dad was . . .' She tried to refocus and put Fred out of her mind, but her gaze was drawn to him like a magnet. 'My dad . . .' Her eyes locked on his and the words began to flow.

'My dad . . . he taught me how to play chess.'

Fred stared back at her, his eyes widening.

'He loved his food, especially sweets, and eating was like a sport for him . . .'

A small chuckle hummed from the audience.

'Though when I had to give up sugar for the baby, he did too. That was just the sort of person he was. The kindest, most grateful, most marvellous man I've ever met. He had time for everyone and always tried to brighten someone's day, no matter who they were. He always put other people before himself and made them feel special. He made *me* feel special. His sense of humour was second to none and he always knew how to make me laugh. What I wouldn't do to hear his laugh again.' Her voice cracked as she gasped through shaky breaths. 'He taught me . . . that love – that *true* love – is unconditional, no matter what you do, or what your name is. He was the sort of dad a little girl dreams about.'

The tears were coming so fast now that she had to stop speaking. The minister passed her a tissue, and she mumbled a quick 'Thank you' into the microphone before taking her seat.

It took every bit of willpower to stay there: there was only one place she wanted to go. As soon as the last hymn was sung, she swung around, scanning the back pew, but he was gone. She rushed down the aisle, past the startled cousins and colleagues, not caring if she was being rude.

Fred had helped her to forgive her dad, and in some strange way she felt her dad was helping her to forgive Fred. She now knew with absolute certainty whom she was grieving. And unlike her father, buried deep below ground, she could get him back.

Fred hobbled down the steep stone steps. He shouldn't have come today. He'd only wanted to creep in unnoticed to pay his respects to Bernard; he'd never intended to bother Hannah. When he saw her crying, he panicked and left. Had he just made things worse?

He recalled her words – surely just his silly old imagination playing tricks on him? But it had sounded like she was talking about him. *Could* she have been talking about him? A whisper of hope rustled in his soul, but his brain didn't dare let him believe it. He didn't want her to feel like she owed him anything.

'*Dad!*'

The word grasped his heart with such force that he could barely stay standing. He turned to see a tear-stained Hannah running out of the church. Instinctively he looked behind him, just as he had at the river that day when Denise had first called him Bernard. This time, though, the name felt one hundred per cent right. He knew deep in his heart that *he* was Dad, even if he wasn't Bernard – that it was possible to be both *Fred* and *Dad*.

'Dad! Wait!' Hannah ploughed into his arms, almost knocking him over. The grief and the guilt and the love erupted from his heart and eyes. Fred held her tight, patting her curly hair as she wept.

'Oh, love, it's okay – it's okay, now.' He glanced up at the sky. The rain had finally stopped, as if he and Hannah had taken on its tears. 'Why don't we go for a walk, hey?'

She nodded and they both looked up to see a white-haired man exiting the church.

'Hi, Stephen,' said Hannah, wiping her eyes.

'Thank you, Hannah dear, that was a lovely service. Your dad would have liked it.' He patted her shoulder and then looked at Fred. 'Hello, we haven't met, I'm a cousin of Ber . . . Ber . . . Bernard!?' The colour drained from his face.

'Good Lord!' he shrieked. Trembling, he took a few steps backwards, grabbed Marjorie's arm and made a mad dash to his car. He threw a handful of something out the window as they sped off.

Whatever it was fluttered slowly to their feet. Three 100-dollar bills.

'That was Dad's cousin,' said Hannah. 'He owed Bernard money.'

They looked at each other for a moment, then burst out laughing.

Chapter 61

Sunlight peeped through the clouds and illuminated Bernard's headstone, shooing away the last trace of frost from the air. Hannah picked a bit of lint off her black maternity dress. The handful of people who'd attended the funeral had left and Hannah and Fred sat side by side, sipping takeaway cappuccinos from a nearby cafe. An unexpected laugh escaped her, breaking the silence.

'Well, I certainly didn't expect to be in this situation.' She took a deep breath, savouring the kind of relief that only comes after a big cry. A weight had lifted, bringing a deliciously light sense of freedom.

'Neither did I,' Fred smiled, staring at the grave where he'd once supposedly been buried.

Hannah turned to face him, taking him in. 'So, were you really going to be homeless?'

'Well, yes.' He stared off into the distance, his blue eyes filled with memories. 'But in all honesty, I was homeless long before I came to the nursing home.'

'What do you mean?'

'My wife Dawn was my true home, you see, and after she died . . . Well, nothing ever felt like home again. I was so lonely.' His eyes met hers. 'Until I met you, that is.'

Hannah looked at him, studying his every detail like a mother seeing her newborn baby for the first time. This man who was not her father, not even a relative, but someone whom she had inexplicably grown to love with all her heart.

Fred took her hands in his, holding them as if he'd never held anything so valuable.

For a second she pretended he was Bernard, her throat burning with a mixture of reflux and guilt. 'I . . . I was too late for him,' she said, grief snatching her breath. 'I was so incredibly hurt, so angry, for so many years. I didn't think he deserved a second chance.'

'Well, maybe he didn't. But you did give him one, only by some stroke of fate, it was me that got that chance. And for that I'm so very grateful.' Fred gazed at the headstone and took a deep breath. 'Hannah, I feel like over the last few months I've developed a strong sense of your dad. I've walked in his shoes, quite literally. I've even taken his medication, some of which was very unpleasant!'

Her eyebrows shot up. Jeepers, he must have wanted to stay very badly.

He chuckled and leaned closer. 'Anyway, what I'm trying to say is I know for certain your dad did love you. That he was truly sorry for the way things went, and that he wanted you to be happy. That will wasn't made recently – he made it decades ago. He's loved you his whole life. You were always his Han, the most precious thing in the world to him – even though he couldn't show it.'

'I know,' she whispered. 'I know.'

'And, Hannah, I think he understands, somehow,' he said, his voice raw with emotion. 'Your dad knows you've forgiven him.'

She exhaled a shaky breath, her eyes swimming with fresh, warm tears.

'Anyway, love, I'm so thankful that I could see you again and that we could talk. I'm truly sorry, Hannah. I never, ever meant to hurt you. I do truly hope there are no hard feelings? The social worker is setting me up in a housing-commission flat, so I'll have a place to live. Don't give a second thought to me, sweetheart. I'll be right as rain.' His wet eyes were like a watercolour painting swirled with kindness and sadness.

Panic rose within her, and she grabbed his hand. 'Don't you dare bolt on me! I can't lose you again!'

'Oh, Hannah, my darling girl,' he said, lips trembling. 'I don't want to bolt. My whole world has been spinning since my Dawnie passed, everything's been blurry and nonsensical. You . . . you've made it all clear again. I want to stand still with you and never let go.'

Hannah looked directly into the eyes of the man who had taught her what love was. 'You will have a new home, but it's going to be with me . . . Dad.' She touched her belly. 'And with her.'

Fred's eyes grew two sizes as tears navigated their way down his crinkled cheeks. He was silent for a minute before stammering, 'No, no, I couldn't possibly intrude on you like that. I'd be such a burden.'

She sniffed. 'Fred, you have to understand that meeting you, getting to know you,' she paused, placing her hand on his soft cheek, 'and loving you, well, it was the greatest gift my dad could ever have given me. You are the dad that he desperately wanted to be, but never could be. You are who I always wanted, who I always waited for as a little girl. And now – now that you are finally here – I am picking you up and never, ever putting you down again.'

Neither of them made any attempt to hold back the crying now, letting the tears fall freely.

Fred moved closer. 'You know, when Dawn died, when her heart stopped beating, I just assumed that mine would too. I wanted it to – so many days I wanted it to. But it didn't. I just couldn't understand how a heart so broken could go on beating. And I never understood why – until now. It was so I could love you. You've given me a reason to live, Hannah.'

Hannah threw herself into Fred's arms, and breathed in his scent. He no longer smelt like the sandalwood of the past, but of a new and even better fragrance: home. When they finally let go, both of their shirts were wet.

Fred removed a tissue from his pocket. 'Are you sure you can handle another crybaby alongside her?' He motioned to her belly.

'Make that three crybabies,' she laughed, pointing to herself. 'I think we'll make the perfect family. Let's go home – I've got some leftover sugar-free lamingtons if you're hungry?'

'That sounds wonderful. I'll meet you at the car in a tick. I just need a moment with your old man.'

Hannah took a few steps towards the parking lot, then stopped and turned back. 'I almost forgot,' she said, placing something on her father's grave.

Fred smiled and nodded at her before she left.

Fred beamed at the ultrasound photo resting on Bernard's grave, taking it all in. Like Bernard, he had won the lottery, though not once, but twice. His darling Dawn, the permanent resident of his heart, finally had company. It didn't matter now that he hadn't come home sooner that dreadful night, because he was home now. Their daughter had finally arrived safely. Like water bursting from a cracked dam, he finally felt Dawn's forgiveness, too, though it had been there all along.

He looked at the final resting place of the man who had given him this incomprehensible gift, for it was through Bernard's death that Fred had been brought back to life.

'Thank you, mate. Thank you so much for letting me borrow your life,' he said, placing his hand gently on the headstone. 'I promise I'm going to take marvellous care of them both – just you wait and see.'

As he turned to leave, a lone scruffy seagull landed on the grave and let out a resounding squawk.

Epilogue

Fred sat on a sun-dappled porch, a large mug of cappuccino warming his fingers. Three Iced VoVos beckoned to him from their mosaic plate. A shy breeze brushed his cheek as a curly-haired toddler giggled in her highchair.

'Peekaboo!' said Hannah, uncovering smiling eyes brimming with love for her daughter. 'This came for us,' she said, handing Fred a white embossed card.

He couldn't wipe the grin off his face. It was Kevin and Linh's wedding invitation.

Hannah beamed. 'I thought you'd like that. Val called too; she's coming over tomorrow for a haircut.'

'Excellent! I'll be able to show her the tiny pink cardigan I made. Only missed one row this time!' He winked.

Hannah turned to her daughter. 'Mummy's just going to get your sippy-cup. You stay out here with Granddad,' she said, patting Fred's shoulder as she rose to go inside the house; *their* house. Fred hadn't just found a place to live, somewhere to merely exist – he'd found a place to love, and to be loved. He would never be homeless again.

He reached up and squeezed Hannah's hand, meeting her gaze as they both looked over to the precious girl, taking in her chubby legs, her perfect dimples, her fabulous eyebrows, her sparkling eyes. Dawn Sadie Greer, his glorious granddaughter. Fred's heart overflowed. He spooned the chocolatey foam from his mug into her sticky little mouth.

'You, my darling, are the froth on my cappuccino.'

Acknowledgements

They say to 'write what you know'. It may, therefore, be rather alarming that my book has so many references to prostates. That aside, if there is one thing I do know, it is love – and it is for this reason that I was able to write this story.

The writing and publication of this novel saw the spectacular merging of my dreams and reality. It's been a journey guided by the love, encouragement and expertise of so many remarkable individuals, and I am grateful to each one for shaping this book into what it is today.

Firstly, to my dearly departed grandparents and precious friends Dawn and Fred Parkes, my beloved Nan and Pa and the seed of inspiration for this story. Thank you for everything. How I wish you could have read this book! I've spent a long time thinking about what attracted multiple people around the world to publish this story and strive to see it on screen. I have come to the conclusion that somehow, your love got into my keyboard and onto the page. Your selflessness, optimism and lifelong adoration of each other – even through health battles, nursing-home care and dementia – inspired all who met you. Your remarkable relationship is a testament to the beauty of lasting marriage, and you breathed life into the characters and stories of Fred, Dawn, Albert and Val. Pa, you not only inspired me as a wordsmith (you would have been the ultimate proofreader!) but taught me the power of kindness, integrity and gratitude. Even the Fred in these pages cannot capture what an utterly delightful human being you were.

To my incredible family. Christine and Nigel Rosen, I truly won the jackpot with parents like you. Growing up, I believed that all love is unconditional – because it's all I ever knew. Your unwavering belief in me and my writing lifted me to a place I never thought possible. Thank you for being among my first readers and sounding-boards throughout the entire process, and for all the practical help that allowed me time to write. To my siblings, Jenni Sanderson and Dave Rosen, I've always admired your fearlessness with every endeavour, and when you touched the stars you inspired me to reach for them too. To Kim, Suzanne, Kate, Ben, Bear and Ayla, thank you for your constant enthusiasm along the way. I love you all so much. Special thanks to Kim for speed-reading when fresh eyes were needed at the last-minute! To my extended family – aunts, uncles, cousins, in-laws, nieces, and nephews – thank you for your support, especially to my lovely great-aunt Wendy (sister/sister-in-law of the real Dawn and Fred). To my late, great-grandfather Michael Morris and paternal grandparents Dulcie and Eric Rosen, the privilege of knowing you for so many years led to my love of working with – and eventually writing about – older people.

To the amazing women in my life who never doubted me, and whose friendship keeps me afloat: Eliza Wilson, Georgia Finlayson, Katie Clark, Tania Rusbridge, Laura Parkes, Sarah Malla, Andrea Pearce, Alice Bannan, Amy Lee, Mel Cassidy, Rita Whyte, Narda McCarthy, Jill Devlin, Belinda Grant, Debbie Keyt, Georgy Charles and Esther Blatt. Special thanks to Tania, for our childhood spent writing and performing plays and short films, instrumental in shaping me as a storyteller; to Eliza, my high-school bestie, for the years of comedy skits we wrote and performed (some as physics assignments, some just for fun) – my sense of humour wouldn't be the same without you; and to Belinda, who encouraged me to do the course that started everything, and became an invaluable beta reader, calmer of nerves and giver of editorial advice throughout – I am so grateful, and wish you all the literary success you so richly deserve.

To my Beaumaris Theatre family, thank you for your unbridled enthusiasm and for providing me with a place to stretch my creative wings and tell dramatic stories on stage well before I began writing.

To my sensational writing group, whom I am lucky to call friends – Terry Phillips, Elyse Harrison, Kate Burns and Veronica Lando – thank you for laughing at my jokes and for loving Fred as much as I did from the outset. Your feedback and encouragement helped shape this story in so many ways, and I could not have arrived here without your company. Terry, I hope we can one day co-author Patricia's *special* cookbook.

To Pamela Freeman, Valerie Khoo and the Australian Writers Centre, your first-rate courses were a pivotal step in my journey to publication. Thank you to my fabulous tutor Bernadette Foley for inspiration and advice both during and after the course. Your initial words of encouragement made me believe that I had a story worth sharing, and you became the voice in my head, pushing me to keep writing. To the Australian Society of Authors, thank you for your guidance and the fantastic Literary Speed Dating event that led to my offer of publication. Special thanks to Sylvia Balog for superb editing advice and to talented author Richard Roper for helping me polish my pitch and giving me the confidence to go for it.

To Joanna Nell, Kerryn Mayne, Amanda Hampson, Ruth Hogan and all the kind-hearted authors who helped me learn the ropes and took the time to read my manuscript and provide endorsement – your support means the world. To my photographer Angelica James, thank you for being such a patient and phenomenal artist.

To the brilliant team at Penguin Random House Australia. First and foremost, to my marvellous (simply marvellous!) publisher and editor Beverley Cousins, who believed in my work from the beginning. Your 'yes' was the catalyst that set this dream in motion, and I am forever grateful for your trust, support, patience and editorial prowess. To esteemed editors Rachel Scully and Katie Purvis for putting my manuscript through the wash so it was shinier than ever, and for making it appear as though I have excellent grammar. To my awesome publicity and marketing team, Anna Tidswell and Tanaya Lowden, for expert buzz generation; to Debra Billson for the gorgeous Australian cover design; to Veronica Eze for audio casting; and to Tim Carroll for breathing life into the narrative.

To my magnificent US publisher and editor Liz Stein of William Morrow of Harper Collins USA. You not only saw the potential in my book, but truly understood its essence. Our initial Zoom call remains one of my most treasured memories of this journey. Thank you for your faith, encouragement, and editorial expertise.

To the terrific team at Nemira Publishers in Romania, thank you for your interest in my work. What an honour to have the book translated into another language!

To my rock-star agent, Pippa Masson from Curtis Brown Australia, who shared my vision for the book and spread it globally within days! I am so grateful for your guidance and support throughout; and to Caitlan Cooper-Trent for your valuable assistance. To the lovely Stacy Testa of Writers House, New York, for securing Fred the perfect home in the US. To Cath Summerhayes of Curtis Brown UK and Kate Cooper of Curtis Brown Australia for your ongoing efforts to secure opportunities for my work. To my sensational US media rights agent Addison Duffy of UTA, thank you for your love of Fred and shared determination to see him on the screen (which was my ultimate ambition before the first word was written). I'm so excited to see what the future holds!

To the generous people who assisted in my research: Geoff Shepherd and Kerryn Mayne for vital input on police procedure, legal eagle Aisha Tzouklis for answering all my questions on estate law and trust funds, Kate Stalker for shedding light on nursing-home protocol, Rachel Newlander Einstein for Americanisation suggestions for the US edition (you are the opposite of a ratbag!), and cousin-in-law and talented screenwriter Phil Enchelmaier for valuable insights into screen adaptation. To all the staff, residents, and families I had the privilege of working with and caring for during my years in aged care, thank you. Our time together was greatly influential in the writing of this novel.

To my wonderful readers. I am incredibly grateful that you chose this book. Thank you to those who have left such beautiful reviews, who have told their friends and spread the love. I would also like to acknowledge all those who have been touched by the issues my characters face – grief, dementia, social isolation, cancer and addiction. To you, I send my love and strength.

To my glorious daughters Eve and Norah. Due to my physical limitations you have never seen me climb a mountain . . . until now. I could not have taken a single step without your love and encouragement. I love that we share a passion for writing and can bounce ideas off each other. Norah, I can't tell you how many times your pride in me kept me going. Eve, thank you for Albert's great line,

'You can't have shadows without light.' You girls are my light. Never stop chasing your dreams, my sweethearts, however impossible they seem.

And lastly, to my husband and best friend Josh – my number one supporter and sounding board, and my very own Fred. I can never thank you enough for walking every step of this journey alongside me. Your adoration, support, and unfaltering belief in me was the ladder to my dreams. Any victory I have is your victory, my love. Any legacy I leave will be your legacy too. There were many things I needed to research to write this book, but the feeling of being cherished was never one of them.

Josh, Eve and Norah . . . you my darlings, are the froth on my cappuccino.